VESTAL VIRGIN:
CHOSEN
FOR
ROME

VESTAL VIRGIN:
CHOSEN
FOR
ROME

Katherine Spada Basto

PAINTED TURTLE PRESS

ISBN: 978-1-7333900-7-1 (paperback)
ISBN: 978-1-7333900-9-5 (ebook)

Library of Congress Cataloging in Publication Data
Library of Congress Control Number: 2019914484

Painted Turtle Press   Painted Turtle Press
                           Hartford, Connecticut

To my mother and father,
my first teachers

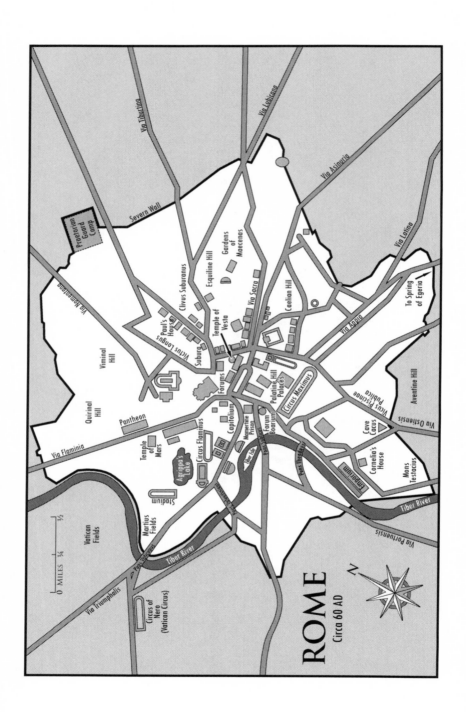

CHAPTER 1

AUGUST 60 AD

On the day of my tenth birthday, the Festival of Diana, a loud knock resounded on the vestibule door. Who could be knocking? I thought my neighbors had presents for me.

My parents spoke with me about exciting news a few weeks before. "Cornelia, you may be a part of a grand celebration soon. We know not when, but we must be prepared. For you might be chosen."

"Chosen for what?" I asked.

But I never received an answer. Maybe today.

I was overjoyed to celebrate my birthday. Visions of rag dolls in silk dresses, toys, a new tunica, and a pair of sandals filled my mind. I thought of all the honeyed figs and dates I'd get to eat today.

My family and my neighbors indulged me. My father always presented me with gifts from his travels: trinkets from

Judea, a small North African drum made of camel's hide, a cedar box from Lebanon, and dyed scarves from Phoenica were among my favorites. I had them neatly lined up in my room.

As the youngest child in the family, when I demanded something, Father made certain I got my wish. Even my older brother Cornelius, fourteen, gave in to my every whim. "Who do you think you are, Queen Cleopatra?" he would ask me.

"Of course, I am Queen Cleopatra. And you are my slave," I'd reply. Cornelius would roll up his eyes, mumble under his breath, and shake his head.

"Taltos, please answer the door," my mother ordered, pointing toward the vestibule. Taltos was one of our slaves and he was the family favorite. Father had traded for him in North Africa years ago. Taltos was seventeen years old, but he was still short, thin, and very dark of complexion. His ringlet curls bobbed about his forehead and hung like little scrolls around his face. His round, brown eyes seemed to spin like marbles when he became nervous. Taltos, like my family, paid me all the attention I desired and made certain my temper was rarely aroused. I loved him like a brother.

My father and mother waited in the atrium for our visitors. They both twisted their hands together and kept wiping and fanning their faces with a cloth. My father wore his best linen toga today. His thick, dark hair was oiled and curled. When he oiled his hair, it made his blue eyes look bigger and brighter. My father was the most handsome of men, more handsome than even the gods!

Over her tunica, Mother had worn her finest sleeveless stola—emerald green with stripes of yellow on the hem. Her dark hair was pulled tightly in a knot, and her brown eyes were outlined in kohl.

I hid behind the pleated folds of my mother's stola, peeking out to see who would bring me gifts. Taltos opened the door, politely bowed to our guests, and led them toward the atrium. Light poured into the room from the open dome onto a rectangular pool filled with red, white and gold fish. A fountain with a statue of Neptune splashed with waters that overflowed into the pool. The sea god's trident—sharp and pointed—glittered in the bright sunlight.

Neptune was my family's patron god. Descended from a long line of merchant seamen, my father traded in wine and Cosa's famous fish sauce.

Taltos escorted our visitors into the atrium where we all waited. Little brown sparrows fluttered about the pool, dipping their wings in for a bath. Two men I didn't know stood before my parents' gazes. They wore the tunics of messengers with the Emperor's seal on their belts. Each carried a messenger bag slung over their shoulders. They both removed a wax tablet with a stylus to write with from their pouches.

"Greetings, Dominus, Domina," they said to my parents.

One of them, a tall thin man with a kindly smile, encouraged me to come out from behind my mother's stola. He bent over, crooking his finger toward me. His chin was long and pointed. His cheeks looked like little red plums. "Where's Cornelia?" he asked as if this was a game. He looked up and down, pretending he couldn't find me. *Does he think I am still a baby?*

"Cornelia, this is not the time for shyness," my mother announced.

I stepped out.

"I am Cornelia Cosa, and it is my tenth birthday."

"Yes, Cornelia, there you are—and such a pretty child," the tall man murmured, patting my head. My hair was washed,

3

scrubbed, dried, and hung loosely down my back. Mother still had to curl it. My relatives told me my hair was the color of the grapes that grew in Etruria—black with streaks of red or blue-violet, depending on the way the light fell on it. My hair was my pride.

Mother loved curling it with hot tongs and pinning it in ringlets. "Your hair complements your eyes, the color of the Tyhrrenian Sea," she'd murmur. My blue eyes had specks of yellow in them. I had inherited my father's eyes and long, black lashes.

"But when you are angry, Cornelia, your eyes are no longer blue with specks of color. They are flames of ice and fire," Taltos once told me shaking his head. The same way all my family shook their heads when it came to me. Especially after I stamped my foot hard or tossed my hair around like a horse demanding I get my way.

I knew I was pretty. My eyes were big, my nose was long and straight, and my skin a deep olive color. I was tall for my age and thin as a reed. I loved the dance and told Taltos some-day I would dance for the Emperor.

One day when mother was curling my hair she said, "When you are older Cornelia, men will line up to ask Father for your hand in marriage."

I squealed with delight, thinking about all my suitors. "But Mother, tell me about men. Are they all like Father?" I asked.

Mother stepped back after pinning another curl around my face. Giving me a grave look, she held a finger to her chin and shook her head.

"Of course all men are *not* like Father. All men are differ-ent. Some are loving and some—"She paused. "Never mind such talk, Cornelia." She sighed, shook her head, and continued pinning my hair in ringlets.

"I pray I find a loving husband just like Father," I said.

"Please Cornelia, keep these thoughts to yourself. There will be time enough for marriage."

I believed her words.

"She looks to be perfect. The Pontifex Maximus will be pleased," the short fat messenger said. His extended stomach made his belt stretch out; he was panting and out of breath.

The two messengers began to speak to one another in whispers. The short man began to scribble words on his wax tablet. What was he writing?

Then the tall man removed a scroll from his bag and unraveled it. "Let us now review the requirements," he said. "First, the physique. Slave, bring us a stool." He motioned to Taltos.

Taltos quickly found a stool by the sidewall of the atrium. Then with a gesture from the fat man, Taltos lifted me to stand on it. To my surprise, the tall man examined my eyes, ears, mouth, arms, underarms, legs, even my teeth for defects, as the short man wrote. Not to my surprise, no defects were found. Next they made me read and enunciate words to ensure my voice was clear and strong. They noted no shortcoming with my speaking and reading ability either. I could have told them this!

Pleased to be deemed perfect, I tilted my chin up with pride.

The tall man continued. "Next, that both parents are alive." Check. "That both parents are Roman by birth." He stared at my father.

5

"Do you have evidence of this? I know your family hails from Cosa," the short man stated, then puffed out his chest and began to wheeze.

My father offered him a small scroll that was hanging from his roped belt. "Here is my proof. I am a true citizen of Rome. My parents left Etruria years ago. Rome is my only home."

The messengers hovered over the opened scroll and scrutinized its contents. Then they handed it back to Father.

"That is good." Check.

"She is obviously between the ages of six and ten?"

"It *is* her tenth birthday today," my father announced. Check.

"Cornelia has one sibling, yes?" the tall man asked.

"That is correct," my mother replied. She gestured toward the library. "Taltos, find Cornelius. Bring him here immediately." She added, "And bring me Cornelia's cedar box from her room." She clapped twice.

One thing was certain. I seemed to have met all the qualifications; for what I didn't know. But all eyes were on me, and after all, it *was* my birthday. So it had to be something good.

Cornelius stumbled into the atrium with his nose buried in a scroll. He saw me and quickly turned away, then pulled a small wrapped gift from his pocket and handed it to me. "Happy Birthday, Cornelia. *Bonam Fortunam!*"

Good luck! I felt I already had the most fortune in the world.

Taltos returned with my cedar box. "Carry this for luck, Cornelia," he said, and handed me the small box filled with my most prized possessions. I slipped my brother's gift into my cedar box.

The two men huddled together conferring. "We are pleased to report that Cornelia qualifies for the lottery today," the tall man decreed. "Let us ready ourselves to depart."

"Depart?" my mother asked. "I thought this was not planned until—"

"Emperor's orders, Domina. We must depart. Other girls await," the fat messenger exclaimed, huffing for another breath. He stretched out his belt before snapping it back in place.

Depart for where? Other girls awaited as well? I wondered. The wondering only got me more excited. And nervous!

Mother started flitting about like the sparrows, patting her coifed hair and pinning up the palla that would cover her head, using a turtle-shaped gold brooch. There would be no time to pin and curl my hair. Father paced about like a caged beast. When he stood still, he tapped his foot up and down and kept greasing back his hair.

"First, let us pray to the Lares," Mother said. The family gods will continue to bless us with good fortune."

We gathered in front of the family shrine in a corner of the atrium. Small statues of Neptune and of the fleet-footed god of messengers, Mercury, stood in the small alcove on the shrine. My father would pray to Mercury for safe travels and prosperous business trades. Another statue of Diana, with her bow and arrow arched and ready, stood in my honor. After all, I was born on her feast day!

For some reason, perhaps for luck, I grabbed my *bulla* to make sure it was still around my neck. Given to me at my naming ceremony when I was but nine days old, the round gold necklace had Neptune's trident carved on it. All of Rome's children were given a bulla at birth.

My bulla warded off evil. It protected me against the evil eye or a curse.

"You shall wear your bulla until you are married. Never take it off," my mother warned me. "Once you marry you will no longer have use of it. Your husband will protect you."

I trusted my bulla would bring me Bonam Fortunam. I jumped up and down, listening to it clank back and forth. I was ready for my birthday adventure to begin.

CHAPTER 2

Taltos had strewn flower petals on the floor of our villa and hung garlands of roses on the walls in honor of my special day. The scent of dried lavender and rose drifted out of the open door. Across the road a white carriage drawn by two white horses awaited us. The seal of the Emperor was displayed on the carriage door. Few people were walking on the road today; many Romans left for the seaside in August to escape the heat.

We lived at the base of the Aventine Hill across from the Tiber River. My father owned a wharf where he received his goods from the Port of Ostia. Nearby stood the cave of the monster Cacus, the fire-breathing beast of legend that Hercules outsmarted. The cave jutted out toward the Tiber, and was now a lookout for people to watch for boats.

I clutched my cedar box to my chest. A few of my neighbors stood outside clapping and wishing me well. Many carried white flowers and thrust them at me as we followed the red-garbed messengers through the crowd. I was waiting for more presents, but I assumed they would come later.

I turned back to look at my family villa; outside stood the stone post with the two-headed Janus on it that protected our household; the head of the New Year stared at me. The other head, the old year, faced our villa.

"Where are we going, Father?" I whispered.

He watched the gathering crowd with a frown on his face. "Why to the Forum, of course," he said, never looking at me. He said this as if it were the most natural way to celebrate my tenth birthday. "If you must know, you are part of the lottery today, Cornelia— you and eleven other girls." He smiled and waved at those who gathered around us, but he didn't smile at me.

Father finally looked at me. "Normally, twenty girls are chosen for the lottery. Emperor Nero could only find twelve this year. Cornelia, I was planning on telling you. I didn't know the lottery would fall on your birthday. Your mother and I had no warning."

"What's a lottery and what's it for?" I asked.

"It's a contest. You may be chosen in the lottery," my father replied.

"I love contests, Father. You know that." Now I was hoping that I would win. "Who else will be there?" I asked.

"Perhaps a crowd of well-wishers. Senators. Important people … I'm not sure. Most important, the Emperor himself will be present. Nero will be there in his role of Pontifex Maximus." Father held up a finger. "Remember how I explained the role of Pontifex Maximus to you?"

I nodded, but at that moment I did not remember what my father spoke of.

"Push back, scatter all of you. Emperor's orders!" the messengers shouted to the onlookers.

The two messengers escorted us to the carriage. It was large enough to fit the family, Taltos included. Cornelius slumped in his seat, sullen and bored. He was still carrying his scroll. But I felt like Cleopatra herself, heading up the Nile to meet my fate.

We advanced slowly around the Aventine Hill; we passed Cacus's Cave, rode up toward the cattle market— the Forum Boarium, and past the Temple of Hercules. I listened to the horses' hooves click-clop against the paved stones wondering what would happen next.

The carriage began to ascend the Capitoline Hill, passing the great Temple of Jupiter. All along the way, people waved and stopped to stare. Then the carriage slowed and took an abrupt right down toward the Via Sacra. Hot air blew around my face and I fanned myself.

"Are we almost to the Forum, Father?" I asked.

"See for yourself, Daughter."

I stretched my neck out of the carriage and looked down on the great marble pillars of the Senate and the many grand temples to all our gods rising up before me a short distance away.

At last we arrived at the entrance to the Forum, the open plaza surrounded by the grandest buildings in Rome. A few carriages waited ahead of us. My excitement spilled over, and I began jumping up and down in my seat. "This is the best birthday ever," I shouted. "Will I receive presents from everyone, even the Emperor himself?" I had my dance already planned.

"Control yourself, Cornelia. The lottery is a serious matter," said my father.

My mother sighed and gave Cornelius a knowing look.

Then she glanced sidelong at Taltos, like she knew something I did not. They all knew something!

I didn't care about the lottery. It was my special day!

Finally, it was my family's turn to enter into the Forum. A soldier stuck his head inside the carriage window. He handed my father a smooth, round piece of wood with a carving on it. "Emperor's orders," he commanded. "Hold onto this marker until it is time for the lottery."

"What is that?" I asked, poking at the little wooden marker with burnt carvings.

Father sighed and wiped sweat from his brow. He turned the marker over and over in the palm of his hand. Then he carefully inspected it.

"Cornelia, you are full of questions today. Please be like every obedient daughter of Rome and stay quiet."

"Yes, Cornelia. Your questions disturb me as well," said my mother fanning herself.

I was becoming impatient. *Why should I be quiet?* "It is my birthday, and I want to know if this is a birthday present," I persisted. "Tell me, Father. Tell me what it means. Please!"

Father shrugged and turned the smooth object over again in his fingers. "This is called a *lot*, Cornelia."

"I want to see what's on it," I whined, and reached out to try to grab it from him.

He handed it over to me.

Carved on one side was a small image of a cat's face with pointed ears, triangle nose, and whiskers.

"Look, there's a cat's face on it. Can I keep it?" I thought for a moment. "I know! I was born under the star of Leo, the big cat. Remember, Taltos, you told me about my star?" Taltos murmured under his breath shaking his head.

I loved all animals, but cats were my favorite. "Does this mean I get a cat for my birthday?"

My father sighed. "We keep this marker for the lottery, Cornelia. If the cat is chosen, you will be the chosen one."

"Chosen for *what?*"

Now I had angered Father.

"Enough of your questions, Cornelia." He held his breath and heaved out another loud sigh. He pinched his lips together before he spoke. "You will be obedient and remain silent until I tell you. No more talk."

I looked to the others for an answer. Cornelius just rolled his eyes and shook his head like he always did. Taltos and Mother stayed silent and gazed out the window, pretending they had not heard anything.

My family left the carriage and made our way through the arched porticoes leading to the Forum. The markets and vendor stalls alongside the Forum were bustling with activity. The smell of rosemary, garlic, and roasted lamb filled the air. Merchants hawked their wares, selling busts of Julius Caesar and small statues of Rome's gods and goddesses. I saw a statuette of the goddess Persephone next to Hades, the Lord of the Underworld. I decided after the lottery, I would ask Father to buy me these statuettes to place in our family shrine.

I noticed my friend Cynthia, who ran up to me and gave me an embrace.

"Happy Birthday, Cornelia. Are you excited to be a part of the lottery?" Her blue eyes looked so bright in the sun.

"Of course I am. Are you part of the lottery too?" I asked her.

"No. I was not deemed perfect enough. You know my speech gets jumbled up at times. I get confused and nervous when I have to recite out loud."

I felt sorry for Cynthia. I was judged perfect and she was not. We said our goodbyes and she ran back to her family.

The families were asked to come close to the center of the open square. A few senators stood talking on the marble stairs of the Senate building watching the proceedings. They wore togas with purple hems and had laurel wreaths on their heads. The priest of Jupiter, the Flamen Dialis, stood with his beautiful wife to the side; they often led rituals and sacrifices in the city. I also saw an older woman dressed in white who accompanied the pair.

My mother kept fanning herself, and Taltos's eyes spun like rolling marbles. His head bobbed up and down, taking in all the sights and people.

Then the noise stopped. Everything became quiet. Even the horses seemed to turn to watch the man stomping into the square. He wore a long, white cloth that covered his head. Flames of curled, dark yellow hair stuck out of his mantle. He had round eyes the color of a gray-blue sky. And they seemed to glow with a strange light. Although his arms bulged with muscle, his toga could not conceal his belly. He paced on thin legs around the center of the plaza.

I nudged Taltos. "Who's that?" I whispered.

"That's the Emperor Nero, silly. He's in his role of Pontifex Maximus, the High Priest. You didn't recognize him because he wears the head covering."

Cornelius put his scroll away. He shuffled his feet and stood there as motionless as a statue. But then he briefly put his hand on my shoulder and shook it. "You'll be all right, sister," he decreed.

Of course, I thought. *Why wouldn't I?*

Several slaves stood in the center of the Forum holding a wide, earthenware pot. My father and the other fathers who held lots were called forth and slowly walked to the center. They spoke among themselves for a brief time with the Emperor. Then they dropped the little markers in the bowl. The markers made a dull, clicking noise as the slaves shook them up.

Mother, Taltos, and Cornelius gathered around me waiting for Father to return.

"You won't get picked, Cornelia," my brother said. "We'll be celebrating your birthday at home tonight."

"Wait—if I'm picked I can't go home?" Cornelius ignored my question. Confused, I clasped my cedar box. Then I felt for my bulla around my neck. It always made me feel safe.

"May Divine Jupiter and the Goddess Vesta bless this lottery," announced the Flamen Dialis. "And now, the Revered Pontifex Maximus."

My father returned and his hands were trembling. "What have I done?" he kept murmuring.

The Pontifex Maximus strutted about the square quieting the crowd. Many of the Senators came forth now, gathering around the bowl.

"We shall now choose a lot that will be drawn by the Pontifex Maximus," shouted the newsreader from the Rostra, the area of the Forum where announcements were made.

"Slaves, hold tight the bowl," commanded the Pontifex Maximus.

The small group around the bowl spoke among themselves in raised, strained voices, as if they were arguing. People in the crowd began to whisper. What was happening? The old woman dressed in white joined the circle of men.

The Pontifex Maximus raised his arm up high, and then I saw his hand plunge into the bowl. He thrust his hand up again, now gripping a single lot high in the air.

"I am pleased to announce that the gods have decreed their choice," he intoned. "The sign of the cat has been chosen!"

My mother fainted right there. Cornelius moaned and stomped his foot. My father crouched to help my mother up. He murmured something to her, asking if she needed salts. Sweat poured down Father's brow. Taltos's eyes bulged from his head. "Oh dear," he kept mumbling.

I could only watch them, waiting for their congratulations on my triumph. I was the chosen one. The gods had decreed it was *I* who won the lottery, for what I did not know. But I figured it was only right—it was my birthday.

CHAPTER 3

The Pontifex Maximus shouted for everyone to step back away from the open square. He stood alone now, except for the Flamens and the old woman in white. Pointing to a corner near the Senate steps, he shouted, "Slaves, bring us that chair." A wooden chair ornately carved with painted images of fruit, flowers, and birds was carried to the center of the Forum.

"I will ask that Cornelius Marcus Cosa, Pater of Cornelia Cosa, come forth to present his daughter," the Pontifex ordered.

Here was my chance. I was ready and prepared to dance for the Pontifex Maximus who was our Emperor. I still clutched my cedar box and would not let it go. "Keep silent now, Cornelia," my father whispered as he grasped my shoulder. His hand was shaking. "Keep your head held high, daughter. Never forget you are a Cosa."

So I kept my head high and imagined I was Cleopatra sailing up the Nile. I turned back and saw my mother crying, tears streaming down her face. Cornelius and Taltos were trying to console her. Wasn't she proud of me for winning?

I was proud of myself. I would not let my family down. Especially when all eyes were on me, Cornelia Cosa!

My father and I strode across the square and stood in front of the Pontifex Maximus. What a strange man with those bulging, wide eyes! He grinned down at me and seemed pleased. The corners of his mouth rose up in a half smile. He seemed to be several years older than my brother. But something about the Emperor Nero scared me!

"Pater of Cornelia, you shall take this seat." He pointed to the chair. My father followed his orders. "Cornelia Cosa, you shall now take a seat upon your father's lap." Since I had done this many times before, I placed my box on the ground, jumped into my father's lap, and threw my arms around his neck. I lay my cheek against his cheek and waited for the Pontifex to continue.

He had turned his back to us and was consulting with the Flamens and the old woman in white.

The newsreader shouted from the Rostra, "And now the Ancient Rite of Vesta will be conducted."

The Pontifex Maximus turned back around looking angry, as if he was a soldier in battle. He walked around a few paces and stopped. He peered so close to me I could hear him whisper, "She's lovely." and proceeded to tickle my chin.

Then he grabbed my arm. Tight. I tried to move away but his grip kept me there on father's lap. In a loud voice that echoed through the Forum, he shouted, "I take you thus, Amata, as a Vestal priestess, who will perform the rites that a Vestal priestess must perform on behalf of the Roman people."

With that, his stubby hands yanked me away from my father, who sat impassively and did not move.

"Emperor, I'm sorry, but my name is *not* Amata. You have the wrong girl," I politely corrected him. "But I am ready to dance for you if you wish."

He placed his hand on my head and gave me a reassuring pat. "I know you are not Amata, Cornelia. You see, Amata was the first Vestal, after Rhea Silvia of course, in a long line of Vestal Virgins. She was pure and good like you will be pure and good. And Amata means 'beloved.'" He bent over to look into my eyes. "You are now a beloved of Rome. You will learn about Amata, Rhea Silvia and the others, Cornelia. And there is none better than the Virgo Maxima, the Chief Vestal, Mother Aurelia, to teach you this sacred history."

The old woman stepped forward. She had bright, kind blue eyes and skin that reminded me of cobwebs. She smiled and her face crinkled up like papyrus paper.

"But what of my family? What of my birthday celebrations?" I asked in confusion. Tears started to gather in my eyes. I remembered what my father had said to me: "Keep your head up high. Never forget you are a Cosa."

"Family?" Nero had removed his head covering and was the Emperor once again. His ringlet-curls, like little horns, twisted all over his head. He glared down into my eyes again. Then he began to chuckle. "The State of Rome is now your family. Mother Aurelia will be like a mother to you. The other Vestals will be like sisters you never had. Your father has given up his *potestas* and has no control over you. You are no longer a part of the Cosa Paternostra. The gods have decreed this."

He watched me closely. "You, Cornelia, have been chosen to serve in the Temple of Vesta." He paused. "For the required thirty years of service to the goddess."

Thirty years? I did not understand. I could not think beyond today my birthday. I stamped my foot hard. I pointed to the old woman. "This old woman is *not* my mother." I pointed to my mother. "She is my mother, and I want to go home." I grabbed my cedar box and held it close to my chest.

"This is no longer possible, Cornelia," the old woman said gently. "You have been chosen by the Great Goddess Vesta herself."

"When can I go home?" I cried.

"You shall be allowed visitations when the time is right," the Emperor said. "And your family may visit you at the temple on special occasions. But we waste time, for there is one last act for the novice before we hand her to the Vestal Order."

The Emperor stood over me. Before I knew it, he had ripped my beloved bulla from my neck.

My bulla!" I shouted. "I need my bulla!"

"You have no need of your bulla now. For thirty years, you will be married to the State of Rome serving Vesta. Heed the rules and laws of the Vestals, for the price you will pay for broken rules and vows could prove harsh."

My beloved bulla lay on the ground between the Emperor and myself. I snatched it up and dropped it inside my cedar box. The Emperor could rip my bulla from my neck, but I would *not* allow him to keep it. I ran back to my family and hugged each one of them.

"We shall see you soon, Cornelia," said Mother, wiping a tear. "The goddess has chosen you. Remember that."

Taltos had tears in his eyes as well. "I will visit you too, Cornelia. Make us proud."

Cornelius was muttering as usual. I embraced him. "Stop mumbling, Cornelius. I'll be home soon," I reassured him.

I clutched my cedar box. It was all I had left. I held my head high and walked back to the chair. Father was still sitting there, his hands covering his face.

The Emperor came forth and addressed Father. "For your service, Cornelius Marcus Cosa, Pater of Cornelia." A slave appeared and dropped three bags of gold at Father's feet. *Clank-clank-thud.* "Behold, three bags of gold worth a million secesteres in full payment," the Emperor announced. Father gazed down at the money. But for some reason, he would not look at me.

A young man now stepped forward. He was dressed in a pale yellow tunic with a cloak of red stripes draped over his shoulders. He held a staff that curved down at the top, like a shepherd's crook. He looked to be a few years older than Cornelius. He bowed, unraveled a scroll, and began to read: "The auguries and omens are good. An eagle was seen flying overhead. Cornelia Cosa could reign as one of the greatest of all Vestals." He then added, "If she obeys the rules and fulfills her vows." He bowed and stepped back.

The Emperor nodded. "This is good."

So I, Cornelia Cosa, had been chosen to serve Vesta. And it seemed my father had received the presents on this day. I guessed I wasn't going to get a cat. This didn't seem fair—but I still thought it was only right I should be chosen.

CHAPTER 4

So I became a Vestal Virgin. I knew not what this all meant. Thirty years had little meaning for me.

I was paraded around the Forum to the cheers of the crowd. Mother Aurelia held one of my trembling hands, and in the other I carried my cedar box. I kept my head high and waved to my admirers. "Cornelia Cosa could reign as one of the greatest of all Vestals." The words of the augur resounded in my head. And then the warning: "If she obeys the rules and fulfills her vows."

I wasn't worried about breaking the rules. Father always forgave me when I broke *his* rules. How could this be any different?

Mother Aurelia squeezed my hand. "We are grateful to have you now, Cornelia. After the Vestal Laelia died unexpectedly, we have been waiting for this day. We must have six vestals at all times. Otherwise Vesta is not pleased."

Leaving my family behind, she led me through the Forum, pointing out the temples and the place where the sacred fig tree grew. We stopped in front of the grounds of a small round building. "This is the Regia," Mother Aurelia explained.

"Who lives here?" I asked.

"No one lives here, Cornelia. The Regia is where many of the sacred relics are kept, relics that date from the time of King Numa. You will see them soon and understand their meaning when your training begins. Our storehouse filled with grain is kept here as well. The Emperor writes out his schedules and the calendar in the Regia. It is his office." Mother Aurelia pointed to the palace above the Regia, on the hillside overlooking the Forum.

"That's the Emperor's palace—but you know this. Sometimes Vestals attend banquets there." The palace, white with many marble pillars, loomed over the gardens. The Emperor could watch from many of his windows all the movement in the Forum.

Mother Aurelia led me to a building on the right. It was surrounded by a grove of pine and elm trees. The white marble columns rose higher than my neck could stretch. In front of the columns, small steps led up to the door. "This is the temple of Castor and Pollux, the twins," she explained. "Many people do business here and come to pay their respects." She showed me the fount in front of the temple. "Here is the spring of Juturna, where we retrieve sacred waters." Then she motioned to a small, square building. "Here is the temple of Julius Caesar."

I sighed. *Didn't Mother Aurelia think I knew anything?*

Mother Aurelia stopped at a small, circular temple with a dome supported by shiny white columns. Wrapped around the hut-size building were designs and what looked like screens woven into the sides. A gnarled tree stood nearby, hanging over the left side of the temple, its twisted branches drooping down at the entrance. Bits of ribbon and string hung off of it. "Why are we stopping here?" I asked.

Mother Aurelia looked surprised. "Why this is the Temple of Vesta, Cornelia."

"I know *that!*" I said.

"Then you know that here is where the sacred fire burns for Rome. It must continually burn, and we Vestals are appointed to guard the sacred flame. The screens are a necessity to let out smoke, lest we breathe in too much of it."

I watched the ribbons of smoke twirl out from the top of the dome.

"Soon you will learn to be a keeper of the sacred hearth-fire. But until your official training begins, we have more that we must do. Come now, little one."

She tugged on my hand gently. We walked the grounds of the Vestals. Cypress and yew trees lined the edges. Statues of Vestals graced the open court. I stared up at the cold, marble images of these women. Who were they? Would a statue be erected to me someday? What was the strange headcovering they wore? I had seen Vestals in Rome traveling by litter or sedan.

One statue was of a Vestal with a mournful look on her face. Her stone gaze watched me with pity. *"Obey your vows and do not break the rules,"* I heard in my mind again.

Mother Aurelia took me around the back of the long building and through a gate in the garden wall. "Let me show you where the mill and stables are," she explained, indicating the wooden structures. On one side stood the mill and she led me into it. "Here is where the grain is ground for our rituals and feasts." The mill had a great stone in the center, blackened from age and use. As if reading my thoughts about the stone, Mother Aurelia said, "Yes, this black stone is volcanic pumice right from Mt. Aetna."

I watched the two donkeys plodding along, turning the millstone, walking in a circle, round and round, with tethers on their necks. An attendant was present, keeping an eye on the animals.

"Cornelia, meet our two donkeys. Strong and Bond. They are a part of our family. Donkeys are sacred to Vesta. Let them be an example of hard work. For the only day off they receive is on the Vestalia—but that's not until June."

One of the donkeys brayed and nodded his head up and down. "Strong seems to like you, Cornelia. You already have a new friend," said Mother Aurelia.

The adjoining building held stalls for the donkeys and was filled with hay and straw for their care. "I like the donkeys," I told Mother Aurelia. "Can I visit them?"

"Of course you can, dear," she said, as if amused. "But now we must proceed back to the Atrium to your new home, the House of the Vestals.

"Here we are," said Mother Aurelia, pointing to a long, two-storied building behind the temple. Seven steps led up to a massive wooden door with carvings on it. "Welcome, Cornelia. Vesta is happy to have you with us."

Several women stood in front of the steps ready to greet me. Looking like a flock of geese, they were dressed from head to foot in white and wore unusual white wrappings and linen mantles on their heads.

"Welcome, Sister Cornelia," they sang out in unison.

An older Vestal, but not nearly as old as Mother Aurelia, stepped forward. Her face was pinched into a scowl. She was tall and thin with sharp black eyes, and her lanky frame hovered over me."I am Junia—Junia Silvani Torquata, thirty-six years of age. You can call me Junia. I will be your teacher and you *will* obey me." She returned to her place by the steps.

"And my name is Cornelia Marcella Cosa. You may address me as Cornelia." I stamped my foot to the ground and turned my nose up to this rude woman. How dare she address me in such a manner?

"You are a spoiled girl I see, and I will have no disrespect shown to me." Junia stared down at me with horror.

"And you are nothing but an old windbag—and an old bag of bones as well!" I shouted, trying to hurt her feelings.

"How dare this girl speak to me this way?" Junia looked to Mother Aurelia for some answers.

"Please, Junia. The girl is distressed. Let's move on for the time," said Mother Aurelia.

The next Vestal came forward, bowed, and flung her open hand toward my new home. "I am Lucretia, and I welcome you."

Lucretia had a sparkle in her light blue eyes and a wide, round face that was red around the cheeks. She looked younger than Junia, and it was clear from her plump shape that she enjoyed food. I liked Lucretia immediately.

The next Vestal to introduce herself was even younger. She had beautiful olive-red skin and brown-green eyes that reminded me of the color of pine boughs. "I am Vibidia, seventeen years of age. I hope I shall be one of your friends. We shall be like sisters." She smiled sweetly and grasped my hand.

"Junia shall be your teacher until she retires from service," said Mother Aurelia. I noticed Vibidia roll up her eyes and let out a loud sigh. "There is one more Vestal. Rubria is presently in the temple guarding the flame," said Mother. "You shall meet her later at dinner."

We all stood before the steps leading to the vast door that led to the House of the Vestals.

"Before you enter your new home, Cornelia, we must complete the sacred ritual of the novice." Mother paused and looked to Junia. "Let us proceed to the sacred tree that stands by the Temple." Mother Aurelia, still holding my hand, led me to the entrance of the temple under the ancient oak tree. "Sister Junia, please bring forth the shears."

Shears?

A shudder came over me and I started to tremble.

Junia marched over and looming over me, withdrew from her pocket thick, bronze shears. Her long nose had wrinkles running up and down it. I wanted to grab that nose, pinch it, and twist it!

"A lock of hair must be cut from the novice's head. We then hang it on the sacred Capetine Oak. Hold still now, Cornelia," ordered Junia.

She moved behind me and snipped off a lock of my black hair. She then wrapped one end in twine and tied it to a low-lying branch of the tree.

I felt relieved that just a lock of my hair was cut off. It hung on the tree looking like the tail of a horse. Pleased with myself, I thought how proud my family would be of my bravery.

"Can we go into the house now?" I asked meekly.

All the other Vestals except for Junia snickered under their breath. Had I said something wrong?

"No, we are not quite ready yet," said Junia in a stern tone. "After a lock of hair is cut and hung on the tree, the novice, as a sacrifice to Vesta, must be completely shorn." She paused, smirking, and held up the glinting shears. "You are sacrificing your old life for the new."

Shorn? Now I hated Junia Silvani Toquata even more. "Shorn? I just gave the goddess a lock of my hair. I'll do no more. My hair is my hair." I stamped my foot again and announced I wanted to go home.

"This *is* your new home," said Lucretia calmly. "We all made this sacrifice. Sacrifices are not meant to be easy, Cornelia."

"No!" I bunched up my fists and stamped my foot over and over."I made a sacrifice with the lock of hair. And I gave up my birthday presents. Isn't that enough? I won't give anymore to this goddess." Tears flowed down my face.

For the first time in my life no one listened to my orders.

Junia, with her shears began to snip and clip. And she didn't stop until she had removed every hair on my head. When it was over, I reached up to feel my scalp. All that was left was fuzz that felt like the skin of a peach. A pile of black hair that looked like crow feathers spread round my feet. I wailed in fury.

"Wipe your eyes." Lucretia laughed. "It will grow back."

"Our new novice may now enter her new home," said Mother Aurelia with a patient smile and a wave of her hand. I clutched my cedar chest even tighter. "Welcome Sister Cornelia to the House of the Vestals."

CHAPTER 5

I climbed the seven steps and entered my new home feeling as bald as a baby bird.

We stood in the atrium, a long wide room made of shiny marble. A grand statue of Vesta holding a torch dominated the room. I didn't know how I felt about Vesta; I just knew I felt uncomfortable because her eyes seemed to watch me. The Vestals gathered around me and anointed my head with olive oil. Then they proceeded to wrap a white band around my head.

The atrium was so large the women's voices echoed off the walls. Other than the bright mosaic tiles on the floor patterned in gold, orange, and red flames, it was colorless. Lanterns hung everywhere; they flickered and cast shadows along the walls and floor. Small passages led to doorways off the atrium. I wondered if I'd get the chance to explore my new home soon. It seemed so gloomy, nothing but cold stone and shadows.

"When your hair grows in, Cornelia, I will teach you the trick of the six braids," said Lucretia. "You will wrap the braids around your head and then they shall be bound with a band called the *infula*. When you are ready, you will be presented with the Vestal hood called the *suffibulum*. We wear the hood when we make sacrifices. And the veil is part of the hood when we sacrifice …"

"Lucretia, mind yourself. You are confusing the girl," Junia snapped. "For now she wears the white band. Remember, *I* am the girl's teacher."

Lucretica whispered to me, "Do not worry. All will be well."

For a moment, I realized I was enjoying the attention bestowed upon me. It was not the attention I had anticipated. But the gods were more powerful; the Goddess Vesta had chosen me.

With the band securely wrapped around my head, Lucretia escorted me along a corridor to the back of the house, then up some winding stairs that led to the second floor. A stone balcony abutting the stairs faced the garden out back. The garden was filled with rows of colorful lilies and wildflowers blooming along the stone-cut pathways. Each row seemed to have a different color. A part of the garden was covered with a canopy for shade. I noticed many potted plants such as ivy, stretching their necks to the sun and then … more statues of Vestal Virgins.

A rectangular fishpond marked the center of the garden. Pine, cypress, and yew trees added a dark green backdrop to the splash of colors. The Via Nova ran along the left side of the walled-in garden, the Via Sacra along the right side. I had a view of the Forum and Vesta's temple from this direction. So here was a peaceful place amid the clamor and noise of Rome.

I followed Lucretia down another faintly lit hallway to a door on the right. "Here is your *cubiculum*, where you will sleep and pray." She opened the door with a small gold key. On the right side of the room stood an unadorned, narrow bed. A washbasin and chamber pot sat at the foot of the bed. A table in a corner held a brazier flickering pale light. A wooden desk with some scrolls on it stood on the left side of the room. A polished metal oval hung over the desk.

My new quarters, drab and sparse, left me feeling more discouraged. But my room had a small window that overlooked the Temple grounds, so I peered out with interest. I could see the Temple of Vesta from my window.

The sun was setting. The cypress trees and the pine groves near the Temple of Castor and Pollux cast long, deep blue shadows that stretched against the ground. "Wash up and rest for a time. When the bell rings, it's time for dinner. After dinner we will have more time to talk," said Lucretia. She softly closed the door.

I set my cedar box on the bed and opened it. On top was my bulla, ripped from my neck. Beneath it were some favorite gifts from Father's travels—a small, ivory elephant from Africa, a gold coin from Greece, one obsidian marble, and several silver necklaces. This was all I had left of my old life.

Cornelius's gift awaited me. I would open it later.

I lifted off my band and stared into the polished oval. The fading sunlight illuminated my eyes. They looked so much bigger now that my hair was gone. But my eyes were red from tears and droopy from such a long day. I watched out of the window; a few people still roamed about the Forum. White puffs of smoke rose from the Temple of Vesta.

I lay down on the bed and tears formed again in my eyes.

I sobbed into my pillow. This was my new home. But I wanted to return to the comforts of my old home. *Perhaps,* I thought, *I will escape.* This thought gave me hope.

Before I realized it, I'd fallen asleep and awoke to the faint tinkling sound of a bell. I remembered this meant it was time for dinner. This was to be my first meal in the House of the Vestals. I could not afford to be late and risk angering Mother Aurelia or worse, Junia.

I quietly pushed open the door. The hallway was empty. It smelled musty, an odd aroma of oil lamps and perfume. I was alone. Or so I thought. A dark, thin woman came forth from the shadows, her black hair wound up around her head. She wore a simple white tunica. Her tawny eyes blinked and a smile came forth from her thick lips. I thought she must be a little older than Vibidia.

"You scared me," I exclaimed.

"You must be Cornelia." She bowed, glancing at my head. "I am a servant to the Vestals. My name is Domicia. I am your personal servant. Now I will escort you to dinner."

How envious I was of Domicia's hair! All I could think of was my bald head and how itchy it was, how ugly I felt. Then I remembered that she was a servant and I, a Vestal.

I followed Domicia out of the narrow hallway. Oil lamps on the walls flickered little motes of light as if I were truly in a world of shadows. Was this what Hades the underworld looked like— nothing but statues and strange ghostly women coming and going—?

At the smell of meat and spices, my stomach began to rumble. "We are almost there," Domicia said and now took my hand. Finally we arrived in the dining area, the *triclinium.* And what a dining room it was! Everything in the room was colored in white and gold. Couches filled up part of the room while a dining table completed the other section. Servants carrying water and food scurried in and out of the room.

"She is here," announced Domicia.

"Sister Cornelia, please make sure you are prompt for meals," Junia said in a strict tone. "Tardiness is unacceptable in a Vestal."

The other Vestals had gathered around a long wooden table. I thought perhaps they would recline on the couches like I'd seen my father and his friends do, stretching their arms out to reach for delicacies. But there was no reclining tonight. Each Vestal sat upright in a high-backed chair. The chairs were carved with fruit, trees, animals and ivy. They reminded me of the chair Father and I sat on during the ceremony. As if reading my mind, Lucretia laughed and said, "Mostly, we use the reclining couches for our meals. Sometimes we do not."

I noticed the Vestal I had not met was now present. Rubria looked at me with curiosity. Thin wisps of red curls poked out from her headdress. She blinked up at me with bright green eyes and long black eyelashes. Her skin was almost as white as her Vestal robes, and her lips a deep red. She smiled a large grin that flashed sharp, white teeth. Like a she-wolf! Rubria was the most beautiful Vestal in the house— far more beautiful than bald, pitiful me.

"You must be Cornelia, Cornelia the bald." Rubria laughed, arching up an eyebrow. "But I can see you are a beauty. Such a pity." She sighed.

"And you must be Rubria," I replied. "It is a pleasure to meet you." And then I promptly sat down for dinner.

"Let us give thanks," said Mother Aurelia. I watched all the Vestals bow their heads.

"Goddess Vesta, we welcome our new sister Cornelia," Mother intoned." May she find solace, wisdom, virtue, and obedience within our sanctified home. We give thanks for bringing us Cornelia, in Your Name, and in the name of Rome."

The meal served by slave girls consisted of beef broth, cucumber, leek and artichoke salad, stuffed dates, quail eggs, and a delicacy my father let me try once from a vendor at the Circus Maximus— roasted dormice. I picked one up by the tail and bit down. It was crunchy, juicy and delicious, even if it did have bones in it!

After dinner a small cake was placed on the table. "Taltos, your family servant brought this cake while you were resting," said Lucretia. "It's a poppy-seed honey cake. He said it was your favorite." I eyed the cake with great interest. So my family remembered my birthday after all!

"Happy birthday, Cornelia. Welcome to your new home," the Vestals shouted. I picked at my slice of the moist, sweet cake. Although the cake was from my home, it didn't taste the same. My thoughts were back with my family. How long would it be until I saw them again?

"Where's Vibidia?" I asked, noticing she was missing.

"She took my place guarding the sacred fire. We all take turns you know," answered Rubria. "Usually in six-hour stretches. You'll have your time soon enough. But of course you will join one of us until you are ready to tend Vesta's fire yourself."

Junia scowled at Rubria, muttering under her breath about all the work to be done.

Mother Aurelia motioned for Lucretia to come over with a whisk of her hand. "Take Cornelia to her room. She must be tired after such a long day. We have much to prepare for tomorrow." She began to blow out the candles.

Lucretia clasped her thick hand around my shoulder. I shuddered thinking about my first night in the House of the Vestals. Again, as if reading my mind, Lucretia said, "Do not worry so, Cornelia. Fear not. You will find peace here."

She opened the door to my cubicle. "Here you are, Cornelia." She pointed to the thick scrolls on the desk. "You might want to start studying these scrolls soon." She squinted in the fading, gray light. "One scroll reviews the festivals the Vestals partake in and what their roles are. In the desk are candles, if you need more light."

"Please don't leave me here alone," I pleaded. "At least sit with me before bedtime."

Lucretia's face softened. "Why of course. For just a moment. I do remember my first night in the House of the Vestals." She plopped down next to me on the bed.

"Lucretia, all I want is to be home with my family again. I want to marry like other young girls do, marry a good man who loves me. I want a family, children of my own. Now this is not possible for me. Now I have nothing but prayers, feasts, rituals and tending the fire. My family is gone from me." I threw my thin arms into the air, then buried my face in my hands and began to sob. "It's just not fair!"

Lucretia eyed me calmly and offered me a gentle embrace. "We've all been through the pain and anguish of separation, Cornelia. We've all suffered the disappointment and feelings of loss … from being chosen." She gazed out of my bedroom's small window. "I also wanted to marry and have children, but the goddess chose me as a Vestal." She paused as if she were remembering when she was my age. "You are not alone, Cornelia. And remember, when a sacrifice is made, much will be given you. You were chosen by the goddess herself." She stroked my shorn head and smiled. "And remember, like all Vestals, you will have something no other girl or woman in Rome has, except the Emperor's wife perhaps." She smiled and glanced out the window again.

"What would that be? What will I have that no other girl in Rome has? Tell me, please!"

"You will have power, Cornelia. Power!"

"Power?" I asked, my eyes starting to droop.

Lucretia laughed. "Now that's for another time. Rest assured Cornelia, I see that you will be a Vestal of great power. But even Vestals need their sleep."

She kissed me on my head. "May Vesta bless you always."

With that she shut the door and was gone.

I was alone in my new home.

Pulling back the bed covering, I thought upon the events of the day. But on this day, when I was told to keep my head up high, I, Cornelia Cosa, could do no more than lower my head onto the pillow and fall fast asleep.

CHAPTER 6

The next morning during breakfast, I asked Mother Aurelia a simple question. "What will I be learning my first day as a novice?" My voice was filled with hope.

I had slept a deep and sound sleep my first night as a Vestal. Perhaps I simply was tired; but perhaps it was a good omen— that truly the Goddess Vesta had blessed me in my sleep. As I waited for Mother Aurelia's answer to me, I busied myself eating the last piece of my breakfast—a third wheat pancake. I soaked it in olive oil and stuffed it into my mouth.

Today I was hoping to explore the vast rooms of my new home—called the *Atrium Vestae*. I did not understand how six Vestals and servants could live in a house with so many rooms.

After all the emotions I'd felt the day before, a calm came over me today. Perhaps the Goddess Vesta had come to me like a vapor of warmth and love in the middle of the night. Then I thought of my bulla. I *must* wear my bulla in secret. I would find time between my training to retrieve it. Perhaps carrying my bulla would free me—for I believed in the power of my amulet. Mother Aurelia stared intently at me and I wondered why she wouldn't answer my question.

"Pay attention, Cornelia." Junia's hard, dark eyes and pinched nose faced my direction. She sniffed and shook her head. "You were daydreaming, something frowned upon by the order. You will need reminding about this."

"We often receive visions while we conduct our sacred rites," said Rubria, smiling.

"Focus is the word, my child. Focus," said Mother Aurelia. Her eyes twinkled like a warm light. "And remembrance, of course."

"And remembrance," said Junia.

I was going to ask Mother what she meant by remembrance. But Junia, never taking her eyes from me, interrupted in her brusque manner.

"If you must know, Cornelia, the first rule of the novice is: 'You will not speak unless spoken to.'"

"For how long?" I blurted out. Then I realized I had just broken the first rule. My hand flew to cover my mouth as the other Vestals tittered.

"For at least half a moon cycle," answered Junia, not amused. "You may address your servants and others such as your *lictor*." I wanted to ask about my lictor, but for at least two weeks, I could speak only when spoken to.

"Cornelia, now is the time to watch, listen and learn," Mother Aurelia said gently, "to take in the teachings of the Vestals, all the way back to the beginning, from King Numa, and then back to Troy. There is much to learn and remember. You will learn that words have power."

Mother arose and approached me. She rested her hands on my shoulders. "And Vesta knows you will do well."

I nodded, afraid to speak.

"Now I must be off to attend to other duties," said Mother.

"And we shall promptly retire to the library," Junia declared. "All available Vestals will attend to the first lesson of our new novice. Let us proceed."

We walked to the library in silence. The vast Vestal library was right off the dining area, where rows of scrolls, papyrus, wax tablets, and other reading materials lined great wooden shelves that reached to the ceiling. Several ladders rested against the shelves—just in case someone needed a scroll from a top shelf. I was surrounded by years of history— the history of Rome and the Vestal Virgins themselves. On one side of the room, a small rounded door colored a burnished red-brown was marked "By Permission Only." I wondered what was behind that door.

I was surrounded by the Vestals as well, staring at me like I was a new doll to be played with. I loved the expanse of the library, the smell of wood and papyrus, how organized it was, and that everything had its place. I thought back to my room at home and how I loved to arrange and rearrange everything to my liking. For some reason, I felt protected in this room.

After we sat down, Junia began. "For your first lesson, Cornelia, please tell us the four elements and what you know of them,"

"Four elements?" I dumbly repeated.

"Yes, the four elements. These are important to a Vestal's learning. We use the elements in our rituals," Junia explained.

All eyes were on me. *I can get this right,* I thought. So I took my time.

"There's the earth, of course," I stated. "The ground we stand on, the rich soil that life grows from."

"Very good," said Junia. "You will soon learn the connection of Vesta and the Earth. Continue."

I thought for a long moment.

"There's the fire—the fire the Vestals must keep alive for the sake of Rome. The fire we must guard, the fire that warms us, the fire that must never go out."

"Next?" Junia asked.

I started feeling rushed and on display; I was being forced to answer when I wasn't ready. I needed time to think. What else? Suddenly the answer came to me.

"Why, there is water of course. The water we need to live and to quench our thirst." I paused and waited.

"Yes, Cornelia. And you shall soon learn the rituals and rites of the water. And the last element?"

I took in a deep breath and thought. And thought some more. It finally came forth into my mind. "The air that we breathe, this is an element. Did I get it right?" I asked.

"Indeed." Junia glanced around at the Vestals gawking at me and nodded.

"But what of the mysterious fifth element?" Rubria spoke up with a mischievous gleam in her eyes.

"Fifth element?" I asked, confused.

Rubria spoke again, even though Junia narrowed her eyes in her direction. "The fifth element is called the ether. It's where all is formed including our thoughts and desires. It's where our prayers and blessings go. We send everything we think onto the ether … and it often returns to us in some form. We protect Rome that way too."

"Is this magic?" I asked.

"Some might call it that," said Junia, casting a mean glance at Rubria. "We use the ether only for the good of Rome and never for our own personal good. Remember this as a warning!"

Junia clapped her hands twice. "Think upon these elements, for as part of your training, you will learn to work with them all—including the mysteries of the ether." She paused and let out a deep breath.

Someone knocked on the door.

"Enter," stated Junia in a very imperious tone, clearly not pleased about being interrupted. In walked Domicia first, followed by the man from the lottery, the Pontifex Maximus, the Emperor Nero himself! He flung his head from side to side, glared around the room, stared into every corner and inspected every space and cubit of the library. Did he think an enemy was hiding in here?

Then his eyes found Rubria, and he gazed deeply at her— as if he was in a trance. *Why is he staring at her this way?* I wondered. Rubria cast her eyes down and her eyelashes started to flutter.

"How is the new novice's training progressing?" The Emperor strode toward me and patted my head.

"She is doing well—as well as can be expected for her first day," Junia replied. She addressed the assembled Vestals. "Let us take a break before lunch. You may have some free time." Clearly the Emperor had business to discuss with Junia.

Lucretia asked me if I cared to walk the temple grounds.

She wanted to explain the purpose of the Regia and some of the surrounding temples to the gods.

We left the library where the Emperor Nero was still speaking with Junia. I noticed Rubria remained as well, fussing with her headdress while watching the Emperor, and then staring down at her hands.

The late morning sunrays sent small flames of light onto the temple grounds. Many people, including senators, walked the Forum grounds, mindless of anything but their conversation. The Forum markets adjacent to the Temple of Vesta started to fill up with chatter, bargaining, and the aromas of hot food cooking.

At that moment my family came into my mind. I was still feeling angry. Would they ever come to get me and take me home?

"Lucretia, when can I see my family again?" I asked.

"Soon child, soon. Remember to focus." She pulled me along already out of breath.

I forgot I had broken the rule of silence. But Lucretia did not chide or scold me. She merely grabbed my arm and tucked it under hers. We stopped in front of the Regia. "Many of the sacred relics are kept here," she explained.

"Yes, Mother Aurelia mentioned the relics. What are they?" I asked.

"The relics tell the story of our past ... what is left of it. You shall see them soon enough. We are the guardians of the sacred relics. They are kept in the Regia, the Emperor's office—with the exception of one ..." Lucretia paused as if she were uncertain whether she should tell me more. "This one special relic is kept in the Temple of Vesta itself. It is housed within the alcove of the temple."

"What relic is that, Lucretia?" I asked.

"Why, it is the Palladium, Cornelia." She sighed and had a far-off look in her eyes. "It is an object of power. We are tasked to guard the Palladium as well."

"But what is it?" I demanded to know.

"It is a small statue of Pallas Athena. That is what the Greeks called her. We call her Minerva, of course. This is not just any statue of this great goddess. The Palladium is *the* statue that we guard."

"But why this statue?" I asked. "What is so special about it?"

"It is special because it was carried by Aeneas to Rome. Legend has it this statue was given to him by the Priestesses of Troy."

"Aeneas? Priestesses of Troy?" I repeated, awestruck.

"Yes. You see when Troy was burning, the Princess Cassandra entrusted the great hero Aeneas with the statue— to make certain that the Palladium was protected—and would forever be safeguarded."

I took a deep breath. This was something for me to look forward to—to behold an ancient relic from the Trojan War!

We continued arm in arm until we finally stopped in front of the Temple of Castor and Pollux. I already loved the grove of pine and elm trees that surrounded the temple. I asked Lucretia if we could walk near them for shade and comfort. Then I heard a loud, persistent drumming against a tree.

"What is that noise?" I asked.

Lucretia squinted, looked up, and pointed, suddenly filled with excitement. "Why, that's Picus, come to greet you," she exclaimed, her hands flapping in joy.

"Picus?"

"Yes, Picus." Her hands started to flap again. "Wait until I tell Mother Aurelia. This is a sign from the gods."

I watched as a green speckled woodpecker with a red pointed crest and black-belly scudded up and down the tree trunk, bobbing his head each time he pierced a hole in the wood. His sharp claws stuck deep in the bark. Then he flew to the ground pecking at pine seeds.

"Why it's just a woodpecker, Lucretia. Why do you call him Picus?"

"You've never heard of Picus?" She shook her head back and forth. "Picus was an ancient woodland god, sacred to Mars, sacred to the founders of Rome, Romulus and Remus. The legend has it that Picus helped feed the abandoned twins, pounding out acorn flesh for the orphans."

"But my father told me that a she-wolf suckled the twins," I said.

"Yes, that's true. But before the she-wolf arrived, Picus flew down and fed the boys." Lucretia stared in awe at the bird. "And this is a sign from the god himself—a sign for you, as the youngest Vestal. Picus is now one of your protectors. Call on him for strength, faith, and perseverance."

The woodpecker took flight and landed on a square vault made from marble in front of the temple stairs. The top of the vault was open. "Look, he's even leading you to the spring we gather water from," Lucretia exclaimed. "The spring of Juturna. In your training with the water element, you will learn about both springs we gather sacred water from."

As we came closer, I saw the water bubbling up from its marble enclosure. Picus flew off, but watched us carefully from a nearby pine.

I knew from my family that Romans were a superstitious people, people who watched for signs. Anything could be taken as an omen. I had once seen the Flamen Dialis sacrifice a sheep, only to declare all was well, because the sheep's liver was healthy. Romans often studied the entrails of animals to get answers to daily questions, and to see what the future might hold.

My father had told me of the College of Augurs. How they studied the flight of eagles, vultures, crows, and other birds important to Rome. They also studied the patterns and directions they flew toward. They especially reviewed the movements of chickens first thing in the morning. What direction the chickens pecked; how many grains they ate—all of these were portents. They were omens of how the day would proceed.

I remembered it was just yesterday when the augur announced that the signs were good— that I would be one of the greatest Vestals. How did he do what he did? I was curious to learn and understand.

Picus watched us from high on a branch. He was quiet now, observing us and resting.

"Wait until I tell the other Vestals. This is a good sign, Cornelia. You are under the protection of Picus. He will help you become adjusted to our way of life. You'll see. Call on him when you are in need."

"Must I be outside waiting for him if I need him?" I asked.

"No, my dear. Remember the ether. You can send your prayers up, and he will answer you … if you are patient enough to wait for an answer."

Not wearing my bulla anymore, I felt relieved that something was protecting me—even if it was just a hungry woodpecker banging on a pine tree.

CHAPTER 7

We turned back toward the Atrium Vestae. Lucretia was so excited she started to run ahead exclaiming she must tell Junia about the encounter with Picus. "Such an omen, such a positive sign," she said, panting. "I will see you inside."

As I walked alone, I saw Rubria rushing toward the temple. "I am late for my shift," she called, whirling by me like a cloud of white smoke. Her face flushed, she grasped the end of her white robe and ran.

As Rubria climbed the stairs to the temple, Vibidia was standing by the door. I paused so we could walk back together. She was the Vestal closest to my age—and I had barely spoken with her. But she was praying, and I heard her mumble under her breath words about forgiveness and the power of Jesus. *What god is this?* I wondered.

"Cornelia? How are you? What are you doing here? Were you listening to me?" Vibidia smiled down at me, her eyes blinking in the light. She seemed the calmest Vestal of all.

"Lucretia showed me the spring of Juturna in front of the Temple of Castor and Pollux. Then Picus came to visit us." I puffed up with pride. "Lucretia says he's a god who will protect me. And who is this Jesus you pray to? Another God with a temple I know not of? I want to learn everything."

"Picus—the woodpecker? Ah, I see." Vibidia had a lost look in her eyes. Would she answer my question? Instead, she asked me a question of her own. "Cornelia, do you believe in the gods?" We stopped for a brief moment under the Capetine Oak. The thick clump of my hair tied to the branch brought back memories of yesterday, of my beloved hair shorn for Vesta.

"Of course I believe in the gods. I was born on the Festival of Diana, so I was dedicated to her as a child. I am now dedicated to Vesta." I pointed to the tree. "And there's my lock of hair to prove it. Yes I believe in the gods."

I eyed Vibidia with curiosity. Why was she asking me such questions? "Don't you believe in our gods and goddesses?" I asked her.

Vibidia gazed up to the clear blue sky as if the answer resided somewhere up there.

"Many times I have tried to believe, Cornelia. And many times I must. But I believe in the Son of God now, the Son of the One God—the one they call Jesus Christ."

"What God is this?" I asked. "Is this the new god you were just praying to? Is there a temple where we can make offerings? Is there a statue we can pray to? Does this god require certain sacrifices? Does—"

Vibidia held up her hand and glanced around to make sure no one else was listening. "Hush, Cornelia. I will tell you more if you swear not to tell a word of this to anyone—not even to Lucretia."

"I swear," I said, in anticipation of learning more secrets.

She lowered her voice to a whisper. "There is a sect in Rome—they call themselves Believers. They are followers of the Nazarene, Jesus. And they need no temple to their god, nor do they require sacrifices. They try to live the teachings of Jesus. They are His disciples. Someday when my time is up as a Vestal, I shall walk with these disciples."

She grabbed my arms and shook my shoulders. "Tell not a soul, and I shall tell you even more later." We silently made our way back to the Atrium. Vibidia had given me much to think about. Perhaps I would learn more about this Jesus, another God for Rome, but described by Vibidia as the Son of the One God.

Lunch was platters of cold meats, olives, and cheese. I ate in silence during the meal.

"This afternoon Cornelia, you will return to your room and commence studying the rules of the Vestals and the festivals … if there is time," said Junia in her usual tone. "You will rest this evening, for tomorrow you will be allowed your first visit into Vesta's Temple."

So tomorrow was the day I would behold Vesta's flame. Thoughts filled my mind like a swarm of bees. I wanted to learn everything I could, but mostly I wanted to see the flame.

"Lucretia shared with me how Picus came to you," Junia remarked. "We Vestals and the Goddess are well pleased."

I felt relieved that she was pleased with *something* about me. I said nothing; like a sponge I soaked in whatever anyone told me. What could I do but listen? Vibidia looked at me with a reassuring serene smile.

"There will be no formal dinner tonight," Junia announced. "Domicia will bring something to your room for dinner tonight to tide you over until the morning. Do you have any questions, Cornelia?"

I shook my head.

"Then that is all for now," Junia said firmly.

I did have many unanswered questions of course. When was I going to guard the flame? When could I participate in festivals? When could I see the Palladium? Who was this Jesus that Vibidia loved so much? My head started to spin, my eyes drooped, and my body felt heavy and tired.

Junia added, "You may take a rest before you review the rules of the novice."

I nodded and Lucretia led me upstairs to my room.

Upon my desk lay a new scroll, one I hadn't seen before. Someone must have left it there during my walk on the grounds. It was held together firmly with the Emperor's seal, a blot of red wax with the faint outline of the God Apollo bathed in rays of sunlight. In bold writing along the side was written, **"Rules for the Novice."**

I quickly broke the seal and began to read:

To the Novice:

Welcome to the House of the Vestals!

Behold the Laws and Rules of the Ancient Order of the Vestals. Guide and guard them well, for they are a part of our tenets of Faith and Law.

I. You must watch the perpetual and pure flame that resides within the Temple of Vesta. If the fire goes out under your watch, you shall be punished. If Rome suffers as a result of your carelessness, then your punishment will be dire.

II. You shall serve and remain with the Vestal Order for 30 years. During this 30-year period, the first 10 years are your training period; the second 10 years will be for duties, and the last 10 years will be for training other novices. After 30 years you will be free to conduct your life as you choose. You may however, remain within the Vestal Order for longer than 30 years.

III. During this 30-year period, you will remain a virgin. If your chastity is brought into question, either before a court or if accused by another, and you are found guilty of this crime, the punishment is death by being buried alive. When a Vestal loses her Virginity, the State of Rome is stained by this impurity. This is a warning.

IV. You shall carry the water in a vessel shaped so it may never rest on the ground. If precious water is spilled, the consequence will be a severe punishment.

V. You will have privileges granted, such as having a lictor, the ability to make a will and own land, and the ability to pardon criminals you may meet on the road. Do not abuse such privileges.

VI. You will be responsible for maintaining records, wills, and important documents located in the library. You must never reveal or expose the contents of this information unless you are told otherwise.

VII. You will only be allowed to walk the streets of Rome with permission from the Chief Virgo Maxima, and never alone. No citizen may touch or grab you, unless you touch the forhead or hand of a citizen with Vesta's blessing.

The Emperor Nero's seal was stamped at the bottom of the scroll next to his name. Beneath it, Mother Aurelia's signature appeared in scratchy writing. A black line indicated where I must sign. *No*, I thought. *I am not ready to sign my life away to Vesta.*

After reading the rules of the novice, I could read no more. Then I remembered my gift from Cornelius. I retrieved my cedar box and set it on top of my desk. I lifted the handle and removed the small wrapped box from its place.

I tore off the wrapping and opened my gift. A green jewel sparkled before my eyes. A little note lay rolled up inside the box. I unraveled the note and read:

For Cornelia on her 10th birthday,
An emerald for you found in the depths of the
Mediterranean Sea.
Love,
Cornelius.

An emerald! How had he gotten such a jewel? This made me miss my brother even more. After all the complaining I'd done about him, he didn't seem so awful now. I realized how much I loved Cornelius—how much I missed him already in my new life as a Vestal.

When would I see my family again? I thought that maybe I would try to use the power of the ether to get my way. I cared not that this power must be used for the good of Rome. What about what was good for *me*?

Sitting on my bed, holding my emerald in my left hand and my bulla in the right, I concentrated all of my thoughts on my family. I saw myself back home with my family who celebrated my return. I vowed I would never be bad again. My parents would come get me and tell me it was all a mistake. They wanted me back as their daughter.

But I had little power or belief in myself. I never felt so alone in my life.

Someone knocked on the door. Domicia pushed the door open and came in quietly with a tray of dried fish, cheese, and fruit. "How are your studies coming, Cornelia?" She raised an eyebrow noticing that I was holding the emerald. What concern was it to *her*? She was a slave and should mind her place.

I stared long and hard at her. "Your timing is perfect because I am hungry. And my studies are coming along. I am taking a rest."

"I see," she said, and placed the tray on the table near the desk. "When you are finished, slip the tray under the door. I'll be back for it soon. I don't want to disturb your studies." She moved in a stealthy manner like one of the panthers at the Circus Maximus, and then silently closed the door. I couldn't decide if I trusted her—or even liked her.

I pounced on my food and ate everything with relish. While I ate, I watched the dwindling activity on the temple grounds.

The sunrays started to fade and melted into thin shadows that sank into the grass. The columns from the Temple of Castor and Pollux also cast shadows that looked like bands of iron bars. Like the bars prisoners sat behind.

But as dusk set in, I observed something else from my window—something that made me think. For as night settled over Rome, I watched the Emperor Nero stomp down the hill with a guard behind him. He ascended the steps of the Temple, and banged his fist on the door. The guard remained by the Temple steps.

What happened next, I would never forget. I watched as Rubria opened the door for Emperor Nero. He entered the Temple then grabbed her to him— just like he grabbed and yanked me to him the day before. And then the door to the temple slammed shut.

CHAPTER 8

I already thought of Emperor Nero as a beast. He couldn't fool me. The way he looked at Rubria. The way he barged into the temple. But he was the Pontifex Maximus; he could do whatever he pleased. I could do nothing of what I pleased anymore. I was just a novice-in-training.

Once again, I slept soundly in my tiny room. When I awoke, the sun was shining, and life was stirring outside on the Forum grounds. I heard the ringing of the breakfast bell and quickly wrapped the white band round my head and flung on my plain white tunica.

I scurried out the door, along the dim-lit hallway, down the back stairs, and finally into the dining room. I found a place and remained silent—as was the rule.

"Eat up, Cornelia," said Junia, frowning. "You missed the morning prayer to Vesta. This will be a busy training day for you. You will visit the temple today. After breakfast, you may return to your room, where you will pray to Vesta. You may also continue to review the festivals and rituals we partake in."

More reading! More work! No dancing or visiting my friends. No fun at all! I felt an overwhelming burden on me. What could I do now but follow Junia's orders? I thought that perhaps I *would* work on the power of the ether to get me home.

Back in my room, I prayed to Vesta, and decided I would use the magic of the ether to get what *I* wanted, not what people wanted from me. I would use the ether to get me back to my family. I had nothing to lose. I concentrated with focus. Over and over, I sent out thoughts and images about my family. Perhaps an hour passed.

There was a loud knock on the door. Someone slowly opened it. Domicia poked her head into the room. "You have visitors, Cornelia," she announced. She stepped back out of the way. My father, mother, and brother stood in the shadows. *My magic is working*, I thought. *They are here to take me home!*

I glared at them. "At last," I cried. "I knew you would come get me. I just need to take my box." My mother gasped and my father shook his head.

"No, Cornelia We come only to visit," said my father.

"Look at me! Look what they've done to me." I pointed to my head. "How *could* you?" I bunched up my fists and snarled at them. The old Cornelia was back.

"The goddess chose you," my father said softly. "We had nothing to do with this."

"Then why did you receive money—for me? Me!" I said, jabbing a finger at my chest. "You always told me I was worth more than gold." And then I pointed at my father. "You lied to me, Father, lied."

My father stared down to the floor. My mother seemed shocked to witness me in such a state. "Your hair will grow again, Cornelia. You'll get used to it." She wiped a stray tear from her face with the hem of her stola. Cornelius blinked and gaped at me as if I were an oddity, someone he no longer knew.

"I demand to go home—now! I am suffering, and you don't care." I sniffled and stood there waiting for an answer.

"What can we do, Cornelia? You were chosen. We came here to see you and brought you some treats," my father said.

My mother's hands were shaking as she handed me the tightly wrapped package. "All of your favorites," she said. I grabbed the box and flung it across the room.

I was more confused than ever. Hadn't the magic of the ether drawn my family to me? "You mean your won't fight for me? To get me away from this—prison?" I cried.

"Cornelia, this may be the last time we shall see you in many moons," said Father. "We have come to say goodbye … know that we love you and care about you."

"If you loved me, you would take me home," I wailed. Red-faced, I felt my tantrum grow. Everything that had worked for me at home no longer seemed to work anymore. "I hate you! I hate you all!" I screamed. "And I will never forget how you have forsaken your only daughter to—this!" I tore the wrapping off my head, pointed to my baldness, and gestured to the sparse surrounding of my room.

"We are sorry, Cornelia. Someday you might forgive us and understand," my father said.

"Understand? Understand what? That you sold me—for three bags of gold? Of course, I do not understand." I flopped onto my bed, covered my face in my trembling hands, and continued to sob. Maybe my display of emotion would melt their hearts.

"I am worth more than gold!" I screamed.

"You are, Cornelia," said my brother. "But—"

"Perhaps it's too soon for a visit," my mother said to my father. I continued to sob and wail.

And when I stopped to look up to see if they were watching, I noticed they were gone. They had left me all alone with nothing but my tears. My thoughts and powers had brought them to me. But my thoughts and powers could not keep me with them. Perhaps I had not yet mastered the mysteries of the ether element. I would have to study harder.

I sat sobbing on my bed until I heard another knock on the door. I mumbled for the person to come in. It was Domicia with two other slave women. "We are here to prepare you for your visit to the temple," she said. They rubbed my head with oils and unguents that smelled like a garden: lavender, rose, and thyme blended together.

Domicia watched me wipe my tears away, but ignored my gesture, and made no reference to my outburst. "I do have good news for you, Cornelia," she said.

"What good news?" I asked, wiping my nose. After the scene with my family, the only good news would be that the Emperor had made a mistake, and I would be able to return home.

"You will be moving down the hall to a much larger apartment soon. Your new living quarters will be spacious with at least four rooms to call your own."

She and the others continued to massage my scalp calmly. "And look, your hair is already sprouting up." She smiled. "It's starting to grow back."

I sprang up and ran to see myself in the polished oval. Sure enough, tiny needles of black hair stuck out from my head.

The other slaves accompanying Domicia soothed me with their soft voices and strong hands. I was now ready to enter the temple and meet Vesta's flame for the first time.

Junia was waiting for me in front of the Temple. "I see you are prepared, Cornelia. Let us make haste." She grabbed my elbow and escorted me up the stairs. I said a silent prayer to Vesta. Junia pushed the bronze door open. Lucretia was inside tending the fire. Her face brightened when she saw me.

I tried to observe everything inside the temple. I counted eighteen white pillars circling around the walls, holding up the great dome. And what a dome it was! Painted gold stars amid an indigo sky sparkled down on me. In the center of the dome, a small, round hole allowed the smoke to rise up and out of the temple. The temple fire burned in a deep, circular pit. Six short stairs descended to the small flame shooting up colored sparks of red, blue, and orange.

A pile of wedge-shaped pieces of wood lay in a carefully arranged stack near the fire. Mosaic designs on the floor showed the many shapes of the fire, glowing, bending, and reaching skyward. Besides the ceiling it was the most colorful part of the temple—except for the flame itself. To one side of the fire, a sunken pit was filled with ashes; I presumed they were ashes collected from the daily burning of all that wood. Six seats sat empty around the fire. A slave girl stood to one side assisting Lucretia. Then I noticed the carved niche with a small, round wooden door off to one side of the temple.

"Do you have any questions?" Junia asked.

"Yes. What is behind the door?"

Junia looked surprised. "That is where we keep our most revered and sacred relic, the Palladium. I believe Lucretia reviewed its history with you?" I nodded. "Now is the time you shall behold it with your own eyes," she announced.

So this was where the statue of Pallas Athena was kept! My breath quickened to think I would soon see this object of power.

Junia led me to the small alcove, pushed away the curtain, and gently opened the door. The space beyond was no more than a small recess. A narrow wooden table sat in the center of the alcove. The statue, covered in a white cloth, looked smaller than I had imagined.

Junia lifted the cloth and displayed the sacred object. The statue looked to be carved of an olive wood; it was blackened by fire and smudged with stains. Carved into the wood was the likeness of Minerva—Pallas Athena! A winged owl-eyed helmet covered her head, as if she were ready for battle; the wise warrior goddess held a spear in one hand and a shield in another. A snake lay crushed underneath one of her feet. Her shield had carvings with a strange, monstrous head in the center. Her battle gown had grooves that flowed down to her feet.

Could this really be the sacred object carried from the burning shores of Troy by Aeneas? "Can I touch Her?" I asked Junia.

"Not yet, Cornelia. Remember, you are still a novice. But

you can pray to Her for guidance as regards your studies. And of course you can pray to Her for the protection and safety of Rome. We guard this statue the way mothers guard their young. If something should happen to the Palladium …" Junia shuddered, "… it could bode badly for Rome."

She quickly replaced the cloth over the statue, gave a mumbled blessing, and promptly shut the door. Then she rearranged the curtain covering the door.

"Do you have any other questions?" She regarded me with a raised eyebrow.

"Yes. What type of wood do the Vestals use to keep the flame burning? Why is the wood shaped in a triangle?"

"These are fine questions. We only use oak from within Rome's sacred groves. If we run low on oak, we use the wood from the maple tree. Maple burns with purity. The wedge shape you call a triangle must be cleaved from the heart of the tree. To please Vesta's heart." Junia paused. "All right?"

"What about the sacred objects in the Regia?" I asked. "What's in there?"

Junia sighed. She was starting to get impatient with me. "The sacred objects are kept in the Regia for safekeeping."

"But what are the objects? I would like to know," I asked.

Lucretia came around and touched me on the shoulder. "One of the objects is the Great Spear that fell from heaven. It is called King Numa's spear. The spear was a sign to the Roman people that Numa would be king, and indeed he was for many years."

I already knew I loved King Numa and wanted to know everything I could about him.

"And then there's the shield of King Numa—"

"That is enough for now, Lucretia. Please resume your duties," commanded Junia. "Too much information into that little head of hers … never good for a novice." She began to mumble under her breath.

By now I was entranced with the fire. I could not take my eyes off the blue-orange flames that rose straight to the heavens, the smoke that rose perfectly out of the hole in the top of the dome. I watched Lucretia carefully position each piece of wood onto the fire.

"We must never throw the wood straight on the fire. We gently lay it down with care," Lucretia explained.

"Cornelia, you will be allowed to return with another Vestal soon," said Junia. "That is all for today." We gave thanks to Vesta and departed the temple.

After a midday lunch of cheese, olives and salted fish, I was told to return to my room for more study. The Feast of Ops Consiva was only a few weeks away. I would attend, but only as a spectator. The other news was that I would meet my new lictor soon. Lucretia explained that the lictors assigned to us were our protectors, bodyguards who announced our arrivals and departures. They also helped to clear the clogged roads in order for us to pass. Vestal guards! How exciting!

If I studied and followed the Vestal rules and rituals, the reward, Junia shared, would be a trip to the Circus Maximus—with box seats close to the Emperor and the Senators. Emperor Nero was always enthusiastic about the chariot races. We must applaud him loudly and cheer for his team.

So now I had something to look forward to. My parents were gone but my hair was growing—like me—from the inside out.

CHAPTER 9

I sat in my room, studying the details of our next ritual, and wondering when I would get to move into my more spacious living quarters. When I had something to look forward to, I started forgetting the past—how hurt and angry I felt over my parents' disregard for me.

I reviewed the calendar with the list of festivals. I now realized that Rome based many of its celebrations around the harvest; the planting times, the reaping times; the animal sacrifices to be made to ensure the crops were bountiful. I studied how the Roman Calendar was influenced by the moon phases—the Kalends, the Nones and the Ides.

My head began to swirl with all this information. I needed a break from my work. Quietly shutting the door behind me, I made my way down the half-lit narrow corridor. I wanted to sit out in the back garden, enjoy the bright sunlight, and say my prayers to Vesta.

A bench under a cypress tree looked like a perfect place for me to sit and pray. The garden statues of long ago Vestals seemed happy to see me—more than happy, they welcomed me today.

"Dear Vesta, Goddess of the Hearth," I prayed, "You have chosen me for a reason. I know not why. Now I am a part of you. Please give me a sign that I am yours." Waited for a sign. I watched the flower heads stretch toward the sun, the wind blowing stem and leaf in a steady rhythm. The walled-off garden was a quiet place that no one but the Vestals could enter. The front of the Atrium Vestae was noisy; visitors to the Forum often roamed the grounds leading to our home. I adored this sacred garden and how much love and care it received from the Vestals and servants.

The noise I heard at first was faint and weak. I turned my head but saw nothing. I heard it again—a slight mewing. "Where are you?" I asked. Rather than get up, I waited patiently. I heard it again. And waited. Finally, I turned around. A black and white head poked out from around the trunk of a cypress tree for a moment—then disappeared.

"Come now ... I'm a friend," I whispered. The tiny head popped out from behind the tree again. It had pointed ears, a triangle nose, eyes the color of my new emerald, and a black mask that outlined its eyes. It was a kitten, half grown and all by itself. It reminded me of my lottery marker, the face of the cat looking out at me.

"Come here, little one." I tried to coax the kitten out from her hiding place. I sat still, turning around every so often. The kitten seemed to be lost, alone, and most likely hungry. My heart went out to the little orphan, this cat that needed me.

After sitting as still as the statues surrounding me, I felt a brief nudge on my legs and heard the purring noise; it sounded like a roar to me. Back and forth the kitten rubbed against me. Then she allowed me to pick her up. She had already spied the fishpond; she jumped down and kept looking in that direction.

But those eyes, like Vesta's flame, had put a spell on me. The cat's green eyes seemed outlined in kohl, just like my mother's eyeliner. Just like Cleopatra. "I shall call you Cleo—after my favorite queen. And you are just as beautiful. Now you are mine," I told her.

I lifted her thin body up toward the sun, and to the statues of the Vestals, then settled Cleo on my lap. She stayed there purring, with a regal contentment that only queens and cats are capable of. I was in love.

I gave thanks to Vesta for hearing my prayers. She had not only given me a sign, she brought me a new friend. I did not feel so alone anymore.

How would I get Cleo back to my room unnoticed? I tucked her in the folds of my tunica. I would get some leftover fish and goat's milk from the kitchen for her. I could tell she was hungry; she was so thin, but she remained quiet while I carried her up to my room.

I set her on the floor, and after sniffing everything in the room she curled up in a ball and fell asleep. There was a loud knock on the door. I picked Cleo up and stuffed her under the bed, telling her to stay quiet.

"Please come in," I commanded. It was Junia, her face as pinched and red as a dried-up grape.

"I hear your parents were here this morning—and you made a scene. Vestals control themselves—and you did not! Why, it sounds like you acted like a spoiled child. We shall not have another display of emotion or anything resembling a tantrum, Cornelia," she said. "If I hear of another outburst, you will be chastised."

I remained quiet.

"For tomorrow's lesson, you will learn about the ritual of carrying the water—from Vibidia," Junia added. That was a relief. Now I would have time to speak with Vibidia and learn more about this new god she worshipped—Jesus Christ. But then Junia concluded, "And I will be there to supervise you."

"Mew." I heard the faint crying and acted as if I had lost something in the room. I fumbled with the box of treats from my family that rattled like a musical instrument.

"Mew."

Junia's eyes darted back and forth, and she made a loud hrrumph. "What is this, Cornelia? What is that noise?" She stiffened, and her pointed nose loomed over me. But it was too late. For Cleo had appeared, stretched out her front paws, and yawned.

"What is the meaning of this? I want an answer—at once!" Junia demanded.

I decided I would tell her the truth—as calmly as I could. No tantrums or outbursts this time.

"I found her in the garden all by herself. She's lonely, thin and starved, and she needs me," I pleaded.

"More like you need *her*," Junia mumbled. "No cats are allowed inside the Atrium Vestae."

Domicia had shown up at the door. "The Atrium could use a cat to catch the mice and rodents that scurry around at night. You know how they find their way into the granary and the mill. They wreak havoc on our sacred grains. And the cold weather will soon be settling in on Rome …"

So although Domicia had told Junia about my earlier outburst, she now defended me.

Junia bristled with anger. "Mind your place, slave. Do what you are told now!" Junia shook her head as if deciding what to say next. "I shall think on the matter. In the meantime, the cat can live in the garden." Junia sniffed the air as if she smelled something unpleasant, and looked around again, making sure I wasn't hiding anything else.

Cleo began to purr and rub herself against Junia's thick white robes. She even wound her tail around Junia's leg and stared at her with those green eyes. Was Junia's hard heart melting? "Take this feline out back. Now!" she ordered Domicia. "And find some goat's milk and scraps of meat for the creature. The House of Vesta cannot and will not be responsible for the death of any such animal. Now!"

Domicia lifted the crying cat and soothed it in her arms. I watched with sadness in my heart. But I refused to cry and scream. Tantrums did not work for me anymore.

But I had ideas—and a plan for my cat. Vesta had answered my prayer. She would not forsake me now.

As dusk settled in once again over the Atrium, I said my prayers, reviewed the Festival of Ops Consiva, and readied myself for bed. A full moon was rising over the Atrium bright and round.

A soft knock sounded against the door. "Who is it?" I asked, thinking about all the visitors I had had today.

"It is Rubria. May I come in?"

"Of course," I replied. I enjoyed company before I went to bed. Rubria slipped in and sat beside me. The red hair poking out of her headdress looked like tiny flames. Even her headdress couldn't contain her curls.

"Come with me, Cornelia. Out to the back garden," she whispered.

"Why?" I asked.

"You'll see," she said. "Stay quiet now."

All was silent within the Atrium walls. I shut the door with care and followed the most colorful and exciting Vestal of all. What did Rubria want with me tonight? Would she help me look for Cleo?

We found a stone bench alongside the garden. I heard the noise of wagon carts creaking and the braying of donkeys along the Via Sacra. Wagons and carts were allowed in Rome only after nightfall; Rome was too crowded with people during the day.

I breathed deeply and waited. Rubria looked in all directions, and then pulled a silver-blue flask from her cloak. "Stand up, Cornelia, and face the full moon," she ordered. I did as I was told. "Stand still now." She unplugged the flask's top and began anointing my head saying prayers to Vesta.

"What are you doing, Rubria?" I asked her, as she massaged the oil deep into my head.

"This sacred blend of oils will make your hair grow faster and thicker under the full moon. Everything grows faster under the full moon," she murmured, fussing over me.

"What's in it?" I asked.

"This is a blend of olive, grapeseed, lavender, and rosemary oils." She began reciting an incantation over and over:

"As above, so below,
Goddess make her hair to grow,
As within, so without,
Make Cornelia's hair grow out."

I had little idea what she was doing, but then I remembered. "Are you working magic with the ether, Rubria?" I asked, for she was the Vestal who had explained this magic to me.

"Of course I am, Cornelia. I send up my prayers through the moon rays right into the ether. The full moon is *always* the best time to work the magic of the ether."

"And what you say rhymes. I love to rhyme."

"Yes, rhymes are a part of our magic. The Goddess Vesta loves rhymes and the rhythm of words. Remember this well." Her soothing words and gentle strokes along my head relaxed me. After she finished anointing my head, I decided I would dance in the garden. I stood in the moonlit garden and began to gently bow to the moon and the sleeping flowers in the evening light. I lifted my arms up to the sky, twirled myself around, and bent down toward the earth. I tried to remember the steps to my favorite dance. And for a moment—I felt free! Even though the night noises from the streets remained around the garden— the grunts of work animals, dogs howling and people arguing— still, somehow the Vestal garden was a sanctuary. My sanctuary.

I followed the cut stones along the path, bowed to the Vestal statues, and remembered how I had wanted to dance for the Emperor. But now I danced in Vesta's honor. Rubria seemed amused; I saw the smile on her face.

"I remember how I used to love the dance, Cornelia," she said.

"Have you danced for the Emperor, Rubria? He would love to watch you; you are so beautiful and graceful." Then I remembered something else. I returned to join Rubria on the bench.

"Why does the Emperor Nero visit you in the temple?" I quietly asked. "At night?"

Rubria, glancing around the moonlit garden, stood and loomed over me. "I know not of what you speak."

"But I saw him bang on the temple door and then he grabbed you—like he grabbed me and yanked me away from my father! He's horrible!"

"Cornelia, please … you imagined it from the shadows … the shadows in your mind. You saw nothing of the sort." She shook my shoulders and lifted my chin up so she could look at me. "And tell not a soul of your imaginings. If the Emperor Nero hears of such lies, you could receive a scourging."

I nodded obediently. My head was soaked with the fragrant herbs. Rubria told me I must not say another word and to sit facing the moon. Only then would the moon's full rays penetrate my head and stimulate new growth.

What I had shared clearly disturbed her. I wished I hadn't been so bold. I was learning there were some subjects I needed to keep to myself.

CHAPTER 10

SEPEMBER 60 AD

Bright sunlight shone into my room as I prepared myself for the lesson on how to carry the spring water to the Atrium Vestae. Lucretia had already explained to me that Vestals never used or drank from waters that ran through pipes. We only drank from the spring of Juturna—near the Temple of Castor and Pollux.

But today I, along with Vibidia with Junia supervising, would proceed in a litter through the Porta Capena, down the Appian Way, to the spring of Egeria. I had learned in my studies that Egeria was a river nymph who fell in love with King Numa over eight hundred years ago. He consulted with the nymph who provided him with wise counsel and gave him many of Rome's laws. We used Egeria's healing water for many of our rituals and sacrifices.

I felt excited because today would be my first official day in public. I must hold myself in a dignified manner. For now I represented Vesta and my new family—the Roman State.

As practice, we began at the well of Juturna. I was shown how to ladle the water into a clay vessel that had a sharp tip at the bottom. It could not be set upon the ground. I watched Vibidia the way a hawk watches a mouse. And Junia looked on me the same way—with those narrowed, slanted eyes and pinched expression of disdain.

After I retrieved the water and carried it back to the Atrium, I poured it into one of the many deep basins we used for drinking. Vibidia had given me a smaller amphora with a pointed tip at the bottom. Hers was much larger of course. I was to imitate everything she did.

"When do we leave?" I asked anxiously.

"Soon," said Junia. "Our litter will carry us along the Appian Way until we reach a fork in the road. There we dismount and walk to the spring. And when we take the fork and begin walking, you, Cornelia, will hold the vessel in both hands. Look straight ahead and hold your head high," Junia ordered.

The litter awaited us on the Via Sacra. Vibidia's lictor commanded that the road be cleared for us. We must proceed with no obstacles in our path.

We set off passing the palace and then the Circus Maximus quiet this morning in its gargantuan splendor. A few men swept the cluttered, dirty streets around the Circus area preparing for the day ahead. But the crowds who lined the street bowed to us with respect and adoration.

After passing through the gate of the Porta Capena, we continued onto the Appian Way, past a set of crumbling tombstones, some piled one on top of the other. A great tufa-and-stone wall rose up on both sides of the road. In between the graves, ancient trees curled upward, their branches bending over the walls. Then the road curved sharply to the left. We had arrived at the fork in the road.

"Let us off here!" Junia demanded.

I followed the path as best I could. I noticed Vibidia at times tucked the water vessel against her hip and leaned it toward her. Other times she lifted it to the air. Junia followed close behind. I could feel her breath on my neck.

And then, out of the corner of my eye, I saw Taltos in the crowd. Short in stature as he was, he had managed to wedge his way to the front of the gathering. He began to wave to me. "Cornelia, Cornelia, here ... here!"

I looked over and instinctively beamed at my dear family servant. Oh how I missed him, and could not contain my joy! I lifted one hand from the vessel and waved enthusiastically to him. Lucretia had already taught me the imperial wave— hand straight out, palm open, and to slowly move my hand back and forth. Now it seemed the perfect time to try out the Vestal hand wave, even at double speed.

But Junia had witnessed my movement. "Foolish girl, pay attention," she hissed. "Keep your eyes forward. Focus." I glanced at Vibidia who seemed to be in her own world.

Then I felt a hard push on my back. Stumbling forward, I tripped on a paving stone as my sandal caught on an uneven edge. Down I fell, flat on my face. The amphora shattered into pieces at my side.

The crowd gasped, then fell silent. Someone ran to help me up, but Junia refused any assistance. "Let her get up herself," she shouted. "She's got to learn. Now get up!"

I pulled myself up. My tunica, torn and bloodied, hung like a limp rag on my body. My chin, scraped and bruised, was bleeding down my tunica. My knee was also scraped. What had I done but wave? I looked for Taltos, but he was gone. I knew he'd return to my family and tell them what happened.

Junia towered over me red-faced and sullen. Her quiet rage was more frightening than her shouts and insults. *Why did she push me?* I wondered. *Did she want me to look like a fool?*

I refused to cry; this was not the time. I was on display and now looked like a clumsy little girl. I vowed Junia would not get away with this. She was my teacher—and she pushed me. *Did she want to see me fail?* I staunched my bloodied chin with the hem of my tunica. The amphora lay in pieces along the Appian Way, a testament to my first failure as a Vestal.

Vibidia had no expression on her face.

"Please proceed, girls," I heard Junia say behind me. I turned to stare hard at my teacher. I gave her a look that said, "Leave me alone." I would make sure she didn't hover over me for the rest of the journey. But this did not work either, for she remained right behind me while I continued to walk, nursing my bruised chin—and pride.

"Keep your head up. Stay erect and look forward," Junia admonished. "We are getting closer."

The paved road started to slope downhill. I noticed others had taken a sharp left and followed the path marked, "To the Spring of Egeria."

I followed Vibidia while I felt Junia eyeing me like an old, wary crow.

"The spring of Egeria is a healing spring," said Vibidia. "Where many are cured of their ailments and maladies."

The path narrowed; a small, pebbled walkway led to the spring. Overarching trees formed a tunnel of branches and leaves. We proceeded through the bower until a clearing opened up before us. There amid an open field, stood a grove of poplar and mulberry trees along with ancient oaks. We walked across the field, following the path leading to the spring. A large aqueduct ran through the field nearby. I could see snow-capped mountains to the west. Truly, I felt far away from noisy center of Rome. This was a place of peace— and power.

Great stone embankments surrounded the spring. Lush ferns of bright green grew in profusion before the sacred waters. Wildflowers of deep purple, red, yellow and white added more color. And what a crowd gathered at the spring! Junia had stepped in front of us; the crowd parted to let us pass.

The people stared, bruised and bloody as I was. I paid no mind to their shocked faces. We approached the spring with a quiet dignity. I noticed the silence, everyone praying and showing reverence to the Spirit of Egeria. Would she give me a message? I sent my prayer out to the ether … and waited.

The spring, lined with moss and lichen-covered stones, gurgled and made bubbling noises. Even the air seemed differ-ent—as if the waters mingled with the air to create a vital mist and healing vapor. Every once in a while, a flash of rainbow colors burst forth from the water's surface.

"*Come closer, child,*" I heard. But the voice speaking to me was not the voice of Junia or Vibidia. "*Dip your hand into my sacred waters and be healed.*"

I listened to the words and followed the order, as if I were under a spell. I slipped a few fingers into the water and dabbed my chin and knee. The drops immediately disappeared into my bruises. Both Vestals watched me closely, but said not a word.

I knew the waters of Egeria would heal my cuts and bruises. And I knew these waters had already touched a deep part of my soul.

Cups with long handles were nestled into the many niches carved into the stone embankment. A white drinking cup etched with a symbol of a flame sat in one of the niches. "This is our Vestal drinking cup," Junia said. "But you are here today to learn to ladle and pour. Here's how we ladle the water into the vessel." Junia lifted the ladle and continued. "We first say silent prayers to Egeria and ask permission. You hold the amphora on your hip, then ladle the water in slowly, ever mindful not to spill a drop."

I watched Vibidia ladle the water into her vessel with perfection. Everything she did was perfect. She was graceful, patient, and looked as if she moved in a sacred rhythm, a dance of sorts. How I admired her talents!

"Would you like to ladle out the water and practice pouring?" Vibidia asked.

"No, she may not. Not today. Not after bloodying herself and making a fool of all of us." Junia sniffed the air and scanned the gathering crowd. Clearly, pilgrims from near and far made the journey to the sacred spring. Crutches, bandages, votives, and gifts, including ribbons, scarves, and even a piece of amber, graced the surrounding stone niches.

In the nearby field I noticed a small crowd had gathered around a young man flashing a long cloth with red stripes on the borders, and pointing a crooked staff in different directions. A tent stood close by. He lifted his staff and tapped the ground several times. Then he raised the staff into the air and sat down on a stool. Was this the augur from the lottery? An older man with a similar stick stood watching him.

I stepped back a few paces from the spring. Junia seemed occupied, making certain that Vibidia properly got the water we needed for the Atrium.

The young man had noticed me. It *was* the augur who had pronounced that I would be "One of the Greatest Vestals." I wanted to watch his performance—he had a dramatic flair. I was drawn to the activity and walked across the field.

"Lucius, what do the omens say about my wife? Is she cheating on me with the baker? asked a burly man in work clothes.

"Why ask me when you know the answer?" the augur scoffed at the man.

As I walked toward him, he pointed his crook in my direction. "And here she is, Cornelia, the novice. The auguries look promising for you to be a grand Vestal. So the Gods have decreed." And there I was, all tattered, torn, and bruised. I felt anything but grand and great. But I could feel my knee and chin had stopped throbbing—the wounds were beginning to heal.

"So you say." I tried to smile.

He bowed low to me, then whipped his striped cloth around, and brandished his staff in all directions. "Welcome to the Spring of Egeria. The Great Spirit of the waters will heal you. This is a place of power and magic." As if this were a part of my lesson, he said, "You do know that you stand in the field where King Numa received his sacred spear? The great spear that fell from heaven? You stand on sacred ground."

I took in all the sights with my eyes, saying nothing.

The augur wore his black hair oiled, with his long ringlets pushed back, exposing a wide forehead, jet black eyes, white teeth, straight nose and a square chin. He looked to be Vibidia's age, eighteen or nineteen. I also guessed that the older man was his teacher.

"I thank you for the knowledge, Augur," I replied, bowing slightly to him.

"Lucius," he stated.

"Lucius."

"You are most welcome, Cornelia. Perhaps we shall meet again—here—soon."

Junia was stomping into the field demanding I remain with her. I was not to go wandering. She warned me I was to take heed on our walk back. I could afford no more blunders. At least Vibidia was ready with *her* amphora of sacred water!

"Perhaps we shall meet again—here—soon." Lucius's words stayed in my mind as we retraced our steps back to the Appian Way, where our litter awaited to take us once again to our home, the Atrium Vestae.

CHAPTER 11

Two months had passed since I was chosen. My life as a Vestal was proceeding forward. I could speak up now when I wanted. The best news of all was that Rubria's full moon spell had worked; my hair was growing back fast! I had an inch of hair now.

The other good news was that I moved into my new spacious quarters down the hall closer to Vibidia. I now had four rooms, including my own bathroom, lined up with the Atrium's latrines. I had a bathtub that the Atrium's water bearers filled with hot water every morning so I could bathe and be clean for Vesta's services. I even had a small balcony that overlooked the temple grounds.

And my plan to care for and tend to Cleo was working. I would venture out to the garden with some dried fish, call for her, and often she would be waiting for me. Once I even found her dipping a paw into the fishpond. Junia would never approve if she noticed any of our fish gone. Cleo had begun to bring me gifts as well—usually small mice that she deposited at my feet. How could I scold her for being so loyal and loving?

And today was a special day. The final anointing of my head would take place. I would be presented with the headdress of the Vestal. I felt excited and nervous at the same time.

At breakfast we lounged on the dining couches. Domicia bowed to me and offered me some wheat bread with olive oil and cheese. "Will you be at my ceremony today, Domicia?" I asked, trying to chew my food politely.

"If Mother Aurelia allows it, of course I will be there."

I was growing to like Domicia. She tended to my every wish. She even helped me sneak Cleo into my rooms for the night when both the cat and I seemed lonely.

I also attended my first official ritual in September—the Feast of Ops Consiva. Ops was one of our goddesses of abundance. The ceremony was little more than Emperor Nero and Mother Aurelia, in her official role as Virgo Maxima, blessing the storehouse filled with grain. I hoped the other festivals would prove more exciting than blessing the grain.

After breakfast everyone was to meet in the library—all except Lucretia, who had fire duty. We proceeded solemnly to the library and waited for Mother Aurelia. What was to happen to me today?

Finally, Mother Aurelia arrived. All of the Vestals wore their *vittae*— badges of honor for their service to Vesta. I had no badges yet, and still wore my long white tunica and band of wool around my head. I did manage to find a small pouch from my cedar box, then placed my bulla and emerald in it, and tied it around my waist, hidden near my undergarments.

"Vestals, we shall now proceed. Please follow me." I heard a rattling noise and watched Mother fumble with a bundle of keys hanging from her belt.

We approached the door that said, "By Permission Only."

"We always enter the sanctity of this place with respect and veneration. Silence please," said Mother as she found the right gold key. "And all Vestals have a key," she added.

"With the exception of *novices*," Junia reminded her.

Mother Aurelia quickly turned the key several times, and the thick door creaked open. "Come now, all of you," she requested.

The door led into a narrow passageway. Only a dim light shone anywhere in this hall. Domicia stayed right behind me, assuring I would not stumble. Another door lay ahead of us. This one was unlocked. "Come in, come in, Vestals," Mother Aurelia said. I stood on my toes to see further inside—I was so impatient.

One by one, the Vestals stepped into a great circular hall lit with lanterns that glowed with a light that reminded me of early morning. The colors of white marble, bronze and gold swirled around the room.

I decided I needed to stand next to Vibidia and made my way to her. She was a calm, reassuring presence in my life.

"Welcome to the Hall of the Gods," Mother Aurelia said. "Here you will find a representation of every god and goddess we worship in Rome. You may now take some time to walk around the hall to pay respect to them."

A life-size, bronze statue of a man holding a shield in one hand and a spear in the other stood in the center of the great hall. His long curled hair and athletic build gave him the look of a deity.

"What god is that?" I asked, pointing to the statue.

"That is no god—that's King Numa. Here his spirit resides," said Rubria sighing. She stared up at the handsome likeness with reverence.

I looked around at the hundreds of carved niches with bronze and gold statuettes of all our gods, including deities from other lands— gods and goddesses we had made our own—Roman. My father had spoken to me about this during one of my lessons.

There was Jupiter, father of the gods, with his thunderbolt; Venus emerging from the sea foam; Mercury with his cap and winged sandals; Minerva with her owl, shield, and spear. An area just for the Vestal Household gods, the Lares and Penates, was in the center near King Numa. Being the gods of our hearth and home, we must keep them happy and honored.

I carefully walked around the hall with Vibidia making sure I prayed to as many deities as possible. I turned and asked Vibidia, perhaps louder than I thought, "Where's Jesus? Jesus Christ? Where's his statue? I don't see *him* anywhere." Vibidia's face grew pale, then turned plum red, and she nudged me. We turned around and there was Junia, holding her breath, glaring at me with clenched fists.

"I heard that, and in our Hall of the Gods, we have no statue of any Jesus Christ," she snapped. "We worship no one by such a name. Who told you about this, Cornelia?"

I shrugged. "When I was strolling the temple grounds, I overheard someone mention his name. I was just curious— trying to learn. I meant no offense." If I wasn't in the Hall of the Gods, I would have stuck out my tongue at her or tried to trip her. She always seemed to be behind me, watching everything I did. Why couldn't she just leave me alone on my special day?

Then I noticed two alcoves on either side of the hall and another in the middle. One alcove was draped in a thick, purple curtain, one in black, and the third, a crimson red. I asked Mother what lay behind the curtains.

"Cornelia, you are ready, and now is the time to see," said Mother Aurelia, beaming with pride. "Domicia, please pull the curtain of the left alcove." Domicia did as she was told and moved the purple curtain aside.

I took in a sharp breath of wonder. Within the alcove, jewelry and precious stones were arranged upon shelves. I recognized the thick, clear glint of diamonds, the pure red of rubies, the blue of sapphires, and the rich green of emeralds. Amber brooches, purple-colored stone necklaces, all glittered and shone with a brilliance of light. A crown studded with diamonds and sapphires lay atop a red cushioned pillow.

I had no words, so taken was I by this sight.

"Here are the jewels of Rome that we are entrusted to care for," said Mother, clearly in awe and reverence. "Once a year in June during the Vestalia we place this crown upon the statue of Vesta in the Atrium. It's the honor we bestow upon our Goddess."

"What about the other alcoves? What lies behind those curtains?" I asked.

Mother Aurelia nodded and lifted up a finger as if I must show more patience. Domicia crossed to the other side of the Hall. Once again she pushed aside the heavy drapes, revealing a series of organized scroll boxes carefully arranged on shelves. For a moment it reminded me of my bedroom at home, everything neatly organized, categorized, and shelved.

"Here in this alcove we keep the wills, licenses, and other

important documents of the leading citizens of Rome, including Senators and the Emperor Nero himself," Junia explained. "We are entrusted to safeguard them here in the Hall of the Gods. We are the guardians of Vesta and Rome's inner sanctum. The State of Rome, King Numa, and the Goddess Vesta herself have chosen us. And they depend on us." Junia paused and took a breath in. "And if we let them down, we do so at our own peril," she warned, "and to the peril of Rome."

"And the third alcove?" I pointed to the red curtain.

"We are about to show you, Cornelia," said Mother as she lifted her flowing white robes. "Vestals follow me please."

All five of us, and Domicia gathered around this mysterious alcove. Mother Aurelia flung the curtain aside. There was nothing but a black wall. But then I noticed the black wooden door that almost blended in with the wall.

Mother Aurelia fumbled again with her key ring until she found a small, silver key, and twisted it into the door lock. The door pushed opened toward the inside. "Tread carefully," Mother commanded. A small landing inside the door led to a narrow band of stone steps that curved sharply downward. The walls had layers of stone wedged and inlaid between stucco. I touched them. They felt warm and I knew they were old. I clung onto the thin rail on the left side as we descended the winding stairs. Deeper and deeper into the depths of the Atrium we moved, one careful step at a time.

A sweet aroma filled my nostrils. "What's that smell?" I asked Vibidia, who was in front of me.

"It is called frankincense, a special Arabic gum used for our rituals. It's very sacred," she whispered.

For some reason, I remembered my pouch with my bulla and emerald in it. I had a feeling about what lay ahead, and

I did not want Junia or Mother Aurelia to find it. I fumbled about under my tunica. "Please, Vibidia, hold this for me until the ceremony is over." She stopped on the stairs, turned around, and I quickly pressed the pouch into the palm of her hand. She would guard them for me.

The descent became a slow procession in the dark. No light shone for our passage with the exception of a dim lamp at the bottom of the landing. This little light seemed shrouded in fog. I gripped the rail and dared not look straight down. I did not want to stumble or fall on the stairs.

I sensed the last step was approaching. Halting a moment, I took a deep breath and noticed that on the landing, Mother Aurelia and Junia were already waiting for the rest of us. Their figures appeared in and out of the shadows. Another door, black and gray and made of thick bars of grooved wood, awaited our entry into yet another room. A red flame insignia was branded onto the door.

This time Mother Aurelia needed no keys. "Welcome to the Inner Sanctuary," she said, "the great womb of Vesta, the great womb of Earth." Mother Aurelia pushed the door wide, and Junia followed close behind her. Then came Vibidia, me, Domicia and finally Rubria.

Heavy perfumed smoke from a brazier filled the circular room. In the center was a raised podium with seats around it. A basin of water stood off to the side. A few small lights winked on the walls. Marks and etchings on the wall told stories of previous Vestal Virgins ...

"Step forward, Cornelia. Now is the time to be purified with the sacred smoke," I heard Junia say. I stepped into the inner circle while the other Vestals sat on the cushioned seats. Junia lifted up the brazier and swung it back and forth, enveloping me in incense from head to foot. The room seemed as if it were a cloud of smoke. "Next, Cornelia, you will wash yourself from this basin of water, water from the spring of Egeria. Bathe yourself now." Wondering if I had to remove my clothes, Junia answered before I had time to ask. "Yes, remove all your items of clothing. Today all will be made new."

I removed my clothes and bathed myself in the cool liquid. While I was bathing I heard Rubria say, "Cornelia, you are letting go of the old to make way for the new." All the others repeated this.

After my purification bath, I was given a robe to cover myself. Then Mother Aurelia stepped forward and pulled a little scroll from her belt. She unraveled it, and showed it to me; I realized this was the scroll I had yet to sign—my commitment for thirty years as a Vestal. She handed it to Junia and stepped into the inner circle.

Mother Aurelia began her recitation: "Vesta, we have before us our new novice, Cornelia, whom we pray has shown and will continue to show her utter devotion to you. Thank you for bringing her to us. Let the anointing begin."

All the other Vestals were given a small cup filled with oil they used to anoint my head, my face, and every part of me, murmuring prayers to Vesta.

Then Mother Aurelia lifted both of her arms toward the ceiling and looked up. I held my breath wondering what was to happen next. She chanted in a slow, deep voice:

"As above, so below
As within, so without
We guard Vesta's fire
May it never go out.

As Vesta's fire burns,
With an eternal glow,
It burns for the State
So Rome can grow."

She slowly brought her arms down and turned her palms toward the earth.

"And now we bring Cornelia our novice her new clothing. Domicia, please," ordered Mother Aurelia.

Domicia came forth with a thick bundle folded in her arms.

"We start with the feet. Please, Domicia, Cornelia's new sandals."

Domicia displayed my new closed-toe sandals gleaming white with gold trimming. She handed them to me.

"Vestals wear sandals made from the skins of sacrificed animals. These were crafted by one of Rome's imperial cobblers," continued Mother Aurelia.

How soft they felt! I noticed at the back of each sandal, a small set of gold wings was carefully sewn on. Mercury be blessed, how I loved my new sandals—and wings! Domicia took my new shoes from me, bent down and placed them on my clean feet.

"So you will be fleet of foot and won't slip or fall when you carry the water vessel," Junia reminded me with a smirk.

All the Vestals with the exception of Junia fussed over me like mother hens.

"And now it is time for the sacred girdle, the rope that ties around your waist," Mother Aurelia called out. Domicia pulled forth from the bundle a small rope. Attached to the belt dangled small strands of red and white twine. "You are bound to Vesta the next thirty years. This is the tie that shall bind," Mother decreed. "Red and white are the colors of Vesta," she explained. "The red of blood and fire, and the white of purity."

After being belted, it was time to honor me with the sacred head coverings of the Vestals. The headdress was meant to bind my hair. "Bring forth the infula, the sacred headdress," Mother Aurelia ordered. She was truly a powerful Virgo Maxima. Her voice held command and authority, a voice that demanded respect. She always wore the suffibulum, the sacred hood, because she *was* the Chief Vestal.

Domicia lifted up my new headdress and handed it to Mother. Mother in turn raised it high in the Inner Sanctum— as if she were displaying it to Vesta herself. I stood in awe of the wide, white headband, with woolen balls that ran across it. But my new infula was different—it had six white braids attached that hung down off the carefully woven cap. Because I had been recently shorn, the braids were a gift of hair, prob-ably made from the hair of a sacrificed horse. "Behold the headdress made for our Sister Cornelia. May she wear this to honor and serve Vesta for thirty years."

"May you serve Vesta with power and honor," the Vestals replied.

Mother gently crowned me; the cap slid snugly over my head, the top of the band along my forehead. The woolen balls decorated my brow, while the braids hung down in a perfect pattern. "We usually wrap the braids around our head and pin them up," explained Mother. "Since you haven't much hair of your own, you can let them remain loose for now. Once your hair grows back, Domicia and the others will help you wrap and weave the braids."

"Isn't this what brides wear on their wedding day?" I asked.

"Yes, Cornelia. You are *now* being wedded to Rome," Mother explained. She gazed at me with pride. "And now for the sacrificial hood."

I watched Domicia produce the sacred Vestal hood—the suffibulum. Mother Aurelia calmly took the hood from Domicia and wrapped it around my headdress.

"You will now wear Vesta's sacred hood. We use this hood only during ceremonies and sacrifices. And this hood will further identify you to the citizens of Rome as a Vestal. This hood will now be blessed, and it is one of Vesta's protections against the world." She held the hood high as she waited for Vesta's protection and blessing. "I raise the new hood of our novice Cornelia, that she may be protected and blessed with the light of the ever-pure fire of Vesta."

She gently draped the hood over my headdress. It was a light hood and had a purple border around the hem. I loved the feel of it hanging to my shoulders.

"And I have just the perfect gift to accompany the hood," said Rubria with a smile. She handed Mother Aurelia a shiny gold brooch. The round pin had an image of the sun on it, with bright sunrays, like arms that spread in all directions.

"When we conduct rituals and sacrifices, we fasten the brooch at the neck—to keep the hood in place," Mother said.

"And it's pure gold," Rubria added. "Pure as the sun."

I felt hands fastening the edges of the hood together, pinning my new sun brooch to my neck.

"Now for the stola, please," intoned Mother Aurelia.

Domicia handed me the heavy white cloth. I drapped it on awkwardly as it fell to my ankles.

"You must gather carefully the ends of the stola and carry

them in your arms. This gathering of the hem will ensure that you walk with dignity and grace," continued Mother.

"May you walk the path of Vesta with dignity and grace," all the Vestals said at once. I wondered if they had rehearsed these words.

"And don't forget her palla," Junia reminded Mother.

"Of course. Please, Domicia, do you have the cloth so Cornelia can wrap it around her headdress?" Domicia came forth with a fresh white cloth. "This falls to your neck, Cornelia. I'm sure you have seen your mother wearing one?" she asked. I nodded.

"And now the time has come—for the signing," exclaimed Mother Aurelia.

Junia gave Mother the scroll that held the "Rules of the Novice," the rules I still had not signed.

"Servant, bring forth the tablet and stylus. Junia, bring forth the sealing wax."

Domicia did so, and Junia displayed a red stick of wax.

"Our sister Cornelia has read the rules of the novice. She has proven herself worthy. Are you ready, Cornelia? Ready to sign?" asked Mother. All eyes were on me waiting and watching my every expression.

"Mark your name on this signing tablet when you are ready. After you sign upon the tablet, Vesta's sacred ashes will be sprinkled on your signature and imprinted on the scroll. Sister Junia, prepare the wax," ordered Mother.

Junia began dripping hot blots of red wax where my name would be imprinted onto the scroll. In the dim light, I noticed my hand was unsteady, and I tried to control my shaking. My new Vestal attire felt heavy; I could barely move. I took in a deep breath and regarded the women around me who had proven in their own ways just how much they cared for me. They were my family now—so I had best prepare to sign.

"I am ready," I announced. "Ready to commit to service for thirty years to the Goddess Vesta."

Domicia passed me the small tablet along with the stylus. There I signed my name along with my life, committing to Vesta for the next thirty years.

"Vesta bless," I heard everyone say.

Mother Aurelia grasped the tablet from me and then dipped my signature into a wide- mouthed urn filled with ashes from the temple. The wax was ready and lay wet and hot on the scroll.

"Now is the time," murmured Mother Aurelia. She placed the ash-covered indentation on the signing tablet against the hot wax on the scroll, pressed it hard, and lifted it. There before me was my name surrounded by ash sealed in the red wax.

"It is done," Mother Aurelia announced. "You, Cornelia, have been found worthy so far in your training. But know you are *still* in training and have much to learn and understand." She held up the signed scroll. "This scroll shall be placed with the other Vestal scrolls in the alcove of wills and documents. There it shall remain for thirty years or until your duty is complete."

All was silent for a reverent moment. Each Vestal came in closer to honor and admire me.

"Congratulations, Cornelia, Goddess Vesta bless!" Rubria said. She pulled a small polished metal from her pouch. "Look at yourself, Sister."

I stared at the new me, shrouded in my new headdress, hood, and stola. How regal I looked with my new sun brooch. My blue eyes glowed in the half- lit room.

"But before this, to end the ceremony, we will call upon Vesta's blessing," said Mother, "and ask of the mysterious fifth element, the ether, for a sign."

We waited. I knew that Vesta approved of me. Had not my lot been a cat and had she not sent Cleo to me? It was quiet as we waited. Nothing happened.

"Our ceremony is finished. Let us each welcome Sister Cornelia," said Mother, clearly disappointed Vesta had given us no sign.

Then I heard loud footsteps coming down the stairs. An urgent knock rapped at the door.

"Who is it?" demanded Mother Aurelia.

The knocking continued.

"Come in," I heard Junia grumble. "This better be important."

The door flung open. A slave stood before us panting and out of breath.

"Come at once! Quick! Lucretia is on fire in the temple!"

CHAPTER 12

What had happened to Lucretia?

What kind of a sign was this?

A blur of activity started up. Candles and incense were quickly extinguished. A flurry of white robes whirled by me and out the door leaving me standing there stunned with only Domicia remaining.

"Let's go, Cornelia. We must find out what happened to Lucretia," she said. I nodded anxiously thinking of how much I had grown to love and trust Lucretia.

I remembered to lift up the hem of my stola, trying not to trip on the stairs. Up we climbed to the landing, through the Hall of the Gods, and back out into the library. We ran through the Atrium, out the front door, and made our way to the temple. The door was open and some *vigiles*, the fire brigade, had arrived. They formed a short line, passing buckets of water into the temple. Although there was a small bucket of water within the temple itself, I assumed Lucretia could not reach it during her accident. Where was her servant?

Domicia and I pushed past the crowd at the temple door. I prayed to Vesta we were not too late. And of course, no one could put out the sacred flame.

The first thing I saw was Lucretia lying on the temple floor in a puddle of water. The Vestals hovered around her praying aloud. Was she still alive? One side of her body especially one arm and hand were badly burned. Angry red blisters marred part of her face. A section of her robe was scorched.

Thankfully, Vesta's fire still burned, a small and tender flame. "Someone mind the fire while we attend to Lucretia," I heard Junia order. I decided that person would be me. *I* could prove I was worthy to Vesta now.

Lucretia remained on the floor motionless. "I tried," she gasped out. "The fire caught onto my hem."

A stretcher arrived at the temple. "Someone call a physician," shouted Mother Aurelia. "Get her onto the stretcher, then take her to the Atrium immediately." She commanded four servants standing nearby to carry the stretcher.

"Cornelia, stay with Vibidia and tend to the flame. The rest of us will accompany Lucretia. Once the physician arrives, we will better know her condition," said Mother.

The servants lifted Lucretia, who tossed and moaned on the stretcher. The rest of the Vestals followed the stretcher back to the Atrium.

As I went to shut the temple door, I saw the Praetorian Guard along with Emperor Nero proceeding down the hill and heading toward the temple. I waited and tried to greet them as calmly as possible.

"What has transpired here? Has Vesta's flame been extinguished?" Nero asked, his eyes narrowing to a slit. He was straining to see inside the temple. I stood there in my full regalia.

"No," I answered. "Vesta's flame still burns. The hem on one of the Vestal's robes caught fire and spread up her body. She has been taken by stretcher to the Atrium."

"What Vestal? Is it the Vestal Rubria that the fire scorched? Was it Rubria? Tell me!" he demanded.

I shook my head back and forth. "No. It was Lucretia. It was an accident. That's all we know."

Emperor Nero nodded, sighed with relief, and under his breath muttered, "Thank the Gods and Vesta it was not Rubria."

I knew what he was thinking. Didn't he care about the fate of Lucretia? I knew the only Vestal he cared about was Rubria.

"This is all we know, my Emperor. We have no other information. The other Vestals are in the Atrium— maybe you can go see how *Lucretia* is doing. Vibidia and I have our work tending the fire." I emphasized the name Lucretia so he might understand that she mattered as well—we all mattered, not just beautiful Rubria.

"Make way for the Emperor," a guard announced. Nero strode through the grounds toward the Atrium where the dispersed crowd from the temple gathered, awaiting any news.

I shut the temple door. Vibidia and I sat near the flame, tending it with the small wedges of wood. It made me feel important that I could remain with Vibidia and help her here. I was still shaking after my signing ceremony.

I spoke in a trembling voice. "Vibidia, was this the sign that Mother Aurelia asked for from Vesta? It happened almost immediately after the ceremony. What can this all mean?"

"Cornelia, we know that many things happen for a reason. Sometimes we must wait and see. And as you know, I really don't believe in such signs." Vibidia paused as she stoked the flame. "But yes, the timing—well, it is strange indeed. I know not the answer. But I know we must pray for Lucretia's recovery."

Vibidia started praying out loud that Lucretia heal and recover from her burns. I noticed she did not pray to Vesta. Rather, she spoke her words to her favorite god, Jesus.

"Do you think you should pray to Jesus inside the temple of Vesta?" I asked, trying to be polite.

"Would you like me to pray silently then?" she asked.

"No, pray to whom you wish." I noticed that her prayers were calming me down. Who was I to judge my friend, she who was now like a sister to me? I decided whatever god or goddess would answer our prayers and heal Lucretia was fine by me. I was just thankful that the Vestals needed me and I could be of some use.

"I thought something like this might happen one day," Vibidia mused. "Our robes are so long, thick and heavy; bending over Vesta's flames can be dangerous. We must be careful in the future. Poor Lucretia." Vibidia sat silent now, staring deep into the small fire. "If Vesta's flame had gone out, Lucretia would still receive a scourging from Emperor Nero. Even with her burns," she said as she looked into the fire. "But now we know not if she will even remain alive, or ever be the same." She met my worried look. "You do not want to anger Emperor Nero, Cornelia. His temper is well known throughout Rome.

I wish he'd turn his watchful eyes away from the Vestals" she murmured.

Did Vibidia really know everything about Emperor Nero's watchful eyes? I knew I could tell no one about what I had seen the night he bounded down the hill to the temple and knocked on the door. And Rubria had let him in! Had he done the same with Vibidia? I doubted he would ever bother with Junia. I decided not to ask Vibidia or tell her anything of this.

I also hoped he would leave us alone. But he was the Pontifex Maximus, the head of our order. We must do as we were told and follow all the rules.

My thoughts focused on Lucretia. Would she survive the fire? Would she be scarred and suffer stares and pain the remainder of her life? All I knew was how kind and sweet she was, and how much time she had spent with me that first miserable night. Nothing must happen to her! So I prayed along with Vibidia. I silently prayed to Vesta, sent it up on the ether, and then I said a short and silent prayer to Jesus Christ. For if Vibidia found him a worthy god, why shouldn't I?

Vibidia and I continued to watch the fire. The door to the temple opened slowly. There was Mother Aurelia accompanied by Domicia. Both appeared solemn and grieved.

"The physician has arrived and has seen Lucretia," Mother Aurelia announced. "She is suffering greatly. She has burns along one side of her face, and down along her body where Vesta's fire scorched her." Mother paused to take a breath.

"Will she live?" Vibidia and I asked at once.

"We don't know yet," Mother continued. "I do know we have a crisis while we wait. The physician is bandaging her wounds. If she recovers, you may not recognize her."

"Oh no!" I cried. "Was this the sign from Vesta you asked for?"

Mother paused, and the wrinkles around her mouth tightened in a sad smile.

"Perhaps it is so, Cornelia. And now Vesta needs *your* service more than ever. You will take Lucretia's place in future ceremonies while we await word on her recovery. Emperor Nero has given his approval. If Lucretia does not heal, a lottery will be held for a new Vestal."

CHAPTER 13

Vesta had answered. She needed me. This made me feel important. The Goddess needed *me*!

"Cornelia, you will double up with Vibidia for fire duty," Mother Aurelia said. "If you are needed for any future rituals and festivals, and most likely you will be, Domicia will be right there to assist you. Hopefully, this will be temporary. We will consider this a part of your training."

"But Lucretia will survive, won't she?" I asked.

"No one knows, Cornelia. No one can say. Only Vesta knows. But Her sign after your crowning ceremony is this— that She has faith in you to fulfill the duties Lucretia carried out. There's no other solution at this time."

"I am honored," I replied. "To serve Vesta as best as I can."

"And that's *all* we can expect," said Mother in a weary voice. She looked old, tired, and so frail. I wondered if she would retire soon. I was starting to worry about her as well.

Then Mother seemed to brighten up as if she could just brush away everything she had just shared with us. "But now a bit of good news. Your lictor, Cornelia is waiting for you on the temple stairs. Domicia stay with Vibidia please."

Mother opened the door of the temple. On the first stair stood my lictor. He looked no older than Cornelius. "Ah, here we are," exclaimed Mother Aurelia, flinging her hand out. "Cornelia, meet your new lictor."

"Petrus at your service, Vestal Cornelia." The young man removed his cap and bowed low to me. He wore a red tunic, and his oiled muscles bulged from both arms and legs. His bright brown eyes held blinking sparks of merriment. I was thrilled to finally have a lictor, a bodyguard and protector.

I bowed back. "It is my pleasure. And I thank you." How I must have looked in my vestal attire with my gold sun brooch gleaming in the bright light and my head covered with my shawl.

Vesta trusted me now. I must prove myself worthy.

After Mother Aurelia left the temple, we continued to carefully lay wedges of wood onto Vesta's fire. "Oh, here's your bulla," said Vibidia softly and handed me my pouch.

"Thank you for protecting it," I said as I took the gold piece from the pouch. Then I did something bold. I held up my bulla with Neptune's trident on it. Then I lowered it for a brief moment into the fire.

"Neptune, as patron God of my family, Cosa, I ask you to guard and protect us from the dangers of fire—any fire. Lord of the Waters deep, protect us."

I held up my bulla toward the painted ceiling of stars, moon and sun. I sent my prayer right up through the apex of the temple dome right into the ether.

"It is done," I said to Vibidia. "We have nothing to worry about. We are safe now."

Vibidia shook her head as if she didn't believe a word I had said. But she smiled at me and told me I was starting to become a real Vestal.

I had invoked my family's patron God Neptune for protection against fire. How proud my family would be of me!

After Rubria relieved us of fire duty, I thought maybe I could visit Lucretia and give her words of encouragement and hope—just like she had given me on my first night in the Atrium. I decided she needed me. And I needed to see her.

I knocked on the chamber door to Mother Aurelia's apartment. No one answered. I knew I needed approval to visit Lucretia; I longed to see my friend, to speak with her. Where could she be?

I saw Mother come from a room down the Atrium Hall. She was speaking with a man I had never seen before. I crept closer, hiding behind a pillar, so I could hear of what they spoke. "Let her rest. We've done everything we can for her. All we can do is wait and hope," I heard the man say.

I remained behind the pillar while Mother escorted the physician out the front door. Then I tiptoed down the hall and gently turned the door handle. I entered trying not to make a sound and quickly shut the door. A servant sat in the corner watching over Lucretia. I ignored her.

There was Lucretia with one side of her face bandaged up. One of her eyes was covered in thick cloth. She had wrappings around one hand and up her arm, torso and leg, all on one side of her body. Her head was wrapped as well. She breathed with heavy gasps for air. I stood over her bed praying—praying that she would recover.

"Lucretia, it is Cornelia." I gently placed my hand on her unburned arm. The exposed eye opened toward me.

"Cornelia," she whispered. The servant got up, gave her stool to me, and left the room.

I grasped her good hand. "How are you?" I asked her. Then I realized what a foolish question this was—I didn't know what to say.

"Pain, Cornelia," she wimpered. "Pain."

"I am so sorry, Lucretia," I replied.

"Water," she suddenly rasped. "Please, water."

I ladled out water from the small basin next to her bed and poured it into a drinking vessel that sat on the bed table. She lifted her head as I helped her drink the water. Her head dropped back to the pillow.

"Lucretia, do you remember what you told me my first night in the Atrium? That no sacrifice is ever easy? And you have made the greatest sacrifice to Vesta—you've given so much."

Her unbandaged eye stared at me. For a moment she looked angry. "Sacrifice? I've been burned by Vesta's flame. It was an accident. I tripped and fell into Vesta's fire, and now I am being punished for my clumsiness."

"But you have sacrificed everything for Vesta, Lucretia. I shall always be grateful for your kindness and patience. Remember Picus the woodpecker you taught me all about? He is one of my guardians now. I will call on this god to help you. I know you will heal, and Vesta in Her power, shall revive you."

"So you say, Cornelia. I know longer understand my fate," she whispered. "or whether I will recover to serve Vesta, as I stated in my vows many years ago." She paused and took a strained breath in. "I can only trust Vesta, as I trust all the gods," she said quietly.

I admired her faith and courage. "If only you had been with us at my ceremony. This never would have happened," I cried. "Why Vesta, why Lucretia?" Thick, wet tears streamed down my face. I wiped them away with my new stola. I had to remain strong for Lucretia's sake.

"Cornelia, we never know when or why a sacrifice may be needed," she told me.

"No, Lucretia, you've given enough. You have almost given your life," I replied.

Lucretia still laboring with her breath gave my hand a squeeze with hers. "I'm tired now, Cornelia. Come visit me again," she said.

I leaned over and kissed her on the forehead.

"Carry on with you duties. Vesta has deemed it so. I am proud of you." She squeezed my hand again and fell back to sleep.

That's all I could do—carry on with my duties until Lucretia recovered from her burns. And I would pray for her healing to every god I knew.

CHAPTER 14

MARCH 1, 61 AD

Almost seven months had passed since I was chosen. Today marked the celebration of the New Year, the beginning of new life and the end of the old. Although we honored New Year's Day on January 1st, the day dedicated to the two-headed god Janus—he who looks in both directions— inside and out— Emperor Nero kept to the old date because March 1st was dedicated to our founding god, Mars.

Every available Vestal was busy preparing for the festival hanging fresh wreaths of laurel leaves around the temple and in the Atrium. All the Vestals except Lucretia. She still lay in bed recovering from her wounds. I visited her every chance I got and tried to cheer her up. Still, no one knew when—or if—she would return to Vesta's service.

Servants scurried like mice, cleaning floors, scouring out vessels, polishing lamps and then filling them with fresh oil.

Garlands and weaves of violets and daffodils added color to the Atrium and the temple.

It seemed all of Rome was preparing for the festival. Already a great gathering of people clustered near the temple of Castor and Pollux, anxiously waiting for the festivities to begin. Many held tapers in anticipation of Vesta's new flame to be rekindled by Emperor Nero.

Junia offered to attend fire duty during the festival. Since Lucretia's accident, Junia did not have much time to concentrate on my training. I was learning by watching the others and imitating what they did.

I was most excited to be included in the yearly rekindling of the sacred flame. I prayed to Vesta and trusted I would do everything correct, prompt, and at the right time.

After breakfast and before the rekindling, Mother Aurelia called us to the library. Emperor Nero wanted to meet with us about something important. What could this be about right before the festival?

We sat and waited, eager to begin the ceremonies. The Emperor finally arrived, wearing a crown of gold laurel leaves and a stiff white toga. Rubria stared up at him as if he were a god himself. But I thought of him as ugly and brutish. His white toga and fresh wreath couldn't fool me.

"Gather around, girls, I have some news," he said with a dramatic gesture of his hands. "I don't have much time. I must practice the songs for my performance."

Rubria had told me of Nero's love of the theater and that he fancied himself a singer and actor.

"I have spoken with the imperial physician regarding Lucretia. Although Lucretia is healing from her burns, the physician says she will be disfigured and scarred for the rest of her life."

Silence seemed to smother the library like a heavy cloak.

"But she can still serve Vesta," I cried out, defending my first friend in the Atrium. "Vesta doesn't care what she looks like. It's what's inside that counts. Her heart is pure!"

"This may be true, Cornelia," the Emperor stated indulgently. "But the people of Rome care. All Vestals must be perfectly presentable, perfect in all ways. Lucretia, with her injuries, will only detract from our work."

"But what will happen to her *now*?" I asked, worried for my Vestal sister.

"Lucretia will retire from the order in a week's time. She will reside in her family's villa in Pompeii. You may say your goodbyes to her soon. She will have a state pension that will provide for her for the rest of her days." Nero paused and his eyes swiveled around the room finding Rubria. "And yes, next week another lottery will be held for a new Vestal." He coughed and his eyes rested on Rubria—again.

A new Vestal?

I would not be the youngest anymore.

"Now we have much to do today. We begin with the relighting of Vesta's sacred flame," Nero continued. He stood up and strode toward me. "Cornelia, you will assist Mother Aurelia in carrying the rekindled light to the temple. The youngest Vestal must walk with the oldest." He leaned over and clasped his hand over my cheek. "You are *still* the youngest Vestal, Cornelia. Show them what you have learned."

This was my chance to prove my worth, my chance to hold the new flame. I dedicated the relighting to Lucretia and sent it up to the ether.

The procession was to start with Mother Aurelia and me, old and young, followed by Vibidia and Rubria. But first, Nero donned the mantle of the Pontifex Maximus. We made a circle in front of the statue of Vesta who seemed to watch with approval. A beam of sunlight flowed into the Atrium for just a brief moment, illuminating Vesta's likeness. I thought this was a positive portent from the goddess.

Domicia came forth through the front door, carrying a bronze sieve with a tiny flame that flickered; she cupped it with her hands. "Here is part of Vesta's old flame. It is ready."

She handed the sieve to Mother Aurelia, who looked especially regal and proud on this day. The badge she wore at her neck was polished and gleaming. I shook my head; I had no time for distractions today.

"Where is the wood?" Nero asked.

Rubria stepped forward with a slab of thin, smooth wood. In the wood was a perfectly round hole.

"Here is the sacred laurel. And here is the stick, also made of laurel," she said as she handed it to Nero.

The Emperor held up the wooden slab and stick to the statue of Vesta. Mother Aurelia held up the old flame.

"To Vesta of the pure flame. All the old is gone—and the new must come in." He snuffed out the old flame. I panicked and then realized Junia was still keeping the old flame going in the temple, until we were ready to place the new flame into the old. Excited by my first real public ritual, I had to focus hard to keep from fidgeting.

Nero inserted the laurel stick that fit perfectly into the slab of wood. Up and down he crammed it until little sparks began to appear from the friction. It seemed like hard work!

After about fifteen minutes, Nero managed to ignite a small flame. Rubria pulled out a taper and handed it to the panting Emperor. He grabbed the taper, stuck it into the new flame, and relit anew the bronze sieve. "It is done," he pronounced out of breath. "The new flame has been rekindled. It is a good sign."

"Vesta be praised," said Mother Aurelia, who looked relieved. Rubria sighed and placed her hand on the Emperor's sleeve. Vibidia looked bored. But my heart was beating so fast and loud, I thought I was starting to shake. Then I remembered I had to carry the flame in honor of Lucretia and calmed myself.

"We are now ready to proceed to Vesta's temple," Nero commanded. "Cornelia, are you ready?" He arched an eyebrow.

"Yes I am." I straightened myself up as tall as I could, because I had already learned how important posture was to a Vestal.

Mother Aurelia was right next to me. She handed me the sieve with the young flame flickering with new life for Rome and all her people.

"I will lead the procession," Nero ordered. "Cornelia and Mother Aurelia will follow me with the flame. Vibidia and Rubria are next. Then Domicia and any other servants available."

We all lined up ready to emerge from the Atrium. I sent my prayers to the ether, to Vesta, that I would not trip—or worse— drop the flame and let it go out.

The door of the Atrium was flung open. Throngs of Romans awaited with their own tapers, eager to get a new flame of their own, to light their hearthfires.

"Hail Caesar," shouted the crowd when they saw the Emperor.

"Hail Vesta," I heard someone shout.

Proudly, I lifted the sieve with the small flame flickering up to the sun and carefully descended the stairs. "As above, so below," I remembered. Now it was time to stop and let people dip their tapers in the flame so they could rush home to relight their own fires. To share Vesta's new flame with the people thrilled me.

After the lighting of hundreds of Roman tapers, it was time to enter the temple. There was Junia on fire duty, her pinched face red from the heat. "Vesta's fire is ready," she announced.

"Gather round now," Mother ordered. "Take your places." The old fire was almost out, smoldering as though awaiting another wedge of wood. But the fire still had life.

"Bring the sieve to the center," commanded Nero.

Carefully I lowered the sieve towards the dying embers, and using the same taper Nero had used in the Atrium, merged the new glowing flame with the old. The fire sparked, bent, then shuddered into a new flame, flashing new life. I thought of the importance of this new flame for me, for Vesta, for Lucretia, for Rome.

"It is done! The new flame is now alive in the temple. And you are all charged to ensure it stays alive," warned the Emperor. "I will go make the announcement." He stepped to the temple door, opened it, and greeted the gathered crowd. We all stood behind him with the exception of Junia, who tended the young flame.

"The sacred fire has been rekindled. Vesta is pleased. Rome will have continued success," the Emperor shouted. He lifted both arms toward the sky and began to sing a few notes of a song, as if he had rehearsed for his performance. The crowd cheered just as they would their favorite charioteer. They held aloft their tapers, burning with Vesta's New Year flame.

"Return home with Vesta's new flame. Clean out your old ashes to make way for the new," Nero called. He paused and puffed his chest out.

"And after this I say, let the festivities begin!"

About an hour after Nero's announcement, people began to gather around the Forum and temple grounds again. Cymbals clanged, drums beat and horns blared, signaling it was time for the celebrations to begin.

We stood around the temple stairs, greeting and blessing citizens. Even I, the youngest, was allowed to bless others.

The clamor grew quiet of a sudden. All eyes seemed to watch the area near the Regia. I nudged Rubria. "What is to happen now?" I asked her.

"You'll see." She sighed and had a glazed look in her eyes.

And then they appeared from behind the Regia. Men dressed in strange costumes. I counted twelve of them. I gasped at the sight. Then I remembered my father taking the family to the New Year's festival several years ago. I recalled they were the priests of Mars. Although I had watched them before as a young child, I now viewed them through the eyes of a Vestal novice.

"Here they come, the Salii, the Priests of Mars," Rubria replied with that faraway look.

The twelve priests of Mars, all young and handsome, were dressed in pointed helmets, red tunics with short red cloaks, and each carried a bronze shield that looked like two circles atop one another, decorated with swirls and designs. In their other hand, the men brandished a club. Suddenly, the priests began to leap, jump, twirl, and thrust, then rushed toward citizens who milled about; they banged their clubs against their shields, *bam-bam-bam*, right in peoples' ears. They danced

109

around in circles, leaping high into the air, landing on one foot, twirling, bowing, and then they were off to the next group of people.

"Why are they banging?" I asked Rubria. My eyes could not leave this dancing group of priests.

"The banging clears away the ghosts ... the ghosts of the old year. And the god Mars hears the banging."

"You mean like the banging of the woodpecker, Picus? Is that why Picus is sacred to Mars?

"That is correct, Cornelia. And Mars, if satisfied will awaken to ensure we receive the grain we need from Egypt

How I wanted to get up and dance with them! They reminded me of wild rabbits, excited to leap, hop, jump and dance away. "Where will they go next?" I asked.

Rubria looked down at me then lifted my chin. "Cornelia, you still have a lot to learn. The Salii dance for twelve days around Rome, leaping like deer, bestowing blessings with their clubs and shields. Remember Mars is the god of war. But he is also the Patron God of Rome."

"Why are there twelve shields and twelve men?" I asked Rubria.

Rubria grinned and patted me on the shoulder. "The legend has it that the great shield of King Numa fell from the heavens as a weapon of protection, a gift from Jupiter. Eleven of the twelve shields are forged to look like King Numa's original shield; only the twelfth is real. No one knows which shield *is* the sacred shield of Numa." Rubria was so patient answering all my questions.

I continued to look on in astonishment. The Salii began to circle around the Vestals, banging their clubs and shouting out the blessings of Mars. The audience was much amused, clapping and demanding more dances. "Who can leap the highest?" a man asked.

"We want to see a New Year's leap," cried another woman.

The leaps continued even higher. These priests had legs like grasshoppers, long and sturdy. Someone began playing a flute. The sound seemed to calm the commotion.

"And before we take our leave to the Campus Martius, we shall now sing a hymn to Mars, God of War, founding father of Rome," shouted the Emperor.

People gathered around the dancing men. The lead Salii priest stepped forward and began:

"Hail to our founding god, Mars, He who fathered the twins, Romulus and Remus. We give thanks for the she-wolf who suckled the boys, and we give thanks for Picus the woodpecker, who helped feed the boys. All are sacred. We beseech you to show us a sign. We wait upon your blessings to ensure our crops ripen and arrive with safety. If we must take up our battle shilds for war, we are ready with our war cry ... "

All twelve Salii began to whoop, screech, and sound battle cries before the people.

"And now we await a sign from the god. We await an augury," shouted Nero.

People spread out as I watched the augur Lucius carry his red striped cloth around him, along with his crooked staff and stool. He put down his stool, held up his staff toward the cloudless sky, and drew the invisible rectangle onto sky then the earth. "From the heavens to the earth, above-below, north-south-east-west, left-right-front-center, we await a sign from you, Mars."

He spun around, and his long cloth followed him, billowing out toward each direction. He had a certain grace and distinguished air. I had a hard time taking my eyes away from his every movement. But I did wrest my eyes away from Lucius for a moment to watch the crowd. I saw my brother Cornelius, mouth agape, staring at me; Taltos, right next to him waved gently toward me. I knew better than to wave back. I nodded. I wanted to run over to embrace and kiss them both and tell them I was all right, that I missed them.

We awaited the sign. Lucius paced around the rectangle and finally settled on his stool in the middle of the sacred space and waited. Then we heard a fluttering, and I counted three doves that flew to the left. Where they came from, I didn't know.

"It is a sign from Mars," Lucius announced. "Three doves of peace. Flying to the left. Peace will reign for a time; this year will be a year of peace." He held up his staff and then thumped on the earth. "The God Mars has given his approval."

"Let the festivities continue," shouted Nero, embracing Lucius. "It is the will of Jupiter and the blessing of Mars that the auguries are good."

The crowd cheered and began dispersing; many followed the dancing Salii towards the Campus Martius. When I searched the crowd for Cornelius and Taltos, they were gone.

I told Vibidia I wanted to speak with the augur before we began our fire watch. Junia needed to be relieved soon. I was intrigued with what he had done—and how these doves just happened to fly over us.

112

"Greetings, Lucius. I love watching your auguries," I said, as he gathered up his stool and staff.

"Cornelia, all dressed in the Vestal regalia now, I see." He smiled and bowed to me. "Will you truly be one of the greatest Vestals? His eyes twinkled.

"Please don't tease me," I said. "I've taken Lucretia's place. I'm learning."

"And so you *are* learning. I watched the procession from the Regia. You did a magnificent job carrying the new flame. You had me enthralled."

Enthralled?

It was my turn to ask him questions. "How did you learn all this? What you just did? I love the movements of your wand and what you do. Is it magic? Maybe it's you that will be one of Rome's greatest augurs."

Lucius chuckled to himself mumbling about magic. "I study and live at the College of the Augurs and Pontiffs." He pointed to the long, low building close to the palace. "In a few years time, I will be Rome's official augur." His face lit up and he gave me a wide smile. "I am sure, Cornelia, with Mother Aurelia's permission, you could visit me sometime. I'd be happy to explain how the auguries work."

"I would love that," I told him.

As he began walking up the hill, he turned and said, "Remember, if you see some birds in flight or something unusual, come to me and I shall read you the signs. I promise. May the blessings of the New Year be upon you, Cornelia."

"And may Vesta bless you with Her protective light," I replied.

He turned again, and with a low bow thanked me.

I would not forget Lucius's promise.

CHAPTER 15

MARCH-APRIL 61 AD

A week after the New Year, I found a letter under my door. I unraveled the scroll. It was from my mother:

My dearest Cornelia,

I hope you are well in your new life as a Vestal Virgin. The whole family misses you. The house is quiet without you. I am sad to report your father is not well. We are hoping for his recovery soon. Cornelius and Taltos told me they saw you at the New Year's Festival and how graceful and beautiful you are. I plan on visiting the temple soon. I will come with the other matrons in June for the Vestalia. Watch for me. With much love, and may the Gods keep you close,

Mother

In just a few months my mother would visit during the Vestalia—the week in June when the Temple of Vesta would be open to the matrons of Rome. I wasn't sure how I felt about this visit.

Lucretia was set to leave the Atrium today. This was her last day as a Vestal—and my heart was sore to see her go. After breakfast, I asked Mother Aurelia when I could visit with Lucretia. "Go ahead, child. Vibidia can do fire duty alone today," Mother assured me.

I didn't know how I felt about Lucretia leaving and another young Vestal taking her place. I knew I would miss Lucretia's cheerful ways and her positive spirit. And I wasn't sure I was ready to give up the attention I received as the youngest Vestal.

I knocked on Lucretia's door and announced myself. I heard her beckon me to come in. I found her packing, dressed in the tunica and stola of a matron; the white garb of the Vestals was gone. Her hair was tied back in a knot.

"Lucretia, I am here to say goodbye." I held back my tears.

Lucretia sat on the bed and called me to come sit with her. The scar that remained on her cheek puckered up like the bloom of a fading rose, all withered and wrinkled. The burn was no longer red and angry-looking. One of her eyes still drooped, and scars remained on her hand and arm.

"How do you feel?" I asked her, and realized I had posed a stupid question. I could see very well how she felt from her grim, drawn face.

She gave a desolate shrug. "I must return home. I have failed in my duties to Vesta." She sounded lost and forlorn.

"Failed in your duties? You have not failed! Vesta knows your heart. Just because Emperor Nero does not approve of your face ..." Oh, why couldn't I think of anything more hopeful to say? I quickly prayed to Vesta under my breath. "I'm so sorry, Lucretia," I added. "You have made a great sacrifice to Vesta."

"The goddess almost claimed my life, Cornelia. It was my fault that I tripped, clumsy Vestal that I am—or was."

I threw my arms around her and began to cry. "I'll never forget what you told me my first night as a Vestal," I reminded her. "Remember you told me that when a sacrifice is made, you will get something in return? Your sacrifice was not made in vain, Lucretia."

"Was it not, Cornelia? All I am left with now are ugly scars, memories of my failure." She began to weep. The two of us sobbed in each other's arms.

"Your scars are your badges," I told her. "And they will continue to heal. And just think, Lucretia, you now have a chance to marry, to have children, and a happy home."

Lucretia just stared out her apartment window. "Who would marry me? Like this?" She brushed a finger over her scar.

"Someone who will love you for you—not how you look. May Vesta bring to you someone who will truly care for you."

"Thank you, Cornelia for this blessing. There are times … I feel no one could ever love me." She reached over and kissed the top of my forehead. "You are a good girl."

I felt stronger than I ever had. I had prayed to find words to give Lucretia a blessing and some words of solace; it seemed Vesta had responded.

"Will you write to me," I asked. "Please tell me you will write."

"Of course I will write. Think of me when you see Picus, the woodpecker. Think of me when you attend to the fire. I will miss my life here in the Atrium."

"And we shall miss you," I cried. "I shall never forget your kindness to me. Never! I shall send prayers to you on the ether—just as you taught me." We wept some more in each other's arms. Lucretia then placed a circlet on her head. An attached black veil helped conceal her face.

"And so I leave the Atrium veiled," she murmured.

Lucretia's servant appeared, letting her know that Emperor Nero and the available Vestals were all waiting.

"Remember the power of love. Love cannot see your scars, only your beauty," I told her. "I love your beauty. Lucretia. May you let the fire in your heart shine."

"It will take time to heal both my heart and my scars," she said sadly. "Now I will have the time."

We closed the door to her apartment as the servant carried her baggage. On the back stairs, Lucretia looked out on the garden one last time. "Take care of the plants and that cat of yours. I saw her yesterday." I watched a smile form under her veil.

Lucretia moved slowly, as if bidding farewell to every statue, every plant, flower, stone and blade of grass on the grounds. When we finally arrived in the Atrium's great hall, Emperor Nero stood in attendance, along with Mother Aurelia, Junia, Rubria, slaves, water bearers, and the cooking staff. Nero had some scrolls in his hand. Everyone had formed a line and started clapping when they saw her.

"Hail, Lucretia. Goddess Vesta bless, Bonam Fortunam!" they shouted and embraced her gently. The Emperor stepped forward in his purple tunic with a circlet of laurel leaves entwined on his head.

"Lucretia, for your faithful service to Vesta, here is a copy of your pension, a generous pension that will provide for you the rest of your days. You need never worry about money." He handed the retired Vestal her papers. "To good health and recovery," he said.

"Thank you. Hail Caesar." She bowed to the Emperor.

We Vestals all fussed over her, making the most of this last moment together.

"You promised to write, Lucretia," I called out.

"You have my word, little one," she said and blew a kiss to me.

Then she entered the imperial carriage. It was headed to the port of Ostia, where a boat would sail her south to Pompeii. The horses pulled away, kicking up dust.

I didn't know how I really felt about Lucretia leaving the Vestal order. Was I just sad, or perhaps a bit envious? I had no time to think, because I needed to join Vibidia for fire duty.

"Did you know the Emperor Nero is rumored to have murdered his mother?" Vibidia whispered to me as we served fire duty alone that evening.

"What?" I sat with Vibidia, helping her arrange the pieces of wood for Vesta's fire.

"I thought you should know."

"Why? How?" I asked her.

"Why? Why not? If anyone gets in the way of Nero's plans, he makes certain he gets them out of the way." She shook her head with a look of disgust.

"How?" I repeated again. "How did he murder his own mother?"

"Some say he hired people to poison her," Vibidia continued. "That is his preferred method. He's gotten rid of many people this way including his half-brother, so they say."

Emperor Nero ordered the murder of his own mother?

"Why are you telling me this, Vibi?" I asked. "Lucretia just left, and I am too sad to think of murder."

Vibidia shook me by the shoulders. "I tell you this lest you think our Emperor is something other than he is. Don't trust him. Don't drink from any goblet he may offer you. Be careful." Vibidia seemed to study my face. "And you are growing more beautiful every day," she murmured. "I worry."

"He would never harm a Vestal, Vibi," I said. And then I thought of Rubria the night he yanked her to him in the Temple.

"Be careful, Cornelia. We all must take care. Emperor Nero is a dangerous man."

I continued my studies with Junia each week in the library. Every week I was given my fire duty schedule created by Emperor Nero and Mother Aurelia. I noticed that the Emperor had assigned me fire duty with Vibidia, never Rubria.

Each week I learned about the different festivals for each month of the year—and there were many. But April's festival of the Fordicidia upset me; witnessing it myself, the image stayed fresh in my mind. For it was demanded an unborn calf be ripped from its pregnant mother's womb, only to be taken and burnt alive by Mother Aurelia in Vesta's fire. We saved the ashes for the next festival, the Feast of the Parilia, dedicated to Rome's shepherds and their flocks. The Parilia was the traditional anniversary of Rome's founding by Romulus and Remus.

The calf's ashes were mixed with the ashes and blood of the slain October Horse. The mixture of blood and ashes was distributed to Rome's shepherds, to ensure fertility for their flocks. The cries of the mother and calf being ripped asunder, was a sound I would not soon forget.

CHAPTER 16

MAY 61 AD

The month of May was busy for the Vestal Virgins. Mother Aurelia and Junia, the two eldest Vestals, were responsible for gathering the sacred wheat called *spelt*. The spelt was to be carried by slaves to the mill. There it would be ground up with the help of the donkeys. In June, before the Vestalia, we added salt and water to the mix and baked it in the granary. We called the wafer the *mola salsa*. The mola salsa was used in many of our rituals, especially to sprinkle atop the heads of animals before sacrifices.

After Lucretia's departure a new Vestal was chosen named Occia, a bright-eyed, eight-year-old girl who seemed happy to be chosen as a Vestal—unlike me. She seemed so innocent and looked so small with her shorn hair. She followed me around whenever she could, asking me endless questions. She reminded me of myself when I was that age, so I tried not to become impatient with her— but even her enthusiasm for learning annoyed me and tested my patience.

Soon after she was chosen, Occia rushed up to me out of breath. "Cornelia, you wouldn't believe what Lucius the augur told me."

"What did he tell you, Occia? That you will be one of the greatest Vestals?" I asked sarcastically.

"How did you know, Cornelia?"

"He told me the same," I said, not amused by her receiving the same message from Lucius.

"Oh good," Occia exclaimed, her expression filled with the joy of an innocent. "We will both be together as the greatest of Vestals ever! Lucius told me the gods have proclaimed this."

I patted her on the head and told her it was true; we *would* be among the greatest Vestals. I was accustomed to being the youngest Vestal and getting all the attention. Occia had now taken my place. But I was proud that I had already sprouted several inches in height and was almost as tall as Vibi now.

I missed Lucretia. Every day I thought of her. Every day I watched for a letter from her. I found time to make sure I embraced Occia when she was confused and distraught over her learning. I made certain each night to send prayers out to the ether that Lucretia remain healthy and that she might find happiness—maybe even happiness with a new husband, a husband who would love her heart and not judge her by the scars she carried on her face.

Today was the last day of the Lemuria. We honored our ancestors on the ninth, eleventh, and thirteenth of May. Each day of the Lemuria, I took the handful of black beans required to appease the family spirits. I stood in the garden, held the beans in my fist, threw them behind me, and shouted, "Ghosts of my father, go out!" Junia explained if I didn't do this ritual, the maleficent ghosts of my ancestors could prove meddlesome.

"Ghosts of my father go out!"

I thought of my father. My mother had written in her letter he was unwell. But why should I care? The Vestals were my family; the State of Rome owned me for thirty years.

But I completed the ritual anyway, then tried to cast the image of my father from my mind, the image of him wringing his hands exclaiming, "What have I done?" I tried to forgive him. I wanted to erase these images from my mind. They still haunted me.

Disturbing dreams overtook my sleep many nights. Time and again, the image of Emperor Nero appeared, his dark yellow hair erupting in flames as he yanked me from my father. In the dream, I clung to my father. But it was no use. My father always let me go. So I tried to let the ancestral spirits of the dead go out, just like I tried to let the image of my father and my family go forth from my mind.

The Ides of May was dedicated to the Feast of the Argeii, the festival of the straw men. Junia explained that twenty-six straw men called dummies, each representing an area of Rome, were thrown into the Tiber. Instead of real human sacrifices, these straw men were substitutes. I was looking forward to the moment I could cast one of the little dummies into the river!

"Remember, the Flaminica will carry the basket with the twenty-six straw men onto the Pons Sublicus," Junia reminded me. "She will be dressed in mourning attire. We will take the basket and throw the straw men into the river, one at a time."

The Pons Sublicus was the oldest bridge in Rome. Father had taken me there on many outings. I wondered if Junia would try to push me off that bridge, just like she had pushed me down on the way to the spring of Egeria.

We began to prepare for the procession. Rubria had fire duty and Occia remained with her in training. I made certain after bathing that Domicia oiled my body and sprinkled me with rose water. I had to be perfect. A large crowd was expected, lined up along both banks of the Tiber. I adjusted my headdress, tightened the cord around my waist, pinched my cheeks for color and I was ready.

A solemn drumbeat signaled the festival would soon start. All of our lictors, ready with their *fasces* out, those bundles of bound rods with an ax at each end, would demand the crowds part to make way for the Vestals.

Domicia knocked on my apartment door. "Are you ready, Cornelia? It is time."

"Yes, I am ready," I called out.

"The other Vestals await you in the Atrium."

I glanced at myself in the polished oval one last time. I wondered who would be watching today. I was excited to think both Vibi and I, along with the others, would throw the straw men over the bridge.

The drumbeat grew louder. I grabbed the pouch with my bulla and emerald and tied it into my undergarments. White and red ribbons hung from my headdress, the vestal colors of purity and Vesta's flame.

I covered my head with my hood, picked up my hem, and scurried downstairs to the atrium. They were all waiting for me. It was mid-morning, and already the sun's rays burned in a fiery haze.

A squat, bald man stood at the front of the line. A drum just as round as he was, hung from a strap around his neck. He kept turning around, watching the vestals prepare for the procession.

"Are we ready?" Mother Aurelia asked, looking us over from headdress to our special soft-toed shoes. She seemed satisfied. "Let us proceed." She came over to me and patted me on the shoulders. "Remember, Cornelia, keep your hands together like this, clasped together—no waving to the crowds today. This is a solemn occasion. Cornelia? Are you listening to me?"

"Yes, Mother," I answered obediently.

Boom-boom-boom. The drumming began again, echoing against the walls. Clasping my hands together, I held them in front of my belt; gazing straight forward, I straightened my back and shoulders.

Out the door we processed, Mother and Junia first. Then Vibi and I descended down the stairs. All of our movements seemed in harmony today.

Our litters were waiting for us.

The road leading to the Aventine Hill was lined with Praetorian Guards to allow us passage. On either side of the road, people waited and watched for glimpses of us, the white-clothed virgins.

The mournful procession continued down the Aventine Hill past the Temple of Hercules, around the Cave of Cacus, and up past my family villa, until we reached the Pons Sublicus.

Today the bridge was festooned with red, white and gold flowered garlands, and violet-blue wildflower wreaths were twisted with ivy; the flower arrangements almost covered the old wood pilings and pikes that held up the bridge. The sound of the drumbeat called to the people; more and more gathered to witness the Festival of the Straw Men.

After departing our litters, we stood by the side of the swollen riverbank awaiting the Flaminica and Emperor Nero. I wondered what mood he would be in today. I never knew. Then out of the corner of my eye, I noticed the solemn parade of the pontifices; the augurs including Lucius; the priests of Mars, and leading the group, Emperor Nero and the Flaminica. Nero had next to him a little man, a dwarf of a man who seemed eager to watch the ritual. The Flaminica was dressed in black; a black mourning veil covered her face.

I whispered to Vibi, "Who's the dwarf?"

"Why, that's Varros, the man who organizes Nero's games at the Circus Maximus. He's in charge of the animals, the betting, the gambling." She dropped her voice. "He's not a nice man."

The drumbeat stopped. "Hail, Caesar!" shouted someone in the crowd.

The Emperor donning the mantle of the Pontifex Maximus strode to the center of the wooden bridge. He held his hand up to silence the crowd. "Citizens of Rome, we are gathered here today to offer the straw men to Father Tiber; twenty-six in number, for we know that twenty-six represents the twenty-six districts of Rome—all represented today."

The crowd burst into applause. "I call forth the Flaminica and the Vestal Virgins to the bridge," Nero commanded. The drummer began beating his drum again.

Vibidia nudged me. "Are you all right?"

I nodded.

The Flaminica carrying the large, woven basket stepped gracefully onto the bridge. She held the basket up high. We Vestals followed her, stepping with care along the worn planks.

"Behold," said Nero, "here is the basket filled with the straw men, substitutes for the sacrifice of human life. Into the Tiber they must fall." He glanced at Mother Aurelia who nodded. He asked, "Vestals, are you ready?"

I knew each of us must take a straw man out and cast it into the Tiber, offering these dummies as a gift—not only to Father Tiber—but to all of Rome's gods.

My breath quickened to be atop this bridge with Rome's most prominent citizens watching. I had to be perfect—no distractions and no mistakes.

The Flaminica handed the basket to Mother and departed the bridge. Now it was our turn. One by one, we each took a straw man and dropped it into the swirling currents of the river, casting blessings to the gods.

While we tossed the straw men into the Tiber, people yelled we should get rid of the old dummies ... no one wanted them! The basket filled with straw made it more difficult to find the little men.

Finally, the last straw man was ready to be drowned in the Tiber. And it was my turn to cast it out. I dug my hand deep into the straw basket. And I could not find the last straw man. Everyone on both sides of the Tiber waited and watched me.

Then I felt something strange; it was slippery, cold and coiled up. What was this? I gripped it, lifted it out, and realized I was holding onto the tail of a small snake, alive and hissing! For a brief moment, I didn't know what to do. But then I did. I swung that snake twice over my head and cast it straight into the Tiber—where it vanished in the waters.

"Aha! A snake! And a snake charmer!" Nero burst into laughter. "Lucius," he demanded, "Read the augury."

Lucius stepped forward. "As we know, the great snake of our God of Healing, Asclepius, fell off a ship into the river, swam to Tiber Island, and because of it, a Temple to the God is on our island. The snake is the symbol of healing and new life," he proudly stated.

Nero and his dwarf seemed to think this was funny. I was trembling; all I wanted to do was return to the Atrium.

"That is enough, Augur. I must speak." Nero approached the center of the bridge, pushing us out of the way.

"People of Rome," he shouted. "A straw man was missing today—because there resides a snake who lives in one of our districts. This snake calls himself a follower of the Nazarene. And perhaps many more snakes lurk in Rome. Let this be a warning. For those who believe in the usurper, this Jesus—take heed." He laughed a deep, roaring laugh and started to sing out a hymn to Apollo.

The realization I had been holding a snake and threw it into the Tiber shocked me. I didn't know how I could have done this. I must have swayed a little, because Junia came up beside me.

"It was *only* a little water snake, Cornelia. Harmless." She raised an eyebrow and shook her head disapprovingly at the Emperor.

The dwarf and the Emperor laughed wildly and shook hands. Was this a bet they had had between them?

We slowly paraded off the bridge. On the way, Nero patted me on the head and called me his snake-charming Vestal. Vibi, quiet, seemed angered by the incident. But my Vestal sisters gathered around me, congratulating me on how calm and brave I was to handle that snake—even if it was a water snake!

CHAPTER 17

JUNE 61 AD

Today marked the day we'd all been waiting for—the Vestalia. Knowing my mother would be visiting, I felt unsettled and nervous. What would she say to me?

It was a perfect June day. The air was crisp and birds fluttered about on the branches of the trees guarding their nests. The sacred rue was in full bloom, its yellow-green blossoms circling the temple. Even Picus flew overhead, bringing insects to the young. It seemed like everyone around the Forum was bustling in anticipation of Vesta's temple opening to the public.

But today only the matrons were allowed inside, matrons like my mother, who would arrive with their offerings to Vesta, remove their sandals, and await the blessing of the Goddess of the Hearthfire. And today all the bakers in Rome had the day off. Even the mill donkeys were given respite from the grind of the millstone.

Earlier in the morning, I helped garland Strong, my favorite mill donkey. I asked the stable boy, Arturo, a short dark servant, if I could have the honors, and he nodded and grinned at me. I slipped the wreath of violets and roses around Strong's neck. He lifted his head and nodded, one ear bent forward and the other bent back.

Strong knew something was different today. He gave me a puzzled look, let out a loud bray, and stamped his hoof. Strong would lead the procession today. Vibi, responsible for the other donkey, Bond, was still in the Atrium getting ready.

At the back of the stable, I noticed Cleo burrowed in a small stack of hay. She stretched her paws out, yawned, blinked up at me, and closed her eyes. She was never too far away. What a positive omen to see Cleo this morning!

I still had to retrieve the loaves of bread to be hung around the donkey's neck. Today Strong had a light burden: a garland of roses and violets, loaves of bread, and a fresh brushing to his silver-gray coat. It shone in the bright June sunlight. "Make us proud," I whispered in his ear, "just like I make Vesta proud."

A trumpet blared, signaling it was time to receive the matrons. Vibi finally arrived at the stables and prepared Bond for his day off. Meanwhile, Arturo led Strong out of the stable toward the temple of Vesta. Even the mill donkeys would greet the matrons.

Rubria and Occia had fire duty. All other Vestals must gather on the temple steps, in anticipation of the mothers with their offerings. I waited for Vibi, and we proceeded to the temple. Domicia and the other servants frantically ran back and forth from the Atrium to the temple, making sure everything was in order. Junia explained that one by one, the matrons would enter the temple and lay down their offerings before the fire. Then the servants, depending upon the gifts, would bring them to the storeroom in the Regia or deposit them in the Atrium.

Flocks of women began to arrive, many barefoot, dressed as they pleased. Some women looked disheveled, as though they hadn't even washed. Vesta cared not how they dressed; it was what lay within their hearts that mattered.

Many of the matrons began to wash first at the spring of Juturna, washing and wiping their hands and feet. One by one or in groups of two, the women lined up for the honor of entering the temple. What a thrill to hold my hand up, place it on a forehead of a woman who looked at me with adoration, and then to whisper, "Vesta bless" or "May Vesta bless you."

Finally I saw her. My mother. She bowed to me—to *me*! I wanted to hug her, to shout, to cry out how much I missed her. But I did not dare! Over the last months, I had learned to control myself—to play the role of a Vestal Virgin.

"May Vesta bless you." My voice cracked with emotion.

"Cornelia, thank you. You are beautiful, stately, and digni-fied," Mother said with pride and sadness in her voice. "We all miss you."

"And I you," I said, turning to meet my mother's gaze.

"Daughter, your father sends his regards. He is better now," Mother said. Although I was relieved to hear Father was recov-ering, today, the first day of the Vestalia was devoted to women.

"Please remember, my father is Rome now," I told her.

My mother's face drooped, etched in hurt and pain. Why did I have such vengeful anger toward my father? I was a Vestal now. Instead of tears and outburst, I could face my mother with a stern dignity and semblance of grace. It had been almost a year since I left my old life behind—now my old life looked me in the face.

"I give you the blessings of Vesta," I continued, touching her forehead. "Please bring your offerings into the temple." Mother carried a basket covered with a white cloth, most likely fresh bread. I didn't care. I had made my offering to Vesta months ago— a service of thirty years. What was a loaf of bread to Vesta when I would give her the best years of my life?

Mother entered the temple, head bowed in reverence. I continued to greet and bless Rome's matrons, blessing them with fruitfulness. What did I know about fruitfulness? Most likely I would never bear a child.

After the temple visit, many matrons walked to the Capitoline Hill to pay homage at the Temple of Jupiter, in honor of Jupiter the Baker. Finally, Mother departed the temple. She had tears in her eyes. She lightly touched my shoulder. "Your father wants to visit you soon. Maybe for your birthday in August." She paused staring at me as though she could not believe it was really me, her daughter. She wiped her eyes. "And some good news ... Taltos will soon be a freedman ... your father will release him from the bonds of slavery soon."

Taltos freed? This truly was good news. "Please tell him how happy I am for him. And tell him—and my brother— to come visit me soon. I miss both of them." I said nothing about my father. My pride prevented me from expressing how much I missed him too. Tears welled up in my eyes.

"Go in peace," I told my mother, giving her a light embrace.

After the last of the matrons were gone, a trumpet sounded, signaling the procession of the Vestalia would soon begin. Led by Emperor Nero, our lictors, Mother Aurelia, and finally the available Vestals, Vibi and I were to ride alongside the festooned donkeys. Our path included proceeding up the Viminal Hill, as far as the Praetorian Guard headquarters.

Arturo brought forth the two mill donkeys both brushed to a shine. Strong kept trying to shake the bread loaves off his neck. But both donkeys groomed and garlanded were ready. I was ready too. I always loved being part of a procession.

Nero arrived with his white mantle on, signaling his role as Pontifex Maximus. A sedan chair awaited him. Our lictors began shouting, "Make way for the Vestals." We had our own special carriage today, the Vestal *carpetum*. Mother Aurelia had her special carriage waiting as well. Junia would ride with the Chief Vestal today!

The Emperor's sedan led the procession, followed by the carriage carrying Mother Aurelia and Junia. We were next in line, followed by the mill donkeys and bakers. We could wave today and bless the crowd. And what a crowd it was! People threw white and red roses at us! "Bless us, Vesta bless us," the crowd shouted. Many people raised up their arms to us, nudging each other out of the way. I gave them the imperial wave.

In my training, I had been taught to raise my hand up high when someone bowed low to me. I was taught to bring Vesta's blessing down from on high, right from the ether into the penitent's body. And I did just that.

Riding next to Strong gave me confidence. He looked so proud and regal today! Many of the bakers behind us pulled their own mill donkeys by a tether. Up, then down around the

Palatine Hill we proceeded, and then we continued up toward the Viminal Hill.

Suddenly I heard a commotion up ahead. Emperor Nero's sedan halted. What was happening? I asked Vibi what she thought.

"I don't know. Shush!" she told me in a whisper. "Just watch and listen." She pushed aside the curtain of the carpetum.

A short man with a balding head, bandy legs, and a thick pointed beard stood on the street, in front of a villa. He was shackled to a guard. He motioned with his free hand, calling out to the crowd. His dark eyes had a determined and fierce look. He waved his fettered arm in the air. Who was this man to disrupt the Vestalia parade?

Nero removed himself from his sedan and proceeded to the side of the road where the scene was unfolding. On the Emperor's approach, the guard forced the disruptive man to kneel. Nero pointed a long finger at the prisoner.

"Why is *he* here on the street?" he bellowed.

"This prisoner," the guard stammered, "calls himself Paul. You know him as Saul. You, Caesar, put him on house arrest. He is out getting his daily air."

The prisoner stood up again, defying the guard's orders. He shouted as if he were speaking to an audience. "Idolaters all! Nothing but vain superstitions! There is no Vesta, there is no Mars, no Apollo, not even Jupiter! There are no gods, but the one true God! Idolaters, turn away from your false gods, your graven images. Jesus Christ, our martyred savior was sent by the one true God!" *So this Jesus was a real man who was killed? I thought in surprise. And still Paul risked his life?*

I thought how bold he was to address the Emperor. I whispered again to Vibi, "Have you heard of this man, Paul?" She nodded, not taking her eyes from the scene. "Will the Emperor have him killed?" I said under my breath.

Vibi pressed up against me, as if I should just keep quiet. "Not on the Vestalia. Cornelia, refrain from questions now. Please."

We continued to watch the events, eager to hear what Paul and Nero said to each another. Strong snorted, brayed, then pawed the paved stones with a determination that told me he wanted to keep going. "Shh!" I turned around and whispered out of the window.

"You who call yourself Paul now," shouted Nero. "You, once a Jew who persecuted Gentiles, many who now call themselves followers of the Cult of the Nazarene—you, now a Jesus follower yourself?" He sneered at the little man as if he was a bug ready to be squashed. "You have no power here, Saul. Your rantings are harmless against the State of Rome. Are you not afraid of the consequences of your words?"

"Caesar, I have no fear of death. Leave your sin-ridden ways behind and call on Jesus, the Messiah who died for you. I demand a hearing, Caesar!"

I thought how brazen and bold this man was to address Nero as Caesar and not Emperor.

Nero laughed, a loud-pitched roar. "You, Saul of Tarsus, are under house arrest, and there you shall stay until I decide your fate. *I* will decide on your hearing. You and your kind disgust me!" He laughed again. "And what does *your* god have that ours do not?"

"Eternal life, Caesar! I care for your soul and all the lost souls of Rome! Repent! I am an apostle for my true Lord and I speak the truth!" The bowlegged man shook his fists; his fetters clanked and rattled as if he were trying to free himself from bondage.

"And what power do you have over me, a Divine Caesar, appointed by the Gods, when you live in chains? Answer!" Nero shouted.

A Divine Caesar?

The little man replied, "It's the power of the Word, His word and the words written by the Prophets. I give of myself, but never to your word or power, Caesar. And you will always be Caesar—never divine."

The guard forced Paul to his knees again, mumbling that he needed to show respect to the Emperor.

Mother Aurelia had stepped out from her carriage. She walked to Emperor Nero and Paul. She seemed so tall standing over them. "What is happening to stop the Vestalia procession?" she asked. "The Gods and Vesta will be angry." Paul glanced up at her, as if she were a statue herself, and then stared down at her shoes. He didn't move or say a word. Mother shook her head in disapproval and returned to her carriage.

"Take him away now," Nero said, huffing with anger. "This man does not deserve to even breathe Rome's air. He insults and angers our gods." He drew close to the prisoner's dirtied face. "Perhaps a few of my favorite lions are hungry for meat—the flesh of a Jesus follower. And I will decide when your hearing is, not you!" Nero seemed to revel in the thought as he rubbed his hands together.

"I will go gladly to die a martyr's death for Jesus Christ," Paul screamed out.

I shook in fear. Vibi sat still through the commotion with the exception of her hands fidgeting on her lap. I knew she must feel concern for this bold and brave believer, but must also admire this little man, who was ready to die for his God.

"Return this prisoner to the bowels of this house," Nero commanded. "He will disturb the Vestalia no more!"

The mood of the procession dampened. The prisoner Paul had broken the spirit of the Vestalia by his fiery words. On the way back to the temple, Strong decided he wouldn't budge any further. I quickly demanded the slaves to stop our sedan, got out, and spoke in the donkey's ear, telling him of the treats waiting for him back at the mill. I think he wanted his real freedom today, to run loose around the fields, to kick his heels up in the air and rejoice in being untethered. But like the prisoner Paul, Strong must return to the mill, his own prison, where the great pumice grindstone awaited him. He seemed to listen to my soothing tones, for he soon began to move again with the others.

Crowds still wandered about the temple grounds. Slaves helped the Emperor from his sedan, and the donkeys finally got their reward: fresh oats, a lump of sugar, and dried fruit.

The Emperor stepped forth to make his pronouncement "The first day of the Vestalia is complete," said Nero. "Now we may continue with the day. And I bless the Vestals, the brides of Rome."

The crowd gathered around the Vestal party just for a glimpse of us. Then I noticed the augur Lucius, who appeared from the Regia, heading in our direction. It had been some time since I had seen him. He wore his light yellow tunic with his red striped cloth that made his hair look even blacker and shinier. He carried his augur's staff with him. He had seen me and made his way in my direction. "Congratulations, Cornelia. May you bestow upon me the blessings of Vesta?"

He bowed low. I raised my hand. "May the blessings of Vesta be upon you always." As I lowered my hand and as he lifted his head, he grabbed my hand. A pulse of warmth went through me. "Thank you, my Vestal," he murmured.

A loud cawing sounded above us. It seemed as though everyone, including the Emperor looked up. A lone eagle was being chased by a crow. Then two more crows appeared and followed the eagle right on his tail feathers. People in the crowd pointed and wondered what this all meant.

"Where is an augur when we need one?" the Emperor shouted.

Lucius stepped forward and held up his augur's crook. "I am here, Caesar," he proclaimed.

"Clear the way. We must have a reading on this portent," Nero ordered.

Lucius then cast his rectangle, quartered the sky and earth, tapped his staff to the ground, and was set to report his augury.

"The eagle is our symbol for Rome, a bird of strength and power. Yet he is chased by not just one crow, but three. The eagle flies toward the Emperor's Palace, but he is not alone. He is harassed by these loud, cawing black birds, intent on making his life a misery." He paused as everyone awaited the rest of the augury.

"Emperor Nero, you have enemies right here in Rome. At least three of these enemies are stirring up forces against you. They are not Romans by birth. They seek your downfall. Beware!"

I thought Emperor Nero's eyes would bulge from his head. He tore off his mantle and pulled at his hair. "And I will find the culprits. Rest assured." He stomped off to his palace, his guards trotting after him up the hill. The rest of us stood there silent.

All I could think about was the prisoner Paul making a scene on the street. Was he one of the crows ready to bring the Emperor down? He had little power in prison on house arrest.

I will ask Vibi during fire duty what she thinks of the augury. And I will ask her what she knows about this man called Paul.

CHAPTER 18

After the matrons departed, Vibidia and I sat alone tending the fire. Domicia left for the Atrium to fetch us dinner. Now was my chance.

"Vibi," I asked her. "Who is this Paul—that strange little man in irons? Do you know of him?"

Vibi blinked her brown-green eyes as if she was remembering something. "I've heard of him," was all she said.

"How?" I asked. "Who told you?"

"I have friends in high places."

"Friends in high places?" I repeated. "You mean Emperor Nero?"

"No, silly." Vibidia dropped a small wedge of wood close to the flame. "I hear things," she said.

"Hear things? What things? From who?" I blushed knowing I sounded just like Occia repeating herself.

"My cousin, of course." Vibidia's green eyes twinkled—just mentioning her cousin lit up her face.

"Your cousin? Is he a Senator?" I asked.

"Cornelia, in the name of Vesta—shush! Domicia will return soon with dinner." She began humming under her breath.

"But—"

"My cousin Marcus is a member of the Praetorian Guard," she whispered."He is often assigned to Paul's prison, the hired house Paul rents near the Praetorian Guard headquarters."

"That's where we saw this Paul. Why does Nero keep him imprisoned? Because he believes in Jesus Christ?"

Vibi tucked her knees in and wrapped her stola round herself. "I don't know. I'd like to find out." She shook her head and shivered. "He must pose some danger to Nero. A threat perhaps to the State of Rome itself."

I watched Vibi. "Can you find out?" I asked. "Maybe you or Rubria could pardon him, maybe convince Nero to set him free. You know, if you met him on the road?" I remembered the Vestal rule— that if a Vestal met a convicted criminal on the road, she could pardon and free him—like a divine intervention of sorts. There was nothing anyone could do, not even Emperor Nero!

I leaned in close, my shoulder next to Vibi's. "Does your cousin tell you much? About Paul and the Jesus followers?"

"Sometimes I see my cousin during my time off, a privilege you will have soon." Although we were still alone, she whispered in my ear, "Marcus tells me this Paul holds late night talks; he might be chained to a guard but he speaks in the spirit—of Jesus."

She sighed, gazed up to the top of the open dome of the temple, and grasped her heart.

"Spirit … of Jesus? Vibidia, we are priestesses of the spirit of Vesta. How can you say this? And what of the eagle and the crows? And what the augur Lucius said to Nero? Vibi, please don't … just stay away."

141

But Vibi appeared not to hear my words. She stared up to the heavens, deep in her own thoughts, deep in prayer. Only then did I turn and notice the shadow lingering on the inside of the open, temple door. Domicia had returned with our dinner.

After fire duty and evening prayers, I lay in bed wondering if Domicia had overheard my conversation with Vibi. Why did she linger by the door? My mind tossed about ideas the way Strong tossed his mane when he was upset.

I could not be sure, but the way my servant had been watching us, and then quickly cast her eyes to the ground led me to suspect her; how her shadow lurked around the open door, how her hands trembled as she gave us our meal. I wondered how much she heard.

Some days I completely trusted Domicia. Those were the times when she treated me like an older sister would, telling me stories of her native Egypt, oiling my body, rubbing fragrances like lavender on me during my bath. And she told me of the men she had loved, and those who professed to love her. She left them behind the day she was sold as a slave in the Egyptian marketplace.

Thoughts of the Goddess Vesta ran through my mind. I sent prayers up to the ether in hopes for a response, some message from the Goddess I was now dedicated to. I prayed in earnest:

"Beloved Vesta, fill me with the light of understanding, Cast light in the darkness; take away my fears for I have Seen much in the last moon. Bless me Vesta, Goddess of the sacred fire."

I rolled over to my side and took a deep breath. I readied to fall asleep. And in between the time of waking and sleeping, I heard a voice speak to me:

"Take good care,
For the eagle watches, he knows,
Others too, watch the eagle
But do not know.
The fish speaks louder
Than the eagle's great cry."

I awoke, sat up in bed and rushed to my desk. In the faint light from the setting sun, I unrolled a blank piece of papyrus, found a stylus and an inkpot, and wrote down the message from Vesta. What did it mean? Was the message connected to the augury today?

Vesta, are you giving me a warning? I asked.

At first I thought I would speak with one of the Vestals about the message. Vibi perhaps could help. But I doubted she believed in these messages. Rubia who loved to stand close to Emperor Nero and bow low to him— what could she tell me? I knew Junia despised me and Mother Aurelia was old. Occia was too young. Then I remembered Lucius. He had invited me to visit him if I experienced anything strange. Could he help explain this message?

I decided I *must* speak with Lucius about this when I had the chance. He might understand being an augur.

143

The Vestalia lasted for another week. During this time I busied myself with escorting people into the temple, blessing the sick and elderly, and tending Vesta's flame.

Today was the last day of the Vestalia, and the temple was set for a thorough cleansing. After the ashes were swept up, the temple would be closed to the public for another year. Although I participated in sweeping up some of the ashes, I had the afternoon off. I tucked the papyrus with the message I had written from Vesta inside the pouch hanging from my belt. Then I set off in search of Lucius.

I knew the augur stayed in the apartments next to the College of Pontifices, between the Regia and the Palatine Hill. I found him in the royal chicken coop, scribbling notes on a wax tablet with a stylus. After I called out to him, he lifted his head and acknowledged me.

"Greetings, Cornelia, the one Vestal who can handle a snake—"

I blushed. "Good morning, Lucius. Am I interrupting an augury?"

"I've just finished. You will be happy to know that all the signs are positive today. The imperial chickens pecked the right number of times and ate an auspicious number of grains. And now to see you! Indeed your presence is timely."

I surveyed the chicken coop. All I saw were clucking fowl making a commotion. How did Lucius read the signs with chickens? I wondered why the Emperor considered this so important. Each passing day as a Vestal, I realized just how strange Roman ways were!

"What honor do I have to see you this morning? Are you enjoying being a Vestal?"

"I'm learning," I said. "There's so much to learn."

"You are doing well as a novice," Lucius said. "I still cannot believe you picked up that snake. Emperor Nero is still talking about this, calling you the next Pythia." He shook his head in disbelief.

"Pythia?" I asked.

"Yes. The Pythia, the priestess of Delphi, she who is sacred to Apollo. Everyone knows how much the Emperor worships this god."

I had had enough of snakes for the rest of my life. I decided to get right to the point. "You told me if anything strange happened, a message or a sign, to come see you." I pulled the papyrus from my pouch. "Here. I received a message from Vesta. Her voice came to me before I fell asleep."

Lucius unraveled the papyrus, and his brow furrowed up with lines. "Hmmm, may I keep this? I need to ponder the meaning. The eagle of course must represent Rome. The fish—I am not so sure."

"Remember the eagle being chased by the crows? And the warning to Nero? Is there a connection?" I asked.

"After I take a final record of my chicken augury, I'll look through the Sibylline Books housed in the Temple of Jupiter. Perhaps one of the books will shed some light on your message from Vesta."

"What are the Sibylline Books?" I asked.

"Originally there were nine books, given to one of our early Kings, King Tarquinius by the Sibyl of Cumae. She burned six of the nine books, since Tarquinius refused to pay for them," Lucius explained.

"And then?"

"And then the King finally paid for the remaining three books. We consult them in times of turmoil and unrest."

"The Goddess in her message seemed angry and distraught," I said.

"I see," Lucius replied, as he tucked the scroll inside his tunic. "Can you meet me at the spring of Juturna later tonight? Will you have fire duty?" he asked.

"Yes I will," I said. "Late night duty."

"That's perfect," he said. "Meet me at the spring of Juturna. I may have some answers for you then."

Lucius was waiting for me at the spring. Vibi told me she would begin fire duty until I arrived. The evening mist began to create a heavy fog over the Forum. A guard stood close by the Temple of Castor and Pollux. Since the back of the temple led to the Emperor's Palace, everyone had to pass the guard's approval. Luckily, we did not need to enter the temple.

The guard glared at us anyhow.

"Please, I must have words with this Vestal. It's urgent," Lucius told the guard, who nodded.

"Did you find anything yet?" I asked him. "Something that might explain Vesta's message?'

"Yes—and no." He directed me toward the stand of trees near the temple.

"I spoke with the Chief Haruspex about your message. We both spoke about what you did with the snake. How you handled it."

"And—"I asked.

"And it's clear, Cornelia, you have the gift of prophecy. Please, any messages you receive, write them down. The

Emperor might want to know—to consult with you like he does the astrologers and soothsayers."

"I don't want Nero to know of my visions!"

"But they may prove useful to him."

"Did you consult the Sibylline Books? What else did the Chief Haruspex say?"

"We studied the message from Vesta. We understand the eagle stands for Rome. But of the fish, we are not sure. We think the fish stands for something submerged, not fully developed. But it's finding its way. Finding its own voice."

"Please do not share this with Nero."

"As you wish, Cornelia."

"What of the Sibylline Books?" I asked again.

"Both the haruspex and I did a reading, prayed to Jupiter for guidance, and were led to this passage in Book II." He pulled out a small scroll of his own. "Read this in private. Perhaps you can help us further understand its meaning."

More work for me! And still I had no clear answer to my vision.

I tucked the scroll inside my belt. "Thank you, Lucius."

"No. Thank *you*, Cornelia."

I heard a voice behind me. "Vibidia awaits you in the temple. You are late."

There was Domicia. The nerve of her! I was almost eleven, old enough to conduct my own business. Had she overheard us, and why did she follow me so closely? I said my goodbyes to Lucius and made my way to the temple, with Domicia on my heels.

I decided I would not even tell Vibi about any of this. Too many ears were listening about the temple.

After fire duty, back in my apartment, I unraveled the scroll. A passage from the Sibylline Books lay before me. I read:

And into outward form all-desolate
For stars from heaven shall fall into the sea
And all the souls of men shall gnash their teeth
Burned both by sulphur stream, and force of fire
In ravenous soil, and ashes hide all things.
And the of the world all the elements
Shall be bereft, air, earth, sea, light, sky, days nights;
And no longer in the air shall fly
Birds without number, nor shall
Living things that swim the sea
Swim any more at all.

I sat and thought for many moments. If I were truly a prophetess, as Lucius claimed, I should know what it meant. I prayed to Vesta and received no answer. I hid the scroll away, too tired to think anymore. But the images of fire and ashes haunted me. As I tossed and turned, the smell of sulphur burned my nostrils. And in my visions, I saw a place as dark, gray and desolate as the underworld, where bad people went, with nothing but ashes floating in the air.

CHAPTER 19

AUGUST 61 AD

A whole year had passed. And today it was my eleventh birthday. I had grown several inches since my arrival to the House of the Vestals. Most people thought my age fifteen or sixteen. My hair was long enough so Domicia could even pull a comb through it, though it mostly remained covered under my fillet and headdress.

I was given the day off. The Vestals brought me a small honey cake ringed with eleven sweets. Then I started to wait. And waited for someone from my family to visit me. I remembered the promise my mother made on the Vestalia—that my father would visit me on my birthday. Where was he? Was he thinking about me, his only daughter, today?

Finally, I could wait no more. Anger seethed inside me, anger that my own family had forgotten my special day. It was late in the day when I made the decision.

"Domicia," I ordered. "Call for a litter for me and Vibi. Now!"

"Why?" she asked.

"It's not your concern,"

How dare she, a servant, question what I chose to do—on my birthday? Her lurking over me like a dark, long-necked bird gave me shivers. She seemed to enjoy living in the shadows. *My shadow,* I thought.

I found Vibi and requested she join me on the trip. She agreed with a shrug.

A white litter with six slaves finally appeared waiting for us along the Via Sacra. "Please carry us to this address," I ordered, as I handed the lead slave a piece of papyrus. Then I advised our lictors to proceed in front of us, parting crowds to the side of the road.

My mind was crowded with thoughts. *How bold of me to go.* I wondered if my family was even at home. Perhaps Emperor Nero had forbidden my father to visit me. Nothing surprised me about Emperor Nero anymore. All he cared about these days was building more rooms, baths, and gardens for his palace.

The slaves hoisted up the litter with a heave and grunt as we settled in for the ride. The roads around the Forum bustled with activity: men preparing carts for their nightly rides through the city, people making final sales before nightfall, gamblers taking bets for tomorrow's chariot races at the Circus Maximus.

The litter proceeded past the Forum and down the Clivus Capitoline, a road leading toward the Aventine Hill, my old home. Everyone stopped for us, bowed, and waved. I enjoyed riding in the litter, looking down on the people. To the right of us flowed the Tiber with its wharves and warehouses, several of them my father's. I hadn't realized how much I missed my old neighborhood.

Finally, the litter stopped in front of my family's house. All seemed quiet. "Please return in an hour's time," I told the slave and handed him a coin from my pouch. "Return on time!"

I felt relieved Vibi was with me. We smoothed out our stolas and straightened our headdresses, then departed the litter. My soft-toed white shoes touched the ground on my father's soil for the first time in a year.

At the vestibule door, I knocked loudly and cleared my throat. Luckily, Taltos answered. "What a surprise!" He bowed low to me and then to Vibi. "Being a Vestal becomes you, Cornelia." His dark eyes took in the sight of us, two young women cloaked in white. "Welcome! Come in, come," he said.

My home looked the same. But it felt different; something was missing. *Perhaps it's just me that's missing,* I thought. I prayed to Vesta for strength. We waited.

My mother was first to appear fluttering about like a moth. "Cornelia, look at you— daughter. We are so proud." She embraced me. She looked over at Vibi.

"Mother, this is Vibidia. My sister in Vesta's name now."

"Of course. Welcome." She beckoned us to the chairs scattered around the atrium. "Please take a seat. It's very nice to meet you, Vibidia. Thank you for watching over our daughter as she learns to be a proper Vestal." Vibi smiled and told Mother it was her duty and pleasure. "And Cornelia," my mother continued, "your feat with the snake at the Feast of the Argeii—it's all people are talking about. How did you do it?" She stared at me in a new and different way. Was it a look of admiration—or fear?

"The Goddess works through me now, Mother. It was not my power that held the snake but—"I had to get off this subject. "Where is my father? My brother?" I asked.

"Cornelius is down at your father's warehouse," she said. "And your father is in the library."

"Did you forget what day it is today?" I asked, trying to keep my temper calm. Vibi watched me and shook her head, as if to tell me to take care what I said.

"Why—"my mother paused.

"Yes, it's my birthday. And you promised Father would visit me," I replied in a haughty voice.

And that was when my father came forth, his hair much grayer now, with many more lines etched on his forehead. He seemed tired—and old.

"Daughter—you've returned," he exclaimed. "How proud we are to have a Vestal in the family." I rose from my chair and we embraced. He pushed me back, still holding me, so he could study me. "You have grown."

"But why haven't you visited me? Not even on my own birthday!" I clenched my fists and kept them stiff by my side. Vibi's eyes widened with shock. *She's hoping I don't have a temper tantrum,* I thought.

"Happy birthday to you," was all he said.

"Why does no one visit me?" I demanded. My father just stood there, as pale as a statue, staring down at me with no expression on his face. Like he had seen a ghost, an ancestral spirit come to haunt him.

"We've suffered losses since you left us, Cornelia. I became ill for a time. Your brother has taken over the business during my illness. I'm better now, but that is not all."

My heart sank. "What else, Father? What has happened?"

"Cornelia, our fortunes have taken a turn for the worse. Two of my ships went down in a violent storm in the Mediterranean. We lost everything and everyone on board." I gasped, sad for my family. Now I had to comfort my father. Even on my own birthday.

"Are you in need of money, Father? I receive a monthly pension now. Money will never be a problem for me."

"Cornelia, this is why I have been hesitant to visit you at the Atrium. I want to do nothing to upset your training. And we will take nothing from your Vestal pension. The Cosas are far too proud for this!"

"What about Emperor Nero? Could you request his help?" I asked.

"Nero? Help? I'd rather be dead than approach that man— if one could even call him a man!" my father said.

"That's why you haven't come to see me? Because you are ashamed?" I realized how far removed I was from my family, how little I knew them anymore.

"Yes, Cornelia, I ... we are ashamed." He hung his head low and began to cry softly.

"Please Father, I beg of you, stop. What happened to the three bags of gold given to you by Nero? For me?"

"Gone, Cornelia. All put into the business—and lost at sea."

"Well," I huffed. "I hope it was all worth it!" I stamped my foot hard. The old Cornelia was back. But then my heart opened for I did not like to see my father in agony. He was humiliated. And I was making it worse.

"Please Father, if you need anything—money, guidance, favors— you come to the House of the Vestals. I will help you." I realized I still loved my family with a fierce pride. I made a vow I would never see my family return to a plebian existence. I needed to know that they were safe and secure.

"And if you can't come, make sure to send Taltos," I said.

My father's eyes lit up for a brief moment. "Did you know, Cornelia, I will be freeing Taltos in a few years? He's served me well. If I am still fully in business by then, I will be a patron to him. He is deserving of his freedom and more."

I watched Taltos standing tall, all puffed up with pride. I congratulated him, and Vibi did the same, in her stately refined manner.

My father came toward me again, embraced me, and held me close to his chest. The smell of pine oil, wine, and that faint odor of fish filled my nose. He still smelled the same. "Thank you for coming today, Cornelia. You have brought me some bright moments in an otherwise dreary life. We miss you more than you can know. And today you've brought your father some happiness, however fleeting it may be, to a father who mourns the loss of his daughter every day."

Everyone seemed to be crying now. Even Taltos wiped a tear from his eye and Vibi sniffled trying to control her own emotions. My family wished me a final happy birthday and we said our goodbyes and left.

The sun was setting over the seven hills of Rome by the time the litter tilted to begin the climb up the Aventine Hill. I expressed a wish that if we had time, I would like to visit the Temple of Diana. But Vibi said we had to get back to the House of the Vestals.

However, it was clear she had something else in mind first. When I saw her pull out her own tattered piece of papyrus and hand it out the window to the head slave, the litter stopped.

"Where are we going?" I asked.

"You'll see," was all she said.

The litter passed the Circus Maximus, and continued past the palaces and the Forum.

"Where are we going?" I asked again. I thought maybe she had a birthday surprise for me. The litter was fast approaching the Subura, an area where many of Rome's poor resided. Julius Caesar was born in the Subura! Look at how far he had risen from the slums.

We continued on a narrow, winding road that twisted like a mosaic. Rows of apartment blocks mixed with markets and shops were crammed in together often one building on top of another. Mist started to fill the air. I hoped Vibi knew where we were going because I could see very little; only shapes and dark figures roaming the streets.

"You'll see," was all she would tell me.

The litter ride, bumpy and uncomfortable was making me dizzy. Carts on one side of the road began their night-time journeys through the city. We finally stopped in front of a two-storied villa between the Viminal and Esquiline Hill. In the shadows of fog-filled twilight, I thought it looked familiar. A guard holding an oil lamp stood out in front of the dwelling.

"That's my cousin, Marcus," Vibi whispered. "He is on duty tonight."

The slaves lowered the litter, and Vibi like a specter in white descended and spoke with her cousin for a few minutes. Lights blinked in the dreary-looking house. I noticed a few people going in after getting a nod from Marcus. Why?

Finally Vibi returned. She had a smile on her face.

"I have a birthday present for you after all, Cornelia," she told me as she settled back into the litter. "It's a surprise. And remember, I joined you today to visit your family. So, get ready to come with me."

"Now? Where?" I asked.

"Here, right here. Not now ... not yet. And no more questions please. I will explain more to you when we have fire duty."

"Who lives there?" I asked.

Vibi sighed and tsked her tongue. I couldn't help that I was always asking questions.

"Don't you remember anything?" she asked. "Paul lives here, Paul the prisoner. Paul, who speaks of Jesus Christ." She let out another long sigh. I was starting to feel like I was a burden. "I've told you enough, Sister," she continued. "Trust me. I know what I'm doing. And this is enough for any eleven-year-old." She leaned over and embraced me. She had that same glow on her face like the one I'd seen during fire duty.

Then she stuck a short, wand-like stick she carried with her out the window and struck the side of the litter three times. "Let us be off. To the House of the Vestals," she ordered. "And be quick about it."

Back at the Atrium, I decided to wash myself at the spring of Juturna. Vibi and I had early fire duty in the morning. For now, I decided to roam about the grounds. My family visit was still on my mind.

"Cornelia, we meet again."

I looked up after pouring water into my drinking vessel. "Lucius, what are you doing here?" I asked.

"Looking for you, I hoped. The gods have answered me.

Were you about Rome this afternoon? I didn't see you any-where around the Atrium."

"It's my birthday. Vibidia and I paid a visit to my family on the Aventine. I miss my old neighborhood."

"But of course. How could I forget today is your birthday? It's been a whole year since I read the auguries in the Forum. Remember?"

"And I heard you read the augury for Occia. So she and I will be two of the greatest Vestals ever?"

"Indeed. It is so," said Lucius with a proud grin.

He smiled down at me, his dark eyes twinkling. "Do you feel at home with the Vestals now?" he asked.

"I've lost my family. But I've gained many new sisters here. They are my family now."

Then Lucius leaned in close and whispered, "Did you read the passage from the Sibylline Book? What do you make of such words, Cornelia?"

"I've had little time with all my duties. I will call upon Vesta tonight. She may have a message for me—for us! Some-times the gods take their time. We must be patient." Then I remembered. "But what of *my* message from Vesta? The eagle and the fish?"

"I am still thinking about this. Why don't we meet in a week's time to discuss this mystery in more depth? I think between the two of us, we can make sense of this riddle."

"Of course," I said, looking forward to meeting this hand-some augur again.

"You'll do no such thing, Cornelia!" I spun around and saw Junia's pointed nose staring down at me. "Vestals in training do not set up times and dates with augurs! Not unless a chap-erone is present." How much else she had overheard, I knew

157

not. "And where have you been? You've missed dinner." She snorted, her body stiff and rigid.

"It's my birthday today." I got up close to her face. "Remember?"

Lucius wore a grin on his face. He filled up his vessel and proceeded back to the Regia nodding at me.

"I am allowed friends, correct? Friends who will help me become a better Vestal, unlike you, who do nothing but make my life a misery." All the anger I felt toward my father seemed to rush back again. I didn't care that I was taking it out on Junia. She was as mean as a street dog; at that moment she reminded me of a vulture, hovering, waiting to pick at anything she could.

"How dare you speak to me in such a manner? *You*— nothing but a novice in training?" Junia, breathing heavily now, stuck a long thin finger right to my face and wagged it back and forth. "I have a mind to speak with Mother Aurelia about that bold tongue of yours. Consider this a warning, young lady."

"I'm fine, and please don't stick your finger in my face. That's rude!"

"Mind yourself, Cornelia. I will be watching you closely. And from now on, I will advise certain others in the Atrium to keep a close eye on your comings and goings. You have been warned!"

I paid no mind to her words but just strode away to the Atrium. My eleventh birthday was not much better than my tenth.

Still sleepless, I decided to walk through the back garden. The noise of the nightly carts and the shouting from the streets did not disturb me. Junia had disturbed me. I found a bench and saw Cleo in the mist playing around the fishpond. Dipping her paws in, she seemed to enjoy batting the fish about, tormenting them and frightening them into the deep corners of the pool. All they could do was hide.

"Cleo," I ordered, "leave the Atrium fish alone." She didn't listen. It seemed like a game to her, to play with the fish, flicking at their fins like I would swat a bug. And she stared and waited with the intensity of a wild beast, like a tiger from the Circus Maximus. The hunter and the hunted. My sweet and loving Cleo by day turned into a huntress by night. I prayed for the fish. I could do no more.

That night in bed, after I said my prayers to Vesta, I thought about my message from Vesta. I thought about the eagle and the fish. I had just seen Cleo try to kill one. What did it all mean? Being so tired, I could think no more. All I could do was pray to Vesta for answers. But none came.

CHAPTER 20

The morning after my birthday, Vibi and I walked to the temple arm and arm. Junia was leaving the temple as we climbed the stairs.

"It's about time," she exclaimed, snorting like an angry bull. Why couldn't she just leave me be? I gave her my "leave me alone" stare and hoped it would work. It did.

We settled into our fire duty. I was exhausted from the visit with my family. Domicia was out getting us some water. Vibi whispered to me, "Are you ready? Tonight's the night."

"Tonight?" I repeated.

"Yes, tonight. Listen for my knock at your door. I will explain more later."

Fire duty and the rest of the afternoon passed by with few occurrences. What could I do but agree to Vibi's request? I owed her that much after she had come with me to visit my parents. I trusted her and was growing to love her. I was up for another adventure.

Darkness fell over the Atrium as I waited. Nothing. Finally as I lay in bed, my eyes drooping, I heard a soft knock on the door. I got up and opened it with caution. There was Vibi in her nightgown, half in shadow, the other half lit by the dim oil lamps in the corridor.

"Are you ready?" she asked.

I nodded. "I think so."

"Here." She thrust a bundle of clothes at me and quickly closed the door behind her. "Tonight we leave behind our Vestal garments. Here is a cloak of a young Jewish girl for you to wear. I will be your older sister. Make sure you wear the Jewish head covering properly. Here, let me show you how to put it on." She dug the headdress out and I watched her teach me to place it correctly over my head. "I will be back in some minutes. And in the bundle there's some extra cloth to stuff in your bed—just in case nosey Domicia peeks in your room. Now get ready!"

I closed the door half asleep and looked at the bundle. I brought it to the flickering oil lamp blinking in the corner of my apartment and unraveled it. Along with a coarse brown cloak, a strange olive-green headcovering and green tunica awaited me. This was the first time in over a year I would wear something other than the white Vestal attire. I slipped on my Vestal soft-toed sandals and was ready.

The tunica fit, but I had problems with the head wrap. A part of the covering included a concealment of my chin and the sides of my face. I thought how much worse Jewish women and girls suffered by wearing such a constricting headdress. I noticed that the green tunica covered most of my inner white tunica; still, a few inches of white hung down around my shoes.

Where did Vibi find such clothing? Everything else seemed to fit. They were just a bit big.

I heard the light footsteps and the soft knock again. "Cornelia, ready?" I heard.

"Yes," I answered and let her in my apartment. When I saw her in her own headdress, with only her eyes, nose, and mouth exposed, I resisted a laugh. *Do I look this foolish?* I tried to suppress a giggle.

"Now is not the time," Vibi responded as if reading my thoughts. "Fix your head covering properly. It's crooked." She stood over me fussing and mumbling. Finally, she seemed satisfied with how I looked. "We are ready now. Let's go."

We crept out to the back staircase facing the garden and huddled together, heads bowed, and hurried toward the Via Sacra.

The evening rain had ended. Night mist slowly filled the air. The street noise was as loud as ever: donkeys braying, people arguing, smells of roasted meat mingled with smoke, dogs barking, children laughing then screaming … for many of Rome's citizens slept during the hottest hours of the day, only to awaken at nightfall.

A cart was waiting on the side of the road. Vibi spoke with the driver. The cart, filled with what looked like sacks of grain and a few amphorae had little room left. Vibi came around to the back of the cart where I was waiting.

"Get in. Kneel down and cover yourself with your cloak. No one will notice the difference between us and a sack of grain." I squeezed into a side of the cart, covered myself, and waited. Vibi crowded in next to me.

"Yah, get a move on." The carter cracked a whip to the donkey's back and we began the forward movement on the Via

Sacra. The ride was bumpy, so Vibi and I clung together and tried to sway with the cart's movement.

"What if someone notices we are missing?" I asked, amid the turns and bumps on the road. "I'm scared."

"Cornelia, I know what I'm doing."

The ride seemed endless. My head was tired and sore from my nose being pressed to the cart's bottom. How I wanted to lift my head and witness Rome's nightlife teeming around us. At last the cart came to a halt.

"We get out here," Vibi said.

I lifted my head. "Where are we?" I asked, shaking bits of grain off my cloak and looking at the rain-glistened shops and apartments lining the street.

The carter came round and acted as if he were fixing something in the back of the wagon. And then he helped us crawl out, as we kept low, bent over like old women.

Vibi thrust a coin in his hand. "For your services. Please return in one hour's time." The carter bowed to her, and just as quickly, the wagon was off.

"Where are we?" I asked her again.

"We must walk through the Subura. It's just a short walk. And if anyone bothers us, we are sisters. Jewish sisters. Anyone who meets us will see the headcovers and recognize us as Jewish."

We followed the narrow, winding streets through the Subura. The smells of thick smoke from cooking fires and the stench of urine burned my nose. But to walk among the common people and to pretend to be someone we were not—this was excitement for me.

"This is the first time in a year I am wearing something other than white," I mused.

"And it will be your last time—if we get caught," Vibi scolded me. "Now keep your thoughts to yourself. Stay silent."

The streets were so crowded with people we blended in. We walked briskly, our heads lowered. Every so often I lifted my head to view the rosy lights coming from many of the two-storied apartments. I wondered what life was like for these people. What they were doing and saying? What were they eating?

Men played knuckles with sheep bones in front of shops, laughing, cursing, then laughing again. Even young children ran through the streets. These people seemed happier than the Emperor or anyone in the Atrium. They were poor, yes, but seemed to have a joy that everyone I had met this year was lacking—all except Lucretia. I wondered if she had met any man who would love her. I was becoming distracted with my own thoughts.

Vibi nudged me. "Pay attention," she warned. "I may be playing the role of your older sister, but please refrain from acting like a child. I have no time to worry over you." She stopped, turned toward me, and grabbed me by the shoulders. "Follow everything I say and do. Understand?"

I nodded as she adjusted my headdress. It kept falling over my eyes. At last we arrived at the vaguely familiar villa on the outskirts of the Subura, located on the Viminal Hill, close to the Esquiline. Dull lights flickered from the inside. A guard stood outside at his post, holding a torch in one hand and a small pouch in the other.

Vibidia reached into her pocket and handed me a round marker. "This marker has the sign of the fish on it," she explained. My mind immediately went back to my vision of the eagle and the fish. Maybe I would get some answers.

"Hand this to the guard. Listen to me and repeat what I say," Vibi reminded me again. The guard looked us over from head to foot. I could see little expression on his face. Vibi pulled out her marker. "The sign of the fish," she said, and bowed slightly. She elbowed me.

"Oh … the fish," I mumbled, and dropped the marker into the pouch.

"You may enter," said the guard, now bowing to us like all of Rome's citizens did when they witnessed a Vestal in public. So he knew. "Shalom to you both," he said.

We climbed the stairs and Vibi opened the door under the arch leading into the villa, and slowly led us in through the vestibule. A great room awaited us; similar to an atrium but smaller than what I was accustomed to. Several groups of people had gathered in the corners of the room. They whispered among themselves. A few people glanced at us but just as quickly looked away. Vibi's plan seemed to work. We were just a pair of Jewish sisters.

Everyone waited. Braziers hanging from the ceiling blinked dim lights. The light and shadows made it seem as if more people were present. A few chairs and couches placed around the room provided seating for attendants.

Then I saw him, the small, bandy-legged man with the balding head and tufts of red and gray hair sticking up on the sides. His pointed beard glowed with a red-gray light, like a burning ember. I thought of how brave he was that day on the street when he stood up to Emperor Nero. I admired his courage.

He was still chained to a guard. But clearly this was not stopping Paul from holding a gathering during his house arrest. He may be Nero's prisoner, I thought, but nothing, not even the Emperor, could quell his passion for sharing his truth. I squinted and saw a light around him—or so I thought. Maybe it was just the flickering lights playing tricks upon my eyes.

Paul's eyes met Vibi's and then he looked at me and nodded. Vibi could not take her eyes from the prisoner. With his free hand he beckoned us forth. "Come. Come closer to hear the word. Sit, please. Do not be shy. All are welcome here."

Two men stood to each side of Paul. One was tall and lean and dark in color with a beard similiar to the many Greek men I had seen in Rome. The other man, younger and pale in complexion, seemed to keep track of the people mingling in the room. His eyes darted back and forth, as if he were another guard protecting his prisoner.

"Here are two of my trusted companions," said Paul. "Let me introduce Luke, my beloved physician, and Timothy, who is like a son to me."

We nodded and bowed. I looked to Vibi, because I had promised to do everything she did.

"Before you sit would you care to introduce yourselves?" he asked.

Vibi gave me a look that told me to keep quiet. "We are Jewish sisters who seek understanding," she replied.

Paul chuckled. "So you have come to the right house. Welcome."

Many people sat while others stood. Paul did not appear angered being chained to the guard; the guard in turn did not seem bothered by Paul. We found a couch near the front and made ourselves comfortable.

Everyone stayed quiet as this strange man with the strange glow began: "Friends, Brothers and Sisters, my journeys have led me to Rome. During this last journey, I have been shipwrecked, I've wrestled with a snake and survived a snake bite, and I've been called a god because of it!

"What adventures I have had that led me to my arrest in Rome! But it was on the road to Damascus that I met my Savior, the Messiah, Jesus Christ, come to fulfill the words of the prophets. Before this, I, Saul of Tarsus, was a sinner, a Pharisee who put many to death with just my word. But now I speak *the* Word, the word of our Lord Jesus who has forgiven me my many sins." He raised his free hand and lifted a finger.

"Upon arriving in Rome, being put under house arrest, I called for the Chief of the Jews in Rome. And others of Jewish persuasion." He glanced around the room. "I see many of you have returned. For this I am pleased." He continued. "I explained to them I had committed no crime— that I am a Roman citizen by birth—but the Jewish authorities listened to me not. Thus I was delivered, a prisoner, into the hands of the Romans. I know that the Leader of the Jews here in Rome and others have spoken against me, and I am forced to appeal to Caesar.

"For this reason, I call Jews and Gentiles to me so I can speak with you about Him! My hope is for Israel. But remember, there is no longer Jew or Roman or Greek, there is no longer slave and free, there's no longer male or female; you are One with the Messiah, Jesus Christ."

He sighed. "And for the preaching of this good news, I am bound to these chains." He rattled the clanking chains about so everyone could see and hear them. The guard on the other end of the chain seemed tired and bored, as if he had heard this speech before.

"I am bound to this chain," Paul held up his fastened wrist again, "because of you. I do it for your souls." I looked over at Vibi. There she sat holding her breath, listening intently to Paul's every word.

"Take courage now. Although you may be amid a den of vipers and idolaters, take heed of the Word. And for tonight's meeting here is the word." Paul paused, wiped his brow with his free hand, and was ready:

"Remember this I say unto you, Go to the people and say:

You will ever be hearing, but never understanding
You will ever be seeing, but never perceiving
For the peoples' heart has become calloused
They hardly hear with their ears
And they have closed their eyes.
Otherwise they might see with their eyes
And hear with their ears
Understand with their hearts

And in turn, I will heal them.
Therefore, I want you to know
That God's salvation has been sent to the Gentiles
And they will listen."

"We are listening," said Vibidia out loud.

What was she thinking? Paul's words seemed to penetrate deep into my spirit as well. Could I understand with my heart?

Some of the Jewish men began arguing amongst themselves."Who is this man to tell us our eyes and ears are closed?"

One man shouted, "This man proclaims the Nazarene is our Messiah? I'll listen no more to such blasphemy!"

Then several of them abruptly left. The room soon cleared, and only a few people mingled around Paul.

"Here is our chance to speak with him. Please behave," Vibi chided me.

"You behave too," I whispered, thinking about Vibi's outburst.

Paul stood by a wall, flanked by his two companions, and then slouched down to the floor with his guard, sitting and awaiting anyone who cared to speak with him. Concerned about the time, I nudged Vibi to remind her we must be leaving soon.

We waited our turn to speak to the prisoner. Finally we approached him. Paul grabbed Vibi's hand with his free hand and clasped it tightly. "Thank you for coming. Blessings of the risen Christ be with you," he said. He then pulled from his pocket a small etching of a man with a dark beard and dark eyes. "Here is an etching of our Savior," he said showing us the image.

"Why, he looks a lot like you," I said.

Paul smiled up at me. "Out of the mouth of a child. Our Savior loved the children and called them unto him."

I was insulted for a moment. "But I'm not a child—anymore!" I told him.

"You are still child enough to listen and learn. Understanding comes like waves of sand in the desert, like waves of water across the ocean. Understanding takes time. Did you hear my words, child?"

I paused to take a breath before I spoke. "Yes, I seek to understand."

"I seek to understand and know the truth as well," Vibi said eagerly.

I felt inspired to be out late with Vibi wearing different clothes and meeting Paul. Remembering that Paul spoke of a snake, I said, "I also grabbed hold of a snake."

He eyed me carefully. "Did you, my child?" His eyes crinkled with delight. "And did it bite you?" he asked.

"No," I said.

"And were you frightened?"

"Yes," I answered, ashamed of my fear.

"As was I." He stretched his arm out to me. "Come closer." The guard attached to Paul lightly snored.

"Did you know that Jesus Christ was scared? Did that stop him? No! You see, Jesus still carried humanity within him—he had a human body and human emotions. While he lived, he became angry, he cried, he laughed. Yet he held within that human body, the light of the living God."

I could not contain my curiosity. "But what of Rome's many gods?" I asked. Vibi nudged me now.

Paul shook his head. "All the gods are man-made shadows of the one true God. It's too much to understand for a young mind." He looked up to the ceiling and shook his head. "And to think that I, a sinner who deserved only punishment, have found redemption."

The Roman guard stirred, grunted, and then opened his eyes a sliver, only to close them again.

"Life is for understanding," Paul continued.

"But isn't that why we have auguries in Rome? To understand and read the omens?" I thought of Lucius and the sacred chickens, and how he read so accurately the flight of birds.

Vibi cleared her throat. "That is enough, sister." She spoke with Paul now. "Please forgive my sister. She has an inquisitive nature."

"What about the sign of the fish?" I asked quickly.

"Ah, the fish," Paul said. "Our Savior called himself a fisher of men. This is our sign. My dear friend Peter was a fisherman— he left it behind to follow our Messiah." Paul smiled. Truly there was a glow about him. I thought of Lucretia and the power of the ether. Was this where the light beaming from his eyes originated?

"What about the power of the ether?" I blurted out.

"Yes, I know of the ether, the fifth element that astrologers and soothsayers speak of." He paused. "And what of the ether, child? What do you know as a good and obedient Jewish daughter?" He glanced over at the man called Luke, who smiled, his eyes alive with understanding.

"I've learned about the ether," I said with pride. Vibidia wrapped her arm around me tight. She was trying to keep me quiet. Faint wisps of perfume, the one I recognized as frankincense, lingered in the air, just as Vibi and I had lingered too long.

"We are leaving now." She pulled her cloak around me. "Thank you kindly."

"Yes. "Paul in a soft voice continued, gazing up at me. "And you have learned it from the Vestal Order." There was silence around us, with the exception of the guard lightly snoring.

"How did you know?" Vibi and I whispered this at the same time.

"Why, look." He cast his eyes down and pointed. Pointed to my white, soft-toed vestal shoes. How could I have forgotten about the shoes?

"Please," Paul continued. "All are welcome here. The Spirit cares nothing about white shoes or ancient orders. You must return again soon. Pray for me, an old sinner who has found his way. I, in turn, shall pray for you. And remember the power of love. It is only by the power of love we are gathered together—a love that understands and will forgive all … if you ask."

Vibi and I bowed in unison and hurried out the front door.

We made our way through the narrow streets of the Subura, cloaks and heads huddled together. The paving stones were slippery under our feet from the early rains, so we held onto one another.

The cart was waiting at the same spot. We clambered to the back and the carter covered us with a coarse sack. All I could think of was how late it was getting, and that we needed to get back home to the Atrium. After enduring bumps and groans from the wagon hitting uneven pavement and getting stuck in rain-filled ruts, the carter shouted, "Whoa."

Vibi got off first and dusted bits of grain and dirt from her cloak. I slid out from the wagon and watched Vibi give the carter another coin. I thought he must be a Jesus Follower as well. Why else would he agree to such a dangerous undertaking?

"Follow me and keep your head down, covering on," she reminded me.

We made our way over the wooden bridge from the Via Sacra, up to the back of the Atrium, and up the stairs overlooking the Vestal garden. No one was around; just the ever-present noises from the street that seemed soothing tonight. We climbed to the back door. It was locked, but Vibi pulled a key from her pouch. She thought of everything!

The door creaked slightly. I felt safer now in the long corridor of the Vestal apartments. "Good night ... Sister," Vibi said, and kissed my forehead. "You were brave to come with me tonight. Think on the words said at the meeting." Then she vanished down the hall like a vapor of mist. I would think on what Paul spoke of—but not now.

For when I glanced back at the other end of the hallway, a shadow led by a faint light, illuminated a wall. I found the knob to my door, opened it, and then peered out. The shadow was gone.

CHAPTER 21

The day after my encounter with the prisoner Paul, I awoke refreshed. I knew I ought to feel tired, perhaps ashamed, but instead I felt a renewal of my spirit. I could not explain the feeling to myself. I think perhaps it was the first real peace I had felt since entering the House of the Vestals.

But then worry pounced upon me. Had anyone seen Vibi and me? What would we say if someone did see us? Worse, the bundle of Jewish clothing remained bunched up in a corner of my apartment. I picked them up, folded them, and hid them at the bottom of my wardrobe chest.

I would ponder Paul's message during my morning prayers. Could I now include Jesus as another god I prayed to? Paul had called him the Son of the One God. I felt more confused than ever.

After breakfast I had free time before my early evening fire duty. I decided to go visit my favorite place on the grounds, the garden of the Vestals. The peaches, plums, and apricots were ripe. The fruit hung heavy and low off the boughs. I plucked a peach and started to roam through the many paths traversing the garden. The herb garden, so tenderly cared for, displayed bright yellow stalks of fragrant chamomile; the lovely scent of bergamot helped to clear my mind. Mint plants bordered the herb garden. It helped keep the insects away.

"Why, it's the young Vestal herself. Turning into quite a beauty, I see."

There was Rubria sitting on a bench; she motioned me to come closer. Cleo sat purring on her lap. I hadn't seen Cleo for some time. Where did she go when I searched for her? I thought perhaps I was like Cleo—escaping into the night like a ghost roaming the streets.

"Good morning, Rubria. I am a still a young Vestal—but not the youngest anymore."

"Yes I know," Rubria mused, petting Cleo and scratching behind her ears. "I am helping little Occia learn to have confidence in herself. You, on the other hand—I can see you have all the confidence in the world. But know your place; you never want this confidence to turn into *boldness*." She laughed under her breath as if she was remembering when she was a young Vestal-in-training.

I thought of how bold Rubria was around Emperor Nero, but I said nothing.

"You are like the child I never had, Cornelia. Occia too. I mourn my barrenness, never to bring life into this world," she murmured.

"But you were chosen by Vesta," I argued, trying to make her feel better.

"Yes. The same way slaves are chosen by their masters."

"I'm sorry," I said, because I could think of nothing else to say. She was right of course. So I got up and hugged her. Cleo yawned, jumped down, and scampered toward the fishpond, her usual amusement. She padded her paw up and down on the water, scaring the fish. How she enjoyed the chase, the game to torment them. And then, as I watched that paw, the claws came out—sharp. She grabbed onto the flesh of a fish that was too foolish to hide and flung it up into the air.

"Stop, Cleo!" I shouted, and tried to shoo her away from the pond. It was too late. The fish, fins flapping, bounced on the ground gasping for air.

I tried to save it. But Cleo guarded her prey, and when I approached her, she hissed at me. Then with a turn of her head, she looked upon the dying fish, took it in her mouth, and trotted off towards the donkey stables.

I heard Rubria calling me. "What can you do, Cornelia? What can any of us do? It's the natural order of things."

"But she's our temple cat," I moaned. "And now she's eating the Atrium's fish."

"It's her bounty, Cornelia. Just like we are bounties for Rome, given no choice. My life could have been different if I'd had a choice."

"What choice would you have made, Rubria?" I asked her. "If you could?"

Rubria sighed a long, melancholy sigh. "Like most women, I wanted children. And a husband I could call my own. Someone to love me."

I decided to be bold. "Rubria." I grabbed her hand. "Do you love Emperor Nero?"

She yanked her hand away.

"Why ask me about *him*?"

"Because I see the way he looks at you—and the way you look at him."

"Love is a strong word, Cornelia. The Emperor cares about me. But you are too young and naïve to understand. The Emperor has a wife, a wife the people love. A wife, rumor has it, that he wants to get rid of. Just like they say he got rid of his mother. And he has a mistress, the beautiful and dangerous Poppaea. How can I compete and measure up to that?" She wrung her hands in frustration and looked up to the heavens as if awaiting an answer.

"Compete? Why should you compete with these women? You are a Vestal!"

Rubria slid close to me and wrapped her arm around my shoulder. She whispered, "Let me explain something to you, Cornelia. Something I hope you understand and never have to endure. It is this—that men are rarely satisfied with what they have. They are always seeking more. It's the conquest they love. And they seek after what they can't have—or are not supposed to have. They seek the unattainable. Until they get it! Once they do, once the hunt is over, that which they seek is discarded, thrown away, like scraps to pigs."

"How cruel!" I replied. "How can this be? My father is not like this."

"Life can be cruel, Cornelia. Every day I try to accept my fate as a Vestal, a fate I never could embrace." Rubria burst into a torrent of tears. And I found myself comforting her.

"It was our fate to be chosen, Rubria. We were chosen by Vesta. I didn't accept my fate at first, but now I seek love … and understanding." Once again, the words of Paul emerged from my mouth. I thought of what he said to us, "Understanding through love." It was so mysterious—for sometimes I felt like I understood nothing.

Rubria echoed my thoughts. "Cornelia, you understand nothing about the vow of chastity. It's only a word to one so young." She sniffed. "Just wait and see. Someday you will understand and know what I speak about."

"I may be young, but I try to accept my fate and understand it. I hope you can do the same."

Rubria smiled down at me and wiped her eyes. "Wisdom— from the mouth of a child," she mused. "I love you like my own, Cornelia," she said again. "You bring happiness to my cold heart. Thank you." She kissed the top of my forehead.

I felt glad I had brightened Rubria's heart, if only for a few minutes.

"And remember Lucretia? She accepted her fate as a Vestal and accepted her fate as a free woman. Her face may be scarred, but she is free. Think of the sacrifice she made to Vesta, to Rome."

"You are right, Cornelia. I should be ashamed of my own selfishness. We cannot know or even understand our fate. All we can do is accept it." We embraced each other. Even the hot sun seemed to smile upon us.

Then I saw little Occia running toward us. She looked so small. She stopped to catch her breath while we waited. "Mother Aurelia wants us all to meet her in the library. She has an important announcement!"

Rubria and I walked arm in arm back to the Atrium, as Occia skipped ahead. I wondered what this announcement could be.

All I could think about was when I would get the chance to speak with Vibi; we had fire duty later in the evening. I had more questions about Paul.

"Gather around," Mother Aurelia said. "I have something important I must discuss. Junia has fire duty and knows already." Mother's hands flitted like the sparrows in the garden, circling the air. "Come round now." We each found a stool to sit on.

I watched as Vibi came through the door at last. Her skin had a gray pale cast to it. Two pink blotches burned on her cheeks. But when she lifted her eyes, brightness filled the room. Her eyes twinkled like polished emeralds. Vibi found a lone stool, sat down, and then fumbled with her headdress fixing it properly.

"You see girls," Mother began. "I have been with the Vestal order for over thirty years. My duty is done. More than thirty years completed with dignity and grace. My bones ache with the rheum, my feet are tired, I can no longer tend the fire like I used to ... and yes, during the days and years of my duty, and especially as Virgo Maxima, my soul has been filled with this fire and spirit." She wiped a tear away, her veined hand brushing against a cheek. "And this is why girls, in December I am retiring."

She began to weep. Tears streamed down her wrinkled face, her eyes like puddles of water. We all sat stone-faced, shocked by the news. Vibi breathed out a sigh. I knew what she was thinking. This was about Mother Aurelia—not about us.

Occia ran to the Virgo Maxima and embraced her. "I will organize a going away party and you shall have a cake!" The other Vestals gathered around Mother, wishing her Bonam Fortunam, and telling her how much we would miss her. I even told her I loved her. And to watch Rubria crying for someone other than herself gave me hope.

"Thank you, my dears." Mother wiped her eyes, coughed, and blew her nose into a cloth. She seemed so old to me; her forehead wrinkles looked like a plowed field. Yet I thought she looked as fragile as a flower, like a spring violet veined white and purple.

"There's more, children," Mother added. "Once I retire, Junia will officially become the Virgo Maxima. Once this happens, Vibidia will be in charge of Occia's training." She looked over at me. "And you, Cornelia. Rubria will begin to work more closely with you once I'm gone."

Mother watched Domicia and the other servants hurrying back and forth from the library. "Please remember that I will assist with all the transitions to ensure everything proceeds smoothly. The Emperor has requested this." Mother Aurelia seemed satisfied with everything she had said; her speech was finished.

But I heard her speaking to herself under her breath, asking what she was to do for the rest of her life. "So many decisions, perhaps not much time, where to go, I know not," she mumbled.

"The Spirit will give you answers … and understanding, if you ask," I told her. "Trust and carry it to the ether. You will always have the power, Mother."

Mother Aurelia's cheeks blushed pink. "You're right, Cornelia. Now I know why the augur pronounced what he did at the lottery you won over a year ago. I'm glad you were chosen, child, for your wisdom is a solace to me."

The remaining Vestals began to leave. Suddenly Mother Aurelia stood straight and cleared her throat; she was back to being the Virgo Maxima. She stiffened up and shouted, "Just one more moment, Vestals. I just remembered something. Vibidia, Cornelia, Emperor Nero would like to speak with you. Four o'clock at the Regia. This is all he told me. Please be prompt!" Mother paused. "And make sure Domicia comes with you."

CHAPTER 22

Why had Emperor Nero requested to see Vibi and me? Why Domicia?

I thought about the night before— the lurking shadow in the hallway. Was that shadow Domicia? Had she seen us slip out into the evening, only to check on us later? Did she report us? Yes, we broke the rules, but it was worth it. The thought of Paul's words steadied my heart.

The hours passed slowly until it was time to see what Emperor Nero wanted with us. We trudged the short distance to the Regia; Domicia trailed closely behind. A guard awaited us at the door. He admitted us with a grunt, nod, and a bow.

"Follow me. I will escort you to the West Room where Emperor Nero awaits you."

Vibi put a finger to her lips. "Say nothing and let me do the speaking," she whispered.

What could we do if we were accused of leaving the Atrium with no permission? I started to shake.

We arrived at the door. The guard banged against it. "They are here, Caesar," he called out.

"Let them in," Nero replied in a gruff voice. The thick door opened and we entered the West Room that held the shrine to Mars. The two-circled shields and lances of the Salii hung on the walls in strange patterns. I glanced at every shield. Which one was the original shield of King Numa? They all appeared exactly the same.

Nero sat behind a grand desk. A beautiful woman in a red stola with upswept gold-red hair lounged nearby on a couch. Nero's favorite dwarf, Varros stood on one side of the room, his tiny fingers gesturing at us.

"Welcome, girls. Please take a seat." Nero pointed to a small couch in front of his desk. We sat down across from the Emperor. Domicia stood by the door.

"Hail Caesar," Vibi said.

After a brisk look from her and on cue, I repeated the words.

Nero seemed pleased. He plucked a date from a bowl on his desk and began sucking the juices from it, keeping his eyes on us the whole time. He wiped his chin with his hand, and then he disposed of the pit into another bowl.

"Would you care for a date?' he asked.

We both shook our heads politely. I certainly did not need any messy juices dripping down my chin.

"Mother Aurelia told us you wanted to speak to us," Vibi said.

"Yes. I've been speaking with certain people … in my palace and here in the Regia. You see … people talk. They say the walls have ears in Rome."

"This is true," said Vibi.

I nodded, keeping calm but trembling inside.

"Have you heard any rumors, girls?"

We shook our heads.

"Heard anything about me while you are out walking amongst the people? Bestowing blessings in the name of Vesta?" he asked.

"We have heard no rumors about you. The people love you, Caesar. And when we bless others, we in turn are blessed. Rome is blessed," said Vibi with perfect dignity.

"The spies around the palace," he continued, "they are plentiful indeed ... just like my enemies are plentiful." He glanced over his shoulder at Domicia. "One never knows the real state of affairs, now do they?" He leaned over and tickled my chin. "My little novice ..." he continued, "my snake-charming prophetess. Yes, I've heard. I've heard! And I may need your prophecies in the future. Just like the Oracle of Delphi in Greece."

He slapped his hand to his knee and began to chuckle soft and slow. Then his laugh became loud and boisterous. What did he find so amusing? Did Lucius share my messages with the Emperor? I felt like one of Cleo's victims tossed around and played with before being killed. "My enemies will never get the best of this Caesar," he said.

The red-clad woman yawned and stretched; she looked bored.

"But I digress," the Emperor continued, staring intently at us. "You both have been chosen for something special. I, as Pontifex Maximus, have chosen you Vestals, my Vestals who look so grand together, to catch the blood drained from the October Horse. You will transport your amphoras of blood from the Campus Martius in a sedan; then you shall walk through the Forum back to the Regia. Once there, you will mingle the horse's blood with the ashes of the unborn calf, slaughtered in April. Remember, no blood of the sacrifice must be spilled. You understand what I speak of, Vibidia? Surely you will teach our novice about carrying the blood come October?"

"It would be my honor, Caesar," said Vibi. I watched her breathe out a sigh. And I did the same.

The dwarf-man, Varros, cackled, twisted up his face, and made gulping noises that caused the Emperor to laugh.

Nero continued. "I will look forward to watching you girls carry your amphoras."

He turned to Varros. "So—Varros, what faction will win the rights to the coveted horse head this year? Will it be the inhabitants from the dark Subura alleys? Or will the victors be from the Via Sacra? Who will claim the horse head this year? I have my notions, and I will place my bets accordingly." Nero chuckled to himself.

"I know not, Caesar," stated Varros. "But I know whatever faction you bet on will surely win." The Emperor and his miniature burst into laughter.

"If you want to know, I'll be betting on the Via Sacra," Nero explained. "Mark my words, this district will fight hard for the head of the sacrificial beast. They want that head hanging from the pole. I cannot wait for this day. Nothing must go wrong!" He popped another date into his mouth and spit out the pit. "I will speak to Mother Aurelia about the honor bestowed on you two. And I will make certain Rubria is present. That miserable Junia can hold fire duty that day. I want only the most attractive Vestals near the October horse."

He paused and leaned towards us. "This ritual harkens back to the Great Horse of Troy. Remember, this is a part of my lineage. I am a direct descendant of Aeneas, the true Founder of Rome. Remember this, my Vestals. Nothing can go wrong on the Ides of October. I know Vibidia you are familiar with the rite. Teach Cornelia well. You may go." He nodded to Domicia, who bowed to him.

Nero was done with us. If he only knew what Vibi was really teaching me! But she could go through the motions of a Vestal. What could I do? I had been chosen once again.

"What an honor to be chosen to carry the blood of the October horse," I remarked to Vibi as we sat around the temple completing our fire duty. "Although it sounds like a gruesome rite."

"So it is," Vibi said. "It's a gruesome honor."

I yawned a loud, slow deep yawn.

"Someone isn't getting proper sleep. Cornelia, you must remember to get your sleep. Or you will forget everything concerning your duties," remarked Domicia, who was sprinkling sacred water around the temple using a laurel sprig.

"Just don't forget *your* duties, Domicia. Duties that don't include lurking—behind doors!" I said in a mean tone. I was tired and cranky.

Domicia's eyes opened wide. The rest of her face had little expression.

"Domicia, please fetch us some drinking water and some food to tide us over. Now!" commanded Vibi. She clapped her hands twice. Domicia opened the door then shut it behind her. She was gone.

"Being chosen for this ritual is an honor … and a relief," Vibi said. "I thought for certain your servant spied on us last night and reported us to Nero. What do you think? Did she see us?" she asked me, gently stoking Vesta's flame.

I leaned close to her. "After you went to your room, I

noticed a shadow down the hallway. The shadow appeared close to the back door." I put my finger to my lips, got up, and flung open the temple door. No one was there. "But it could have been any restless servant in the Atrium. I don't think we have to worry," I reassured her.

Vibidia seemed satisfied. "I hope you are right. If that's the case, why not imagine the two of us going to see Paul again? Let's send the wish right up to the ether." Vibi's eyes followed the trail of smoke up through the hole in the dome, the smoke from the sacred fire that burned for the safety of Rome.

I thought to myself, *Why not?* We had already broken the rules. Then I thought again.

"We broke the rules once, Vibi. And got away with it. But remember what the augur said about me being a great Vestal, as long as I didn't break the rules?"

Vibi shook her head and carefully placed another wedge of wood on the dancing flame.

"He was referring to the most serious rule, Cornelia. Regarding your chastity. That's what he meant."

We sat quiet for a time waiting for Domicia to return. I listened to the fire breath with soft hissing sounds. I stared into it, breathing in its sacred essence, waiting for a sign, a message from Vesta.

I remembered what Paul said to me about the fish—the meaning of it for Jesus Followers. And then I remembered my message from Vesta.

"Let's see, Vibi. Let's see what happens."

After fire duty, I returned to my room. At my feet I found a tightly bound papyrus scroll that had been placed under the door. I bent to pick it up, tore off the seal, and opened the letter.

It was from Lucretia. At long last!

I brought it to my desk and read:

"Dear Cornelia,

Greetings from Pompeii. How is my favorite Vestal doing? I am well here in my new life. Every day I grow stronger. Although I miss the life of a Vestal, I have exciting news. I have met a man whom I love and who loves me for myself. He has asked for my hand in marriage. He accepts me scars and all. He even took me to see Emperor Nero perform in Naples several months ago. I never knew my heart could be this happy.

The other good news is I have received an invitation to Mother Aurelia's retirement party in December. You, my Vestal child will move up in the ranks. I will attend the festivities in December, perhaps even attend the Festival of the Bona Dea. I look forward to seeing you and all the other Vestals soon. Until then, stay the course, do your duty, and follow the rules.

Write to me soon or send a message to me on the ether. Be well, my dear one. Give my love to everyone in the Atrium, even your cat!

Love,
Lucretia"

So Lucretia would visit in December! I couldn't wait to see my Vestal sister and friend again—although I admitted to myself I felt a tinge of jealousy that she could now marry.

CHAPTER 23

SEPTEMBER 61 AD

My favorite Vestal duty was to retrieve water from the spring of Egeria. Every week I hoped to be chosen. It gave me freedom, a feeling of importance, and time away from the dank, dreary Atrium. For today, Vibi and I were chosen to travel the Appian Way. This time we would go unescorted without horrid Junia accompanying us.

After morning prayers and breakfast, we set off in a litter with our amphoras. The sun's slanted rays spilled light upon the paving stones; the air was crisp and cool, refreshing my mood.

Our lictors led the way carrying their *fasces*, the bundle of ax-headed sticks, and announced that the Vestals were passing. How we were honored when the common people saluted us!

The litter stopped at the fork leading to the spring. I knew how to walk now—with elegance and grace, staring straight ahead, not minding the throng of curious onlookers. The rows of cypress pines and olive trees bent toward us. Gnarled boughs stretched across the road on both sides, a tangled arbor of dried leaves and vines that made me feel like I was entering another world.

Vibi and I followed the path to the great field that opened up near the spring.

We approached the spring, and I reverently said a prayer to Egeria, the consort to our beloved order's founder, King Numa. But before we filled our water vessels, I remembered I had brought my bulla to wash under the sacred waters. I did not carry it every day, just when I thought I needed it.

"Vibi, can you hold my amphora? I need to clean my bulla first." She nodded and hoisted the vessel from me. I took my bulla from my pouch. Neptune's trident needed a good cleansing. I let my bulla stay under the running water as Vibi looked on, explaining to me I needed to cleanse both sides of it.

"May I?" I heard a voice from behind me. I turned around. There was Lucius, the augur. He peered from behind my shoulder seemingly fascinated with the gold medallion.

"May you—what?" I asked.

"May I take a look at this?"

I shrugged and handed it to him.

"What a extraordinary piece," he exclaimed, as Vibi returned my amphora. We sat on one of the stone benches nearby. Lucius turned the medallion over and over in his hands.

"May I borrow this?" he asked me.

"Borrow my bulla? I'm not even *supposed* to have my bulla anymore," I reminded him. I couldn't understand what use my bulla could have for him.

"Are you aware that the fury of Neptune is destroying ships filled with grain, grain the Roman people desperately need to survive? Storm after storm hits the Mediterranean Sea almost daily. At least thirty ships have perished. The Emperor is desperate. People are hungry. This might help."

I thought for a moment and remembered what my father told me about his ships.

"Yes," I said. "If it helps Rome, you can borrow it. For just a week." I did not like the thought of giving my bulla away.

Lucius secured the cleansed bulla in a pocket. "Bless you. Bless you both." He kneeled, took one of my hands, and placed it palm down to his forehead. Then he did the same to Vibi. "Before you fill your amphoras, let me please bless you further," he said.

Vibi and I just stared at each other and shrugged. We watched Lucius fill a vessel from one of the thousands of niches carved into the stone. He returned and said, "Please let me do the honor of washing your feet."

He knelt again and took Vibi's shoes off first. He dipped his hand to the water, wiped Vibi's dusty feet, and pulled a red cloth from his cloak. I could see Vibi was enjoying this attention. My turn was next. Lucius gently removed my soft-toed sandals and began cleansing my feet. I enjoyed the attention of Lucius as well. "Why are you doing this, Lucius?" I asked.

"We augurs know the power of one's feet. We stand on the earth with our feet—clean feet—to listen to messages from the Earth below. You must learn to do the same." He smiled at us. "And did you know that having one's feet washed with the sacred waters of Egeria, communing with Vesta, not only with the fire, but with the power of the earth and the water, all lead to greater understanding?"

There was that word again. Spoken by Paul and now Lucius. I listened because I truly longed to understand.

"Our feet are under the rest of the body. They are what allow you to stand. Under-stand-ing!"

"How wise," Vibi murmured, blushing at the same time. "And true to make such deep connections."

"I try,"said Lucius. "My job as augur involves making deep connections."

There was so much to understand in my new life as a Vestal. And how good it felt to receive this attention.

Lucius wiped our feet, lowered his forehead to the ground, and mumbled a prayer under his breath. Then he stood and bowed to us, flashing his red striped cloth around himself. And then he was gone.

Vibi and I returned to the flowing spring and filled our amphoras. I thanked Egeria for such a gift and wondered if the River Goddess had washed the feet of King Numa, the same way Lucius had washed my feet. In my mind I knew it was so.

CHAPTER 24

I noticed that Mother Aurelia had started to keep Vibi and I apart. Did she think Vibi was a bad influence? I felt the opposite was true. Vibi uplifted my spirits, brought adventure to my life, and gave me so much to think about. We still managed to speak and to sit near one another at meals and prayers.

After breakfast one morning, while the Vestals mingled before duties, exchanging news and pleasantries, Vibi approached me and whispered in my ear, "My cousin gave me the message. Tonight under the bridge leading to the Via Nova."

"Tonight?" I asked. Why could I not stop repeating things out loud?

"Tonight it is. Paul is holding a special gathering. It may be his last." Her forehead wrinkled in thought. But her olive-colored cheeks blushed red; her eyes glowed like light reflecting off a pine branch.

"I'll be ready—I guess." I paused and looked around. No one seemed to notice us speaking.

Vibi whispered, "I'll knock lightly. Four times. Have your clothing together … Sister. Remember to wear the right shoes this time for our trip."

Vibi smiled and brought a finger to her lips.

She had something to look forward to. So did I.

Night settled over the Atrium. I waited. Waited for the four knocks. This time I made sure I wore my old sandals. I kept my Vestal attire underneath my Jewish robes. Just in case. I stared at myself in the polished metal oval, and noticed how long my hair was now—almost to my neck. I paced about my room. Where was she? At last I heard the faint knocks, all four of them. I cracked open the door until I could see Vibi's eyes watching me.

"Are you ready?"

"Yes."

"We will follow the same path out, down the back stairs to cross the bridge onto the stairs leading to the road. And then we will cross to the Via Sacra."

"I will follow you."

Tonight's full moon lit up the back gardens. But I had no time to stare up at the moon. We made our way down and quietly crossed to the Via Sacra. The cart was waiting for us.

"Get in," the carter ordered. "Tonight you will be a part of a wagon full of onions." We both climbed in the back and a great cloth sack was thrown over us.

All I could do, head down in the cart, was listen to the sounds of people in the streets, fighting, singing and shouting, all the while hoping I could endure the bumpy ride. And the smell of the onions! My eyes started to water. I tried to wipe my eyes, and Vibi nudged me. "Stop moving."

The cart ambled up the road. After a few minutes, the cart began to lean to one side. I lifted my head as I felt the cart slowing down. I heard a loud moan and a grinding of the wheels. "Whoa!" shouted the carter. The cart jolted to a full stop. And when it halted, my head banged with a thump against the wooden bottom. I touched my forehead and felt pain; a hard bump was forming on my forehead.

I heard the carter get off the wagon. He spoke a few words to his mule, cursed, and walked to the back of the wagon.

"Bad news. The back wheel of the cart is damaged. Hit something in the road," he mumbled. "You'll have to get off here." He paused. "Unless you want to wait for an hour."

We both raised our heads. Vibi watched my face with concern. "You've got a bump on your forehead. Does it hurt?"

"No," I replied, trying to sound brave.

"Let's go," Vibi said.

The carter made certain no one was around the wagon, then stood there fussing with the vegetables, while we slid out from the back.

Vibi reached into her pouch and handed him some coins that made a clinking sound.

"Can you pick us up in two hours time?" she asked. "Will the cart be fixed by then?"

"All I can do is try. I make no promises." He smiled at us, the full moon illuminating the gap in his missing teeth.

"Then we trust you will be here," said Vibi, placing another coin in his palm.

My forehead throbbed in pain. I kept touching the small bump over my left eye. But we had to keep going. And this meant walking through the Subura— again.

But for some reason, I never felt as scared when I was with Vibi. She stayed calm I guessed, because she had faith, faith in Jesus, faith in Paul, faith in the One God. Still, I sent a prayer to Vesta. I had to remain faithful to this goddess I made a vow to over a year ago.

The winding streets through the Subura were crowded with people as usual; some sitting in front of stores, others like us scurrying up the roads and through narrow alleyways. Others just stood around talking, arguing, and taking in the nighttime air. Women stood at street corners, beckoning men to come closer. Dogs ran back and forth across the road, stealing any bit of food from overflowing trash bins in the neighborhood.

Vibi and I stayed close together, heads down and hands clasped. Wagons whipped around the bends of narrow streets, and the sound of carters' whips striking the beasts gave me chills. We had the light of the moon to guide us, but torchbearers roamed the streets in case someone wanted to hire them for light and protection. A few nightwatchmen lingered on street corners, just in case a riot broke out. Nero was known to love to visit the Subura at night; I shuddered at the thought of it.

We passed a shop that clearly sold fruit and vegetables during the day. All was dark now. Just old crates and boxes stood in front of the market. A huddle of bunched-up rags sat near the road. A face appeared from the hood. A wrinkled old woman who looked like a tiny bird with a long, pointed beak glanced up at us. She seemed coated in dirt. A claw reached out and grabbed my wrist holding me tight.

"Help me," she cried. "Bless me now." She let go of my wrist and stared at each of us with shrunken black eyes. Her bony hand, palm up, stretched out toward us.

"Please ... coins ... for grandmother."

I looked over at Vibi, who fumbled again for her purse.

"You girls ... I know are special. That I can see." The woman blinked, squinted, and watched us with her round, mouse eyes.

"Here you are, grandmother," Vibi said, and placed two coins in the outstretched palm. The woman stared at the coins, held them up in the air as if making a prayer, and quickly deposited them into the depths of her rags.

"And what of you, my sweet?" She bent forward; her breath smelled as foul as a sewer drain. She grinned at me and waited. "What have *you* to give me?" she cackled.

"I have nothing," I said. Then something came to me—an idea.

"I do have something, grandmother." I leaned over and kissed her thin cheek that felt as soft as a feather. I reached into my pouch and pulled out the emerald, my birthday gift from Cornelius and handed it to her. At that moment, I didn't care. She needed the jewel more than I did.

She held it up to the bright moonlight and shrieked with delight. "Why, the gods be blessed." She gripped my shoulder and her sharp nails dug into my skin. "And because of your gifts to grandmother tonight, I will tell you what I see ... for the gods speak through me. And so it is ..." She mumbled to herself and began to speak aloud as she gazed toward the moon. "The gods have just told me ... yes, the gods ... that both of you, yes, both of you shall live. But others ... others shall perish into the grey and black of day. Some shall see the truth, while others … remain in shadows."

She shook her covered head and rattled the coins in her pocket. Then she took the emerald and lifted it into the air again. "You both shall live … while others …" She quickly folded her fingers around the gem, and dropped it in her pocket.

I gasped and shuddered. What could she mean?

She began to chuckle under her breath. "If Caesar only knew what I know. The gods tell me things, dears. But no one listens to poor grandmother or pays me mind." She pointed a bony finger toward us. "But you have listened and gifted me. You are blessed now, girls. Be off. Grandmother is pleased. The gods are pleased."

At least, I thought, *this is a good portent for the evening.*

We left the poor woman sitting alone, muttering to herself and fondling her coins and her emerald. Vibi exclaimed that she was a batty old thing who didn't really know what she spoke of. I felt differently, for no one else bothered us the rest of the way, just one carter who stopped to ask if we needed a ride. Vibi told him no, we were walking from synagogue toward our home.

Finally, we arrived at Paul's villa. A crowd gathered outside waiting to enter. A different guard stood before the door tonight, stiff and looking straight ahead. As each person approached him, they whispered the word, the guard nodded, and they were let in.

"The sign of the fish," Vibi mumbled, and I did the same. The guard grunted and pointed a finger to the vestibule.

Tonight's gathering seemed filled with many Roman Jews. I recognized their dress. Lanterns hung from the wall and a great pitcher sat on a table. A white candle burned next to it. Vases of sunflowers had been placed around the room. *It is hard*, I thought, *to think this a prison*.

I saw that Paul was still chained—to a different guard this time. His face looked flushed and filled with excitement. "Follow me," said Vibi, as we moved closer to the little man. We found a shadowed corner where we could stand. But Paul glanced over and a smile lifted up his face.

"Ah yes, the sisters, back once again. Come closer." He beckoned to us.

People began to gather around Paul, quieting down, waiting upon his every word. He began: "Friends, Gentiles, Romans, Jews, adherents to the words of our Savior, listen. Now is the time, now is the hour. Now is the time for forgiveness. As my own Savior, Jesus Christ, forgave me … on the road to Damascus so many years ago. We must forgive others, as I was forgiven."

I thought of my family and how angry I was that they had deserted me. As if someone in the crowd was reading my mind, a man shouted, "What of our families? They do not understand this new god, this new belief."

Paul watched the crowd. "We believers die each day to our old self, and are born anew. We forgive our families, and if we must, we leave them behind. Never forsake them in your heart. You carry your family with you, as Jesus carried his own cross."

Paul stood and began pacing, dragging the guard by the rattling chain. It seemed to me the guard was more of a prisoner than Paul. "People, friends, we are asked to forget. Forget the past, for we must press forward, making our mark, never giving up. Forgive, I say, forgive. And forget!"

At that moment, my heart opened and I felt forgiveness enter it. Could I live Paul's words with forgiveness for all? I knew I carried anger toward my family, anger toward my father, Junia, Nero. My heart pounded as if in response to the words of this man.

"We Believers live these words and keep them alive in our hearts. Carry them with you always ... in your hearts," Paul concluded.

Everyone in the audience seemed moved: some sobbed, some embraced one another, others just stood as if in a dream. Tears glistened in Vibi's eyes. A Jewish man with a thick, bushy beard raised his hand.

"We are Jews, believers in the One God. But for many of us, our god has no name. Or rather names we dare not utter. Why should we believe in this Jesus Christ as the Son of the one true God? Gods come and go in Rome—but our god has remained with us long before this Jesus."

A furor started among the Jewish crowd and because we wore Jewish clothing, we suddenly became a part of it. "Please, calm down," Paul reminded the crowd.

The guard scoffed and then shouted, "Order!"

"Please let me explain," continued Paul. "Jesus was a Jew, come to fulfill the prophecies. Ask Him to come into your heart. Jews, Gentiles, search your soul. While you Gentiles sacrifice animals and pay tribute to the gods in your temples, remember the one true God, through Jesus Christ, who sacrificed His life."

"This is true," I heard one person say.

"And I ask each and every one of you to pray for me. Soon I will make an appeal to Caesar. I shall request an audience with the Emperor himself."

A hush fell over the crowd. I heard Vibi gasp and watched her bring a hand over her mouth. "No," she whispered.

"Have no fear," Paul said gently. "I press forward, making my mark, never giving up. Bless you all."

The crowd began to disperse, people murmuring and speaking in small groups. I noticed Vibi staring intently at a Jewish woman, with wisps of blonde hair and reddened lips, speaking with one of the Jewish leaders. The woman lifted her head and then turned, staring in our direction.

Vibi whispered, "We must leave—now!"

"Why?" I asked.

"That woman staring at us … she looks like the Emperor's mistress, Poppaea."

I realized now that Vibi had mentioned it, she did look like the woman who had been lounging on the couch at the Regia the day Emperor Nero met with us.

But it was too late. She came toward us. "Shalom, girls. Do I know you? I think I've seen you before. Perhaps around the synagogue?"

"Yes, we attend synagogue," Vibi replied quickly. "We are sisters come to hear the word." She eyed the exit, as if she was trying to make a rapid retreat.

The woman nodded. "That is good. I am friends with many Jews. I shall look for you again."

We mumbled a quick Shalom and made certain to thank Paul, the small prophet with a big message.

The wagon was waiting. Our return home to the Atrium was uneventful. I still had the bruise on my forehead; the Jewish head covering partially concealed it, but I knew my Vestal headdress wouldn't. I just hoped tomorrow it would be gone. How could I explain the bruise? I would think of something.

The wagon parked in a dark corner of the Via Sacra. Vibi gave the carter more coins and suggested we remove our Jewish clothing in a deserted alley nearby. "If we get caught, it's best to be in our Vestal robes, not Jewish ones," she said.

I lifted the heavy robes over my head, straightened out my fillet, and rolled the worn clothing into a bundle. We made our way silently up the stairs, over the bridge, around the temples, up the back garden stairs, and once again, Vibi had the key to let us in.

"Goodnight. I'm proud of you, little sister." She bent down and kissed the bruise on my forehead. "Nothing worthwhile is easy, Cornelia." She floated down the hallway, entered her apartment, and was gone.

I stood before the door of my apartment holding onto the bundle of clothes. But then, when I glanced at the back door, I noticed we had forgotten to shut it. The door was slightly open, and the moonlight was shining in. I tiptoed to the door to close it, the clothing still in my hands. I opened it slightly and felt the door bump into something hard.

"Why Domicia," I said. "What are you doing out here?" There was my servant, a candle in her hand, staring down at me.

"I could ask the same of you," she said. "What's that bundle of clothes for?" she asked, peering closer at the pile. She brought the candle flame to my face. "And what's that on your forehead? I didn't see that at dinner."

I could think of no good answer. "That's none of your business," I said. And with that, I slammed the door in her face, locking her out.

CHAPTER 25

September 61 AD

The next morning the lump on my forehead was hard and sore. I stood in front of the polished oval, peering at the black-and-violet-colored bruise. It stung and my whole head hurt.

A knock sounded at the door. "Who is it?" I asked.

"It is me, Domicia." I heard the soft voice.

"All right, come in," I huffed. I thought Domicia might know how to conceal and perhaps hasten the healing of my bruise. Or at least have a salve ready to sooth the pain. Domicia entered carrying a basin of hot water for my morning bath. She lowered the basin to the floor and then pulled a small bottle from one of her pockets.

"I've brought a special Egyptian oil to rub on that bruise. Then I'll oil your body down. Today's a big day, remember?" she asked.

"Leave the bottle of healing oil. I can do it myself." I pointed to the table.

"I am your servant, Cornelia."

Then I remembered what she had said. "What is so special about today, anyway, Domicia? I bumped my head on one of the marble columns—that's why I'm so forgetful and ill-tempered today." I touched my hand to the bruise and was proud of my lie. The bump felt as hard as the little marbles my brother and I once played with. For now, I thought, it was another badge of honor.

"Remember— today is the day the Vestals are to attend the chariot races at the Circus Maximus. The Emperor will be there. It's the start of his September games. Get ready now. You can't be late."

"Vestals, Vestals!" Mother Aurelia clapped her hands and gathered us around her. "The litters are waiting. Are we ready?" She waved her hands up and down like the wings of a goose. I noticed Vibi was missing. She must have fire duty with Occia. Junia looked like a long white bird. Her long neck stretched up, her beaked nose poked down and her black beady eyes seemed to watch everyone in the Atrium.

Domicia stood behind me waiting. My head still hurt, and all I could think about was the roaring noises I'd have to suffer through at the Circus.

Our lictors, fasces tight and prepared, stood on guard tapping their toes and looking fresh in their new tunics. Who were we waiting for? Then Rubria came forth with a glow and an exotic look about her, like Cleopatra herself. *No*, I thought, *she looks more like Venus, her skin the color of the dawn.* I noticed the green ribbons hanging off the side of her belt tucked under her stola. *She's cheering the Green Team*, I thought. The Green Team was Emperor Nero's favorite.

Rubria's exposed strands of red hair sparkled with gold. Her green eyes had a hint of color on the lids. The black outline around her eyes reminded me of Cleo's eyes.

Everyone in the Atrium paused to stare at Rubria. In her vestal white, she was a vision. She certainly had made an entrance.

"Are we ready?" Mother Aurelia said. "You ladies are a picture of dignified loveliness," she added.

Junia raised up a finger and said, "Except for that bump on Cornelia's head. Due to clumsiness, I presume." All eyes in the Atrium found me. Carefully, I pulled my fillet down. I grabbed a bit of my black hair and stretched it over the bump. *There, I* thought, *that's better.*

"No one will notice, Cornelia," Domicia whispered. "Everyone seems to notice your eyes first. Pretend it's not there."

How could Domica be so kind when I was nothing but cruel and heartless to her, especially this morning?

"And further," Mother Aurelia continued, "I have decided to stay behind with little Occia today to tend the fire. I will relieve Vibidia so she may join you. I remember as a young Vestal how much I enjoyed a day at the Circus. Vibidia needs a day away as well." So Vibi would join us after all!

The gold litters with the Emperor's seals awaited us outside the Atrium. I was to ride with Rubria; our lictors would lead the way, shouting out our arrival, while our servants would follow the procession.

The Circus Maximus, the horse-shoed shaped arena, already shook with the roar of thousands of people. Vendors and hawkers lined up around the Circus; the smell of sweet honeycakes and the strange-looking women hovering around the columns made me feel overwhelmed and small.

At the entrance to the arena, a mob of people waited to get in. There, the slaves lowered our litters. People gathered around us, greeting us and bowing low. Our lictors continued to brandish their bundle of rods and axes at the crowd, shooing them away.

We made our way toward the arena. Then I turned my head and saw my old friend Cynthia and her family pressing toward me. Had they been waiting for me, or was this a coincidence? Of all the thousands of people, why Cynthia? Why now?

"Cornelia," Cynthia gushed. "You look lovely as a Vestal. I have missed you. And I love how your look in your dress."

I nodded. The last thing I wanted to think about was Cynthia and my old life.

"I ask for your blessing today." She seemed so happy and excited. She jumped up and down, brushing her golden hair to the side.

"Blessing? Right now?" I asked.

Junia glared at me as we moved toward the entrance.

"Yes, please. You see, Cornelia," Cynthia continued, almost out of breath. "I am betrothed. And in two year's time, I shall marry. And start a family!" Her parents smiled down on me and nodded.

At that moment, I felt angry and jealous. I wondered if Cynthia noticed my reaction, because my cheeks burned. And my bruise throbbed. To hear this right now was a bad omen. But then I remembered the words of Paul—to forget the past, forgive, and move forward. If Paul could live those words, the least I could do was try.

"Of course I bless you, Cynthia. In the name of Vesta, I bless your hearth, your marriage, and the many healthy children you will have. May you have children that you hold dear, children Rome will be proud of ..." I could say or do no more.

"Thank you, Cornelia. I will never forget this kindness. And when I have my first child, I shall bring him to the Atrium so you can bless him." She squealed with delight like a child herself. "And you will be invited to my wedding."

I thanked Cynthia and decided I had no time to dwell on my hurt feelings. Rubria poked me, urging me to pay attention. In front of the procession, Junia clapped her hands twice—just like Mother Aurelia. "Vestals, we are now ready for our official entrance. Let us proceed."

CHAPTER 26

The Circus Maximus was a sea of people. Everywhere I looked crowds were gathered on the wooden steps struggling to find their seats. We proceeded through the stone archways and walked up the wooden steps to the Emperor's podium, draped with white and gold silk banners, known as his Golden Box. The Vestal box was right next to the Emperor's.

Wave upon wave of spectators roared with cheers, then jeers, hoots and curses. The first race had just ended. Now the entertainment came forth to amuse the restless crowd, while the white sands of the arena were raked smooth in preparation for the next race.

First, several dwarves came tumbling out from a gate. They began somersaulting into the air, then landed in vats of water, causing raucous laughter and screams from the crowd. A juggler appeared balancing balls while walking on stilts. Next, a chariot drawn by two black panthers paraded around the arena, the charioteer blowing kisses to the crowd. I was relieved when Rubria told me there would be no wild animal fights in the arena today. This was a day to celebrate the chariot races.

"The Emperor will arrive soon," Rubria whispered to me. She chose a seat close to the Emperor's chair. "Wait until I catch his eye."

Each Vestal had a special seat. Once seated, we were treated to a fruity drink handed to us in gold goblets. The hot food vendors climbed up and down the steep stairs, shouting what they had to offer today. "Roasted dormice for sale. Roasted vegetables-on-a-stick. Fresh honeycakes."

I reached into a pocket, removed a coin, and ordered a roasted dormouse. Although I tried to eat it with grace, juices dripped down my chin, soiling my Vestal whites. I didn't care; no one would notice my ravenous need to devour the cooked rodent!

At last the Emperor appeared, dressed in his purple toga with a laurel wreath of gold atop his head. Green ribbons fluttered from his toga. His eyes flashed with a wild excitement. Behind him, his mistress Poppaea, several slave girls, Burrus, the Prefect of the Praetorian Guard, and his favorite companion, the dwarf Varros, accompanied him to his Golden Box.

Trumpets blared as Caesar waved to the crowd. The juggler, dwarves, and charioteer proceeded to the exit gate, blowing kisses.

"Let the races begin," the Emperor proclaimed.

The official near the entrance of the starting gate dropped a white cloth; slaves opened the gates, and four chariots, each drawn by four horses, burst out into the arena.

Every part of the Circus had its own team cheering section: red, white, green, and blue. Colored streamers, silk banners, and signs indicated each section's favorite team. At the center of the arena, an obelisk, the *spina,* stood in the middle of the oval racetrack; another obelisk at the east end marked the turning point in the race. At the west end of the Circus, a large pole with seven egg-shaped balls stood; each ball represented a lap of the race; they would be pushed down the pole when a lap was complete. This was a seven-lap race.

Nero paced in his box shouting for the Greens. Two laps in, after a slow start, the Greens' chariot took the sharp curve around the east end obelisk and pulled ahead. I tried to feign enthusiasm; Vibidia looked bored and tired as well. In truth, I was more interested in the crowd, and how they screamed and cheered for their team.

I did enjoy watching the charioteers wrap the horses' reins tightly around their waists, causing the chariots to sway. The harder they pulled, the faster and more dangerous the race became!

Finally, the race ended. The Green team had prevailed, and Emperor Nero clasped the shoulder of Burrus and shook him back and forth. "By Jove's thunderbolt, I knew my team would win." He snickered and nodded his head up and down. "And how angry my friends on the White team must be. Ha!"

Entertainment started up again as the white sand had to be smoothed for the next race. Then someone in the Red section started jeering at the Emperor. Others began to join him. They were in the section closest to us, and perhaps angry their team had lost.

"Caesar, what happened to your mother?" they shouted. "Remember her name? Agrippina?"

"Mother killer!" I heard someone else scream.

"And where is your wife, Octavia? The woman you are married to? The kind and good Octavia? Where is she?" Shouts and curses filled the air.

"We care not for your slutty mistress, Caesar!" someone else bellowed out from the Red's section.

"A woman's voice rose above the others. "We want our grain, Caesar. You give us the Circus—now give us our grain!"

The whole section of Reds, as enraged as their team color might show, began demanding their grain. Where was their wheat dole? Just because they were plebes, they still had to eat and feed their families.

I thought about my bulla and what was happening to the boats from Egypt sailing for Rome with grain—sinking to the bottom of the ocean because of Neptune's storms. The people were hungry. Was my bulla helping?

"We starve, Caesar. Our children hunger for food." They started chanting, "Caesar, Caesar" waiting for a response.

Most of the senators were nodding and conferring with one another. I remembered Rubria telling me Nero's problems with the Senate were growing worse—now it was the plebes! My head throbbed from the noise. And if that weren't bad enough, as I pressed my hand to my bruise, I caught Poppaea studying Vibi and myself. As Nero stood to address the crowd, Poppaea began speaking to him, then pointed at us, and quickly looked away.

A trumpet sounded, signaling the crowd to silence.

"Quiet!" shouted Nero and held up his hand. He stepped to the end of the podium and spoke to the crowd. "Be thankful for the Circus. I give you people entertainment. My people and I are working on the grain problem. You soon shall see barges from the Port of Ostia on the Tiber again, making their way to Rome. Have faith in your Emperor, as you have faith in the gods!"

The voices clamored over one another. "Faith? Faith won't put food on our table! How can we have faith in a man who had his mother murdered? Where is your real wife, the kind Octavia? Where is she?"

The crowd was becoming unruly. Trumpets began to blast again, signaling silence. The next race was about to begin. "We shall take care of the people—all of the people," shouted the Emperor with a wave.

I noticed Nero blew a quick kiss at Rubria before he turned to Poppaea. He grabbed his mistress by the neck, and kissed her on the mouth, as if to proclaim Poppaea was his true wife. The crowd started to jeer again.

When I looked over at Rubria, she was gazing at Nero as if he were a god. How could she? *No*, I thought, *he's a monster with eyes that flash like a wild beast!*

After the races finished— naturally the Greens won every single race— we preceeded down the wobbly steps of the Circus. Junia and the others seemed distracted in the procession out of the Circus.

I noticed Lucius ahead in the line. He turned, saw me, and waited. I moved up to get closer, acting as though I didn't see him. "Cornelia."

I turned to him. "Lucius, did you enjoy the races? I didn't see you near the podium."

"I have your bulla." He pulled it from his cloak. Neptune's trident flashed in the sunlight. "It's working. Just a few more days." He twirled the gold medallion over and over in his hands. His brown eyes met mine. "Why don't you come up to the coop while I'm reading the movements of the chickens— after I feed them, of course." He smiled. "I'll give it back then. Thank you, my Vestal." He bowed and returned to the line.

I loved the way Lucius respected me— an eleven-year-old novice.

CHAPTER 27

A few days had passed since our trip to the Circus Maximus. Now I finally had time to walk to the Imperial Chicken Coop. I wondered how the chickens performed today—and if Lucius was about collecting the portents.

I was in luck. Lucius, with his wax tablet was scribbling down the movements of the clucking fowl. He raised his eyes up and smiled at me. "Cornelia, it has been a morning of auspicious omens. The chickens predicted this, and here you are." He looked carefully at me, studying my face. "I see that awful bump on your forehead is slow to heal," he murmured.

I touched the bruise, now a yellow-violet color, a reminder of my night out with Vibi. But I didn't want to remember that right now. "Thank you, Lucius. It is healing. And I can only hope you are right about the omens."

He came close to me. "Your bulla has brought Rome great luck. I've been working with the Priest of Jupiter who has blessed the bulla. We've sent the message out through the ether in the name of Great Neptune—to have mercy on us all."

He clasped my shoulder. "And the best news is because of your bulla and our hymns to the god, Neptune's storms have subsided. One ship from Egypt carrying grain has reached the Port of Ostia already. Many of the plebes will have their free dole of grain after all."

"Anything to help the State of Rome," I replied, just wanting my bulla back.

"Nero will be pleased. He need not know from where the power flows."

"Caesar hasn't asked where you got this?" I asked.

"He doesn't know, of course. All he cares about are results. And this bulla is getting results."

"And if he doesn't get the results he desires?" I asked.

"It could mean my life is in danger. I fear for my life—if the Emperor doesn't get the results he demands."

"He would think it's your fault?" I pressed on.

"Yes," Lucius nodded. "Nero must blame someone or something for the problems that plague him."

Lucius pulled the bulla from his pocket. It truly seemed to have a new luster, a new glow that was never there before. "Here you are, Cornelia," he said, handing it over to me. "Many thanks. By the power of Jove, King of the Gods, may you continue to be blessed. Your bulla is now an amulet, blessed by the Priest of Jupiter."

He paused and thought a moment. "And this bulla has saved me from a dreadful fate. I'm grateful, Cornelia." He gazed down at me. "We augurs have a tenuous position in the court of Nero. We never know which way the wind blows with this Emperor." He bowed to me.

I pocketed the bulla that now felt heavier than before. I wasn't even sure I wanted it anymore; the weight felt burdensome. The chickens started to make a fuss, squawking for more feed.

"Back to business," Lucius said with a grin.

"If you need use of my bulla again, please call on me," I said.

"Thank you, Cornelia. And remember, this is our secret!"

I was making my way down the slope back toward the Atrium grounds when I saw Mother Aurelia beckoning to me. "Child, where have you been? I've been looking for you." She seemed weary; as if she was all used up and there was nothing left of her.

I was honest. Partially. "I have been up to the Imperial Coop inquiring as to the portents set out by the chickens for today," I answered.

"Portents? Portents indeed. I know not what the portents are for today. I *do* know that Emperor Nero has called for you and Vibidia to come up to the Regia. Only this time he wants me there as well. Do you have any idea, Cornelia, what he could want … now?" She looked flustered and confused, as if she had other things on her mind.

I saw Vibidia walking down the steps of the Atrium coming towards us. "Were you looking for me, Mother?" she inquired.

"Yes I was," Mother Aurelia said. "I just explained to Cornelia that the Emperor requests to see you both."

Vibi yawned, stretching her arms out and said, "Now?" She seemed unconcerned.

"Yes, now. Right now. And I am to accompany the two of you."

"The last time Nero called for us, he explained we were chosen—chosen to carry the blood of the October horse back to the Regia," Vibi mused.

"So perhaps as the Ides of October nears, he will review what you two must do. This is quite an honor, girls, and I am proud of both of you." She gathered us close to her. She started twittering to herself like a bird fussing over a brood of fledglings, speaking to herself more than to us. She embraced us both. I thought how much I would miss her when she retired.

"Let us go to the Regia— the Emperor awaits us."

"Of course, Mother. Let's go," said Vibidia, never afraid of anything.

A servant knocked and announced our arrival.

"Enter," I heard Nero command. There he was, sitting at his desk, strumming a stringed instrument. He plucked away on a few strings before he set it down. His mistress Poppaea, dressed in a red flowing tunica with a red palla wrapped around her gold hair lay on a couch dangling a bunch of grapes over her head. She plucked them one by one with her lips. Next to her stood Burrus looking bored and tired.

"Girls—Mother Aurelia," said the Emperor, picking up a stylus and twirling it in his fingers, "Please … sit down."

We found a place on a couch across from Poppaea. Now that we had arrived, she dropped the grapes on a nearby table. Her red lips glistened with the juice of the fruit, and her skin seemed as white as our robes. Even her hair shimmered with specks of red-gold.

She sat up and stared us down. "Oh, I know what you are thinking, Vestals." She gazed right at me. "How I can be this beautiful? Well, bathing in the milk of one hundred asses every day makes my skin such a translucent white … and my lips …"

"Poppi, that is enough. These Vestals are not here to listen to your beauty secrets."

"But Caesar," she purred.

"Enough." Nero pointed to us. "Are these the girls, Poppi? The girls disguised in Jewish clothing?"

Poppaea stood and glided close to us. I could feel her breath on me. "Caesar, I recognize the eyes … and oh yes, that bump … the young one tried to hide. And the older one … I recognize those green-brown eyes, the olive skin …"

Mother Aurelia looked stricken, as if someone had just slapped her across the face "What are you implying, Caesar? Poppaea? That my Vestals were somewhere they were not supposed to be?

"Indeed Mother Aurelia," Nero answered. "I have my spies. Spies I trust. You must know and realize that Rome is swarming with traitors, people who would see me, Caesar, scion of Aeneas, fail in my mission to bring Rome to a Golden Age."

With that he rose and approached; his heavy shoulders and body atop his skinny legs hung right over us. Vibi did not flinch.

"So, girls, tell me … were you out walking the streets of Rome … at night?"

"What is wrong with this?" Vibi complained. "We needed the night air. Cornelia had hurt her head—"

"But why ... tell me, why did you visit the house of that man Paul, the man who preaches about the Nazarene? *My* prisoner?"

I wondered what Vibi would say next.

"Because we were curious ... that's all," Vibi muttered.

"That is all? All?" he bellowed. "Vestals dedicated to protecting the fire that keeps Rome safe ... merely curious? By the shield of Mars, you tell me a tale!"

Mother Aurelia, her face flushed and wrinkled, chimed in. "Caesar, you must be mistaken. My girls would never—"

"Rest assured, my Emperor, to whom I am entirely devoted, it was *these* two I saw," Poppaea interjected. "I have no doubt."

Nero addressed Vibi with a stern look in his eye. "So, you who know better would take a young Vestal out through the dangerous streets of Rome at night and expose her to the teachings of a traitor? A usurper? Please tell me how you could risk this young Vestal's reputation, never mind your own. Speak!"

"Poppaea was there," Vibi pointed out.

"Never mind Poppaea. You, Vibidia, have broken a rule of the Vestals. Going out alone at night is strictly forbidden. And to enter the house of *my* prisoner, a prisoner who preaches the cult of the Nazarene—"

"We were not alone, Caesar. The two of us went together," said Vibi.

"It makes no matter. You had no permission. You broke the rules and for this—"He paused and pointed at Vibi, "You shall be punished!"

Both Vibi and I started to shake. Mother Aurelia seemed confused by this news, looking first at the Emperor, then to Poppaea, and back at us, shaking her head in disbelief.

Nero continued his rant. "Take heed, Vibidia. You are older than Cornelia and know better. You have broken a cardinal rule of the Vestals. And you will be punished."

"Punished?" The word flew from my mouth.

"Quiet, little snake charmer. Yes, punished." He motioned to Burrus. "Go tell a slave to get the East Room ready. Now!"

Burrus left. Poppaea sat staring at us with a grin across her face.

"So sorry, girls." She half smiled. "I am honest."

"What does this mean, Caesar? This punishment?" Mother Aurelia asked weakly.

"It means that the older Vestal will get a scourging. The young Vestal will watch in order to learn a lesson—lest she be next."

Vibi remained calm, standing still, ready to accept her punishment—all for Paul and his Savior, Jesus. I hoped she thought it worth it; I knew she did. Her faith was that strong. She looked like a statue, rigid and drawn of any color.

I, on the other hand, was on the verge of tears. I knew that Poppaea had betrayed us after she recognized us and identified us that day at the races. *It is all my fault*, I thought. If it weren't for my hideous bruise, now a greenish yellow, we'd be safe.

Mother Aurelia, her face still flushed, scurried from the room, claiming she had work to do and she would deal with the matter later. Later? How much punishment would we have to suffer?

Burrus returned to the West Room. "All is ready, Caesar."

"Thank you, Burrus. That is all for now."

We followed the Emperor down the narrow hall to the East Room, the room over the granary. *Maybe my bulla will help,* I thought. But how could it help Vibidia—now?

A slave was waiting next to the door and opened it for us. We followed Nero, his heavy body swaying with each step. A single lamp flickered on the wall, making the room seem gray and dusky. In a corner of the room, a damask curtain hung from ropes. Next to the curtain, a table set with a strange array of whips and other objects of torture awaited.

"You, traitorous girl, get behind the curtain and disrobe," Nero ordered. Then he looked over at me. "You, little charmer, will hold the curtain while I take pleasure in scourging your friend." I pulled the silk curtain over and Vibi began to disrobe, her vestal attire dropping with a whoosh to the floor. I could see her shadow behind the curtain and how she crossed her arms over her chest.

The Emperor hefted up several whips; one had sharp metal barbs at the end wrapped in pieces of leather. He held it up to examine it closely. The metal glinted in the half-light. I shivered as he placed it back down on the table.

"At last I have found the right scourge for this occasion," Nero announced. He brandished a leather whip with three straps hanging off the end. On the ends of each strap hung little white, grooved stones. Nero clicked them together.

"I've chosen a scourge with the hooves of newborn lambs for your punishment. Baby lambs that were slaughtered." He laughed aloud and started swinging the whip about, and then slammed it down hard against the table. I flinched, hearing the noise, and saw Vibi's shadow shaking and hovering behind the curtain.

"Hold the curtain. Do not move," he ordered me. I tried not to shake; after all, I wasn't being whipped. Yet Vibi was my friend, my sister who would suffer for her love of Jesus Christ, the Narazene. Nero strode behind the curtain.

The whip struck and I heard Vibi groan and bend over.

"Stand up straight," the Emperor demanded. Over and over the whip slashed against her back. "This should teach you, Vibidia, and your little charge too, to obey the rules of the Order. You are dedicated to Vesta, to me, to the State of Rome, not some new god who was but a man!"

The whipping continued until it seemed like the Emperor was slashing Vibidia apart. Yet Vibi remained brave, barely flinching. The only words I heard her repeat over and over were, " … God forgive me … Christ forgive them …", in a whispered tone as if she was praying.

Nero shouted that prayer would not save her from punishment. No God or Savior would come to her rescue.

Finally, Vibi crumbled to the floor on her knees and began crying softly. The scourging was over. Nero emerged from behind the curtain, his eyes afire, the whip stained with my sister's blood.

I could not contain my anger. "You tempt the Fates, Caesar! You tempt the Gods and Vesta by spilling the blood of a Vestal," I screamed. "You bring curses onto Rome, onto all of us," I cried out.

"Make no mind of any curses and fate. Worry about your own fate," Nero panted. "And next time I hear of you girls walking Rome's streets at night, visiting my prisoner, the punishment will be far worse," he said. He chuckled to himself. "Far worse. You'll both get a hot poker thrust down your throat. And I mean both of you!"

He started laughing again to himself. More punishments! And then his laughter rose to a high-pitched howl. Nero seemed to think the idea was funny; perhaps he enjoyed tormenting young girls. Perhaps he just enjoyed inflicting pain.

"How can you laugh when Vibidia suffers?" I asked.

"Just do as you are told and follow the rules!" His shadowed face came close to mine. He pointed his finger right at my face. "Stay out of the streets. It will only get worse for you if you don't. This is a warning. And mark my words. It will give me great pleasure to drive that hot poker down your throats— if you don't obey!"

CHAPTER 28

Nero still insisted Vibidia and I carry the vessels of blood from the slain October horse. What could we do but obey the Emperor's commands? Mother Aurelia had little to say to us after the scene at the Regia. Junia, however, turned her nose up at us and treated us like we were an embarrassment to the order. She told us she was ashamed of us and how could we disgrace Vesta? We said nothing. Life continued on in the Atrium.

Now Rome was astir getting ready for the yearly event. After the scourging Vibi became withdrawn and subdued— at times she barely ate. She was in her own world. But she carried her scars with dignity. She showed me the rough bruise marks; three-pronged grooves ran up and down her back like deep ruts in a road.

"I can bear this burden. We all must carry them with us, Cornelia," she told me, faintly smiling.

We had little time to talk. Vibi was allowed, of course, to teach me about the Rites of the October Horse. Otherwise, Mother Aurelia kept us separated—as best she could.

Today was the Ides of October, the Festival of the October Horse. After breakfast, Junia was finishing up with my weekly tutoring lesson in the library. She asked me question after question. What steps did I need to take during the sacrifice while the animal's throat was slit? What about when the Priest of Mars stabbed the horse in the heart? How was I to comport myself?

"When the horse begins his death throes, you will pray to the departing spirit of the horse, while the blood drips into the vat," she explained. "Once it is poured into the amphora, you will carry it with great care!" She peered close to me, her bird eyes blinking and observing every part of my face. "Well?"

"And after the carriage lets us off … I must walk quickly, walk tall, keep a good pace, but I must not run," I parroted back.

"Hmph! I'm glad you are listening to me today. For a change! A lot rests on this Festival, Cornelia. I will be tending Vesta's fire today. But I expect the best from you, and rest assured, I will hear about your performance from the other girls." She glanced away for a moment. "Never one of my favorite festivals. My stomach churns—at the sight of blood."

This was the first time Junia had admitted anything like this to me. *She is a real person,* I thought. *Sometimes.* Then she stiffened up and was back to her usual self, grumpier than the donkeys on a rainy day. "We will complete this lesson, Cornelia, by you telling me what you remember from last week's lesson."

I thought for a moment. "I learned that Vestals write out their wills and own property," I said.

"Indeed," Junia replied. "What else did I teach you?"

225

I paused. "That if a Vestal meets one convicted of a crime on his way to execution, she may pardon him."

"That is correct. And what else can you remember?"

"I've studied the scrolls about King Numa and his consort, Egeria."

"Consort? My, my. I guess river nymphs can never be real wives to kings, now can they?"

"Just like we Vestals can never be real wives to any earthly husband—now can we?" I decided I would stare her down after my own sharp response.

"And neither can we be consorts! Never forget, the greatest crime for an active duty Vestal is to be any man's consort or mistress. This must never, ever happen to a Vestal."

Her small mouth, pointed chin, and pinched nose came close to my face. She smelled like rose water and olive oil. "The price for a Vestal being with a man—even once, is death—death by being buried alive, if you must know." She shook as if she were remembering something or someone. "Let us move on. From the beginning, Cornelia, please recite the names of all the Caesars—in order."

This was easy. "Julius Caesar, Augustus Caesar ..."

A sharp, urgent knock sounded at the door. Junia held up her hand, indicating she wanted me to stop talking. "Enter," she commanded.

Domicia walked in. "The Emperor's carriages have arrived. They are waiting."

Junia gathered her scrolls and wax tablets and returned them to the library shelves. "Make us proud, Cornelia. Stand firm aside the October Horse."

It was just three Vestals today—Rubria, Vibi, and myself. What a relief that Junia would stay behind along with Mother and Occia. I had freedom from my tutor.

Our first stop along the way was at the Temple of Mars. Rubria explained that here, at the temple of Rome's founding father, the rite of the October Horse would take place. People hurried around the temple, making offerings of flowers, pine branches, and pots of unguents.

After we paid our brief respects, the carriage continued along the east bank of the Tiber. Our lictors rushed ahead of us and shouted to people to clear the way and make room; the Emperor's carriage was headed to the Vatican Circus, the race-track alongside the Campus Martius. We crossed over one of the many bridges spanning the Tiber. We passed small houses, shops, and warehouses along the fringes of the Campus. They looked like little boxes one atop the other.

The racetrack had been smoothed out and raked in antici-pation of the most important race of the season.

The Festival of the October Horse featured a two-char-iot race; each chariot had two horses. The chariots would race around the track seven times. The winning horse, the horse on the right side would be proclaimed the October Horse.

A small podium erected for the Emperor, the priests, sena-tors and Vestals was in place. Silk banners and streamers, along with signs and flags blew in the crisp breezes. The sun blasted rays along the track, as if the golden orb itself had an interest in the race.

I thought with dread about the winning horse, the sacrifice to Mars. *Why*, I thought, *must we kill a triumphant animal?* Then I thought about my own comportment; how I must carry myself with dignity and honor. Yet the words of Paul stayed with me— how Rome was superstitious.

Throngs of people began to arrive, chattering with excitement. People huddled in groups, most likely waging bets on who would win. Food vendors started to appear, setting up booths and lighting small fires for roasting meats and vegetables to suit the crowd's appetites.

Finally, Nero emerged from his carriage along with Poppaea; both were smiling and waving to the cheering crowds. Vibi and I glanced at the Emperor's mistress, who we now knew was a spy; she was the reason Vibi would wear scars down her back for life.

On one side of the arena stood the group representing the Subura, a boisterous crowd exclaiming the horse's head was going to be theirs this year. On the other side, the inhabitants of the Via Sacra waited patiently, as if they assumed they would win this year—again.

We followed Nero and his entourage to the makeshift podium and found our seats. Two chariots finally appeared; one with a pair of white horses yoked to a golden harness, the other, a pair of black stallions harnessed in silver. They made a striking contrast on the field. The charioteers held the reins tightly, yet managed to blow kisses and waves to the cheering audience. Both of the muscled charioteers had their hair slicked and oiled. *Maybe this is what Hercules looked like,* I thought.

The Emperor stood and gestured to the crowd signaling silence. "My fellow Romans, today we honor our founding god, Mars, first by this chariot race, and then the sacrifice of the October Horse. We liken this back to the memory of Troy, part of our history we shall never forget. May the race and the sacrifice find favor with Mars."

Each chariot took its place in the assigned lane. An official announced silence, dropped a white cloth to the ground and shouted, "Let the race begin!" The two chariots bolted, the horses kicking up dust everywhere.

Vibi, Rubria, and I, along with Nero and all the senators and pontiffs cheered for the black team, the team that represented the Via Sacra. It made sense, since we all lived so close to the thoroughfare. So I joined them and shouted just as loudly as the rest.

The race was tight and at times, neck to neck. Each turn on the track inched the white chariot closer, but then the black chariot edged forward. I could see the puffs of hot breath coming from the black horses' nostrils. The charioteer of the black team drew the reins in, wrapped them tight around his waist, then cracked his riding whip to their backs— and the black team pulled ahead.

With that move, the black team left the white team behind for the remainder of the laps—left the white team in the dirt and dust— winning by over a lap.

"It is done! The blacks win. We have the October Horse, the chosen one," Nero announced.

The winning charioteer trotted his horses around the stadium in a victory lap. Flowers, ribbons, and streamers flowed down covering much of the track. Then after waving to the crowd, the charioteer unyoked the horse on the right side of the chariot. Several young men entered the field and garlanded the October Horse with loaves of bread around his neck.

How proud he looks, I thought. *He knows he won the race. But does he understand his fate? The regal stallion has been chosen as a sacrifice. Chosen. Just like me and the other Vestals. Did any of us ever really understand our fate?*

The black stallion was paraded around the field, led by a tether. The horse kept his head full up and even gave the audience a trot or two. He was rewarded with a handful of oats and chopped apples.

"Let us proceed to the Temple of Mars," Nero cried out.

It was time for the sacrifice!

Nero's sedan led the way, crossed back to the other side of the Campus Martius, followed closely by the High Priest of Mars and his band of Salii. The Salii, with their spears and shields, kept a solemn pace along the path. I thought how different they were today compared to the leaps and dances they performed on the New Year.

Following the priests came the pontiffs, flamens, the augurs and haruspices, and then the Vestals. I made sure I had my sacrificial hood on properly and that the special vial of ashes from the sacrificed calf in April was secured in my pouch.

A lone drumbeat started up that helped us march in the somber line, following the path southward to the Temple of Mars. Romans lined the street, throwing more flowers at the victorious horse.

The altar in front of the temple was festooned with garlands, including many pine boughs, sacred to Mars. The marble portico leading into the temple behind the altar was graced with more garlands of flowers, vine branches, and pine sprigs. On the altar lay a large vat, a spear, several small amphoras and a sharp, curved knife. At the sight of the knife, my stomach started to churn.

"You can do this," Vibi said to me quietly, as if she understood my struggles.

The crowd surrounded the altar, anxiously waiting for the rite to begin. The High Priest of Mars stepped forward. The horse was then led up to the altar. Nearby lay a straw pallet awaiting the sacrificial victim. This was his funeral bier; his remains to be burnt to ashes.

The Priest of Mars grabbed the knife from the altar and held it up. The sun's light glinted off the blade, displaying its deadly point. "Behold," exclaimed the priest. "Rome's October Horse." The crowd cheered. The horse raised its head and then pawed the ground several times. *Does he know*, I wondered, *that the knife is meant for him?*

Then the High Priest called us to the altar.

"Our Vestals will remain near the horse, sprinke the sacred ashes on his head, then collect his sacred blood. They will assist in sending his spirit up onto the ether, where the God Mars will receive it, and will bestow on Rome bounty and good fortune. He added, "If it is the will of the God!" He paused to take a breath. "And now, the invocation to Rome's patron God, Mars."

The priest held the knife high over his head and began:

"To the Great God Mars, you who keep Rome safe, during battles and plagues, great Warrior and Soldier God, Father of Romulus and Remus, we dedicate this horse in your honor and name, to protect Rome against her enemies, to welcome in the harvest. We call on you, Mars, to give us a sign so we know you have accepted this sacrifice."

He bowed his head toward the altar, lowered the knife, and kissed the blade.

The horse started to become restless. He bucked back and forth, and sweat began to pour down his flanks and neck. His silky black coat looked as if it was covered in dew. Slaves grabbed at the ropes, trying to keep the horse from pushing back and forth.

I decided to approach the horse. "Let me calm him," I told the priest. "I will talk with him, his spirit." But first I took out the bottle with the sacred ashes, and dabbed his forhead with them.

I placed my hand alongside his thick neck and held it there. I spoke to the horse without actually speaking. I told him his win would allow him to live in glory and his sacrifice was for Rome's safety and protection. And with Vesta's help, I would see that his spirit followed the path of the ether and would lead him to a peaceful pasture.

The horse's ears perked up as if he could truly hear and understand me. I whispered into his ear, "You were chosen by the gods, just as I was chosen. It is an honor. Receive it well."

The horse grew quiet and remained in place. He turned his great black head in my direction and seemed to nod. His huge eyes blinked at me—as if he knew. And then I noticed all the eyes of the crowd, including those of Nero and the Priest of Mars, looking at me with wonder. I had calmed the October Horse. He seemed ready to accept his Fate.

Now was the time. From behind the altar a Salii appeared brandishing a spear. "Behold, the spear of Mars," he shouted. "Greatest weapon of Rome held sacred to this god. The sacrifice is pierced by the spear." And with these words, he proceeded to stab the spear into the horse's heart.

The horse, dazed, lowered his head and let forth a pitiful bawl. His legs started to wobble and he released a loud groan. The spear remained stuck. "Now is the time, Mars. We beseech you to receive this sacrifice," intoned the Priest of Mars. "Gather around the horse. Vestals, prepare the vat."

And then it happened. The priest grabbed hold of the blade and sliced a great crevice along the beast's throat. The horse's eyes rolled upward and then down, looking at me, as if asking for my help. I couldn't save him. I continued my silent prayers for the horse, careful not to show my true emotions.

The blood began to flow like thick honey into the vat. And how brave the horse was, trying to remain upright on his unsteady legs. My stomach churned. I grew dizzy, while my skin soaked my robes with perspiration. I prayed to Vesta to help me get through this. I knew I was supposed to watch the horse and pray for his spirit; the other Vestals seemed to have no problem observing the victorious horse in the midst of death throes.

My legs started to buckle—just like the horse. The fear of fainting overtook me. I knew at that moment I would collapse. Then I felt a strong presence behind me. A pair of muscled shoulders leaned against me. "Have no fear." It was Lucius, standing there, holding me up. "Lean back. You will be fine."

I wiped the sweat from my face and took in a deep breath. Lucky for me, everyone was watching the dying horse. How grateful I was that Lucius had noticed my distress. Turning around toward him, I mouthed the words, "Thank you." He nodded.

The rite of death continued. The blood continued gushing and oozing into the vat while the crowd looked on. At last the horse, sensing this was the end, let loose a final groan and collapsed on his side—dead. At that moment, his spirit left his body, I knew he was upon the ether, up onto other realms, where perhaps Mars was nodding with favor.

"It is done! The October horse is dead. Now is the time to cut the tail off," exclaimed the priest, looking pleased with the outcome. "Runner, are you ready?"

A young boy appeared from the crowd, dressed in a light tunic with running sandals.

"Ready," he exclaimed.

The priest used his bloodied knife to slice the horse's tail off. The runner had with him a gold plate on which to carry it. He was careful to place the bloodied section in the center of the plate; the long black strands of tail hung off the edge.

A group of people at the front of the horse started sawing his head off. Most of the blood had been drained, and our amphorae were filled with the thick liquid that made my stomach churn. I wondered how anyone could get used to the smell of fresh blood!

Nero shouted suddenly, "Augurs, haruspices, stay behind. You must examine the entrails and report the omens."

Lucius and the others gathered around the Emperor. But first Lucius turned to me with a look of concern, to ensure I was myself again.

"Thank you. I am fine," I said, thinking about how grateful I felt that the augur understood my distress.

Lucius bowed and turned away to report the omens to the Emperor.

The ride back to the Via Sacra seemed to take a long time. A small crowd followed us until we dismounted just after we passed the Capitoline Hill. Bearing a vessel filled with the blood of a newly slaughtered horse upset me. My stomach still had a dull, achy pain that would not go away. But the dizzy feelings and thoughts of a faint seemed to have vanished. I could not and would not spill a drop of this poor horse's blood.

We began our descent down the Capitoline Hill toward the Forum; I tried not to become distracted by the cheering crowds. I remembered what Junia had taught me—to walk with grace, look straight ahead, and carry myself with dignity.

I thought I had recovered well from the shock of the blood and violence. Rubria, Vibidia, and I were making our way toward the Regia when I heard something that made me turn my head. "Cornelia, we are so proud of you!" Out of the corner of my eye, I noticed my family watching the procession. There was Father, Mother, Cornelius, and Taltos, waving to me, trying to get my attention.

I looked and nodded and when I nodded, my amphora started to wobble and a great glob of blood shot up into the air. In an instant, I held up the amphora and the blood seemed to land back inside the vessel. But I wasn't certain if I had spilled any blood on me or on the ground. All I could do was to keep going, back to the Regia, back to the Atrium. *Away from my family. Away from the crowds. Away from the sight of the mutilated horse whose head would hang off a pole somewhere in Rome.*

My stomach still ached, but I was determined to walk with grace alongside my sisters. Finally we approached the entrance of the Regia. The runner, who arrived long before us, was wiping the horse's tail across the entrance.

I had made the journey without spilling a drop of the sacred blood; or so I thought. The three of us Vestals stood while the runner brushed the hearth with the horseclotted blood, deep crimson in color. I took in some deep breaths and waited until the runner had finished this important task.

Then I looked down. A large spot of blood stained the front of my clothing. Something wasn't right; I didn't feel right. My head hurt, my stomach hurt, and I felt I had failed in one of my Vestal duties.

Tears streamed down my face. I turned to Rubria. "I spilled some of the horse's blood. I am so sorry. I failed this task."

Rubria came around toward me and examined the stains. Then she turned me around and examined my back.

"What's wrong?" I asked her. "What is wrong with me?"

Rubria laughed and put a hand on my shaking shoulder.

"That's *not* horse's blood, Cornelia. That's your blood. You are a woman now."

CHAPTER 29

DECEMBER AD 61

So I was a woman now. Rubria explained to me what it all meant; my blood would flow each month. Changes started happening with my body as well. I noticed and everyone else took notice too.

The head of the slain October Horse hung on a pole in front of the Regia, it's eyes long since pecked away by crows. The Emperor's team from the Via Sacra won the right to keep the head. His face looked so black and so lifeless, like dark night itself. How long would it remain there, staring at nothing?

Today was the Festival of the Bona Dea, something I eagerly looked forward to for weeks. I knew not what to expect; I was too young last year to attend. I did study about it; it was a secret rite for women only.

Mother Aurelia's party would be celebrated after the Rites of the Bona Dea. How sad I was to think of her leaving us, only to have the miserable Junia replace her. Perhaps she would become kinder and more generous once she became Chief Vestal. My greatest fear with Junia as the new Virgo Maxima was that she would become even more imperious, more domineering. I shuddered to think of those beady eyes watching my every move.

It was sometime after early evening prayers that we gathered together in the Atrium. Vibidia was assigned to fire duty with Occia; she would miss out on the celebrations. She didn't seem to care; she was trapped in a world of her own, thinking about nothing but Paul and his words about Jesus and salvation.

I wanted to shake her by the shoulders and shout, "Enough!" But Vibi had endured so much already. She bore the scars from her awful scourging. The scars were more than just on her tattered back. They were a lasting blot on her soul.

This evening though, all I could think of was seeing Lucretia again and attending the Bona Dea. With Lucretia! The festival was to be held at the home of the Prefect Burrus. His domus was located just east of the Forum on the outskirts of the Subura.

All the available Vestals gathered twittering like little sparrows hopping from bush to branch never keeping still. Mother reviewed with us the details of the ritual. Why was there always something more to remember?

A loud knock sounded on the door. Domicia scurried to open it. Like a fresh wind, in blew Lucretia, dressed in a lovely green stola. She still wore a thin black veil over her face to hide the scars. I didn't care. I ran to her and hugged her around her stomach. Her hard stomach! She always loved her sweets, so I thought she was enjoying them more than ever.

"Why, Cornelia. Here, let me have a look at you."

She pushed me slightly away and gazed at me up and down. "You are a beautiful young woman now, I see," she murmured.

I embraced her again. "I have missed you for so long."

Mother Aurelia came tottering over with Junia following behind her.

"Look who is here— Lucretia. Welcome!" Mother stood back and eyed Lucretia's protruding stomach. "Well?" she asked gently. "What is this now?" Mother chuckled to herself and patted Lucretia's belly.

"I am with child, Mother. I have found and married a wonderful man who accepts me as I am. I am a matron now."

"Bonam Fortunam!" we all shouted as we gathered around her and bestowed blessings on our former Vestal sister.

"And I ask you all to bless this child. I have already in my mind dedicated him—or her— to Vesta, for protection and good health."

Mother Aurelia gazed up to the high ceiling. "Vesta, we now send prayers to you by the power of the perpetual fire that burns in Your Name. Your daughter Lucretia carries the scars from your flame. Protect our dear sister, Lucretia and her future child. May it be so," Mother decreed. We all murmured in agreement.

I could not contain my excitement. "I'm so happy for you, Lucretia. You made my life much easier when I arrived. You welcomed me. How can I thank you?" I hugged her again. I didn't want to let her go.

"Cornelia, the spirit, your spirit that you brought to the Atrium was enough thanks for me." Then she bent over and whispered in my ear, "If I have a girl child, I will name her after my favorite Vestal, Cornelia." Tears sprouted from my eyes. Truly, it was an honor.

We all nodded and prepared to remove to the domus of Burrus. It was getting late. The Festival of the Bona Dea would start soon.

The Emperor's carriages had arrived. Occia would stay behind guarding the temple flame with Vibi. Mother Aurelia told our youngest vestal that of course she was not allowed to attend the Bona Dea, just like I wasn't allowed to attend last year. Occia was too young.

But she could attend the retirement party later that evening. I felt envious that Occia would have time with Vibi now. Would she fill Occia's head with stories about Jesus and Paul? I hoped not, because it was our special bond. I knew I should spend more time with Occia, but I liked the attention from the older Vestals.

The sun was starting to set, casting pale heavenly light over Rome; even the carriages shone in the fading sunrays. The best news was I got to ride along with Lucretia and Rubria. How grown up I felt with these two Vestals!

The carriage proceeded along the stone-paved Via Sacra until we arrived at the domus of Burrus. Mother Aurelia and Junia alighted first. They both carried boxes with items clearly meant for the rite.

Burrus's wife awaited us, welcoming us into the vestibule and then the grand atrium of the domus. I noticed many of the portraits hanging around the atrium were covered with heavy cloth. Even statues and busts sitting atop pillars were draped over. "Why are these pictures covered? And all the busts?" I asked Junia.

"No man's eyes must observe the secret rites of the Bona Dea," she whispered. "Not even the eyes of a likeness of a man painted on canvas or sculpted. Remember, all things have a spirit, even paintings—and especially statues."

We followed the domina who led us down a long hallway. The hall was filled with twisted vines, branches, and garlands that hung over us like a great bower. Finally we came to the end of the hallway; on the right a room was waiting for us. An altar was set with more twisted vines, twigs, and branches. Everything in the room seemed tangled; it made me feel as if I was in the woods.

Other women had already gathered in the room. The Flaminica Dialis, with her yellow and orange veil was there, as well as a group of selected matrons who clustered around the altar. Light cloths covered all the windows. Oil lamps hung from the ceiling and walls. On the altar a lone white pillar candle burned. Mother Aurelia and Junia ordered some slave girls to lay the special boxes in front of the altar.

Mother looked over at the Flaminica. "Are we ready for the sacrifice? Is the pregnant sow ready?" she asked.

"The sow has been sacrificed. I completed it with my sacred knife. The other matronae witnessed the sacrifice," said the Flaminica.

Mother seemed perturbed. "But why ... why didn't you wait for the Vestals? This is not a good omen," she murmured.

"You are late tonight," said the Flaminica. "The sun was setting and the sacrifice needed completion. We do not want to risk upsetting the Bona Dea." The Flaminica paused, seeming to think what to say next. "And this is your last true ritual, Mother. We did not want you to dirty your hands with the blood. It is done."

"Then this is good," said Mother. "Let us proceed."

Facing the altar with their backs turned to us, Mother and Junia began to lift the items from the boxes, and placed them carefully upon the altar. "Gather around Matrons of Rome, you who have been selected to attend this secret rite. Now is the time," exclaimed Mother Aurelia, fluttering her hands in a forward, beckoning motion. "I am honored to conduct this ritual ... my last as the Virgo Maxima."

Mother sighed and I heard gasps from many of the women. Not everyone had known of her retirement. Mother Aurelia was a beloved Chief Vestal— purity and goodness ran deep in her soul.

"But now is not the time to think on the future—my future," Mother continued. "Tonight we pay homage to the good goddess of Rome. I will now share the story of the Bona Dea. As many of us know, her father was named Faunus, a nature god, a god of the woods. One day, Faunus thought his daughter Bona Dea was drunk on wine. Knowing no young girl or woman may drink of the wine he beat his daughter with the branch of a myrtle tree. Imagine. This is why we allow no myrtle on the altar of Bona Dea—or anywhere in the room we dwell in.

"As part of the ritual, I must inspect every corner of the room. To find a sprig of myrtle on the Festival of the Bona Dea may incur the wrath of the Good Goddess, something Rome cannot afford. In the meantime, Domicia, check the doors. Make sure no man is lurking about."

Mother made her way to each corner of the room, like a mouse searching for crumbs of cheese. She looked under the curtains, stared up to the ceiling, and seemed to check every inch of the mosaic floor.

"All is clear, I am happy to report," she said. "We are ready to begin. Junia, please— the first sacred item of the Bona Dea."

Junia approached the object in the center of the altar and uncovered it. A small, elegant statue of a Goddess stood before us, with flowing hair that twisted and twined down her body. In her left hand was a cornucopia. Her right arm had a serpent coiled around it. The serpent was feeding from a bowl.

"Behold, a statue of the Bona Dea, borrowed from Her temple on the Aventine Hill. Thanks be to Her priestesses who kindly blessed the use of Her image for our private ritual," said Junia.

Several of the matrons exclaimed in wonder, chatting to one another about the statue. I immediately loved the Bona Dea. Was it the power of the snake wrapped around her? Or was it the flowing hair and the horn of plenty?

"Thank you, Junia," Mother said, "Now Rubria, please come forth. Continue."

Rubia stepped up and grasped the next item on the altar. She held up a covered bowl-shaped object. Then she removed the cloth and displayed a small round pot with a white top. The pot had several red and black markings on it.

"Behold, the honey pot sacred to Bona Dea, Goddess of Fertility." She lifted the pot up high so all could see. "Matrons and daughters of Rome, when you drink from the honey pot, you drink of the Good Goddess. You drink Her milk. You drink to Her and for Her."

I had never seen Rubria like this—so filled with the Spirit! Even Junia and Mother stood in complete wonderment at the power of Rubria's words. I felt my body quiver—as if I was receiving the message inside myself as well.

"We call this milk," Rubria continued. "Men may call it wine each day of the year. And we know that women may not drink of it. But tonight, *all* women may partake in Bona Dea's milk. So let us bless Bona Dea's milk … for the Good Goddess brings us the sacred liquid of the grape." She placed the pot again on the altar. "Within this pot of milk are a few drops of blood from the sacrifice. Drink of the sow's blood within the wine. It will ensure fertility for Rome! Let us now bless this honey pot." She held the pot aloft again and faced each direction as she proclaimed, "As above, so below, as within, so without, to you Bona Dea, you without spot."

With that, Rubria drank from the pot in a dramatic and impassioned manner and proceeded to gulp the liquid down. I thought, *I am a woman now. Can I drink of the Bona Dea's milk? Yes, I can certainly drink of the Bona Dea's milk.*

"Let the Festival begin," shouted Rubria, smacking her lips of the red juices around her mouth and holding up the wine pot. As if on cue, Domicia and the other slave girls burst forward carrying amphoras and vats of wine. Other servant women provided goblets and gave them to each woman. Even me. They stood by the vessels ladling out Bona Dea's milk.

I sipped my first taste of the liquid and decided I liked it. Then I took a long gulp. It tasted like honey mixed with grapes, strawberries, and spices. I finished my first cup and realized I wanted more.

"No more for you, Cornelia." Rubria was standing behind me. She winked and took a sip from her goblet. Then she flung her arm over my shoulder. "How did I do tonight?" she asked. "My invocation to the Good Goddess?"

"Better than good, Rubria … magnificent in fact. You were glorious. The Bona Dea will be well pleased."

"Women, women, gather around. It's time for the drama of the Bona Dea." Burros's wife clapped her hands twice. "Please," she said to the servants."Move these amphorae to the side. The floor must be cleared for the performers."

I followed the servant girls who dragged the wine vessels to the side of the room. Soon after another request, my wine goblet was filled— again.

No one seemed to notice. The women laughed, told jokes, danced and giggled, the way Cynthia and I had giggled as little girls. Some removed their stolas and danced in their tunicas. Many approached the altar to admire the statue of Bona Dea— making certain to touch the horn of plenty and the head of the snake—for good fortune and fertility.

Suddenly, my head started to spin and my face began to feel warm and flushed, as if I'd been burned by the sun. I thought it was the wine that warmed me.

The space in front of the altar was finally cleared. A few props, such as a small pointed tree, several bushes, and a fence provided the painted backdrop that made for a rustic setting. The characters paraded in. Faunus the nature God, pater of Bona Dea, arrived on stage first. Enraptured, I listened to his accusations against his innocent daughter. But then my stomach started to churn and the room spun around. My mouth became dry and my legs started to feel unsteady.

The need for air became great. No one seemed to notice anything— for all eyes were on Faunus and now Bona Dea. Even Domicia was watching with great interest. I felt sick and desired fresh air. For truly I thought I must vomit. But I didn't know where the vomitorium was in the domus. I was too ashamed to ask.

Keeping my head low and taking in several breaths, I made my way to the door, guarded by a servant girl. "Please let me by," I said. "I am in need of air." She watched me with a wary look. "Just for a few moments," I said. "I don't want to disturb the play."

The servant girl bowed her head. "Of course," she murmured and slowly opened the door. I ran down the hall, into the atrium, and through the vestibule, holding my hand over my mouth. Out of the vestibule I ran, taking no notice of the servant girls slinking about the halls. My legs felt unsteady like I would tumble over. My hands trembled but I kept going.

Finally, I saw some bushes. I dashed behind them, my hands clasping my throat, then I opened my mouth and vomited all of Bona Dea's milk right out of me. Drops of water beaded on my forehead, and then the sweat began dripping down my face. I collapsed next to the bush and just lay there, panting for air, grabbing onto my stomach.

As I wiped my mouth, my senses started to return. Feeling better, I remained hidden behind the bushes. No one from the party could witness me sick from the wine. I waited for my chance to return to the party—without anyone seeing me.

Then I noticed something. A dark shape was lurking behind one of the trees. It seemed to pop out from the trunk, only to return to the shadows. I suddenly felt cold and started to shiver. Who was this? I decided not to move.

The dark figure moved behind another tree—closer to Burrus's domus. How dare this intruder spy on the Festival of the Bona Dea? Feeling brave of a sudden, I decided I would confront the intruder. This would gain me favor with the Bona Dea—and all the others.

I left the safety of the bushes. The shadow was in the shape of a man. He seemed to be watching the house, waiting for his chance to peer inside.

"You are intruding … on the private rites of the Bona Dea," I pronounced, hands on my hips and slurring my words. But I felt braver than I had ever felt in my life. "Leave or I will report you to the Emperor."

The stranger turned around. He looked strangely familiar.

"Who are you?" I whispered.

"I'm Marcus, Vibidia's cousin," he replied.

"Marcus, Marcus, what are *you* doing here now?" I whispered loudly. "No men are allowed near or at the Festival of the Bona Dea."

He approached me and grabbed my shoulders. "Where's Vibidia?" he asked, not listening to what I had said.

"What?"

"Vibidia. My cousin. Is she in there?" he asked, breathing hard. "I have some important news for her."

"Vibidia is tending Vesta's flame in the temple. She's on fire duty tonight." I paused. "Do you want me to give her a message?" I wasn't sure in my condition if I could remember it, but I would try.

"Cornelia, are you …"

"Drunk?" I slurred. "Of course not!" I proceeded to stagger around the bushes trying to stand up straight.

Marcus glanced around the grounds and motioned me to the tree. "Tell her it is about Paul. Here." He thrust a small scroll into my hand. "Give this to Vibidia for me."

"Cornelia, where are you?" I heard Junia's screech coming from the vestibule. "Are you out there?" I heard Lucretia start to shout my name as well.

"Marcus, I must get back. It might be bad luck to run into you—a man on the Bona Dea." I tried to speak but the words were mumbled. I concentrated as best I could. "Go! I will deliver this message to Vibi."

With that said, I dashed back to the domus and explained to the concerned Vestals I had needed the cold night air for a few minutes and that I was fine.

The rest of the evening, I drank no more of Bona Dea's milk. I wondered what Marcus's message said. All I knew was it had something to do with the prisoner Paul. I planned to deliver the message after Mother Aurelia's party. I had as many emotions as the number of goblets of wine running through my veins.

Soon it was time to go home—to the next party.

CHAPTER 30

The carriage ride home was uneventful. I still managed to ask Lucretia every possible question about her new life. What was her husband like? Did she think she would have a boy or girl? What was Pompeii like?

I realized how much I missed her. I wanted to share with her every bit of my life as a Vestal. Then I realized how many things I could not share with her. "The walls of Rome have ears," I remembered Nero saying. So I let Lucretia do the talking and listened; the bumpy carriage ride prevented me from sleeping anyway.

When we arrived back to the Atrium, it was dark with the exception of a sliver moon. But inside, lights blinked brightly. I wished Vibidia could be a part of the celebration. Thinking of my friend tending the fire, I remembered my promise to bring her a piece of cake—and the note from Marcus.

The Atrium was aglow with oil lamps and candles. A special seat under the statue of Vesta was ready for our Chief Vestal—the Vestal of Honor. I wondered if Emperor Nero would be present.

Several of Rome's matrons, attendees of the Festival of the Bona Dea, began to arrive, flushed from the wine. Junia called us together and escorted Mother to her seat. Although Mother held her head high, I could see her hands were shaking. "We pay respect to the services of Mother Aurelia, who has given Vesta and Rome over thirty years of her life. For this we are truly grateful," said Junia, who bowed before Mother Aurelia and stepped away.

Mother looked flustered. It was also Junia's moment because I knew she savored the idea of being Chief Vestal soon. Then Junia came forth again, this time with a small box. "From all of us, to you." She handed it to our Chief Vestal.

Mother carefully unwrapped it, and held up a necklace with a large gold key attached. "This is your key, your key to Rome. May new doors and adventures open up for you, Mother Aurelia. Vesta bless you always," said Junia with enthusiasm and respect in her voice. We all clapped wildly.

All I could think of was the cake. But then an urgent knock pounded at the door. Domicia quietly trod to the door to see who was there. Shortly, she returned. "Message from Emperor Nero for Mother Aurelia. It is to be read out loud according to his orders."

"How considerate! Caesar remembering my special day," Mother mused. She tore open the wax-sealed scroll and read it aloud to the audience:

"To Mother Aurelia, one of Rome's greatest Vestals:

I congratulate and honor you for your more than thirty years service. Your skills, leadership, and patience are part of the reason Rome prospers. I have already commissioned Rome's finest sculptor to fashion your likeness in marble. Your image shall live on forever in the Atrium. However, the situation is dire for Rome. We cannot afford to lose your guidance, your skills and experience. They are needed now more then ever. Too many young Vestals to train at once could prove troubling for the fate of Rome. Please stay on with the Vestal Order. You may decide otherwise, but I ask you in the name of Pax Romana.

–Emperor Nero"

"Why—why, I don't know what to say," exclaimed Mother, in a state of confusion. "If the Emperor claims I am needed here, then I will stay as long as you—my Vestals—and Rome need me." She paused. "And really, what was I going to do with myself anyway? Get married?"

Everyone laughed but Junia, who looked like she got just got stung by a bug.

With this announcement, a loud cheer echoed through the Atrium. The drunken matrons and most of the Vestals seemed happy—all except Junia who stood stiff and glared at Mother. So it was decided Mother Aurelia would remain after all—as long as Caesar and Rome needed her. Junia would have to continue to wait her turn.

After embracing Mother and congratulating her, I cut a slice of almond date honey cake for me, and one for Vibidia. Occia had run back from the temple to the party, so I knew Vibi was alone tending to fire duty. I wanted to share some of the celebration with her, to share the news about Mother remaining with the order, and to deliver Marcus's urgent message.

Before I could leave, Occia ran up to me and looked forlorn. "Cornelia, why can't I be like you? You do everything right. Everyone loves you. And I never can go to special rituals." Her lips puckered up into a pout and then she stared at the floor.

"I didn't get to go to the Bona Dea last year either, Occia," I told her. "You'll have your chance. And everyone loves me?" I repeated. "Are you sure of that?"

"I love you. I want to be just like you." Her big brown eyes watched me.

"Well," I said. "You can't be me, but I'll give you something instead. Wait here."

I ran upstairs to my apartment and found my cedar box with all my trinkets. I would gift them to Occia give her a part of my old life. After all, this was a night of celebrations!

I rushed back down the stairs. There she was waiting, looking small and fragile.

"Here," I thrust the box at her. "My treasures are now your treasures."

"Does that mean we are truly sisters? That together we will be the greatest Vestals ever?" Her eyes widened.

"Yes, it does mean that. We *are* sisters now."

"Thank you, Cornelia," Occia exclaimed, jumping up and down. She ran off showing the box to anyone who would pay attention to her.

I left the Atrium with a slice of cake for Vibi, and proceeded to the temple. All seemed quiet. When I knocked,
Vibidia's servant met me.

"Please leave us," Vibidia ordered. "There's cake in the
Atrium for you." The servant quickly left.

Vibidia added another wedge of wood to the sputtering
flame. Her heart-shaped face had a ruddy glow.

"Vibi, I have some news," I said, as I handed her the slice of
cake. "Mother Aurelia is going to stay on with us. Nero asked
her and Rome needs her. We all need her!"

"Yes, this is good, "Vibi said, as she took a bite of cake.

"And your cousin Marcus was looking for you. He was
prowling around the festival. I was outside—too much of Bona
Dea's milk. Your cousin, what he did was dangerous— I almost
got in trouble because of him." I pulled the scroll from my pouch
and thrust it at her. "Here, he wanted me to give you this."

She took the scroll, unraveled it, and silently read the news.
Then she placed it into Vesta's flame and it burned to ashes.

"What's the news, Vibi? I'll tell no one."

"I *do* know this, Cornelia. I trust you!"

"Well? What is it?"

Vibi leaned to me and whispered, "Nero will release Paul
soon. Release him from house arrest. He will be freed. And
free to preach the Word!"

"Freed? Will he stay in Rome?" I asked.

"No, of course not," she said. "He is banished from Rome.
Nero probably thinks if Paul leaves by order, all the Jesus Followers will leave as well. Remember, he is their leader. Marcus
did write that Paul might depart for Spain. We don't know for
sure. The only thing we know is Paul will soon be free ... free
of Rome, free of Nero ... free!"

I hugged Vibi. Tears of relief and joy filled her eyes.

"This is the best news!" I wiped a tear from her eye.

"I will miss his words, for he's been a true teacher to me," Vibi said. Then she sighed. "If only I could follow him."

"I know, Vibi. But remember, we carry his words in our hearts— always." But then I wondered: *Would Vibi follow her heart?* I shuddered to think what would happen if she was caught. It was forbidden to spill the blood of a Vestal. But I had witnessed her scourging by Nero. Nothing was sacred to Caesar, but Caesar.

CHAPTER 31

MAY 64 AD

Almost a year and a half had passed since Paul was officially freed; the time to prepare for next month's Vestalia was at hand. So much had happened. The Emperor Nero officially divorced his wife Octavia, so he could marry his mistress Poppaea. But the divorce wasn't good enough for Nero's Poppi.

Instead of just banishment, the Emperor's wife Octavia was murdered and her head sent to the Regia, so Nero and Poppaea could, with certainty, know she was dead. According to the rumors, Poppi, upon seeing the head of her rival, laughed and exclaimed Octavia would never present a problem again.

And the old Prefect, Burrus, died right after the Bona Dea. Rumors circulated that Nero poisoned him. A new Prefect of the Praetorian Guard, Tigillenus, had taken his place. He was tall like a pole and wiry; his face looked like a rat. His long nose dominated his face, making his black eyes seem small and shrunken. He had moved up from working the wharves. Everyone said he was mean, greedy and wanted power.

Both Tigillenus, Poppaea, and Varros filled the Emperor's head with ideas. Nero's old advisor, Seneca, no longer could influence the Emperor. Tigillenus, Poppaea, and the ever-present dwarf Varros had the Emperor's ear. The only good news was that Vibi heard Paul made it safely to Spain, and that he was spreading the word about his Savior. At least he was alive and safe from Nero's clutches.

Life in the Atrium had changed little. Mother Aurelia remained as Chief Vestal, much to Junia's anger. And today, the two eldest Vestals gathered the spelt used to make the mola salsa. It was also the Feast of the Lemuria ... again.

We awaited them in the storeroom. At last they arrived with the harvest baskets filled with spelt. We crushed and pounded the grain in our mortars with our pestles, and left it to dry. In just a month we would add both the boiled salt and then the hard salt, baking it into the sacred wafer. The rest of the blend would be used in many of our other rituals that included mixing it with the ashes of our sacrifices.

Finally, my duties in the storeroom were complete. Having a few hours to spare, I decided to sit in the garden for a time. Since it was the Lemuria, I brought a bunch of black beans to throw behind me and shout, "Ghosts of my fathers, go out!"

But I was distracted. New life was emerging everywhere. Plants and flowers opened up to the strengthening sun and a fresh spring breeze blew their stems making them look as if they were bowing. After the long winter, the bright new greens and colorful clusters of irises and flowering herbs helped to renew my spirit.

I sat on one of the benches watching the fishpond. As usual, small birds alighted to dip their beaks into the pool for a drink. Then I heard a distressing sound coming from the pines near the Temple of Castor and Pollux.

I ran to the temple where I heard the sound. But it was too late. Cleo, now fully grown, came toward me with Picus in her mouth! So upset was I that I couldn't tell whether the woodpecker was the male or female. I could hear the babies crying though, making desperate twittering noises. Cleo dropped the dead bird at my feet and purred around my legs.

All this on the Lemuria! Right before I could throw the black beans and keep curses away from me!

"Bad cat! Awful cat!" I scolded. But how could she understand? She hunted mice all the time. Why did she have to kill the woodpecker, sacred to Mars, Romulus and Remus, and me? What did this mean? I knew what I must do.

I left the dead bird on the path and ran straight to the Regia, crying in search of Lucius. He would explain the portent. Lucius had moved up in ranks in the last two years and now was Nero's Assistant Chief Augur.

I entered the Regia and almost bumped into a slave. "Where's Lucius? I need to see him," I panted out of breath, wiping my tears.

"I think he's in the courtyard," the slave murmured, rolling his eyes.

I ran down the hall that led out to the courtyard.

There he was, sitting on a bench reviewing some scrolls and tablets. He looked up at me in surprise. "Cornelia, what is the matter? Here, sit." He patted the bench beside him. I sat down and burst into a fresh round of tears.

"I've—I have received a terrible, awful omen. You see ..." I could barely speak.

"Come now. Tell me. I bet it's not all that bad. What happened? You didn't let Vesta's fire burn out, did you?" I shook my head. "So it can't be that horrible. Tell me what happened," he persisted.

I began. "Lucius, my first omen as a Vestal was Picus. Lucretia told me the woodpecker was a guardian. He welcomed me to the Atrium like the other Vestals did."

"Picus?"

"Yes, that was my name—or should I say Lucretia's name—for the green woodpecker that lives near the temple. We named him Picus after the woodpecker who helped feed Romulus and Remus." I wiped my nose and eyes, trying to get the words out.

"And—"

"And then my cat Cleo came to befriend me. The cat that lives in the stable."

"You mean the black and white mouser? I've seen that cat."

"Today the worst possible thing happened." I shook my head and hid my face in my hands trying to block out the image.

"Go on," he gently urged.

"I was out in the garden. I heard a shriek, and then Cleo appeared with Picus in her mouth and laid the bird at my feet. Dead. My guardian is dead! Dead! Killed by Cleo— for me. What does it mean? Right on the Feast of the Lemuria!"

Lucius reached out for my hand and held it for a brief moment. "I agree this is not a good omen, Cornelia. But I don't think you need to take it personally. You are growing up now … how old are you?"

"I am thirteen. I will be fourteen in August."

"You look older than thirteen. But given your age, I can understand being upset. We know your birthday is in August … the sign of the cat."

"That is true, Lucius. But what does it *mean?*" I asked again."It's more than just about me, right?"

Lucius stared forward, looking at what I knew not.

"You are right to bring this information to me, Cornelia. And you could be right—this does not bode well for Rome. But tell me, from what direction did your cat come when she carried the dead bird?"

I thought for a moment. "She came from the west and brought the bird to me in the garden—the east."

I could see Lucius pondering the information. I heard him mumbling the words west, east, cat, bird, and then he stared up into the heavens as if the answer was in the clouds. While he worked his augur skills, I sent a prayer to Vesta on the ether.

"The old order of Rome is dying. The west is the place of endings, the east beginnings. It is a time of endings. Rome will go through her own turmoil. It will not be easy."

"What do you mean endings? Beginnings? Who's in danger? Are we in danger?" My hands and body kept shaking.

"All of Rome may be in danger. It's hard to say. I must think more on this. Remember, cats signify the south, the place of fire. Birds signify east, the air. There could be those who bring new ideas into Rome. For many reasons, this is a danger-ous time for Rome and its citizens."

"What about Nero?" I asked.

"What about him?"

"Is he in danger, too?"

"Perhaps," he allowed. "I will consult with the Priest of Jupiter and the haruspex. They may have added insights." He patted me on the shoulder. Just his touch gave me strength.

"You did well to come to me today, Cornelia. I will think further on this. And I will review some of the lines from the

Sibylline Books and your dreams from a few years ago. Your visions and messages may shed more light on this omen. I know how sad you are at the death of Picus. But you did the right thing coming to me with your concerns."

All day I was sad. How could I get angry with Cleo whose nature it was to hunt and kill? She was still my cat and I loved her.

Before my scheduled fire duty, I decided to devote time to my studies in the library— one of my favorite rooms in the Atrium. Often it was only I, surrounded by hundreds of scrolls, tablets, and papyrus sheaves. I loved the smell of the oiled paper, the wooden shelves, and the mystery of all the knowledge that resided here. How many years of Rome's history were recorded within these walls? Not to mention inside the walls of the Inner Sanctum?

I started to review the history of early Rome. Junia would test me later in the week. I studied the stories of King Numa and some of the first Vestals. The door to the library opened. In walked Rubria, followed by Emperor Nero. They both glanced over at me and frowned.

"What are *you* doing here, Cornelia?" Rubria asked.

"I'm studying. Learning my history," I replied, wondering what *they* were doing in the library today.

As if reading my mind, Nero answered, "I must review some of the wills in the Hall of the Gods. Rubria offered me her assistance."

Rubria blushed, as if she were embarrassed, and pulled out a silver key. She pushed the cloth drapes away from the door and stuck her key in the lock.

"Here, Cornelia, take this key and lock the door. This is a private showing. No one most know," Rubria explained. "You can let us out after we are finished."

"Of course," I said, accepting the key from her.

"You've become a true guardian, haven't you?" Nero seemed pleased with this arrangement. He patted me on the head like I was still a little child.

They entered and were gone. I approached the door and was prepared to lock it, but I heard noises coming from within. I wanted to know more. Silently, I opened the door and crept to the closed door that led to the Inner Sanctum, the Hall of the Gods. I was worried about Rubria—is this what she wanted?

I listened at the inner door.

"Now is the time, Rubria. Show me." The Emperor's voice sounded rough and his command urgent.

"Show you what?" I heard Rubria say.

"You know. You made me a promise."

"Promise?"

"Here is your chance, Rubria. You want me. I know you do. Tell me you want me!"

There was silence.

"Not like this, Caesar. Not here."

"You'll do as I say. You know you want me!"

"Here?" I heard Rubria's voice pleading.

"Why not? I will have what I want from you. I am Emperor, lest you forget!"

"What do you want?"

"You know what I want. Now kiss me!"

What should I do? I wondered. How could I save Rubria from the beastly Nero? How could she go alone—with him— into the Hall of the Gods? But did she have a choice?

261

I heard noises that disturbed me. So they had both lied to me. They didn't care about wills. And *I* must be the guardian of their lies. I thought about barging through the door—and I thought again. I would not intrude on the Emperor and Rubria; I was old enough now to understand what was happening.

The noises became muffled, as though Nero had his hand over Rubria's mouth. I felt powerless to do anything. If this was what Nero commanded, I could do nothing. *Rubria, my sister Vestal was being defiled by the Emperor, a man who supposedly killed his mother, had his wife beheaded, married his mistress, and slept with his slaves!*

All I could do was return to the library, lock the door, and act as if nothing was wrong. I looked up to the ceiling and prayed to Vesta that this defilement of Rubria would not bring a shower of curses on Rome. Between the omen of the dead woodpecker and now this—I did not know what to think or what to expect anymore. But I knew the omens were not good.

CHAPTER 32

JUNE 64 AD

Today was the first day of the Vestalia. The mola salsa was prepared and ready; it sat inside a great vat ready to be distributed to the people. The donkeys, washed, brushed, and garlanded were ready for the procession. And my fourteenth birthday was just two months away. Summer was almost here.

Since May I had thought about dead Picus and what had happened with Rubria and Nero in the Hall of the Gods. Rubria did not seem distressed or disturbed, so why should I? I remembered in my studies that Romulus and Remus were conceived when the God Mars raped Rhea Silvia—the first Vestal Virgin. Did Nero justify his behavior because he thought himself a god?

I told not a soul—not even Vibi—what I had heard. As a novice, I had learned to keep certain things to myself. *The gods know all*, I thought.

Together, the six Vestals waited in the temple for Nero's arrival. He had requested a blessing from Vesta before he embarked on his eagerly anticipated trip to Egypt.

"Why is the Emperor going to Egypt—*now*?" asked Occia, so curious about everything. "During the Vestalia?"

"It appears the Emperor does not change his plans for any goddess—unless that Goddess is Isis," Rubria said smiling. "He wants to be initiated into Her cult. And I think he wants to bring more of Egypt back to Rome."

"What? Another obelisk?" Vibi asked sarcastically.

"No, Vibidia. Rome has enough obelisks. But he will go to Alexandria," said Rubria, as if she knew all of the Emperor's plans. "Perhaps he will bring some new ideas back to Rome. Perhaps he will bring me some gifts as well, and …"

"That is enough! The Emperor's carriage has arrived," said Mother Aurelia having just spoken with the imperial lictor. "Please, let us gather around and welcome our Emperor into the temple."

The temple had already been swept and cleaned. Domicia and the other slaves stood to the side. On the first day of the Vestalia, the temple fire burned evenly and blazed up blue and orange sparks toward the open dome. *A good sign,* I thought.

After Nero's lictors announced his arrival, I noticed Lucius was with him and several of the Praetorian guards.

"Hail, Caesar," we all chorused. "Welcome, Emperor Nero!"

The Emperor was out of breath. "I have just come from the Temple of Jupiter on the Capitoline. I made the proper offerings for a safe journey to Egypt. If I receive a propitious omen from Vesta, all you Vestals will receive gifts from the land of Isis and Osiris."

He looked at Rubria and winked. She blushed. What had overcome her since that day in the library? Had she broken her vows to Vesta?

One of the Emperor's slaves held a small bouquet of white and red flowers. He handed it to Nero, who in turn held it out to Mother Aurelia. "For the Temple of Vesta, esteemed Virgo Maxima."

I noticed Lucius staring at me shaking his head. He looked uncomfortable today, as though he carried a heavy burden. Perhaps he had further messages about the death of Picus—what it all meant.

"Let us proceed into Vesta's temple," Nero said, "for a blessing of safe travels."

He dramatically stepped up to climb the stairs leading to the temple. We all stood bowing to the Emperor in our whitest of freshly laundered white robes, welcoming him into our sacred Temple.

"Please, come in, Caesar." Mother Aurelia extended her hand. The door was now open and we stood along the sides allowing him entry.

But then something happened, something very strange. For when the Emperor tried to enter, a brisk wind started up and began to blow around the temple. Why was Nero not moving or entering the temple? Why was his cloak flapping up and down? I soon saw why. His cloak had become stuck and twisted in the door hinge. And no matter what we tried to do, his heavy cloak would not budge.

"What is this? Now?" he moaned. "What can this mean?" He turned to Lucius, as if Lucius had all the answers.

"Halt, Caesar," was all he said.

"Halt?"

"It is clear, Caesar. Vesta has made it clear you must stay in Rome. The gods have decreed that now is not the time for you to travel to Egypt. Your people need you here—during the Vestalia and through the summer months," said Lucius.

"You mean, I am stuck—here?" asked Nero, as if the gods were meting out a punishment. "Is this why I am trembling all over?" He looked up toward the heavens. "By Jupiter's bolt, why am I trembling so?" The Emperor was indeed shaking, as if he had seen some ghostly shade come to haunt him. His face turned pale, and I feared he was going to be ill.

"You shall not be stuck *here*," said Junia, pulling out her shears. She promptly snipped off a part of his cloak to free him from the dreaded door hinge. Nero wrested himself from the door and shook his head.

"Make certain this door hinge is oiled," he muttered.

Nero never made it into the temple. Instead, he gathered his entourage about him. "Let us return to the palace at once," he proclaimed. "I must continue to consult the augurs and priests concerning my trip." Then I heard him speak under his breath, "Isis, I *must* go."

Nero never left for Egypt.

Instead, after consulting the many priests at his service, he decided he would remain among his people. The omen from Vesta was clear: you are stuck here.

And he wasn't a happy Emperor having his trip to Egypt postponed. I thought that Vesta, our chaste Goddess of the flames, was angry about what he did to Rubria. I hoped Nero wasn't angered with Lucius—the messenger.

The Vestalia continued for the week. I saw and heard little about the Emperor until one afternoon, Rubria burst into my apartment, out of breath. "We've been invited, just the two of us Vestals, to a banquet on Agrippa's lake. Tigillenus has arranged a banquet to appease Nero's sore feeling about his canceled trip to Egypt. They are calling it the Grand Vestalia banquet. I hear many women will be dressed in Egyptian costumes."

"Do I have to go, Rubria?" I asked.

"Mother gave her permission. We are exempt from fire duty tonight. Caesar requests it, Cornelia."

"Whatever Caesar requests, Caesar gets," I said ruefully.

Rubria shrugged off my comment. "I have heard what Tigellinus has done to ready Agrippa's lake," she told me. "There will be moving rafts, music, food. I can't wait."

Agrippa's lake, located at the Campus Martius had been created by Nero's great-grandfather and was linked to the Tiber River by a small canal. An aqueduct fed water into the lake. Gardens surrounded the lake and a lovely basilica, where Nero met with dignitaries, sat along the banks.

What could I do but go? I had no choice. Whatever Emperor Nero proclaimed in Rome was close to the words of a god.

The sun hung over the Forum's temples hot and brazen today. The sky was a typical Roman blue, clear and soothing. It seemed all of the rooftops were tinged with golden fire. Domicia let me know the carriage had arrived and was waiting for us. Before this, she had scraped my body with a stigil and then oiled me down with lavender-and-rose essences.

"Why must I attend this event, Domicia? I want to stay in the Atrium tonight. With you and Vibi … and Vesta," I murmured, as she fixed my headdress and pinned my new vittae on my chest—my first true Vestal badge.

"You must do what the Emperor requests," she said. "Remember, as a servant, I must do what everyone requests," she reminded me.

"Do you wish for your freedom, Domicia?" I asked, realizing it was a foolish question.

"What servant does not wish their freedom?" she replied.

"I'm not free either, Domicia. I am a slave to Junia, to Nero, to Vesta—to Rome!"

"You were chosen, Cornelia," she gently said.

"The same way Romans choose their slaves—at the market!" Now I sounded like Rubria. I realized how cruel and insensitive I sounded, how cruel to compare my plight to that of my devoted servant. At times, I wanted to leave this dark, damp Atrium and escape Rome. Why couldn't I travel to Pompeii to visit Lucretia, who was happy and fulfilled in motherhood? Instead I was being forced to attend the Lake Banquet.

"I am sorry, Domicia. I will be careful what words I choose next time. You've been kind and loving to me." Domicia nodded and bowed to me. She seemed to understand in her quiet way.

Rubria was already awaiting me in the litter. Sure enough, she had outlined her eyes with deep black kohl—like true Egyptian women.

"Look what one of the Priests of Isis lent me." She lifted up a small wood stringed instrument from a cushion next to her.

"What is it?" I asked.

"It's a kittara. The Priests of Isis use it in their rituals." She laughed. "If we can't bring Nero to Egypt, then we will bring Egypt to Nero."

I did not understand how Rubria could bother about the Emperor. He had a new wife Poppaea, plenty of mistresses judging by rumors going around, and then, of course, Rubria herself. Where did she fit in? If she didn't care, why should I? She was always the Vestal who loved attention.

Just as the carriage was about to leave, a knock pounded against the window. It was Junia. Rubria frowned and asked, "Yes? What is it?"

"I have decided I'm coming with you," said Junia. "I am off fire duty and Mother has given me permission. She wants a report on this banquet in *honor* of the Vestalia."

Junia climbed in, snorted, blinked, and squinted at Rubria, clearly alarmed by her black-lined eyes and reddened lips. But she said not a word. *So much for fun*, I thought.

The golden carriage finally arrived at the lake on the Campus Martius. My eyes widened at the sights around the lake. Each section had makeshift inns and taverns set up for the enjoyment of the people. A raft set in the center of the lake was made from wide planks fastened on top of empty wine caskets bobbing in the water. Most of the raft was covered with purple carpets, reclining couches, and pillows. There was even a bed on it! Attached to the raft were several small boats with oarsmen ready to row the raft around the lake.

"This is a banquet to honor the Vestalia?" I asked Rubria. I saw no signs this was a festival to Vesta. Junia stood stiff and tall her nostrils flaring in disapproval.

269

"Hush, Cornelia. This is not the time ..." Rubria said, as she stepped forth near the shore, and gave her imperial wave to the growing crowd.

A few lone boats rowed back and forth, picking up guests and bringing them to the great raft. Other boats delivered food and drink. The sounds of drums, flutes, and trumpets echoed around the lake.

Soon it was our turn to step into a boat and embark toward the raft. "The Emperor has spared nothing for this banquet," Rubria said, rubbing her fingers along the gold and ivory plating that lined the boat. I thought that yes, he could spare money for *his* banquets, while many of Rome's plebes continued to starve.

The boatman strained hard, pulling his oars deep into the water. He seemed miserable, as if he would rather be anywhere but on this lake. I dragged my fingers through the cool water. I saw a brown-green branch floating ... but then a leathery spine emerged with thick bumps all over it. "What's that?" I asked, yanking my hand from the water.

The oarsman chuckled. "We have crocodiles swimming in the lake today—to please Caesar. Just like the crocodiles that lurk in the Nile. It makes the banquet more exotic."

"Will they bite and eat you?" I asked. I decided to keep my hand out of the water.

"Not usually. Unless you are a young, tasty Vestal morsel." The oarsman laughed out loud.

"Row oarsman with your mouth shut," ordered Junia. "Or we will make sure you are the first course for this reptile!"

At the raft, we disembarked from the boat and climbed the few stairs with a railing to help us up. Each corner of the raft had stairs to allow people access. I was surprised to see how many people the raft could hold. I recognized many senators, priests, Lucius, and of course, Tigillenus, Varros, and Poppaea, who happened to be dressed as Cleopatra herself.

In the center of the raft on a lounging couch sat Nero, strumming his stringed instrument, the lyre. He wore a purple toga and a gold, laurel leaf crown. A slave was feeding him grapes.

Then he stood up to greet us. When he saw Junia his face turned downward into a scowl. "We welcome our brides of Rome to the banquet in honor of the Vestalia. All may eat and drink for free. And for this we have Tigillenus to thank." A crowd of cheers arose from the raft.

Tigillenus merely bowed and exclaimed, "Anything for my Emperor."

Nero stared at Junia in disdain and pulled Rubria close to him. I stood there listening.

"What's *she* doing here?" he hissed. "Junia was *not* invited."

"She demanded she come," was all Rubria could say. "There was nothing I could—"

"I will answer your question, Caesar," intruded Junia, who always seemed to overhear everything. "Mother Aurelia gave me permission because she wants a report about the banquet— how you and the people will honor Vesta today."

A great laugh burst forth from Nero's mouth, and his thick neck bobbed up and down. "Oh, she'll get a report all right. And I for one, do not care what is in that report!" His blood-red face drew close to Junia's pale one. "Lest you forget, I am Emperor. Lest you forget, I requested these two Vestals—my favorites if it be known— to attend *my* banquet. Not you!"

Junia started to mumble a reply, but it was too late. Ignoring her comments, Nero moved on, greeting the incoming dignitaries and guests. Then he swung his purple cloak around, raised his silver goblet, and made a toast. "I have chosen to remain in Rome for the love of my people. The augurs have decreed I stay. I know there are people in Rome who conspire against me. And people who preach against me in other lands. We will soon stop this slander against me, against our gods—against the glories of Rome. We'll bring him back in chains again, if need be! I've heard and seen enough of the Cult of the Nazarene. Bah!"

Nero glanced around at the captivated crowd. "So let us drink to all the gods that reside in Rome … be they Apollo, Isis, Jupiter …" and he looked over at us, "… even Vesta. To the Gods and Goddesses!"

Many lifted their goblets and shouted, "To the Gods and Goddesses! Hail, Caesar" and drank to the health of their Emperor and Rome.

"Let the banquet commence," shouted Nero.

And what a banquet! I didn't know where to look first. I couldn't take my eyes off the hundreds of multicolored parrots flying around the lake, landing anywhere they chose—even on noblewomen's heads.

Then Nero ordered the rowers to pull the lengthy raft along the lake's edge.

"There's my little snake charmer." He pointed to me. "So tell me, Cornelia, do you see any snakes around me?" He stared at Lucius, Varros, Tigillenus, Poppaea, and then gestured to the crowd.

"No, Caesar, but I saw a crocodile."

That made the Emperor laugh. As the raft was slowly pulled around the lake, I noticed a cluster of women milling under one of the tents. They waved and smiled; they wore plumed headdresses and batted bright fans in front of their faces. Many of them dressed in bright-colored stolas, red and orange. I wondered why they were standing there waving.

"Play for me, my Vestal," Nero ordered Rubria, who displayed her kittara and began strumming it and then managed a few twirls of her robes on the bobbing raft. With Rubria busy and Junia glaring at the festivities, I noticed Lucius coming toward me.

"Greetings, Cornelia," he said. He looked tired, his eyes glazed. I asked him how the auguries looked. Had he discussed Picus's death with anyone?

"Can you come to the Regia sometime after the Vestalia? I must speak with you," he whispered. "It's important."

"I'll try," I said.

"What's all this?" Nero appeared from behind us. "We do not talk business at a banquet. Now, my little snake charmer, dance for me."

So I danced. Alongside Rubria, we performed for the Emperor. I had gotten my wish after all. Nero seemed pleased.

The raft continued around the lake, the oarsmen groaning under its weight. A flock of red and blue parrots circled around us, acting as if they were lost and confused. One even dared to hover close to one of the crocodiles, only to be snapped up in its jaws.

The raft headed toward a remote, secluded part of the lake. Several makeshift huts held by poles stood with markings emblazoned on their roofs. Many of the markings were crude symbols I had seen on Rome's walls—graffiti. Then several women under the huts came forth, and began stripping their clothes off. The woman gestured obscenely in the direction of the raft. Tigillenus, Varros, Nero, and even Poppaea thought this amusing; they laughed and chuckled with each other.

"Who are these women?" I asked Rubria.

"Common prostitutes hired by Nero," Rubria said.

"Why?" I asked.

I felt a cold hand cover my eyes. "You should *not* see this, Cornelia. It's not a sight for young eyes, certainly not a novice Vestal." Then Junia cleared her throat, dropped her hand away from my eyes, and marched up to Nero.

"We will not endure such vile entertainment, Caesar. Not during the Vestalia. My novice-in-training has no business watching such … such crude behavior. Take us back immediately. I will report my findings to the Chief Virgo Maxima."

Nero laughed in her face. "And what is *she* going to do—to *me*? The Emperor of Rome? Scourge me?" His laugh, loud and raucous, caused the raft to quake.

"Why, Caesar, this defilement is tempting the fates," Junia said firmly. "This could cause Vesta's fire to be put out. How dare you tempt the wrath of Vesta?"

"Remember your place, Junia. And Vulcan's fire is far stronger than Vesta's puny flame." Nero laughed again, and everyone around him joined in. They did appear to be tempting fate and did not care. As long as Nero had Egypt brought to him, he was happy. I noticed Lucius shaking his head in disgust.

"Take these Vestals back to shore. They have seen enough," Nero ordered the oarsman. "But not before I take this," and before I knew it, he grabbed Rubria and kissed her full on the lips. "Take them away," he shouted, roaring with laughter, "Back to the Atrium."

CHAPTER 33

JULY 15TH 64 AD

After the banquet I suffered nightmares and strange dreams. The images all melded together like a mosaic, but I could not see the whole picture. Everything seemed cloaked in gray. I saw the dead woodpecker and the wanton women along the shores of Agrippa's lake, provocatively luring the Emperor and his men closer and closer. Then the old woman from the Subura appeared, cackling and telling me many would perish.

It was a month after the Vestalia ended; life in the Atrium was busy. I shared with Vibi about what I'd seen at the banquet, and how dismayed I was to witness such disrespect to Vesta. I told her what Nero said about Paul. Why now, when Nero had freed him two years ago? How was Paul a threat when he was preaching in Spain?

Today I finally had time before late afternoon fire duty. I decided I must find Lucius. Whatever he wanted to discuss with me sounded urgent. As I walked the short distance to the Regia, I saw Cleo appear from under a bush. "How could you?" I scolded her, still angry over her killing Picus. She just blinked at me so innocent looking. How could I remain angry with her? I picked her up and nestled her into the folds of my stola. The familiar purring started up and it reassured me.

Lucius was sitting in the Regia courtyard, putting in order a set of wooden tablets. "Good morning," I said.

He looked up at me and saw the cat, whose black and white face appeared from the folds of my stola. "I see you brought the murderess with you," he said, a faint smile on his face.

"I have forgiven Cleo her wrong. That's what Paul told us to do. Forgive." *What had I just said?* The words seemed to flutter right out of my mouth.

"Paul? The one who was imprisoned years ago on house arrest?"

"Yes— so I've heard. That is the message he shared with Rome. I'm glad he's free now."

"I see." That was all he said. Lucius flipped over the wooden tablets that made a clicking noise, and then rubbed his chin with the blunt end of the stylus.

"Cornelia, we have been consulting the Sibylline Books. And of course, I have been reviewing all the portents you have previously given to me."

I felt honored to hear that my visions and dreams mattered. "And …"

Cleo, becoming restless, leapt from my arms and bounded into some nearby bushes, back to her hunter's mode. I couldn't stop her. I felt as if I could stop nothing from happening in Rome. But perhaps I could help—a little.

"Nero is not pleased with my auguries, Cornelia," Lucius said, shaking his head. "Sometimes I think I would be better off feeding him lies instead of the truth. When the omens are bad, the augurs get the blame. My ancestors from Etruria must tremble in their tombs, thinking of how debased this sacred art has become under Nero's reign."

"Etruria? My ancestors are also from Etruria," I said. "Cosa, in fact."

Lucius laughed. "I thought as much." His eyes twinkled for a moment. "You have Etruscan eyes, wide, blue, and filled with light and intelligence."

I must have blushed because my face felt hot.

Then he stood up and came closer to me. "The Emperor has gone mad, I tell you. Mad! The demise of the woodpecker, the Lake Banquet so debased, and the Sibylline Books ... I'm concerned, Cornelia."

"Would you like to use my bulla again?" I pulled it from my pouch and offered it to him.

"By Jupiter's throne, I am not sure even *that* would work. I tell you this because Nero has just left on a trip."

"Trip? He just canceled his trip to Egypt. On account of his wanting to be with the people," I said.

"Indeed. He is now traveling to Antium just twenty miles away from Rome. To his ocean resort. But it's far enough, Cornelia, to cause a commotion among the people. You see, the omens are such that Nero may be scheming. The city is unsettled. Something is brewing in the air ... I can feel it. The piercing of the woodpecker, the direction the wind blows, recent recordings of the flight of birds ... it's not good. Cornelia, have you seen or heard anything else ... anything unusual?"

I thought for a moment. "No ... but I have had strange dreams."

He sat back down on the bench and patted the area next to him. "Sit down. Tell me please." He took a deep breath and was ready to listen.

"They were nightmares all strung together. There was Picus, dead and bloodied; the image of Nero's raft on the lake; and then the old woman appeared to me, cackling with laughter."

"An old woman cackling?" he repeated.

"Yes. She told me many would perish … but I would be safe."

"Hmm." He shook his head. "I will ponder further your visions. And we shall talk again soon."

I decided to visit Vibi during her fire duty in the temple. Vibi sat as always, face expressionless, placing wedges of wood gently onto Vesta's flame. The smell of the sacred wood burning always soothed me. I loved to watch the yellow, red, orange, blue, and black flames bend up, then down and around, as though they danced.

Vibi had gone through so much; yet she seemed stronger than ever. It didn't matter to me what god she had faith in. My heart was filled with love for her. I respected her faith, her courage, her secret beliefs; and her willingness to suffer for her beliefs, for her God, Jesus Christ and His prophet, Paul. I would never tell a soul.

Vibi lifted her head from her private reverie and smiled. How are things?" she asked me.

"I don't know, Vibi. I am still haunted by Nero's words at the banquet— that he wants the prisoner Paul back in chains. He is distrustful and accuses people of speaking about him.

Should we send our messages unto the ether to try to keep Paul free?"

Vibi shook her head. "I think it best not to play with another's fate. Jesus made the ultimate sacrifice ... and Paul follows in his Master's footsteps."

Do nothing? Did she know something? I had an idea. "I feel like viewing the Palladium. Maybe the ancient spirit of the statue has a message for me—for us!"

Vibi nodded still in her own world.

I approached the alcove with reverence, pulled the curtain aside, and opened the little cupboard containing the sacred statue we Vestals protected. There she was, the smooth olive wood smudged from the countless hands that had held it, blackened from the fires that burned in Troy. Her armored breastplate glowed with specks of light from Vesta's flame. I noticed the deep grooves carved with great care into her flowing robe. And the faint outline of the monstrous face leering out from her shield frightened me. What stories did she hold within her? What stories could she tell me?

Her face looked serene, sad yet calm. I gazed into the eyes of the Goddess of Wisdom. Was this truly the statue carried in the arms of Aeneas from the burning flames of Troy?

I gathered in my breath, held it, and then released it with a deep sigh. What message did Minerva have for me? I waited. I listened. And then I heard:

"My child, the armor I wear is the price of freedom and wisdom.
Yet sorrows lie under my breastplate.
There shall be sorrows.
And then there shall be a new day."

I thanked the Goddess and rushed back to Vibi to share the message I had just received.

"Sorrows? I could have told you *that*," she muttered, stoking the flame.

"And then there shall be a new day," I reminded her.

"In Rome, each new day brings nothing but vulgarity, defilement, and disregard," she said.

"But Vibi, where is *your* faith?" I asked her.

"I have no faith in Nero nor in the gods and goddesses. What have the gods done to save Rome from this monster we call Caesar?" She stirred the ashes that sent sparks up into the air. They floated toward the open dome. "Nero is filled with himself. Nothing else," she quietly mused.

"But Vibi—"

"Cornelia, you know where my faith lies," she told me. "My faith, like these sparks, is with the unseen world. My faith lies with the one true God."

I could speak with her no more on this. But I could share this with Lucius, who wanted to know more about my messages.

I found him in the West Wing of the Regia, carefully stacking tablets in a secure place.

"Back so soon?" He smiled at me, his head leaning to the side. "Why, you're out of breath. What has happened now?"

"Is it safe to speak here?" I asked.

"Let's return to the courtyard. It's better in the open air. More private as well."

We sat once again while I shared with him the message from the Palladium.

"So there will be sorrows," he repeated. "And then there will be a new day. More and more senators rebuke Nero's debased ways. Just after the banquet, he arranged a mock marriage with his freed slave."

"I thought he was already married—to Poppaea," I said.

"It was a mock marriage, Cornelia. A marriage based on the lust of his loins. People are now comparing him to his uncle, the Emperor Caligula."

Caligula? I shuddered.

"But the end of the message bodes well. Rome will survive Nero, but will Nero survive Rome?" Lucius asked, wondering.

That, I thought, was the question. Suddenly feeling tired I told Lucius that if any more messages came to me, he would be the first and only person to know. I could keep others' secrets. Surely Lucius would keep mine

CHAPTER 34

JULY 18-20TH 64 AD

After my fire duty with Vibi, I decided to sit in the garden to cool myself. It was twilight; a half moon rose bright and stars began to blink in the sky. I thought I was alone. But there was Rubria walking along the garden path.

"Rubria," I called out to her. She turned and came toward me.

"Cornelia, I thought you had fire duty," she said.

"I'm finished," I told her. "It's so hot this summer, hotter than ever."

"I know. All those dark clouds that threatened rain did nothing—the wind that stirred only blew the clouds out to sea."

The wind had started up, blowing from the north. And what a hot, wicked wind it was—nothing like the crisp autumn and spring breezes that picked up my spirits. But the thought of my fourteenth birthday next month gave me something to look forward to.

Maybe the wicked breezes put another thought into my head.

"Rubria, what happened between you and Emperor Nero—when I was studying in the library?"

She came close to me. "What do you mean … what happened?" she asked.

"Did you … did you break your vows to Vesta?"

"Cornelia, please. Whatever Caesar wants, Caesar gets."

"So you did break your vows," I said, trying not to judge her. "And if you did, I will not tell a soul."

Rubria embraced me and began to cry. "I had no choice, Cornelia. He wanted me."

"And you wanted—*him*?"

"You shall understand someday … how all women desire love and attention from a man. What could I do? What could the first Vestal, Rhea Silvia, do when she was raped by Mars?"

"Nero is not a god," I reminded her.

"But he thinks he is!"

I understood she had little choice. The Emperor forced himself on her. But why did she display herself in front of him? I thought of her conduct at the Lake Banquet.

Others might report her, tattle, and condemn her. But once again, I remembered the words of Paul—the words about leaving the past behind and of forgiveness.

"Vesta forgives you, Rubria," I told her.

She crumpled into my arms, like a child looking for comfort from a mother. I realized now was the time, especially now, that we Vestals must be united. All we had was each other.

"Rubria, look!" I glanced over the garden walls, staring up at the palaces surrounding us. Between the buildings, coming from what looked like the east end of the Circus Maximus, puffs of gray smoke rose like thick clouds. In between the plumes of smoke, tiny flames started to appear, shooting up into the air every so often.

"Look Rubria!" I pointed toward the smoke.

"Just another fire from a food vendor who doesn't clean his greasy stone," she declared. "I am sure they will send out the *vigiles cohorts* with their water buckets. They always manage to put out these pesky fires."

The next day I woke up early. After I took my morning bath, and said my prayers to Vesta, I decided to spend time in the garden again. Junia had tutored me about the stars in the heavens, and that this was the time of year that Sirius the dogstar rose early in the morning. There it was blinking blue sparks of light. I watched it for a moment before it faded behind the clouds.

As I looked up through the palace walls, I realized that the clouds that blocked my view were from a fire. Puffs of smoke continued to bloom in the air.

So Rubria was wrong. The vigiles did not or could not put out this persistent fire! I did not know if this was the same fire or a new one. Rome always suffered from fires started by vendors or people cooking around a flame. And Rome's wicked winds had a mind of their own; they often blew sparks of flames across the seven hills.

I decided to run up to the Emperor's palace so I could get a better view of where the smoke was coming from. I wanted to see for myself. Standing next to one of the Emperor's walls, I looked down at the great hill below me.

The Circus Maximus was on fire!

Flames encircled the great horseshoe shaped arena. I could see many of the wooden structures becoming engulfed in flames, collapsing on top of one another, folding together like burning scrolls. The alarm bell was ringing, and the vigiles ran up and down the hill with buckets. The sounds of women screeching, men shouting for help, children crying, animals howling—made me understand this fire was serious—and dangerous.

Plumes of smoke continued to rise high over Rome. The smell of burning wood, the crashing sounds, the ashes circling around the great flames that leaped higher and higher made me shake. A giant haze started to hang over parts of Rome.

The hot wind still blew in from the north. *Perhaps we are safe,* I thought. *The wind will fan this fire south. But what of my family on the Aventine Hill?* With the Emperor gone to Antium, who would be in charge of the Roman people, some of who may be in grave danger?

I ran back down the hill right into Domicia. She was searching for me out of breath, and looked alarmed. "That horrid fire from last night still burns, Domicia. I'm scared," I told her. I thought of the Sibylline Books, my dreams, my family, Vesta, the message from the Palladium—the sorrows before a new day.

"Cornelia, Mother Aurelia has requested a meeting in the temple. Now!"

We rushed to the temple where all the vestals stood waiting for me. Thankfully, Vesta's flame burned steady.

"Vestals," Mother calmly stated, "I have just received the latest reports. A fire has broken out along the Circus Maximus. It's a stubborn flame, fanned by this northerly wind. The vigiles are working to put it out. Reports are the flame is continuing south toward the Aventine Hill."

"Aventine Hill? That's where my family lives," I cried. "I must find out if they are all right." I started trembling again, thinking my family home could burn to the ground.

Mother Aurelia approached me and placed her hand on my shoulder.

"There's not much we can do for the rest of Rome or your family, Cornelia, except to send out prayers. Have faith," was all she said.

I thought of the crone's words to us that night. *"Many will perish, but you will be safe."*

Addressing all of us now, Mother said, "And there is good news for us. The wind continues to blow from the north. I'm happy to report that this troublesome fire is heading away from the Forum, away from Vesta's temple, and away from the Atrium. We are safe. Vesta's fire burns with purity. The relics are safe. Let us give thanks and let us pray for those suffering due to this fire."

Rome's fire kept burning. We Vestals continued to carry on with our duties. As long as the fire burned to the south, we were safe.

Vibi and I sat in the temple, stirring up embers and staring into Vesta's pure light.

"So the sorrows do begin," Vibi muttered. "For a new day."

"Now you finally believe the message from Minerva?" I asked her.

"Many people *shall* die. I see that now, Cornelia. And many shall die for their faith. All for a new day."

"Would *you* die for your faith, Vibi?"

"Yes, of course I would. My faith as a follower of Jesus Christ!"

"Vibi, shush! Others might be listening."

"True, Cornelia, but my faith is stronger than my duties, stronger than my scars, or even my vows to Vesta. I cling to my faith. That's all I have—that's all any of us have."

Where did my faith lie? With Vesta? With the words of Lucius? With the words of Paul that still resided in my heart? Certainly not with Caesar—or even with Rome.

The next day the fire raged on. The smell of charred wood, embers, soot, and smoke continued to fill the air, clogging my nose and throat and making me feel ill. Maybe it was a new and distinctive smell I could not recognize; I thought it must be the smell of death itself. Was it burning flesh that the fire also consumed?

We were given reports that the fire had engulfed the Aventine, Caeline, and parts of the Palatine Hill. All we could do was pray that the Forum, Vesta's temple, and the Atrium remain untouched. So far we were safe.

A messenger arrived announcing that Emperor Nero was on his way home from Antium. His planned theatrical performance by the ocean was thwarted; rumors of looting in the city were spreading like the fire itself. Rome, like her Emperor, seemed to have gone mad—consumed by an inferno that now seemed unstoppable.

All I could do was pray and continue my devotions to Rome's wellbeing and safety, and tend to Vesta's flame. We had to place our faith in the vigiles cohorts, Rome's fire brigade, buckets in hand, throwing water at the raging flames. My view from the Atrium made me feel as though I was on an island surrounded by a sea of fire.

CHAPTER 35

JULY 22ND 64 AD

And still we carried on guarding Vesta's flame. So far the Forum, the Regia, the Atrium, and the Temple of Vesta had been spared. But the fire fanned by the wind continued to consume the shops along the Circus; the sound of timber upon timber collapsing and crashing down on each other unnerved me. But it was the continuous cries of babies, the howls of dogs, and desperate screams from people that penetrated my soul. Embers floated in the air like dust motes, a danger to anything they landed on.

It was the third day of the fire. According to Rubria, the Emperor had returned home and was surveying the damage the fire had wrought. And according to Mother Aurelia, we *still* had nothing to worry about. She told us that those in danger, those near the Circus who had lost everything, were forced to make their way to the Campus Martius, a place of safety.

I prepared for my fire duty with Vibidia again. Although she claimed she had her faith, she looked tired and pale, as if she had gone somewhere deep inside herself. Domicia would aid us today in the temple, delivering sacred water for the daily cleansing. Life went on as normal for the Vestals ... as Rome continued to burn.

Vibi and I walked to the temple to relieve Junia and little Occia. A haze of smoke hung over Rome, with a flick of a flame springing to life every now and then. I had my bulla with me today. I would call on the powers of Neptune if need be. Perhaps my prayers would be heeded; perhaps Neptune would send us the rain needed to quell this horrible blaze.

Vibi nudged me. "Look," was all she said and pointed up. New flames now snaked up dangerously close to the Capitoline Hill.

"Do you think it is headed this way?" I asked her.

"We will know soon enough," she said.

"It's about time," Junia exclaimed when she saw us. "We've been waiting and we both are tired and hungry. Is there any news about the fire? Are they containing it?"

"We have heard nothing today," said Vibi. "But it's clear the flames are closing in. Look up at the Capitoline ..."

They left with Junia muttering about how incompetent these vigiles were in their attempt to extinguish the fire.

"Maybe my bulla with Neptune's trident will help. I am willing to pray to Neptune, my family's patron God," I said.

"Pray to whatever god you want," Vibi said, stoking Vesta's flame with fresh wood. She seemed resigned to accept whatever fate had for her.

We continued our fire duty as if nothing was amiss. Domicia reported that the vigiles had created a bucket line from the spring of Juturna. They needed any water they could find. She told us there were bucket lines all over the city; from the Tiber River, they doused parts of the Aventine, all along the Caelian Hill, and now they focused on the Capitoline. I thought of my family on the Aventine and prayed for their safety.

Even in Vesta's temple, I could sense the destruction around me; the acrid smell of smoke, the floating ashes, and the screams of people, perhaps jumping from their apartments to either safety or to death. But in Vesta's temple, I still felt safe, protected and insulated from the chaos enveloping Rome. All I could do was place my faith in Vesta—and Neptune.

Domicia appeared at the door with more water. "The fire brigade has managed to quell parts of the inferno," she told us. "But now they say that a new fire has sprung up on the Capitoline, near the house of Tigellinus."

Tigellinus?

"Mother Aurelia said if there's any danger she will inform us. Until then we continue to tend to Vesta's fire."

And so we did. In between the horns blasting and bells ringing, we continued on as if nothing mattered but our Vestal duties. *We will get through this,* I thought. *We must.* But I felt differently in my heart as these new flames crept ever closer. I could feel the heat in my bones— then for some reason I began to shiver.

After a few hours of silent reflection and somber moments, Domicia burst into the temple out of breath. "Mother Aurelia has been given the orders. Everything and everybody along the Capitoline and the Forum is in danger. We must leave the premises immediately!"

I looked up through the hole in the temple dome. I could no longer see the sky. I couldn't tell if it was Vesta's smoke, and if it now mingled with the new fire of Rome. A blanket of haze hung over the Temple ... I could feel it ... a gray cloud that kept growing.

I coughed and tried to catch my breath. I stood over Vesta's fire, lifted my bulla from my pouch, and prayed to Neptune out loud. "Neptune, my family patron, bring us the rains to put this inferno out. The Temple of Vesta must be saved," I shouted. "For the sake of Rome!"

I knew what I must do. "As within, so without," I said aloud, sending the message unto the ether. Then, with a great flourish, I threw my bulla right onto Vesta's unwavering flame.

Vibi raised her eyebrows, and we both stared at my bulla glowing in Vesta's fire.

"Please, girls, we must leave now," said Domicia. Sweat dripped down her face. She kept returning to the temple door. "Hurry!"

I ran to the door. Sure enough, high atop the Capitoline Hill, the flames arched downward toward the Forum. The wind blew the flames sideways. I heard the great temples groan under the fire's power; pillars began to crumble and topple over. Now our sacred temples were a danger to all of us, weapons that could easily crush anyone beneath them.

"Wait," I shouted. "What about the Palladium?" I approached the alcove, drew back the curtain and began to grasp for Minerva.

"Yes, yes, take the statue," Vibi said, "and place her in the stone box next to the altar." I grabbed the covered Palladium off the pedestal, found the box, settled her inside and carefully fastened the latch. Then I tucked it in my stola.

"Let's go," I said, and the three of us left the temple now unguarded.

All of the other Vestals stood in front of the Atrium await-ing us. Poor Occia was crying and coughing. Carts were being filled up with the sacred relics, the wills from the library and the Inner Sanctum— and anything else of importance.

"We have word from the Emperor. There's a firebreak to the side of the Esquiline. We make our way to the Gardens of Maecenas. The Emperor is setting up tents for us," announced Mother.

This new fire fueled by a new wind was consuming the Capitoline Hill. It was still day in Rome. Yet it seemed the city was enveloped in endless night, so dark and black was the smoke. The fire was now a giant, a great black beast that stam-peded across Rome, devouring everything in its path.

"Quick, get into the carts. We must go now!" shouted Mother. "Junia and I will travel by litter. Cover your faces. And don't look back. May Vesta bless us all."

Domicia, already in the cart held out her arms. I handed her the sacred statue. She placed it with the other relics, and helped me into the packed wagon.

The wagon pushed through the tangled mass of people along the Via Sacra, past the top of the Palatine until we reached the entrance to the Esquiline Hill. Great villas and buildings recently knocked down for the sake of the firewall stood in a heap; a homely honor of what was. Stragglers making their way up the greatest hill of Rome trudged slowly, as if they were not certain of where to go. The putrid smells of smoke mixed with floating cinders made it hard to breathe. The wind and fire shrieked a dreadful hissing noise as the stench of burning wood mingled with flesh filled my nose. I covered my face with my stola. My Vestal robes looked as gray as the Roman sky, soiled and ashy.

I thought of our nocturnal visits to Paul—his words and reminders about pressing forward and leaving the past behind; all seemed so true to me at this moment. Not only had I left my family four years ago, now I must leave my home, the Atrium, and the Temple of Vesta behind.

I grabbed the box that held the statue of Minerva and clutched it close to me, She who had survived the fires of Troy! I would make certain she would survive this as well. But what of those I loved? I knew not the fate of my family or my friend Cynthia.

Up the hill we progressed, bumping and bounding, as the wagoneer cursed at anyone in our way. He shouted that he carried the sacred Vestals and the relics, so get out of the road!

We arrived at the untouched Gardens of Maecenas, where a great tower stood at the entrance. We watched in silence from the great hill, staring out at the destruction that once was Rome.

I started to feel sick; my stomach began heaving. Maybe it was the smoke, the blackness of day, the cries for help … still I clung to the statue. And I clung to hope.

"Vibi, I feel sick," I told her and began to cry.

"I know, I know," was all she said. She put her arm around me. Others had started to arrive. I grasped my throat with one hand, while I held the Palladium in the other.

"I can't breathe, Vibi. Am I dying?" I asked her. My world as I knew it was disappearing into flames.

"Cornelia, we are safe. The Palladium is safe. All the relics are safe," she assured me. "We are far enough away from danger."

But when I closed my eyes, all I saw were the flames, the heavy clouds of smoke and destruction. I needed a rest from this nighmare.

"I need to sleep, Vibi." Maybe when I woke up, it would prove to be just that—a nightmare.

"There will be time to rest, Cornelia," she said.

But all I could do was fall to the ground, curl myself into a ball, and cradle the box holding our sacred statue, hoping this was a bad dream. And then, like a bad dream, all went dark.

CHAPTER 36

Did I dream that fateful night on the Esquiline? And was my dream real? For when I awoke in the middle of the night, I thought I saw Emperor Nero atop the tower behind the gardens gesturing to the flames. He stood with his arms stretched and was singing! He looked to be in a trance, as if the fire possessed him! He wore a gold laurel wreath that glowed on his head.

A few days passed with no word. We awaited news—any news. And the news finally came. A messenger arrived late in the morning. "The Capitol is gone. The Forum is gone. All the temples are destroyed," he solemnly announced. "There's nothing left."

"What of the Atrium? Our home?" Mother Aurelia inquired, fretting like a hen.

"Gone I'm afraid," he said, shaking his head. "Nothing but ash and rubble." He paused regarding our downcast faces. "But the good news is the fire is almost out."

Most of the Vestals burst into tears. The Atrium had been their home for years. We clung to one another for solace. We had no temple, no sacred fire to tend, and I knew now that Rome's blaze had consumed and engulfed Vesta's flames, taking the safety and protection of Rome with it.

We really had not much to do besides welcome and help other lucky stragglers into tents. Most of the plebes of the city, those who managed to escape, had taken refuge at the Campus Martius. We also received word that Nero was offering free grain to the people as consolation.

Restless, I asked Vibi if she would come with me to the Aventine. I needed to know the fate of my family. "Rome has just burned for the second time, Cornelia. Now is not the time," she told me.

"You owe me this request, Vibi. I need to see if my family and my family villa are safe. Can we hire a litter?"

"Hire a litter? There are no litters available, Cornelia," she said. "Can you not see that everything has changed?"

"Then we can take a wagon," I said, my stubbornness returning. "Or walk." Vibi sat across from me in the tent, staring out into the gray haze that still hung over Rome.

People were coming and going now, reporting to the Emperor, who had his tents set up near ours. Rumors were starting to spread, according to many of the arrivals, that Nero was responsible for the blaze.

While I sat with Vibi considering ways I could check on my family villa, Lucius appeared from the top of the hill and approached us. His face and hair were filled with soot and ashes; he smelled like burned wood.

"Are you missing something?" he asked me.

"I am missing everything," I told him. "My family, my new home ... all is lost."

"Not all, Cornelia."

Vibi suddenly appeared interested in what the augur had to say and raised her eyes to look at him. Lucius rummaged through his cloak and pulled forth a lump of gold.

"On my way back from the Capitoline Hill, where I'd gone to check on the Temple of Jupiter to make sure we retrieved the Sibylline Books, my augur's staff led me to the Forum. The Emperor commanded I record any auguries on the Capitol and the Forum. And yes, I found the remains of Vesta's Temple. This is the first time I have ever been allowed in!"

Both Vibi and I smiled. We needed some light talk and a bit of humor. We all knew that Emperor Nero was the *only* man allowed in the temple. I remembered the day Vesta had refused him entry when his cloak got stuck in the door. I hoped Vesta had not taken revenge on the Emperor—on all of us—for what he did to Rubria.

"Here you are, Cornelia. And I take this as an auspicious omen."

I looked at his outstretched palm. There was my bulla, partially melted and broken off at one end. But Neptune's trident still remained with a new blackened gleam upon it—gold touched by fire.

"Thank you, Lucius. I am grateful. This gives me hope,"

I convinced Junia I must go see if my family had survived the inferno. The voice of the crone haunted me the voice that exclaimed many would perish. I was tired of waiting for messengers while I had nothing to do. I told Junia that Vibi would accompany me.

Junia frowned but gave us permission saying we must be back soon. She even found a litter for us. Junia explained that later in the day, the Emperor wanted to rekindle a small flame for Vesta at the gardens, a pale substitute, but one of necessity for the future of Rome. Nero also called for a meeting later that afternoon that included the Vestals, the flamens, the varied priests, and the augurs. Junia ordered we must return on time for this important meeting.

We began our descent down the Esquiline. Although the fire was officially out, each side of the road was heaped with still-smoldering ruins. Signs of looting were evident.

I clutched my bulla with great hope. But when we finally turned past the Circus Maximus to proceed down the Aventine, my heart dropped. The Circus was now nothing but a hollowed-out crater, a gray- black monster still fuming with puffs of smoke. The horror that people had suffered! Could Emperor Nero possibly be responsible for so much loss? And so much pain?

As if reading my mind, Vibi said, "They say Nero sang the 'Ode to Troy' from the tower in the gardens while he watched Rome burn to the ground. Could you believe that?"

"Yes, I believe it," I said.

"People are whispering that he was behind the destruction. That *he* wanted Rome to burn."

"But why, Vibi? I asked.

"Why? He wants the land, Cornelia. For himself, that's why. He wants a newer and bigger palace." She turned to look at me. "You are too young to understand the greed that hides in men's hearts." She shook her head.

"No, I am not." I started to defend myself. "My father received three bags of gold for me. That's all he cared about on that day—my birthday, too!"

"Have you forgiven him his greed?" she asked me.

I thought for a moment. "Yes, I think so. But maybe not …" My voice trailed off as the litter turned right onto the road along the Tiber and passed the Cave of Cacus.

"Look Vibi!"

Written on the side of the cave big, bold black letters proclaimed, "Nero Arsonist."

"So this *is* what people think," said Vibi. "They are probably right."

"I don't know, Vibi. I just need to know if my family is alive."

I was relieved to see that not all of the Aventine had burned to the ground. The fact my family villa was so close to the Tiber reassured me. I imagined the vigiles using the waters of Father Tiber, filling bucket after bucket in their long lines to save whatever they could.

We finally arrived at the place where the wharves began. "Let us out here," I commanded. I began to survey the area. My family villa was not far away. But something told me to look among the wharves. Several were just blackened piles of wood now. Others remained barely intact.

I noticed several men milling around the docks, speaking among themselves in low voices. Nearby, two lone figures sat on the stone steps leading to a dock. Maybe they knew. "Let's go, Vibi." I tugged at her stola. Our robes had turned a blackish-gray, as if they had been permanently stained by smoke and ash. All of Rome seemed covered in a film of gray cinder and soot. There wasn't enough water in Rome for a washing.

We hastened down the steps toward the dock. Then I gasped for a breath! I recognized now that it was my father seated with our servant, Taltos.

"Father," I shouted. "Father!" My father stood up glancing around for the voice. He looked dishelved. His hair had turned as gray as Rome itself. Taltos had grown taller and still retained his graceful bearing. He wore the pointed cap of a freedman.

"Who calls?" said father, turning around to behold us. Then he rubbed his hands over his eyes for a brief moment. "Can it be my daughter? Returned to me?" he cried.

"Yes, it is me, Cornelia. I had to see if my family was safe."

We embraced. All the smells of my father came back to me, the fish oil, the wine, smells I hated as a child. I didn't care that he smelled like fish oil and smoke. He was my father—and he was alive! I saw Vibi and Taltos wiping tears from their eyes.

"Where's the rest of the family? Did they make it to safety?"

Father continued to hold me, his body shaking. "The family escaped. Mother and Cornelius are at the Campus Martius—living under a tent."

"With the plebes?" I asked, my eyes wide.

"Cornelia, the Campus Martius was the closest place for us to escape. Thousands await word from Nero."

"Why are you here now, Father?" I asked him.

"I am awaiting shipments from Ostia. I have word the port is backed up with goods. So my new freedman, Taltos and I wait."

Taltos stood up straight, beaming with a newfound pride. I pushed away from my father and embraced Taltos.

"I am so happy for you, Taltos. What will you do now?"

"Thank you, Cornelia. I am free, yet I choose to remain with your father. He is my patron now."

"More like a business partner," said my father, with respect in his voice.

"And you will always be a part of the family—my family."
I burst into tears of relief and joy. "What of the villa, father?"
I finally asked.

"The fire burned out the back of the house, destroying
the garden and cooking areas. The front of the house and the
atrium, thanks to the hard work of the vigiles, was saved."

"What of my friend Cynthia? Did she survive?"

Father looked away to the ever-flowing current of the
Tiber. "I'm sorry to tell you this, Cornelia. Cynthia and her
family did not make it out in time. She is gone." He embraced
me again, and I sobbed with sorrow over my friend's death—
and the death of her dreams of marriage and motherhood.

Father pulled me away and looked into my eyes. "Daughter, I am so proud of you. Your mother, brother, and I miss you
every day."

I wanted to ask him why no one from my family visited
me in the Atrium, and why I wasn't invited to Taltos's freeing
ceremony, but now was not the time. I looked deep into my
father's Etruscan eyes, eyes I had inherited from him.

"Do you need anything from me—from us, the Vestal
order?" I asked him, signaling Vibi over.

Father thought for a moment. "We may need some money,
Cornelia. For the business."

"Whatever you need, Father, I will make certain you get it,
even if I have to request a private audience with Nero. Soon I
will come into my own money, money that I can do with what
I will, even if it means buying my family a villa in Cosa—or
Pompeii. Money is never a worry with the Vestal Order," I
assured him.

Vibi rolled her eyes, as if once again, I was failing to consider how everything might be changed.

"Now is not the time to discuss money, Cornelia," Father told me. "So much has been destroyed. It will cost Rome millions and millions of sesterces to rebuild our city to its former glory." Of course, he was right. Now was not the time to talk about money. "Where are you staying?" he asked me.

"We are safe on the Esquiline. At the Gardens of Maecenas," I answered.

Vibidia nodded. "She's in good hands, Dominus." Father nodded, relieved we were safe.

"We must go now, Father," I said.

"Go with my blessing and thanks. And may the blessings of our patron God Neptune continue to watch over you."

For the first time in weeks, dark clouds moved in from the south. Fat drops of rain began to plunk down on us. "You called the rain in, Father! Something I couldn't do."

"All we can do is our best, Cornelia. Remember that."

"Vesta bless you," Vibi and I exclaimed at the same time. And then we ran back to the waiting litter.

"You have forgiven your father, Cornelia. I could feel it," said Vibi.

"What about your family, Vibi? Are you concerned about them?" I asked her.

"What family?" she responded.

I realized I had never asked her about her family; she had never shared anything with me. "Your parents? Relatives?"

"My parents are gone now. I have one older sister in Ostia. And you have already met my cousin Marcus. That is all that is left of my family."

Vibi leaned over in the litter and whispered to me, "My family is with those who believe. I left my family of origin years ago for my Vestal family. Now Paul and the Jesus followers are my *true* family."

I let the conversation die out. I wanted to see what my family villa looked like after the fire. My father's description was accurate. The front part of the villa, the vestibule with the statue of two-headed Janus was still there, along with the atrium. But half the roof had collapsed. My childhood room looked to be nothing but charred ashes covered with fallen rafters.

I gave thanks to Vesta. My family was alive. I was alive—and I knew that Rome would survive.

CHAPTER 37

By the time we arrived back to the Gardens of Maecenas, I noticed Emperor Nero had gathered a group of people under one of the tents. After Vibidia gave the litter bearers a generous sum of money for their efforts, we made our way to the tent. The Emperor was pacing; his heavy neck hung low like a bull ready to charge.

The pontiffs, flamens, augurs, and Vestals stood watching and listening to the Emperor rant as several Praetorian Guards huddled around him. Tigillenus, Poppaea, and Nero's favorite amusement, the dwarf Varros, were by his side.

Nero spun around, lifted his head, and pointed to us. All eyes fell on Vibi and myself.

"As Pontifex Maxiumus, I demand to know why you Vestals are late for my council!"

He approached Vibi who had little expression on her face. "Visiting any Jesus Believers lately?" he sneered, his puffed lips close to her face. His wide-set eyes glowered with a mad rage.

"Of course she did *not*!" I announced. "*I* needed to see if my family survived the inferno. My family is alive. But now my father's warehouses are nothing but cinder and rubble." I wanted to cry out against the Emperor. Like Hercules fighting the monster Cacus, I could face down this beast!

"Your family? What is so special about *your* family? Nothing but merchants. Bah!"

I wanted to scream insults right in his face. But no words would I speak.

"You were chosen, Cornelia Cosa, because no senators' daughters were available. How does that make you feel, snake charmer? Perhaps your father will help load Rome's rubble onto the barges headed for Ostia."

How dare he speak to me this way? That was slaves' work. I ignored his cruel words. Clearly, he was angered over more than my family situation.

"Gather around then," he commanded. We found a place under the crowded tent and listened. "It is clear from the graffiti all over Rome, that I, Emperor Nero, am being accused of setting this blaze. I am being called an arsonist, accused of destroying Rome. Nothing could be further from the truth. The people of Rome demand answers. And while we rebuild, the people *will* have answers." Nero paced a few steps. "And let's not forget this fact," he declared, "The area most of these Jesus Followers are said to reside in was spared the inferno."

Tigillenus approached the Emperor. Privately they conversed while we waited. I wondered what they could be discussing. I didn't have to wait long.

"I, Caesar, through Tigillenus, shall issue an edict through-out Rome. We are working on this presently." He nodded to Tigillenus. "Read what we have so far."

Tigillenus unraveled a scroll and read: "I, Nero, and the Praetorian Guard have just reason to suspect the arsonists who destroyed our city are none other than the Jesus Followers, who with malicious intent, continue to seek to destroy our city. Let it be known that all those who espouse to the Cult of the Nazarene here in Rome are now suspected of this crime. If you know where these criminals hide in Rome, report them to the Praetorian Guard immediately. A reward will be forthcoming. These zealots, also called Believers, will be rounded up and will be executed at the Vatican Circus. No Roman will want to miss this event. Remember, rewards will be given to those who report the arsonists to authorities." Tigillenus wrapped up the scroll again and slid it into his belt.

Nero concluded, "Once we finalize this edict, Tigillenus and his guards will post this throughout Rome." He started to laugh, pleased with this idea. "And how I look forward to the torture, the spectacle. It's what I—and all good Romans need— so I can move on, rebuild Rome, and work on my new palace." He blew dust off his hands and rubbed them together.

I watched Vibidia, who once again showed little expression on her face. But I could see and feel the pain in her eyes.

"And now, for an augury concerning my edict," Nero announced. "Lucius, prepare to receive the portents."

We gathered around Lucius who had his augur's crook and stool. With his staff, he drew the rectangle in the grass, divided the rectangle into the quadrants, said some prayers, and sat on his stool while we waited. And waited.

Finally, Lucius stood up and walked around the rectangle. He glanced up at the sky. Right at that moment, two vultures began circling around us. Soon after, two crows flew in a straight line right over us.

So here was an omen, an augury. Nero began pacing again, his legs carrying his thick body. "All right, Augur. What say you?"

Poor Lucius! Everyone's eyes were on him.

"We have the omen, Caesar. And I have recorded the omens I witnessed just last evening. Together they create a picture."

I knew this would be Lucius at his best—filled with drama and spectacle.

"Last evening I recorded two bolts of lightning seen over the Palatine. I watched and recorded this from the great tower. But then in the western sky, I spotted that pesky comet seen some time ago. It's visible again."

"You know I don't like to hear of comets," Nero sputtered. "Everyone knows they are bad omens. What say you, Augur?"

"Caesar, you requested a reading. Here are the portents. Listen to what the Gods say."

"I am listening!" Nero yelled, impatient to hear—what *he* wanted to hear.

"The augury says, Caesar, there are men within your own ranks—those who seek your downfall. This is evident from the vultures circling overhead."

"Who are these men, Augur? Are they Jesus Followers?" Nero roared. "And if I am not mistaken, I have heard these words from you before!"

"The gods are silent on this, Caesar." Lucius bravely muttered, then immediately added, "And the crows fly straight. This indicates a successful rebuilding of Rome."

"Of course, of course!" shouted Nero. "I plan to make the new streets of Rome straight—unlike the old narrow, crooked streets I despise."

"The lightning bolts from Jupiter last evening indicate your new palace will be even more magnificent," continued Lucius. "Brighter, bigger—"

"This again makes sense. My new palace will be called the Golden House of course." Nero looked pleased with Lucius for a moment. "And what about the comet?" he asked.

"The comet, Caesar, indicates that a new order will topple the old."

"What do you mean, a new order will topple the old?

Nero was clearly enraged by this declaration. Why didn't Lucius fill him with lies so he would be satisfied?

"We are pondering the power of the comet, Caesar," said Lucius.

"And what of the vultures? The insiders? What does it mean?"

"It means you must watch your back, Caesar, be guarded against many whom you think your friends," Lucius replied.

"It is the blasted Jesus followers who seek to destroy my city. They are my enemies, our enemies," said Nero.

"Perhaps, Caesar," was all Lucius said.

Nero stomped away, crimson with fury. Tigillenus and Poppaea narrowed their eyes at him and whispered in each other's ears. These were not the answers they wanted either. I acknowledged to myself that Lucius was brave to speak his truth, so much braver than Nero, Tigillenus, and the others set to sacrifice any Jesus Follower who remained in our city.

Rome started to clear out the rubble left from the fire. True to Nero's words, slaves began to fill ox carts with slabs of earth, fragments of broken marble, and whatever else remained from the fire: ashes, cinder, planks of burned wood, debris— all shoveled together. They would be carted to the Tiber, unloaded onto barges, and sent to the Port of Ostia to be dumped into the marshes. There were separate carts for the charred bodies; I couldn't even think about how many had perished in the blaze.

We soon heard that a bigger and grander Atrium would be built for the Vestal Order. This plan included a new Temple for Vesta as well. All we could do was wait. This was welcome news for the Vestals, but I dreaded to think what would happen when Nero's edict accusing the Believers was posted throughout Rome.

CHAPTER 38

OCTOBER 64 AD

Three months after the fire, Rome continued to rebuild. To my relief, there would be no Feast of the October Horse this year. The Vestals and other dignitaries were still living on the Esquiline. The Emperor began issuing orders for his new palace, his "Golden House" to be built—larger, more elaborate, and more expensive than his previous palace. A new colossal statue of the Emperor himself was being commissioned. Nero wanted to call the new Rome "Neropolis."

The graffiti accusing Nero of arson was smudged off any remaining temple pillars and rocks. Posts of the notice about the Jesus Followers began circulating in Rome. The Praetorian Guard already held over one hundred Believers at their camp, Believers who awaited their sentence.

Vibi's cousin Marcus told us more news in private. He shared with us that one special prisoner, a fisherman named Simon Peter, was among the unfortunate group.

"So he is one of the fishers of men too," I said, remembering what Paul had told me about the meaning of the fish. Vesta's message made sense now, the message of the eagle and the fish.

"Peter knew the Nazarene. Although he denied Jesus Christ many times, he was overcome with the love for his Lord," Marcus explained.

"What of Paul?" Vibi asked, concerned for her prophet.

"As far as we know, he still preaches in Spain," Marcus answered.

"That is good," said Vibi with relief. "May he carry the message of the Nazarene throughout the world, and may he remain far away from Rome."

At least Paul was safe.

Rubria was not acting like herself. She had sunk into a deep despondency. Did she blame herself for the fire—because of what she and Nero had done that day in the Hall of the Gods? Did she feel that Vesta, angry with her, had cursed Rome with the fire?

We took turns guarding the little flame to Vesta— as if we were in the temple again. But I wondered if life would ever be the same.

"Rubria, why are you so sad?" I asked her, as she stoked the flame gently.

"I committed a wrong, Cornelia. And Vesta along with Vulcan himself took revenge on us all," she stated. "It's all my fault."

"Rubria, nothing is your fault. You couldn't deny Caesar." I hoped to ease her mind, free her of this unwanted burden she carried with her.

But all Rubria did was shake her head and push me away.

We heard the announcement circulating through Rome: all of Rome's people were invited to the Vatican Circus, where a hundred or more Jesus followers would be punished for setting fire to Rome. The festivities, as the announcement stated, would begin tomorrow. Mother Aurelia, along with Occia said they would remain on the hill, tending to our little flame.

I knew not what to expect. Did these Jesus followers even have a trial? What of this Simon Peter? *How convenient*, I thought, *to rid Rome of all these innocent people! How convenient for Caesar to blame them for the fire!*

The next day, after crossing the Tiber, our litters arrived to the other side of the Campus Martius. I could see the Vatican Circus filling with people. The Vatican Circus, a smaller model of the Circus Maximus, had been spared the fire. This was where the October Horse had run his last race. The Vatican Circus was also Nero's special place to practice his skills as a charioteer.

Vibi, pale as ivory, held her head high. Did she expect the worse possible outcome? Who knew what the worst could be? I watched hundreds of plebes lined up holding green tickets, their admittance to the show. Food vendors pushing carts were positioning themselves around the Circus, serving up savory Roman delights. Nero declared today a free day for Romans—and promised free grain.

Our litter bearers, with lictors shouting in front and shaking their ax bundles, pushed through the crowds and arrived at the entrance. After we departed our litter, we made our way to the Imperial Boxes. The usual group of Nero's closest cronies—Tigillenus, the dwarf Varros, Poppaea—already sat waiting for the start of Nero's festivities. The senators were also present and sitting nearby in their special boxes. Next to us, the college of pontifices, priests, and augurs watched dutifully.

After we were seated in our assigned box, Junia stood up and addressed the row of Vestals. "Remember," she said in a low voice, "Vestals show no emotion in public."

Trumpets and various horns blasted and whistles blew, signaling the time had come for the festivities to begin. An official appeared holding a white cloth, as if this was the start of a chariot race.

"Let the race begin!" he shouted, as he dropped the white cloth to the ground. The people in the audience began to cheer and hoot for their team, and then began chanting Nero's name.

From one of the Circus gate archways, Nero appeared, riding a two-horse chariot. Dressed in a green tunic with a gold wreath on his head, he whipped the white horses with a fury. All eyes were on the Emperor showing off his skills. Faster and faster he circled around the spina, a miniature version of the Circus Maximus's obelisk.

Finally, after the traditional seven laps, he reined in the horses with a wild pull, halted the chariot, and got off. He waved and blew kisses to the crowd. This was his moment. The people cheered wildly for their Emperor. But I sat like a stone, refusing to applaud for him. Why should I, when Junia had warned us not to show any emotions? Vibi also sat there in her usual dreamlike state suffering through another Roman spectacle.

"Greetings, people of Rome," Nero shouted. "I welcome you to the festivites today, festivities that I sponsor. What you

will see today will surely ease your minds. Our glorious Rome
has been destroyed by fire. But let it be known, we have found
the culprits. Thanks to Tigillenus and others, we have rounded
up these criminals—arsonists bent on destroying our beloved
city and our way of life. Please—applause for Tigillenus!"

The crowd cheered as Tigillenus stood up, grinned, waved,
and sat back down again. This tall thin Prefect of the Praetorian Guard gave me the shivers.

Nero raised both hands high in the air and gestured to
the sky, as if he spoke to Jupiter himself. "Justice will now be
served! Let the ceremonies begin!"

The crowd again broke into a deafening cheer. *Vestals show
no emotion in public,* I kept reminding myself again and again.
Vibi was in her own world and Rubria seemed lost; the truth
about Nero had pained her deeply. All we could do was stare
straight ahead and watch.

From another archway came forth at least fifty people,
mostly men. They wore animal skins over their naked bodies.
They crouched and crawled around the track, howling and
growling. Was this humiliation their punishment? To be
treated as lowly beasts?

Judging by the gasps and roars of laughter, the crowd
thought it funny. I watched people poke each other, laughing
and grinning, pointing at the spectacle of people covered in
animal skins, forced to perform like animals.

But then I saw something that made me shudder. I lurched
forward. The gate beneath one of the arches on the other side
of the circus opened slowly. Out skulked a pack of wild dogs
about twenty in number. They were thin, mangy, and mean
looking. They started to snarl and circled around these men,
who huddled together in fear. But many got on their knees

and shouted, "Hallelujah, praise Jesus!" and stared up to the sky.

The low growling of the dogs continued as they circled the accused. They reminded me of jackals, like the Egyptian god Anubis, black with mottled brown spots. I felt Vibi next to me shaking. I grabbed for her hand.

And then the bloodlust began. I refused to watch, but I knew what was happening; the prisoners were being torn apart. The terrified shrieking echoed through the Circus. But the worst noises I heard were the din of laughter and cheering, as innocent people were led to a brutal slaughter. I knew not how people could find this amusing! Would *this* appease Rome's gods?

I knew the horrific spectacle pleased Nero. He had found the perfect victims for his scheme, scapegoats blamed for setting fire to Rome. He looked on, well pleased with the carnage before us. I felt sick, but knew I had to stare ahead and show no feeling. Inside myself though, I was repulsed by Rome, her Emperor and her citizens; the bloodlust that ran through the veins of our Roman ancestors was alive. I felt ashamed to witness such cruelty. Yet many of these Jesus followers seemed to go to their death rejoicing and giving thanks!

After the wild dogs devoured the remains of these Followers of the Way, the dogs were goaded back to their pens. Then two thin lions were released and four more men were pushed into the arena. They had no weapons, no armor, nothing to fight with or protect themselves. The lions, as starved-looking as the dogs, crouched low and stalked the accused around the arena.

The men tried to run, but all the arched gates were closed. Finally, they gave themselves willingly, to the might of the beasts and succumbed to death with silent dignity.

The carnage! The screams of anguish! The roars! I wanted to escape to a vomitorium, for my stomach felt sick. But when I looked at Vibi, so brave, I felt her silent but strong faith.

There was more. As the sun began to set, wooden crosses were brought forth and erected in the center of the Circus. Nero stood up to make the announcement. "These Jesus followers ... like their proclaimed Messiah ... will be nailed to the cross and set afire, just as they set my beloved city—our beloved city—on fire!"

Along with three men, each fitted with a tight vest, a burly man in a long tunic with a shock of white hair appeared. He struggled with the guard. Then he shouted to the crowd, "I, Peter, am not worthy to be crucified in the manner of my Lord. I request to be hung upside down."

"You request is granted, fishmonger!" shouted Nero. He indicated to the guards to hang him upside down. "No need to torch him, just torch the others," he cried. "He will die the slow, painful death of suffocation." The Emperor rubbed his hands together with relish, a big grin filling his wide face.

The crowd started to get restless. I thought the idea of more flames, more fire, no longer appealed to them. Why would it? Rome was little more than rubble, soot, ash, and cinders. Now we must witness Jesus Followers burn on crosses?

We watched the guards douse something on the Believers' vests and then light them on fire. A few remained silent, while one screamed out in agony. Their bodies provided light for spectators to witness the crucifixion of Peter—hanging upside down.

While Peter suffered on the cross and those around him burned for their faith, Nero ordered the guards to lift Peter's cross and parade it around the Circus, so people could witness the man in full torture. *This is what Hades must be like,* I thought. *Filled with hate, lies, torture, and murder.* I felt I was in the middle of a living nightmare, powerless to do anything.

But this was no dream. People were being executed in front of us. Finally, it was over. *For now,* I thought. No suspected follower of Jesus was safe in Rome. I wondered who would be next.

CHAPTER 39

JANUARY 65 AD

At last we were back living at the Forum. Emperor Nero ordered huts to be erected for us—made from tufa. No wooden structures were allowed in Rome. After the fire it was deemed too dangerous. We even had a makeshift hut replicated as a temple for Vesta. The Palladium and all the sacred relics we guarded as well as the wills were secured inside our main hut. It would all have to do while our new Temple to Vesta was being built.

The noise of workmen clearing out the rubble disturbed my peace. The clacking, banging and pounding noises disrupted my thoughts. But Rome was rebuilding; rebuilding straighter, wider streets with new materials and new jobs for people—all according to Nero's big plans.

Soon after the spectacle at the Vatican Circus, Vibi said to me, "I have bad news. My cousin Marcus has informed me that Paul has returned to Rome."

"No! Returned to Rome? Why?" I was confused. I thought Paul had been banished from Rome, preaching somewhere out of danger.

"Paul got word about the killing of the Jesus followers—and news of his friend Peter's crucifixion. Paul has given himself up to the Praetorian Guard—given himself up to Nero." She gasped and let out a sob.

My hand flew to my mouth. "What's going to happen to him now?"

"He's been arrested, Cornelia. No house arrest this time. According to Marcus, he is in the dungeon of the Mamertine Prison on the Capitoline Hill."

"Dungeon? Will he even get a trial?"

"I doubt it," she said. "Did any of the other Followers get a trial? I think at most he will get a hearing."

I thought for a moment."Do you think we can save him? You know the Vestal rule, Vibi. If a Vestal meets a convicted criminal going to his execution, she can pardon him. It's worth a try."

Vibi brightened for a moment, but then her face grew dark again. "Let me think on what you say, Cornelia. Perhaps Paul doesn't want to be saved. Perhaps he is ready to sacrifice himself—for his faith."

For some reason, I could not let go of the idea of saving Paul.

"We could visit him in prison," I suggested. "We could ask him— or at least attend his hearing."

Vibi shook her head and looked annoyed, as if I were

disturbing her thoughts. "Let me think on such matters," she told me. "The answers will come."

True to Vibi's word, Paul's hearing was to be held in a few days. We decided to try to attend. I spoke with Rubria about covering any fire duty we might have that day. Perhaps, if Paul were convicted, Vibi and I would meet him on the road to his execution. I knew in my heart Nero wanted him dead. And I knew like the Jesus followers executed at the Circus, he would accept his fate with a glad heart.

On the day of Paul's hearing, we proceeded up to a newly rebuilt portion of Nero's Golden House—grander and more extravagant than the old one. Wagons filled with charred and cracked pieces of marble and rubble headed down to the Tiber, while more wagons came up the Palatine, filled with gold, ivory, and new stone.

Vibi and I discussed standing in the back, but close enough to listen to what was being said. The hearing was open to all; several groups of citizens already made their way to the half-built theater within the palace walls.

The theater was starting to fill up with people: Poppaea, Tigillenus, the various priests and augurs, all were present. Would any Jesus Followers, spared from the cross or the jaws of a starved beast dare expose themselves? I doubted it. We knew we were taking our chances as well. Vibi already had her scourging. I shuddered thinking about it.

Nero sat on what looked like a throne wearing his usual gold wreath with gold leaves encircling his head. Tigillenus stood by his side as always, looking like a long, lanky wharf rat. Then I heard a loud banging and a guard shouted, "The prisoner is here."

Gasps were heard as Paul entered the chamber bound in fetters, one around his neck and one on each of his arms and legs. He seemed so small and resigned before Caesar. What had he done? He had been banished for almost two years. He was gone when the fire broke out months ago. How could *he* possibly be blamed?

But no logic or arguing worked with Nero. He had publically declared the Jesus followers had set fire to Rome, looted goods from burned-out buildings, and that they set forth to destroy Rome. Those believing and speaking about Jesus were Nero's enemies. They were a threat to his way of life.

And here was the showdown, the moment the Emperor had been waiting for. Why had Paul returned? I thought he must have a message, perhaps a final message for the Emperor. Nero stood up, stepped down from his throne, and shouted, "This is a hearing, not a trial. Bring the prisoner forth. I want to see this apostle of the dead Nazarene up close."

The guards pulled the chained prisoner to the front. Paul was dressed in tattered clothes, hair a grizzled gray, and he was dirty from the dungeon where he had been held.

Nero rose from his seat and proceeded to jab a finger in the little man's face. "You," he shouted, "are guilty of inciting violence against my city." He flung his arms into the air. "Our city!" I heard people murmuring in agreement and nodding.

"How, Caesar, could I possibly incite violence in Rome when I've been preaching elsewhere?" Paul asked. "You … Caesar, freed me. *You* let me go. I have returned to speak of the crimes you committed and continue to commit against my brethren."

"You incite others through you letters, Paul," Nero continued." I know you communicate with people here in Rome, those you address as *the brethren*. Did you know that many of your brethren were served to the lions and wild dogs—as a meal?" Nero had a smug and punishing look on his face, but he grinned at the thought of it and laughed out loud.

"This is *why* I have returned, Caesar," Paul responded. "To denounce the murders of innocents who died for the cause. You, Caesar, have turned Rome into a Babylon!"

Nero roared with laughter. "Babylon?" he shouted. "Ha! Indeed— Babylon."

Vibi clenched her fists together, stiff with anger. I reached for my bulla and squeezed it hard.

Nero addressed the crowd of onlookers. "The reason I let this man remain on house arrest for two years is due to my kind nature. I freed him because he is a Roman citizen by birth. Yes, a Jew— and an old Pharisee as well. Perhaps you forget, Saul of Tarsus, how many Jesus Lovers *you* put to death years ago? Remember Saul— or Paul, I let you go and now you have returned." Nero gave Paul a diabolic sneer. "You can't keep away, can you? You have found me. But rest assured, I would have found you. You just made my life easier by giving yourself up." He thrust himself into the prisoner's face. "Fool!" he shouted.

"Caesar, you wanted me returned," Paul stiffly remarked.

Nero intoned, "My spies would have found you soon enough. I sent the edict out for your arrest months ago."

"Before the fire, Caesar?" Paul asked.

"Perhaps. But what matters only is that you are here now. Speak, criminal!"

"My greatest sin in your eyes, Caesar, is that I have preached the true gospel. Not Nero's gospel or the gospel of Isis, Venus,

Apollo, or the host of other deities you worship. I preach the gospel of my Lord, Jesus Christ!"

The room was silent. Color had returned to Vibi's face. Once again she was moved by the words of this brave apostle. So was I.

"And what of my soldiers, my guards that you minister to? What spell have you placed on them that makes them desire to know more about the Nazarene? Tell me!" Then Nero shouted, "What magic do you work?"

"It is no spell I cast, Caesar. I speak the truth, and the Spirit speaks through me."

"And soon you shall speak no more." Nero started pacing around the chamber. "You may say your last words now ... false prophet."

Nero returned to his great chair, placed his elbows on his knees, and bent down to listen.

"Caesar, it is clear that the Kingdom of God does not reside in Rome," Paul began. "We, the Followers of the Way, Believers, cannot worship Christ in his glory and also worship Caesar. You are not a god, Caesar. And you will never be one."

Nero shook his head and waved his hand, dismissing such comments. "Your time is almost finished, prophet of a false god. Deliver your last words, so I can have my dinner on time."

Paul turned away from Nero and addressed all of us, holding up his fettered arms. "I tell you, I am already at the point of being sacrificed; the time of my departure has come. I have fought the good fight. I have finished the race. I have kept my faith."

Vibi held a hankerchief in her hand and quickly wiped her eyes. I reached for her arm and squeezed it.

"Is that all?" Nero asked.

"Yes, I am finished," Paul said solemnly.

"That is correct. You *are* finished. You speak the truth for once. For you Paul, will be beheaded at noon tomorrow, just outside the walls of Rome on the Ostian Way. Because you are a Roman citizen by birth … travesty though this may be … this is where you shall be executed. And this will be your end, false prophet— for I will never have to hear another word out of your lying, deceptive mouth. And remember, when you are gone at last, the world will forget you and remember me!"

"So you say, Caesar," Paul said, now resigned to his fate.

"And that's all *you* will say," said Nero in a voice filled with hatred. "For tomorrow your voice will be silenced forever and your name shall never be spoken again in Rome. Or the name of your false god— Jesus of Nazareth—a mere man! Bah!"

He beckoned to the guards. "Take him away," he shouted. "That is all. Now, where's my dinner?" he asked. "I have worked up an appetite."

The next day everything was calm. The January sun brought forth a crisp, cool, and bright day. The air was still; everything seemed so quiet.

Today was the day of Paul's planned execution. I still felt that with our Vestal privileges we could save him. I spoke to Vibi again. Could we meet Paul on the road to his execution and pardon him? What could Nero say or do?

"One thing I do know, Cornelia," Vibi said, "we must be present. We must be witnesses to this execution. We must be there to pray for Paul. And if the timing is right, perhaps we could pardon him." I was relieved Vibi was starting to accept

my logic; if Paul wanted his freedom, we possibly could give
it to him.

Late-night fire duty was over, and my morning prayers
and breakfast were finished, so I sat watching the sections of
marble pillars for Vesta's new temple being slowly raised with
ropes and hooks. Life continued on in Rome—a constant tear-
ing down of the old to build anew.

Vibi came forth from our hut. "I have hired a litter," she
told me, out of breath. "I've heard Paul will be led around the
Palatine past the Circus Maximus, down the Aventine to the
Ostian Way. But I think we can go down the other side of the
Aventine, the way past your house along the Tiber, and go up
the other side of the hill. This way we will be there before the
procession." Vibi had hope in her eyes.

"What time?"

"In a few hours. Be ready."

I walked up toward the Capitoline Hill, turned back to look at
the Forum, and noticed Domicia following me. "Yes?" I asked
her. "What do you want?"

"Where are you going, Cornelia?"

"I want to see the prison where Paul resides."

"Cornelia, do not tempt fate." She leaned close to me "I am
here for you. If you need help with anything ... I know of Paul
and his Savior, Jesus Christ as well ...

So Domicia knew. Did she overhear our plan to save Paul?
I wanted to trust her. But at that moment, she was an annoy-
ance and a distraction.

"Thank you, Domicia. I—"

"Wait," she said. "Something arrived for you. Mother told me to deliver it to you." She pulled forth a letter. "From Lucretia," she said and handed it to me. I thanked her and left her there to return to the Forum—alone.

An angry crowd had gathered in front of the prison. People pushed each other out of the way as guards tried to hold them back.

"This man had no trial! When will the murder stop?" someone screamed.

A guard shouted, "Not until every Believer is purged from Rome. On the Emperor's orders, there shall be no gatherings in front of this prison. We prepare to ready and accompany the prisoner to his place of execution."

Then I saw Marcus, Vibi's cousin, another Follower in his heart. He had seen me and his brow furrowed up.

"Cornelia, you should not be here. Not now," he said. "Return to the Forum."

"We have hired a litter, Marcus. Vibi and I have a plan," I quietly explained.

He looked shocked, shook his head, and pointed toward the Forum. "Return to the Forum at once. Immediately. Emperor's orders."

After the quiet of the morning, the commotion on the Capitoline Hill grew louder. Our litter arrived at last, and Rubria, also free, decided to join us. Junia inquired where we were going.

Vibi told her we wanted to check on my family again and those living in tents at the Campus Martius. Did she believe us?

The litter bearers carried us through the burned-out streets of Rome, our lictors shouting our arrival so people would let us by. I managed to wave, smile, and bless the people who always treated a litter carrying Vestals with reverence.

The litter followed the road down the Aventine Hill close to the Tiber. We knew Paul would be led past the Circus Maximus and straight down the other side of the Aventine. Our litter turned left near the Cave of Cacus, and made its way up the backside of the Aventine to head him off.

At last we reached the point we knew the procession must pass. I looked at Vibi for guidance. She pulled back the curtain and shouted to the lead bearer to stop. "Leave us off here," she ordered. "Return in an hour's time." She handed him some coins.

Vibi explained we would wait at this spot. And when we looked up the far side of the hill, we could see Paul's procession slowly making its way down the Aventine. I could see Paul in his chains struggling to walk, pushed forward by guards and surrounded by people. Where was Nero?

We stood at the entrance of the Ostian Way like three white geese, uneasy and restless. I could hear a mournful drumbeat. Some people shouted for Paul's freedom, but most people joined in and claimed the man was a traitor to Rome. He must die a traitor's death— for Rome's sake.

Finally, the prisoner approached and I could see the pained expression on his face. As he was about to pass us, Rubria stepped forward. Rubria!

"Stop!" she commanded. "I, as a Vestal, have the power to pardon this man, deemed a criminal by the Emperor." All eyes were on Rubria.

Paul glanced at Vibidia and me with a look of recognition. Then he spoke to Rubria. "Indeed you do, dear Vestal. But I go to my death willingly. I go to join my Savior, the Son of the One Living God. He carried His cross; I carry His light. Have faith, for I fear not death." He studied Rubria as if he knew her thoughts. "And know this, kind Vestal. You are now forgiven for what you could not control. You are innocent, cleansed of any wrongs. Forget the past! All is forgiven!" he shouted to the growing crowd. "As my Lord forgave those who crucified him."

Many will perish ... yet you will be safe. The old woman's words haunted me again.

Rubria burst into a flood of tears that began flowing onto her robes. Paul continued to shout to the crowd, "The Lord knows your hearts and what resides therein. I, once a sinner, I, who condemned Gentiles and Followers, the way Caesar has condemned me, forgive you all. May the message, the good news, spread throughout Rome. My task is finished. I have fought a hard battle—and I have won back my soul."

He quickly turned to Vibi and me. "I know you. And I know what resides in your hearts. My Lord knows you. Fill your hearts with forgiveness and love—it's the only way. Rejoice!"

Many of the crowd began to shout, "Rejoice, rejoice." I noticed the tall, handsome man accompanying Paul to his death. He looked familiar.

"And my dear physician, Luke, will carry the message onward after my death. Rest assured." Paul stared into my eyes as if he was consuming a part of my soul. The physician nodded to us.

"Rejoice, rejoice in the good news, people of Rome! Give thanks!" Paul continued to shout, as the guards pulled him toward the gate. And the procession continued on, leaving Rubria, Vibi, and I clutching each other in tears.

We had tried to save Paul. Instead, it felt like he had saved us. He was ready to go to his death, a prisoner in fetters, who would soon be free of any earthly burdens.

CHAPTER 40

We decided to return to the Forum. We had seen enough. Paul had chosen to give up his good fight. His fate lay on the Ostian Way; nothing could save him from Nero's greedy clutches. The thought of his head being severed, rolling to the ground, and then hearing the cruel laughs of Nero and Tigillenus was more than we needed to bear. The three of us sobbed quietly in the litter; our tears seemed cleansing, as if they cleansed the parched, blackened earth of Rome itself.

"I'll never be a Jesus follower," cried Rubria. "But the man's words touched me deeply. Touched me right here." She pressed a hand to her heart. "I call it genuine love. Something that is missing from Rome."

"But it won't be missing forever," I said.

Vibi reached over and gave me a strong embrace. "You have been with me and you have been understanding of me,

Cornelia. I will never forget our journeys—and how brave you were—and are."

"Nor I," said Rubria. "I feel the same. Cornelia, you listen and seem to understand. You don't pass judgment on your Vestal sisters. The love and forgiveness Paul bestowed upon me, why, I would do the same for you."

"As well as I," said Vibi, her eyes still wet with tears.

So among the death, the destruction, and defilement of Rome, I realized that love did survive.

I rushed back to our makeshift living quarters, anxious to open Lucretia's letter. I was relieved she was still in Pompeii with her new baby. I tore open the waxed seal on the papyrus and read:

My dear Cornelia,

I have heard about the dreadful fire, heard how it destroyed our old home, the Atrium. My heart pains to think of the misery you and the other Vestals have suffered. The loss of Vesta's temple brings me to tears. I have heard of the mass killings of the Jesus Followers. My heart cries for all of you, cries for Rome. I have sent my prayers up on the ether.

Remember what I told you that first night in the Atrium when you were so much younger? Cornelia, you were chosen! Chosen for Rome! Chosen for power! Continue to use your power wisely.

I am safe and happy with my husband and my son, who now walks and calls out for his mother. I could not ask for anything more gratifying in my life.

With love,
Lucretia

I folded up the letter, a treasure in the midst of gloom. Lucretia was a light to me; her words strengthened me and gave me courage. I thanked Vesta for this gift.

The words seemed to ring out throughout all of Rome— Paul was dead!

Rumors began circulating about the prophet's death. That his head glowed after the ax man chopped it off; that his head spoke to others; that it was still alive while his body lay dying. And with his death came new life. For many people, instead of supporting Nero's madness began to elevate the martyr, saying that he had died unjustly with no trial, and that the death and destruction must stop. How could Nero rebuild Rome yet still be bent on destroying and murdering a new sect in Rome? Why was he threatened by this small group? He accepted all the other religions of the Empire. Why not the Jesus followers?

But it was convenient for the Emperor to blame anyone who disagreed with him, who spoke out against his wishes. Nero was like a wounded animal, lashing out against others who got in his way. He would have his new palace, his new Rome, his Neropolis, even if it meant ferreting out and killing every Believer within the city walls.

No one was safe in Rome. Anyone could be accused—if they defied the Emperor.

Mother Aurelia finally announced her retirement. She had seen enough and told us all that she was tired. She needed peace and calm. By next spring, Junia would take her place as the official Virgo Maxima.

I thought how she truly deserved her retirement; after all, she had given more than forty years of her life in service to Vesta. And this time there would be no party, just a quiet farewell. She was like a kind grandmother to me; her wisdom and understanding would be missed. The sorrows were with me, with Vibi, with Rome. Yet I held out hope for the message I had received from Minerva … the hope for a new day.

CHAPTER 41

FEBRUARY 65 AD

The cold rains of winter pelted down on Rome. The Emperor continued his frantic rebuilding. And he continued his relentless attacks on Jesus followers—or anyone he deemed a traitor.

It still would be months before our home, the new Atrium, would be ready. Workmen wrangled round slabs of marble, raising them atop each other with pulleys, creating more unadorned pillars— the pillars would be fluted by masons who carved the perfect lines on the outside. Our new Atrium was going to be grander, taller, wider, and bigger than the old one.

I was sad that Nero had chosen to use most of our Vestal garden area for part of his new palace. The garden would be much smaller! And right beside the old garden, he was demanding a giant bath be built next to the colossal statue of him.

But I had other worries. Walking around the Forum before my fire duty, I saw Lucius coming toward me. He held his augur's staff and his striped cloth swung back and forth over his tunic. He frowned with a concerned look—as if he carried a great burden.

"Cornelia," was all he said with a long sigh.

"Lucius, how are your new living quarters on the Palatine coming?" I asked, trying to make light conversation.

"Bigger and better according to Nero's grand schemes."

I nodded. "You must be relieved and feeling more settled."

"Settled? No, not quite," he said. "Unsettled is more like it." He pressed closer, a desperate look in his eyes.

"Unsettled?"

"Cornelia, there are rumors abounding—that Nero is unhappy with my auguries! He claims the omens I have read have incited the people, causing many to blame him for the fire. People are asking about the Sibylline Books, demanding answers. They are finding explanations about the fire and the murders in our sacred books. Now Nero is filled with more suspicions." He paused to look around the Forum to make sure no one was listening. He whispered, "Yes, I have consulted and read from the Sibylline Books and the fire was predicted. Remember the passage I gave you? And ever since I warned him of enemies within, Nero thinks *I* am now one of them. He only hears what he wants to hear; everything else he considers treason. He has no problem blaming the messenger."

"Lucius, you know it's unsafe to tell Nero the truth!" I reminded him.

"But this is my job. I take it seriously." He paused, glanced around the Forum, and whispered, "He is aware and is afraid of the most dire prophecy of all."

"What is that?" I asked him.

Lucius was so close to me now that he whispered in my ear:

*"He, courting by his voice, all-musical
applause for his sweet songs, shall put to death
his mother and many men.
From Babylon shall flee the fearful Lord:
For he slew many and laid hands upon the womb:
Against his wives he sinned
And of men stained with blood had he been formed."*

He watched me, his eyes red and swollen.

"It's all true, Lucius," I said, barely breathing. "The rumors of Nero killing his mother, having his wife Octavia murdered, the fire, the killing of Jesus Believers. The oracle speaks the truth."

"I know, Cornelia. That is why Nero wants my head—and my blood. My hearing with him is tomorrow."

"Hearing?" I gasped. "Can I come? To support you?"

"I will send word to you. Pray to the Palladium, for truth and justice. The truth may save me," he said hopefully.

And the truth may condemn you, I thought, but held my tongue.

The next day I awaited any word about Lucius's hearing. What lies was Nero proclaiming against his trusted augur? What could I do but wait and send messages up to the ether? I knew that sadly, the truth condemned the innocent, and lies freed the guilty in Rome.

I found time to speak with Vibi again. We walked together around the Forum and stood close to the sacred fig tree. Miraculously, the tree had survived; its wide gnarly branches stretched upward, as if it somehow defied the fire.

"Vibi, I need your help," I told her.

"Help?"

"I think Lucius is in trouble with the Emperor. He has a hearing today. Nero is unhappy with his auguries."

"But Nero likes Lucius," Vibi said. "I'm sure he will get a light sentence. Nero just wants to straighten him out. Rest assured most augurs lie to the Emperor in order to avoid the executioner's block."

"But this is not right, Vibi. You know that yourself. Lucius takes his job seriously. He trained to be an augur for years. I don't think he will lie."

"So what would you have me do?"

"Could you take a litter up to the camp of the Praetorian Guard, speak with Marcus, and find out what is happening? He might know." I hooked my arm through hers. "I'm worried."

"I know, Cornelia. I'll see what I can do for you."

The afternoon dragged on. I had little appetite for the roasted meat, cheese, and a platter of figs, olives, and dates for our early dinner. I picked at the food; my mind and body lay elsewhere. Vibi had gone in search of her cousin and all I could do was wait.

When she finally returned, my heart sank with one look at her face.

"The news is bad, Cornelia. According to Marcus, Nero wants Lucius gone—gone from this earthly realm, that is."

"Gone? Condemned to death?" I started shaking with rage. "What are you telling me? Speak!" I thought back to all the times I had watched Lucius read the omens, how much he had taught me, how he had trusted the messages I received and how, when he washed our feet at the spring of Egeria, he explained the true meaning of under-standing.

"I'm grieved to tell you that Lucius *has* been condemned to death. The execution, another beheading, is scheduled to occur at the Praetorian Guard Camp, right in front of the Severn Gate. Tomorrow at noon." She paused and looked away. "I am sorry to bring you this news, Cornelia."

I thought for a moment, my teeth grinding together in anger. "But—"

"But what?" she asked me.

"We can—we *must* save him," I told her.

"Save him? We couldn't save Paul."

"Paul didn't want to be saved. He accepted and welcomed death. Lucius is only twenty-two."

Vibi asked me again for the second time that day, "What would you have me do?"

"Let me think on this, Vibi. I have an idea."

A plan had formed in my mind, a plan I thought about for the rest of the day. I spoke to no one and kept my thoughts and feelings to myself, everything a good Vestal Virgin was supposed to do. I had learned in my training as a novice that timing was everything. One wrong move at a festival, at a ritual, and the Gods could become angered. Worse was the anger of Emperor Nero.

That night at fire duty, after excusing Domicia to retrieve us some water, I spoke with Vibi about my plan. When Domicia returned, she had a note for me. After she left, I opened it and read:

Cornelia,

I am sentenced to death near the Praetorian Guard Camp next to the Severn Wall at noon. I go to my death an innocent man.

–Lucius

I read it quietly to Vibi and then cast it into the flames. Any evidence was now destroyed.

We spoke of our plan in hushed tones. Vibi had her doubts. "Does Nero follow any laws now? He is still murdering innocent Believers for their faith alone, accusing them of starting the blaze, when everyone knows he and his men were responsible. The Emperor himself is behind the infernal blaze. I just know it!"

"Vibi, please!" I said. "This is *not* the time. Nero may not follow Rome's laws, but he must follow Vesta's laws, the laws of King Numa. He must!"

"He must?" Vibi shook her head calmly. "Whatever you say, Cornelia. Whatever you want."

I wanted to give Lucius his freedom. There was not a lot of time left. Tomorrow was the day. Vibidia would help me. For now, all we could do was wait—and pray.

CHAPTER 42

The day began with heavy rain as if the sky cried its own tears. Then the rains stopped, the clouds parted, and the sun appeared blazing down on Rome.

My day began as usual: a bath, breakfast, prayers to Vesta, and then my morning walk around the Forum. Workmen with carts of new building materials arrived, while others *still* cleared away the remaining debris from the fire. I overheard a group of senators discussing Nero's extravagant spending on his Golden House—while many in Rome remained homeless, still living in tents. I wondered if my family was still living in a tent on the Campus Martius. All I could do was trust Vesta and trust Neptune they were safe.

I walked to the sacred fig tree with nothing but crumbled and damaged ruins behind it. There was life still among the death and destruction. The tree gave me hope. But what gave me even more hope and joy was what I saw that crawled out from under a pile of ruins. It was Cleo! She had survived the fire. I had assumed she was dead, burned in the flames. How clever she was! But Cleo looked thin, her eyes masked in dirt and gray dust, her tail singed at its tip. "Cleo," I shouted. "You are alive!"

Cleo approached me wrapping her body under my concealed legs. The purring became louder. I reached down and picked her up, caressing her thin body.

"Cleo," I murmured again, squeezing her close to me. "You've come home, back to the Atrium," I whispered in her ear. "Never leave me again!" She blinked her green eyes at me, as if she understood. I touched my nose to her nose and kissed the top of her dirtied head.

It was clear Cleo needed some food. Still clutching her to my breast, I returned to the Atrium huts, thinking of how I could convince the cook to spare some dried fish and milk for my half-starved cat. After making sure Cleo was fed, all of the Vestals and sevants celebrated her return. Rubria shouted that it was as if Cleo had returned from the dead!

I knew I had to find time to speak with Vibi soon. We did not have fire duty until later that evening.

Finally, I found her. Here was my chance. "Is everything ready?" I asked her.

"As ready as it will be," she replied.

The litter was waiting for us. Lictors stood by, but we told them to walk beside the litter today, not in front of it. We need no one announcing our presence along the road.

"I heard from Marcus that Nero's procession will follow the Clivus Suburanus near the Viminal Hill until they reach the road to the Praetorian Guard Camp," Vibi told me. "We should follow the Vicus Longus and take the fork in the road toward the Viminal Hill. This way leads right to the Praetorian Camp," she suggested.

I agreed that this sounded like the best plan. Vibi gave the head litter bearer directions, and we began traveling the Via Sacra, until we came to the entrance of the Viminal, so close to the Subura. "You think of everything," I told her, starting to feel tense.

"I have had experience—as you know," she replied.

We entered the Vicus Longus; the Subura was the only area that separated us from the procession. I knew it was already late morning by the sun's position.

"Can't you tell them to go faster?" I urged. But the streets were crowded today with people heading down to the open market near the Tiber. We finally came to the fork in the road—the road that led to the Praetorian Camp.

"Leave me off—right here!" I suddenly commanded. "Wait for me here!"

"You don't want me to—"Vibi said.

"No! I can do this myself. You've had enough problems with Caesar, Vibi!"

Vibi opened the curtain and shouted to the litter bearers to stop.

"We will be waiting for you. May Vesta bless you and may the brave spirit of Paul reside within you," she said to me. "And may the spirit of Jesus Christ go with you," she added.

I thanked her for the blessing. She was a true sister to me. We embraced and I departed the litter. I was already breaking a Vestal rule—walking the streets alone. But I didn't feel alone. I knew the spirit was with me giving me strength. Whether it was the spirit of Vesta, the spirit of Paul, or the spirit of his Savior, Jesus, I knew not. Or cared anymore.

I followed the road until I reached the fork. I took the left at the fork and kept going. There was no procession, nothing I could see. I kept walking thinking I might be too late. I remembered every Vestal rule I had been taught: walk with dignity, hold my head high with a staight back, show no emotion, and act as if nothing was a bother. Perhaps I had, after all, learned the mannerisms of a true Vestal.

I continued to walk to the guard camp. From behind me I heard the doleful sound of a single drumbeat. Assuming it was the procession, I waited behind a pile of rubble on the side of the road, hoping no one would notice me in my white robes.

But Romans had other cares these days. I peeked around the rubble. The drumbeat grew louder. Then I saw the Emperor's carriage leading the procession. The drummer followed and I saw the prisoner, surrounded by a group of guards. Clearly this must be Lucius struggling in his chains. The procession moved slowly— it seemed to crawl up the hill.

The time was drawing near. My time. My training years had taught me this: one wrong move and the outcome could be destroyed. Worse, the person completing the wrong move could be killed.

I saw my chance. And I knew that now was *my* time.

"Stop!" I shouted, as I stepped out and made my way toward the procession. "Stop, I say, in the name of Vesta!"

The Emperor's carriage abruptly halted, as did the procession. I proceeded forward, head erect, as proud as the ostriches that paraded around the Circus Maximus. Nero, Tigillenus, and others stepped from the carriage. I ignored them and walked straight toward the prisoner, my friend Lucius, whose face was white with fear.

I lay my hand on Lucius's shoulder, and lifted up a finger to the air. "Remember the rule of Vesta. If a man convicted meets a Vestal Virgin on the way to his death, this Vestal may pardon the man and free him!"

Nero looked amused. "Is that so, snake charmer?" He always enjoyed the drama. And he would get plenty of drama from me today. The Emperor and his men laughed aloud, slapping their knees and bowing over in hysteria. Death was always a laughing matter for the Emperor.

"Death is no joke, Caesar. You may not follow any of Rome's laws—but you *will* follow the laws of Vesta!"

"And what if I don't, snake charmer?" he asked, bending down to tickle my chin. I pulled myself back and glared at him.

"Know this, Caesar. Over the last four years, I have learned much about the rules of Vesta, and the laws of Rome, laws that are being broken every day. I have knowledge, Caesar! I understand! Think on that day in the library— remember? When I was studying? I have seen and heard much. I understand, Caesar. Perhaps the people would care to know what happened in the library between you and—"

"Enough," bellowed the Emperor.

Is he concerned I will blurt out the truth? I was concerned he would just lie and deny everything as he usually did.

"Obey the laws of Vesta, Caesar! Or else!" I shouted.

"Or else what?" Nero asked.

"Or else, Caesar, you shall bring more curses upon Rome, and upon yourself in due time. I do not wish to think you would anger Vesta—anymore than you already have." I looked at him, facing him fully, feeling a sense of authority and power.

"I, Cornelia Cosa, now declare this augur innocent! I command that he is pardoned through my word, and the word of

Vestal Law." I stamped my foot hard and gritted my teeth at the Emperor staring into his wide eyes.

Lucius watched me with what I thought was a look of respect and admiration—even love. Poor man! He kept trying to wipe his forehead.

"I will confer with my advisors," was all Nero said to me, regarding me coldly with his watery blue-gray eyes. He gathered his men around him while I made myself stand as tall as possible. I, Cornelia Cosa!

Finally, Nero came forth. All he said was, "The prisoner may go free. The Vestal rule has been enforced." I watched Lucius who sighed with relief and mouthed the silent words, "Thank you."

"But," Nero continued, "Let it be known that the freed prisoner will now be banished from Rome—never to return again!" Nero pointed to Lucius. "You must leave at once! You will leave through the Severn Wall past the Praetorian Camp. Return to Etruria—and good riddance to a lying augur. Feed someone else your lies. Now be gone!"

Nero was huffing and mumbling under his breath. But the guards unshackled Lucius and set him free. He still held his augur's staff—a proud testament to his profession.

"And *I* shall escort the freed prisoner to the gate," I proclaimed.

The guards and the growing crowd murmured their disapproval and disappointment. They had anticipated the execution as another of Rome's spectacles—for their entertainment.

Lucius and I walked together until we finally arrived at the Praetorian Guard Camp. A wooden block had been set up in anticipation of the beheading.

"My head would be on that block if it wasn't for you, Cornelia. My life taken with a single blow of the ax."

"Speak no more on this," was all I said, remembering Paul's words about pressing forward and leaving the past behind.

A lone guard stood as sentinel by the gate.

"The prisoner is now free. Open the gate!" I ordered. The guard followed my command. "Now, please ... our privacy," I demanded.

"How can I ever thank you, Cornelia? What can I do," Lucius begged, "to repay you?" I thought for a moment.

"Here." I reached deep into my pocket and pulled out my beloved bulla. "Take this. I have no use for it anymore." I handed him my bulla, my childhood amulet that had helped me through so much. It was burnt and broken from Rome's flames. Yet Neptune's trident still shone clear in the sun.

"What would you have me do with it, Cornelia?" he asked.

"When you reach Etruria, your home and the home of my ancestors, bury it in the soil. Or throw it into the Tyrhennian Sea and say a blessing to Neptune. Let it go. Think of me and our ancestors."

"Of course," he said, staring down at my birth amulet. "I will carry this close to my heart. And when I do return to Rome—"

"Return?"

"Yes, return. According to the auguries, Nero has fewer years left in his reign than the number of fingers on one of my hands."

"And do you believe the auguries? I asked him.

Lucius smiled, as if surprised. "Yes, I do. I believe in the portents. I believe in the words of the Sibylline Books. And I trust in my own dreams, my own omens—the ones that reside in my soul."

"Then may it be so," I told him. "When Nero's reign comes to an end, as you predict, I hope to see you once again ... on a new day ... in a new Rome."

"I am indebted to you, Cornelia," he added tearfully.

"All I ask is that you go. Now. And I will hold the hope you will return to Rome once again."

"And remember the augury I read those years ago. 'Cornelia Cosa will be one of the greatest Vestals.' You are on your way ..."

"*You* must be on your way," I said, my face wet with tears. "May Vesta and the Gods bless and sustain you. And may the spirit of Jesus Christ keep you safe as well."

Lucius's eyebrows shot high. "And you, Cornelia, may the gods who protect Rome watch over you and keep you safe."

I turned around and saw the litter with Vibi had arrived.

"I must go now," I said, "to tend Vesta's fire. I shall await your return. To a new Rome. On a new day."

EPILOGUE

68 AD

Nero was dead. Dead by his own hands. Poison was how he did it. He died a coward's death. For the last three years, plots against the Emperor had risen and fallen like the rushing waves of the Tiber. Rather than be killed by his enemies, he took his own life.

In the same year Lucius was pardoned, Poppaea became pregnant with Nero's child. But one night he kicked her in the stomach, causing his wife and unborn child to perish. Stricken with grief, the already-mad Emperor became haunted, a mere specter of himself; indeed the Sibylline Books and the prophecies had come to pass—in due time.

It took but a few years before Nero's horrific reign ended. I wondered when Lucius would return to Rome. But I had other matters to think upon. Because I had proven myself as a novice, I would move up to the next ten years of my service. And maybe it was just as well Lucius was gone; for as I grew older, I began to feel the burden of the vow of purity I had given so little thought to as a child.

Mother Aurelia retired and Junia was now Virgo Maxima. A new Vestal was once again chosen. Vibi had risen to the level of teacher. She was still like a sister to me, holding Christ in her heart. Rubria strugged on, watching with despair the destruction of her Emperor. Lucretia came to visit us in the

Atrium—with her new daughter, Cornelia! And Cleo grew plump again and began terrorizing the birds near the Atrium and Forum.

Jesus followers, now sometimes known as Christians, were growing in number, converting Gentiles, Roman Jews, and others to "the Way." They never feared death for they believed in new life.

My family came to visit me now. My father rebuilt his business—with my financial help. All was well once again with the Cosas.

There would be a new Emperor. The rebuilding of Rome continued, along with our seasonal festivals and rituals. The Palladium was safe in our new Temple of Vestal. Life continued on.

The sorrows were over ... for now.

AUTHOR'S NOTE

I became interested in the Vestal Virgins because I wondered and imagined what it must be like to be "chosen" at such a young age, removed from one's family, and then to make a vow to Vestal for thirty years. Vestals were always chosen between the ages of 6-10 and there were strict requirements before they could participate in the lottery. What if a young girl really didn't want to be "chosen?"

The Vestal Order began under the reign of King Numa, over 800 years before my story begins. The legend says that Numa received guidance from the river nymph, Egeria who gave him the laws and rules for the Order to obey. The legend of the woodpecker, Picus feeding the twins Romulus and Remus is authentic, and can be found in Ovid's *Metamorphosis*.

"Vestal Virgin: Chosen for Rome" is based on a true character, Cornelia Cosa. Because little is known of her early life and family, I tried for the sake of the story, to create a realistic scenerio for how Cornelia might have been chosen, her reaction, and her entry into a strange, new world.

I chose this time period because Rome was at a crossroads between the new sect, the "Jesus Followers" (soon to be known as "Christians") led by Paul, who was under house arrest in Rome from AD 60-62, and the myriad Pagan religions in Rome, complete with temples to foreign and homespun Gods and Goddesses located all over the city.

Paul indeed held meetings at his rented villa, preached the power and message of Jesus and finally raised the ire of Emperor Nero, who then judged and scapegoated Rome's Christians and blamed them for starting the fire. He did meet his fate along the Ostian Way, beheaded on Nero's orders. Of course, the Great Fire of Rome, the execution of Christians including Peter is true. I tried to keep to the true chronology based on several sources of what happened, how it happened, and why it happened.

Some aspects of the novel are surprisingly true. The chapter on the Lake House Banquet complete with crocodiles and bawdy women is authentic. The portent with Nero's cloak getting stuck in the Temple's doorway is also true. The "In Captio" rite of the novice Vestal is true as the lottery held for choosing a Vestal. All the rites, rituals and festivals are based on the truth. As the author, I had to fill many aspects in and I chose the Vestals using the four elements and added the fifth element the ether as well.

I added the story of Cornelia grabbing hold of the snake on the Pons Sublicus during the Feast of the Argeii as a way of establishing a foundation for her ability as a prophetess. Also, I included the chapter with Lucretia getting burned by Vestal's flame. In my mind, I considered this a possibility and added it for the sake of the story.

The rape of Rubria by Nero is another aspect mentioned by ancient authors, including Tacitus; as regards Nero, all women, girls, men and boys were fair game for his pleasures. The punishment of Vibidia is also based on how the Pontifex Maximus would either scourge or inflict pain upon a Vestal who broke the rules. However, if a Vestal broke the most serious rule, losing her chastity or being accused of this, the punishment was being buried alive in an underground chamber.

The Romans were a superstitious lot. Everything was taken as an omen—from the cries of birds, what directions they flew, how many— it all made a difference. Nero was an exceedingly superstitious Emperor often consulting astrologers, sooth-sayers, harispex (those who read the entrails of a slain beast) the Sibylline Books, and most certainly his augurs. I enjoyed learning about the role of the augur and how critical the por-tents were to Rome.

I'm grateful I was able to take a trip to Rome last year and walk the grounds of these sacred sites, including the Forum, the remains of the Atrium Vestae and the Temple of Vesta, the Circus Maximus, the Aventine Hill, the Tiber River with the ancient Pons Sublicus still arched over those rushing waters and many more wonderful sites featured in this book. For those wondering where the Colisseum was, during the time period I write about, it wasn't built yet. The Colisseum came several years later.

A highlight of my trip to Rome was finding the Spring of Egeria off of the Appian Way. It's a few miles walk, but well worth it; when you arrive, the Appenine Mountains in the distance take one's breath away. It is amidst a lovely park with mulberry trees and open land. Unfortunately the spring is closed off, but a small walkway allows visitors to behold the moss and lichen covered spring. Other areas of Rome we visited included the Subura, the Esquiline Hill, the Pons Sub-licus, and the Praetorian Guard headquarters.

Readers may wonder about the October Horse. This is all true. When writing this chapter, all I could think of was the horse's head from the movie, *The Godfather.* Connection?

Perhaps the competitions and rivalries were a carry over from this ancient rite.

Slaves were common in Roman Society. Many eventually became "freedmen', the process known as manumission. Although Taltos and Domicia are fictional, the Vestals had slaves and servants, as did most well to do families in Rome.

Vestals were indeed chosen through a lottery and in years when Senators' daughters were unavailable, the Emperor had to be satisfied with traditional middle class girls. The Vestals had rituals and festivals to prepare for and the best source of this information is Ovid's *Fasti* that provides details for at least half of the year. Many may recognize the lines, "As above, so below." from the Emerald Tablet of Hermes Trismegistus. Plutarch mentions this Hermes from early in the 1st century AD, but this was known centuries before the time I write— so it's clear the Romans knew about this and were experts anyway, at "syncretism."

Exotic animals were a source of brutal entertainment for the Ancient Romans. Chariot races were the NASCAR of the times. The Romans were a gambling and betting people. They certainly enjoyed their entertainment immensely— their Bread and Circus—even if it meant watching a lion devour an innocent Christian. For 21st century readers, it's shocking and barbaric. I believe our consciousness regarding animals has come quite a ways since the time of Nero.

I tried to be as accurate with my chronology and timeline as possible. During my research, I'd often come upon conflicting information and tried as best I could to get to the truth. As I said earlier, Paul was on house arrest between AD 60-62. There's conflicting evidence of where his house actually was. Nero released him in 62 and most likely, Paul preached in Spain. But after the fire of AD 64 that destroyed most of Rome, Paul returned, was arrested, and thus met his fate on the Ostian Way. Also, much of Paul's dialogue in *Vestal Virgin: Chosen for Rome* is paraphrased and based on his Epistles and the Book of Acts.

Many people know about Nero scapegoating the Jesus followers, and that he threw these early Christians to the lions, or had them crucified like Peter. All of the feasts, rituals and rites are based on truth. There is strong archeological evidence as well, that the Vestals did have an Inner Sanctum within the Atrium. I added many of the details since so little is known of the sanctum and made part of it into a "Hall of the Gods."

Most of the Vestals in *Vestal Virgin: Chosen For Rome* are based on true individuals. Because so little is known of their personalities, I created them for the story. Although the character of Lucius is fictionalized, the role of the augur and the Vestal seemed strongly connected, both offering a crucial service to the State.

I enjoyed writing *Vestal Virgin: Chosen for Rome.* I hope I gave my readers a glimpse into the past and what it might be like to be "chosen" for 30 years to the service to Vesta.

This book represents the first 10 years of Cornelia's service to Vesta. Stay turned for the next part of her journey toward becoming the Virgo Maxima and perhaps, "One of the Greatest Vestals" ever.

Katherine Spada Basto
September 19, 2019

SELECTED
BIBLIOGRAPHY

Although I do not profess to be a Roman scholar, I did quite a bit of research for this book.

From the ancient sources, I used: Ovid's, *Fasti*, Ovid's, *Metamorphosis*, Suetonius's, *Lives of the Twelve Caesars*, Plutarch's, *Lives* (there's a whole chapter on King Numa) Tacitus, *The Annals*, Livy's, *Early History of Rome*, *The Holy Bible*, Virgil's *The Aeneid*, and a replica of the *Sibylline Oracles*.

There are so many excellent books on the Vestal Virgins, far too many for me to list here. However, I will list the books and novels that made a helpful impact on me during my research and writing and thus, I would highly recommend them.

1. Baddeley, Wilbore St Clair and Lina Duff Gordon. *Rome and Its Story:* JM Dent and Co, London, 1904.

2. Bailey, Cyril. *The Religion of Ancient Rome:* Constable and Co, London, 1907.

3. Bonnefoy, Yves. *Roman and European Mythologies:* University of Chicago Press, Chicago and London. 1991.

4. Church, Alfred. *The Burning of Rome:* Palatine Press, New York, NY. 1891

5. Champlin, Edward. *Nero:* Harvard University Press, Cambridge, Mass. 2005

6. Collins, Stephen. *The Great Fire of Rome:* DeCapo Press, Cambridge, Mass. 2010

7. DiLuzio, Meghan. *A Place at the Altar: Priestesses in Republican Rome:* Princeton University Press. 2016

8. Lindar, Molly M. *Portraits of the Vestal Virgins, Priestesses of Ancient Rome:* University of Michigan Press, Ann Arbor, MI. 2015

9. Staples, Ariadne. *From Good Goddesses to Vestal Virgins: Sex and Category in Ancient Rome:* Routledge, New York, NY. 1998

10. Wildfang, Robin. *Rome's Vestal Virgins: A Study of Rome's Vestal Priestesses in the late Republic and early Empire:* Routledge, New York, NY. 2006

11. Worsfold, T. Cato. *History of the Vestal Virgins of Rome:* Mayflower Press, New York, NY. 1934

12. Wright, N.T. *Paul:* Harper Collins, New York, NY. 2018

Here are some of novels I would recommend and those that helped in my learning and research.

1. Argo, John. *The Sibyl's Urn:* Argo Press. 2004

2. Knipe, Humphrey. *The Nero Prediction:* Self- Published. 2017

3. Maier, Paul. *The Flames of Rome:* Kriegal Publications, Grand Rapids, MI. 1981

4. Montgomery, Virginia. *Pagan Princess: A Story of the Greatest Career Women of Ancient Times, The Vestal Virgins of Rome:* Literary Licensing. 2011

5. Tyrpak, Suzanne. *Vestal Virgin:* Createspace, N.C. 2010

6.   White, Edward Lucas. *The Unwilling Vestal:* E.P. Dutton. New York, NY. 1918

7.   Yarbro, Chelsea Quinn. *Blood Games:* Time-Warner, New York, NY. 1979

ACKNOWLEDGEMENTS

First and foremost, I would like to thank my husband, Ronald Basto for reading and rereading this manuscript in its early drafts. Because Ron has a Ph.D in the Classics, with his thesis on Roman mythology, he was able to help me with certain points and sources. The trip we took together to Rome was unforgettable; to be able to traverse the ancient landscape blended in with the modern was truly a blessing. We enjoyed every minute visiting some of the places in the book.

Many thanks to my editor, Carol Gaskin of Editorial Alchemy. Her suggestions and notes truly helped this become a better book. Thanks to my readers, Trish Truitt, Paul Francoeur who also made a difference with helpful comments. A special thanks to Duncan Eagleson of Corvid Design for a magnificent book cover, a map and for also reading the manuscript in its early form. A special thanks to my dear friend Alvis, and of course, all the support I received from my family, God/Goddess, Christ Spirit and the Holy Spirit; I was touched deeply throughout the research and writing of this book. Thank you all!

ABOUT THE AUTHOR

Katherine Spada Basto was a teacher for many years before becoming a full time writer. Born in Hartford, Connecticut, she is the award-winning author of, "Days to the Gallows: A Novel of the Hartford Witch Panic." Katherine did many years of research on the Witches of Hartford and never knew witch hangings occurred in her own home city.

A worldwide traveler, Katherine lived for three years in South Africa and traveled extensively to Europe and the UK on several occasions. She loves to travel and enjoys traveling to sites she is researching to authentic her work in order to bring her writing to life, including her most recent trip to Rome.

A lover of history, Katherine was involved with the creation of the Hartford Circus Fire Memorial, a tribute to the 168 people who lost their lives in the tragedy of July 6, 1944. Katherine's mother, a survivor, was the inspiration behind the work for the Memorial. An animal activist and environmentalist, Katherine often includes animals in her books.

Katherine is presently working on her next book.

For more information,
please visit Katherine's website at
www.katherinespadabasto.com

If you enjoyed *Chosen for Rome...*

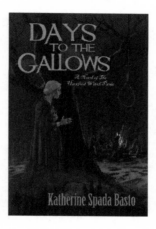

Before the Salem Witch Trials...
in 1662, a witch panic struck Hartford, Connecticut.

Seventeen year old Hester Hosmer is a neighbor and friend to Ann Cole, despite Ann's reputation for being "strange" and a mooncalf. One night when Hester tries to drag Ann home from one of her moonlight walks, the girls stumble upon a strange fire-lit gathering on the South Green. But in 1662, such gatherings are strictly forbidden.

When a child dies mysteriously, Ann's hysteria begins and she accuses certain townspeople of witchcraft. A witch panic envelopes Hartford and paranoia runs rampant.

Hester tries to discourage Ann's hysterics and the more she discovers, the more conflicted she becomes about her own loyalties. Hester's budding romance with Tom, the peddler's son only makes Ann jealous and increases the tension.

With the ruthless Marshal Gilbert, the Puritan Elders and the Acting Governor himself at her beck and call, Ann can prove to be a dangerous enemy.

After all, anyone in Hartford might be a witch.

After years of research, Ms. Spada Basto has brought to life a turbulent and disturbing period of Colonial Connecticut History. It is a time when wolves prowled near the town and superstitions about witches often brought people to an untimely death-hanging by a noose on Gallows' Hill.

Now available on Amazon and from other booksellers.

Made in the USA
Middletown, DE
23 January 2020